# FINDING HAPPINESS AT PENVENNAN COVE

## Also by Linn B. Halton

### The Penvennan Cove Series

*Coming Home to Penvennan Cove*
*Making Waves at Penvennan Cove*
*Finding Happiness At Penvennan Cove*

### Writing as Lucy Coleman

*Magic Under the Mistletoe*
*Summer on the Italian Lakes*
*Snowflakes Over Holly Cove*
*The French Adventure*

# FINDING HAPPINESS AT PENVENNAN COVE

Linn B. Halton

*An Aria Book*

First published in the UK in 2022 by Head of Zeus Ltd,
part of Bloomsbury Publishing Plc



9 7 5 3 2 4 6 8

A catalogue record for this book is available from the British Library.

ISBN (PB): 9781803289366
ISBN (E): 9781838938024

Cover design: Leah Jacobs-Gordon

Typeset by Siliconchips Services Ltd UK

Printed and bound in Great Britain by
CPI Group (UK) Ltd, Croydon CRO 4YY

Head of Zeus Ltd
First Floor East
5–8 Hardwick Street
London EC1R 4RG

WWW.HEADOFZEUS.COM

When the dream you've been chasing has to change,
it can turn your life upside down.

Be guided by your heart and tap into your gut instincts.
Then take a deep breath and a leap of faith.

If you currently find yourself in that situation,
then this story is dedicated to you.

Change can be unexpectedly liberating.

# April

# 1

## Living in Harmony

Waking up each morning next to the man who first stole my heart more than a decade ago is still a novelty. But it's also a reminder to count my blessings. No matter what problems the new day ahead might bring, each night when we fall asleep in each other's arms the irritating worries simply fade away. As for the bigger issues – well, it's a case of acknowledging there are some things that are outside of my control, no matter how difficult that is to accept.

'I can almost hear your mind ticking over,' Ross murmurs, sleepily. 'Did the birds wake you again?' He rolls into me, snaking his arm around my waist and giving it a comforting squeeze.

'Yes,' I grumble, unappreciatively. 'It is a wonderful way to wake up and it does lift my spirits, but it's not even five o'clock. I've had less than four hours sleep and they're so… enthusiastic.'

Loud actually, but it's not their fault I'm feeling sleep

deprived. The garden of Pedrevan Cottage backs onto a swathe of trees leading down to a picturesque stream. Even though it's slightly smaller than the one at the front of the property, Ross says this is the best of the two bedrooms because it has such a lovely outlook. But at this unearthly hour of the morning, it sounds as if every robin, blackbird and thrush in the area has come to Penvennan to celebrate the dawn chorus. Another two blissful hours and it would be the perfect start to the day, because I'm sorely in need of my beauty sleep.

'It's a male thing I'm afraid,' Ross informs me, soberly. 'The most dominant of the males need to assert ownership of their territory. They like to show off to the females and leave the other males in no doubt about how strong they are.' Ross stifles a yawn, but his eyes are now open.

'Strong?'

'After a chilly night and on an empty stomach, they need to be well-fed to sing the loudest. It requires a great deal of energy to impress their partners. It's the *me Tarzan, you Jane* mentality.'

'Is that why you sing in the shower?' I start giggling. Ross sings off-key and he knows it, but it warms my heart to hear him. He pulls me even closer, snuggling his chin into my hair.

'No. That's not a territorial thing. Pedrevan is your cottage. I'm just the poor, homeless guy you took in out of the kindness of your heart. Can you hear that woodpigeon joining in?'

I listen carefully, but all the birds are clamouring to be heard. 'I'm not sure which sound to focus on.'

'Well, people say they *coo*, but it's that *vooo* sound, which usually means the male is defending a nest.'

Ross is right. It's intermittent and there is a sense of urgency to the woodpigeon's call. 'You're surprisingly knowledgeable about birds,' I remark, casually.

'It's only stuff I've picked up from Gawen up at Treeve Perran Farm. Before you arrived back in Penvennan Cove I used to spend my Sundays there giving a hand in return for one of Yvonne's hearty roast dinners.'

Goodness, I learn something new about Ross with every passing day, but this is a real surprise.

'And, of course, our feathered friends are enthusiastic; it's not their fault that sounds carry further before the world around them begins to wake up,' he continues. 'There's no background noise to mask the birdsong, plus it's courting season. Once they have young ones to feed, they'll have less time to sit in the trees and sing. A bit like humans when they settle down.' The bed begins to shake as he chuckles softly to himself. I nudge him gently in his side to discourage him.

I'm still awaiting that proposal he promised me back in November, but I know the timing hasn't been right. It will come once we have a new routine established, but it's still early days.

'What exactly did you do up at the farm? I thought you knew Gawen because you attended Tai Chi classes with Yvonne. Although I notice the two of you don't go anymore.'

Ross rolls away, easing himself upright and adjusting his pillows so he can sit back and stare out the window. It is annoying having to keep the curtains open but Ripley, the boss of the house, is a typically vocal Bengal cat. She howls if she can't jump up onto the windowsill to peer out over the garden, no matter what time of the day or night it is. And as soon as the birds are awake, she's out there hunting. In between, Ripley keeps coming back inside to keep an eye on everything from her privileged vantage point. Fortunately for the birds, she has more luck with mice than she does with any of our feathered friends.

'Not since you came back and started monopolising my spare time,' Ross points out, stifling a yawn.

'That was most definitely not a part of my action plan,' I reply adamantly, seeking out his hand to interlace my fingers with his.

'Maybe not. But the moment you saw me again you couldn't help yourself, could you?' He grins at me in the gloom.

I love the strands of tousled, dark curly hair that flop down onto his forehead, in stark contrast to the shaved back and sides. And that close-cropped beard, which often leaves pink marks on my skin whenever he rubs up against my cheeks.

'No. And neither could you. Are you hungry?' I ask, hoping he'll say *yes*.

'You want me to make pancakes for you at this unearthly hour?'

'No… but you could tempt me with your special scrambled eggs.'

Ross runs his fingertips playfully down the edge of my cheek.

'You mean my Treeve Perran Farm Burford Brown eggs, with freshly chopped tarragon and a sprinkling of home-grown parsley, courtesy of my kitchen windowsill garden?'

That makes me smile.

'When you sold Treylya to your father, I was half-hoping you'd at least bring that beautiful, bespoke off-white leather sofa with you! I wasn't expecting you to turn up with just your clothes, a small cardboard box of personal items and five pots of herbs.'

'Oh, I'm sorry to have disappointed you,' he teases. 'I wasn't about to hire a van for one item of furniture. There wasn't really anything of *me* in that house that wouldn't fit into a few suitcases.'

I was only joking, and I didn't mean to remind him of his ex-wife, Bailey. He built that house to please her and she chose the furnishings, but, as magnificent as it is, Ross could never relax there because it's a show house, not a home. Here in Pedrevan Cottage we're cosy together and now he's here with me forever.

'The herbs were a welcome bonus, believe me. I do know how lucky I am to be living with a builder who also happens to be a budding chef,' I add softly, easing myself up to kiss his neck and work my way slowly across to his mouth.

When we pull away, I can see there's a gleam in his eyes making them shine. 'Well, one of us has to be prepared to roll up their sleeves instead of diving into the freezer.'

He's right and I'm certainly not going to deny it, because it's another of the things I love about him. And my stomach is happy about it too. Even in my wildest daydreams as a teenager, it was never anything more than wanting to catch Ross Treloar's eye and maybe even a kiss. I simply wanted him to find me interesting, more than just a school friend. I never dared to imagine a future where I was *the* woman in his life, because I instinctively knew that the world outside of Penvennan Cove had much to offer. And I was eager to prove myself.

'I love you, Kerra Shaw,' Ross whispers, his breath warm on my cheek. 'I'm sorry for the trouble my father has caused, and I hope that now he's returned to his villa in Spain we can begin to repair the damage.'

In a perfect world that might be the case, but Jago Treloar is used to creating chaos and walking away. Unfortunately, my dad Eddie is a stubborn man – I should know, as I take after him. After Mum died, I returned home and we supported each other for a while, until Dad found out that Ross and I were seeing each other. It's complicated because it isn't just about Ross's disastrous first marriage, but a bitter dispute between the Shaws and the Treloars going way back.

Ross and I hung out in the same little group at school. All the girls chased after him and the few he did date saw it as a status symbol to be referred to as his girlfriend. Others implied a connection to him that simply wasn't true. Several years after I left for London, my best friend – Tegan – mentioned in one of our catch-up phone calls that Ross was married. His new wife, Bailey, was both sophisticated and came from the *right* family, according to Ross's parents. By all accounts, he was dazzled by her and who could blame him? Even I was intrigued when Tegan was describing her to me. It wasn't until after I returned to Penvennan Cove that Ross told me the reason for their divorce. Not only did Bailey run up excessive debts in his name, but she'd had an affair with a local golf caddie. I felt gutted for him because the Ross I know deserves better than that. Dad, on the other hand, saw that as proof Ross couldn't make a relationship work.

'Let's think of this as the start of the next phase in our relationship,' I reply, with more positivity than I'm feeling right now. I miss my father and no longer being welcome in my family home is tough to handle. But I understand that Dad will need time to get used to the idea of me and Ross living together permanently. The situation would probably be a little less volatile if we didn't live almost opposite each other on the High Street. Penvennan is a small community, and nothing remains a secret for long here unless it goes on behind closed doors.

'Anyway, I'm starving,' I continue. 'They do say it's unwise to go to bed on an empty stomach and that was your fault.'

'I was tired and how was I to know you were hungry?' Ross responds, but we both know that wasn't the case at all. However, I was more than willing to be guided upstairs and food was the last thing on my mind last night.

*Miaow, miaow, miaoooooow*. The greyish outline of our little tiger strolls through the bedroom door.

'Hey, Ripley. Don't tell me you've come back in for food, too?' Ross groans as Ripley jumps up onto the bed. Her usually bright, cinnamon-coloured coat is masked in shadows in the half-light. She headbutts Ross's arm, her tail flicking back and forth as she seeks his attention. He stops to smooth her ears for a few moments, but she's obviously in a hurry to eat and get back to stalking her prey.

*Miaow, miaoooooow. Miaoooooow!*

'I guess we're all having an early breakfast this morning,' I confirm, beaming at Ross.

Ripley concurs with another loud *miaoooooow*.

'Okay, I'm getting up now – right this minute.' Ross

clambers out of bed, mumbling to himself. 'That'll teach me for insisting on having an early night.'

I hope he can make out the playful expression on my face. 'It wasn't quite as early as we planned,' I retort. 'But I'm not complaining.'

'You're not tempted to give me my marching orders, then?' he banters with me, and I shake my head enthusiastically.

'You're a keeper, I thought I'd made that clear. Are we wrapping up warmly so we can enjoy breakfast out on the deck? It will be lovely watching the sun rise.'

Ross yanks on his jeans, then leans forward to kiss me and I know what he really wants is to jump back into bed. 'I know we've been in limbo,' he declares, his voice now in serious mode. 'But it won't be for much longer. I needed to sell the house and draw a line under that part of my life forever. Now I'm finally here, it's just you and me going forward with no distractions. Oh, and Ripley too, of course! With my father out of the frame, I feel I can breathe a huge sigh of relief.'

Insisting that his father's plans for setting up a new depot and office is done as a separate entity was a hard-fought battle but one that Ross succeeded in winning.

However, the day Jago walked into our local public house, The Lark and Lantern, he was out to cause trouble. He announced to anyone who was listening that Ross had big plans and wouldn't be staying in Penvennan Cove. That's so typical of the way Jago operates. The mistake he made was in lingering long enough for my dad to catch him in the act.

Jago said that it was time the lonely, single women around here stopped taking advantage of his son. Everyone gasped apparently, when they realised Jago was referring to me because Ross and I have been careful to keep our relationship private.

My father is a proud man, and rightly so. He stands for truth and honesty. However, while Dad sees Ross as a hard-working businessman, he also thinks that he's a man with commitment issues and that I deserve better. What Dad can't see is that Ross is the man Jago would like to be. Jago sacrificed his principles to get where he is today – kicking-back in Spain with a successful business run by his hard-working son, and money piling up in the bank.

Ross and I have been left to deal with the gossip and speculation. As we know from the past, rumours can quickly get out of hand and Ross moving in with me is a way of showing the world they'd better get over it. Every little thing either of us does is now being watched like a drama unfolding, not least the fallout with my dad – and people are taking sides.

Hopefully, by the time Jago returns to the UK for a visit to check that his master plan is going in the right direction, Ross and I will no longer be hot news. Jago will have no choice but to accept the situation because it's none of his business. As for my dad... well, I can only hope and pray that he gets over his prejudice and comes to see that Ross is, and always was, a true gentleman. But more importantly, that Ross's heart is in the right place, which is here, with me.

# 2

## A New Kind of Normal

My phone kicks into life and it's Tegan. We sat next to each other all through our school years and were inseparable. A friendship like that lasts forever, no matter how different the paths you travel might be – and ours couldn't be more diverse.

'I was passing and I'm standing on your doorstep. Do you have time for a coffee break? No problem if it's not convenient,' she says, brightly.

'No, it's fine. Perfect timing in fact, as I've been working since six this morning. I was in the garden office, but I'm walking back up to the cottage as we speak.'

There is no way Tegan was merely passing, as Penvennan Village is a detour off the main road, and I seriously doubt she would be heading down to the cove on a workday.

She waves a greaseproof bag in front of me as I swing open the front door. 'I come bearing gifts. Mrs Moyle's saffron buns and I brought an extra one for Ross.'

We exchange a brief hug as I let her pass and find myself

checking the street before closing the door. Dad usually walks down to the little newsagent's shop for his paper around this time, but he's nowhere to be seen and I heave a heavy sigh.

'Were you hoping to see Eddie?' Tegan comments, as I follow her into the sitting area of the open plan ground floor.

I nod, unable to deny that fact as she hands me the bag and begins to slip off her coat.

'It's lovely to see you and a bun is just the sugar hit I need right now,' I confess. 'I'll pop the kettle on. Aren't you working today?'

Tegan follows me into the kitchen and takes a seat at the lovingly hand-painted and distressed pine table.

When I headed off to London, an ambitious eighteen-year-old, Tegan stayed in Penvennan. She became my eyes and ears, keeping me up to date with news of home as I kick-started my career. She even kept a look out for Dad after my mum died, until I was able to return home for good. Lifestyle changes are a lot easier to accommodate when you know that your future is financially secure and, fortunately, I've reached that point but I'm keen not to advertise the fact.

'I thought I'd pop in to see how it's going.' She raises her eyebrows and we both know exactly to what she's referring – Ross moving in.

Ripley comes running downstairs having heard Tegan's voice, and I busy myself making coffee while she fusses over the feline boss of the house.

'Oh, Rippers – you're such a beauty. I know that I told Sy I wanted a dog, but I'm sorely tempted to get a Bengal cat.'

Sy was my assistant at the company I ran in London, called The Happy Hive. The website allowed fee-paying members to connect by matching those with a need for something specific to people with the necessary skills. When I sold the business, he stayed behind for a while but ended up walking out a few months later. I enticed him down to Cornwall for a break, to get his head around what he was going to do next. At the time Tegan's cleaning business, Clean and Shine, was struggling to survive. I thought that Sy's expertise could help them both; Sy because he needed a confidence boost as he's not usually a quitter, and Tegan to recover from the slide following the death of her husband Pete, two years before. Never in a million years did I ever think that Sy and Tegan would fall for each other. But against all the odds, my two closest friends ended up getting married at the end of November last year.

*Miaow, miaow, miaow, miaow, miaow.*

Tegan leans forward to rub Ripley's chin, which immediately sets her off purring. She flops down and rolls over onto her back, waving her paws languidly in the air.

Watching Ripley makes me smile. 'She's such a diva.'

'You want a tummy rub, don't you!' Tegan coos. 'Diva, or not, you're adorable.'

I stretch my arms, stifling a yawn. 'Well, between the birds and Ripley I'm only getting a few hours' sleep each night, so I'd say get a dog,' I warn Tegan. 'No offence, Ripley, but Bertie next door is a lot less demanding.'

Tegan smiles up at me. 'And I hear that this little princess is being nicer to Bertie these days.'

'Well, it was about time.'

Ripley is – was – my neighbour Drew's cat. Drew is an architect and designed the extensions built onto the rear of both semi-detached cottages. While I was cat sitting Ripley last year when Drew was away, intruders found their way into my garden on three separate occasions, after which Ripley refused to leave my side.

'They do say cats choose their owners and not the other way around,' Tegan reflects.

'And I believe that's true.' At the time I assumed the intruders were after the building materials stacked in the garden, but they were looking for my former tenant. The man I was renting my cottage to didn't look like the sort of person to be involved in stealing cars. It's always the quiet ones, isn't it?

'You can't blame Ripley for deciding that you needed looking after more than Drew. I know the poor guy was devastated when she flatly refused to go home, but you were lonely here – admit it.'

'It was scary at the time and the irony is that between them, Ripley and Ross kept me safe. Now that Drew has Bertie, I don't feel quite so guilty. Seriously, those two are kindred souls.

'It's been a nightmare, but Drew has been very understanding. Here you go, one coffee and one bun. I promise not to scoff Ross's, although it will be a temptation as he won't get back until well after six this evening.'

I take a seat opposite Tegan, noticing that she's already tucking in as if she hasn't eaten in ages.

'Oh, these are so good and it's worth taking a detour to The Penvennan Convenience Store for one of Mrs Moyle's. Hers are way better than any of the other bakeries in the area.' Tegan groans as she chews, pausing for a moment. 'Anyway, talking of Ross… how's it going?' She stares at me wide-eyed, and I break out into a huge, glowing smile.

'Wonderful… surreal at times still, I will admit.' Tegan

is watching me like a hawk, and I glance away as Ripley pads off to slink back upstairs. She's too tired to leap the treads two at a time as she usually does. 'He turned up with a car full of bags and a couple of suitcases, and that was it. I'm not sure what I was expecting, as I know he sold the furniture with the house, but it just felt like he was coming to stay for a holiday.'

'Well, it's going to be one long and adventurous holiday. The two of you were meant to be together. I always thought that, but you were always so… cool towards him, the poor guy. How was he to know that he was your first love?' Tegan reminds me, and I give her a stern look.

'He was my first real *crush*, that's all,' I reply, feeling defensive.

Tegan snorts. 'If you say so, but how long did it take you to fall in love with Ross after he first appeared at your door last year, when the building work was about to begin?'

The instant his eyes met mine my legs turned to jelly, but I'm keeping that to myself. 'Oh, he wormed his way into my affections by getting Ripley on his side. That was a clever move,' I reply, nonchalantly.

I haven't told anyone about the question Ross asked me on the day that Tegan and Sy got married. As midnight approached, the two of us were sitting on a blanket in front of the wall of glass doors looking out over Pedrevan's garden. We toasted what had been a gloriously happy day. Then Ross asked me what my answer would be if he were to ask me to marry him. He made it clear it wasn't a formal proposal, but he sounded nervous. It doesn't hurt to keep a man guessing, so I gave him a theoretical *yes* while trying to sound low-key. I mean, no one likes to be taken for granted, do they? Since then, life has been totally chaotic and it still is, because it's been one stumbling block after another.

'It was agony being apart. Plus, the more that Dad sees us together, the quicker it will sink in that my future really is with Ross.'

I begin eating, fascinated as Tegan collects the last few crumbs on the plate with the tip of her finger and licks them off with great satisfaction.

'Well, that hit the spot for me,' she states, grinning. 'It's bound to be a period of adjustment for you both, Kerra. I mean, your mum was born in Pedrevan Cottage, and you were the one who renovated and furnished it. Ross has moved into your territory and considering that you're both used to living on your own, that's a huge step.'

I take a swig of coffee, wondering how honest I should be with Tegan. 'I do understand that, and it does worry me. I'm trying hard to make Ross feel this is *our* home and we sorted out the wardrobes together into *his* and *her* zones. I even bought a second desk to go into the garden office for him, but he said it wasn't necessary. I got the delivery man to stack the box in the cupboard under the stairs as I haven't given up. It would be fun working side by side and I'm sure there's a lot of paperwork he could easily do from home. But you know how laid back he is, he says he's happy to work from his laptop here in the kitchen if necessary.'

'He's trying to ease himself into your life without turning everything upside down,' Tegan remarks, wistfully.

Tegan is trying not to point out the obvious, which is that Treylya is a huge house and Pedrevan is probably only a third of the size, even with the fabulous new extension.

'What concerns me is that when we were joking around

early this morning, Ross referred to himself as the poor, homeless guy I took in out of the goodness of my heart. I was hoping he'd feel differently, relieved that we are finally setting up home together. I know we're not starting from scratch, but I'm open to change.'

Tegan leans back in her chair, deep in thought. 'He's a proud man, Kerra, and if he wasn't renting his other house – The Forge – to me and Sy, think about how you'd feel moving in there with him. It lacked a woman's touch, but it's what he'd grown used to when Treylya was a holiday rental. Having recently extended Pedrevan Cottage, Ross is well aware of how much every item in here means to you. Let's face it, you didn't bring much with you that day you arrived back from London, did you?'

'No, that's true – but what if Ross doesn't feel comfortable here and he's keeping that to himself for fear of upsetting me?' Voicing my concerns is hard, but Tegan can sense the inner turmoil.

'Look, it was the same when Sy came to live with me. At first, we were a little awkward around each other. Admittedly, it was the house that Pete and I bought together and, as it turned out, there are too many memories there for me to deal with. Finding the perfect tenants for it, and renting The Forge from Ross, was a great solution for me and Sy. At some point I will be able to let the past go and sell the house, then Sy and I can decide what happens next. But for now, The Forge feels like ours, even though it isn't. But Pedrevan is different. Ross oversaw the building of the extension and the renovations. It's a beautiful cottage, full of character and yet with a contemporary feel. What's not to like?'

The look we exchange is one of empathy. 'I did consider

surprising Ross and asking Drew to draw up plans for a loft extension. His books are still at The Forge and his library is a big deal for him. If he had his own study, a place that is entirely his, then he might feel more settled.'

Tegan's forehead wrinkles up into a frown. 'I honestly think that whatever you do next should be a joint decision, Kerra. Look at it from Ross's point of view. If you *surprise* him with a set of plans in which he's had no involvement whatsoever, it sort of gives off the wrong signal, doesn't it?'

Tegan makes a valid point. 'I'm so glad you called in. You're right and I simply need to be patient. I guess when Ross starts thinking about where to build the shelves for his books that will confirm he no longer feels like a lodger.'

We laugh and suddenly that little knot in my stomach starts to unravel, enough that I take a huge bite of bun and chomp away quite happily.

Tegan fiddles with her hair, nervously. 'I also dropped in to give you an update on where things stand with regard to our delayed party and to ask if you'd do me a huge favour.'

I really feel for Tegan and Sy, as after a registry office wedding last November with only Ross and me as witnesses, they were hoping to get their respective families and friends together to celebrate. 'Of course, anything for you!'

'Hmm... well, I'll understand if you say no, given the situation. But I'm desperate because until I've reconciled with my brother, who is still refusing to meet up with me to talk things through, I simply can't set a date.'

'Look, Tegan, it was my cousin Alice's careless chatter that started the whole unfortunate episode to begin with. I feel bad that you and Trev haven't spoken since my first trip back, the summer after I left the cove.'

We sigh in tandem.

'If it hadn't been Alice, it would have been someone else. I don't blame her because I, too, was stopped in my tracks by the rumours. But it's not just that. Sy reached out to his family, and it will be the first time they've got together in many years. It took a lot of courage for him to do that, considering how badly his father has treated him in the past. And now I feel awful that we still can't set a date because Trev won't reply to my calls, or emails. My parents don't know what to do, as they've had to remain neutral to avoid getting drawn into something only Trev and I can resolve face to face. It's an impossible situation if he continues to ignore me.'

'What can I do to help?'

'Would you reach out to him, Kerra, and try to talk him into meeting with me? He always looked up to you when we were at school. You came out guns blazing to shoot down the gossip-mongers in his defence and I'm sure that wasn't lost on him.'

It's so sad because Trev and Tegan were close growing up and the whole family have been affected by what happened.

'Text me his details – maybe I can follow him on social media and then send him a brief message to say hi. We haven't spoken in years, so I can't be too obvious. What do you think?'

'I think tact is the way to go and I'm grateful to you, my dear friend. I'm all out of options and it breaks my heart only ever having seen photos of my nephew. Mum and Dad say that he's a witty, intelligent boy and the spitting image of Trev when he was young.' Tegan is getting emotional and her eyes well up. 'Oh, is that the time already?' She stares at the clock on the wall. 'I'd best get going as I'm on my way to sign up a new cleaning contract. Sy is preparing the accounts ready for the end of the financial year. He has way more patience than me!'

As I see her out, the hug she gives me is one of grateful thanks and I can only hope Trev is receptive when I try to make contact. After everything that Tegan has done for me over the years, I need to make this happen for her. I'm going to give it my best shot, anyway.

'How was your day?' Sitting here with a glass of wine in my hand watching Ross cooking, it's hard not to feel smug. My man is happy making dinner for me and looking very at home indeed.

'Good. In fact, we have a start date for the new build on that large parcel of land next to Treylya and I spent all day re-jigging the schedules. The timing is perfect, as I will be on site most days and it's so convenient being on our doorstep.'

Ross said *our* and a fuzzy feeling begins to wrap itself around me.

'You're excited about this project, aren't you?'

'I am because it's unusual. It's a single-storey stone-built property and I think you'd approve of it. It will blend in with the landscape as it's on that flat ledge in front of the rocky outcrop that leads up onto the moor. It's partially set back into the hillside, which explains the massive budget. The owner also has a castle up in Scotland, and this is going to be his Cornish holiday home. A cool one-point-two-million-pound price tag didn't even make him bat an eyelid.'

I gasp. 'Ross, that's incredible. If your father were here, he'd be popping a champagne cork!'

Ross turns off the ring beneath the pan of pasta and I study him for a second or two. He's wearing his navy striped apron around his waist with style and is looking simply gorgeous in a pale blue linen shirt with his sleeves rolled up, and I could sit here gazing at him forever. Instinctively, I jump up to head over and grab a kiss – just because I can.

'He might when I tell him. But for now, it's just between you and me.' His eyes are playful as our lips touch. 'You lika di pasta di pollo e funghi?' Ross enquires in the most appalling Italian accent before he pulls away.

'Yes.' I grin back at him. 'I love pasta with chicken and mushrooms, but I've never seen them that colour before,' I muse, glancing over his shoulder at the frying pan.

'I dropped in on Gawen. It's another of his new partnerships and they're called *wine caps*, hence the maroon colour and I think they're rather elegant.' He holds a raw one up to show me.

'Interesting. What do they taste like?'

'A combination of Portobello mushrooms, red wine and – rather bizarrely – white potatoes. We're the first to taste Gawen's crop, so this is an honour. Anyway, what sort of day did you have?'

When Jago was around Ross wasn't himself. It was like having a dark cloud constantly hovering over us, wondering whether lightning would strike. Tonight, he's so happy and carefree that my heart is leaping inside my chest. And this kitchen was made for him; he's in chef heaven. You see, you don't have to be a cook to design the perfect kitchen, you simply need to appreciate good food and the essentials required to make it. I start chuckling to myself as Ross turns back around to stare at me, his left eyebrow raised enquiringly.

'What?' he demands, the wooden spoon in his hand tilted at an angle to stop the sauce from dripping off.

'I was just thinking that it's true what they say – visualise what you want to manifest in your life, and you'll get it.'

Ross laughs. 'And you imagined me?' he queries, feigning surprise.

'Yes, I did. Now turn back around as I don't want you to burn that delicious smelling sauce.'

I had no idea Ross would ever be involved in my life – well, outside of my dreams, that is. And yet when I look at him now, he was the one I imagined standing there cooking dinner for me as Drew and I designed the kitchen in 3D. Now that's fate, because I had no idea Ross enjoyed cooking – not until our first real date at The Forge.

'If you could learn how to cut hair, you'd be my perfect dream come true!' I tease and Ross bursts out laughing.

'Oh, so I get my team to build your extension, then I personally install the storage solution in your garden office and now I'm cooking for you – but it's still not enough. Has anyone ever told you that you're high maintenance, Kerra Shaw?'

'Great expectations come with high standards. For which I make no apology at all,' I flutter my eyelashes at him. 'After all, I waited for you for a reason!'

Ross grins to himself as he strains pans and fusses over the presentation of the various components of the dish. He yanks the tea towel off his shoulder, undoes the tie on his apron and proudly walks towards the table carrying the special pasta bowls he bought me for Christmas.

Placing them down quite proudly, he doesn't take his eyes off me as he watches for my initial reaction.

'Magnificent. Now that's worthy of a top-class restaurant. Well done, you!'

'This chef tastes as he goes, so it's seasoned to perfection. You can dive straight in.'

The little mountain of ribbon pasta is lightly coated in the creamy mushroom sauce, which is a scarlet colour. A sprinkling of freshly chopped parsley adds a freshness to the wonderful fusion of smells as I breathe in.

'I'm surprised that the mushrooms have turned the sauce such a rich, red colour.'

He grins at me across the table.

'It's Yvonne's recipe and she suggested adding a little grated beetroot with the cream to enhance the colour, otherwise the mushrooms turn it more of a delicate pink, which spoils the dish. She's still experimenting, but I'd say it smells like a winner, although the proof is in the eating.'

Yvonne and Gawen make such a perfect team. You can tell when people are in synch with each other. Ross is eagerly awaiting my feedback as I twirl the fork to secure my first mouthful. And it's divine. I want to react instantly, but instinctively my hand flies up to my mouth as I savour it, because it's so good.

'That,' I state, staring across at him, 'is heaven on a plate.'

Ross gives me one of his cheeky grins, the sort that bubbles up quite naturally when he's feeling relaxed. Those mesmerizingly dark-brown eyes of his sparkle back at me and I quiver with pure happiness as he shovels a huge forkful of food into his mouth.

'Oh, there's a saffron bun in the cake tin for you. Tegan

popped in for coffee this morning and she'd been to Mrs Moyle's.'

'This morning? That's unusual for her to be socialising on a Thursday morning. Was she in the village taking on a new customer?'

'No. She called in to ask a favour. I'm going to try to talk Trev into meeting up with her.'

'Oh, I see. Tough one. Good luck with that!'

'She's run out of options. If I'm successful, would you mind them coming here one evening to talk? At least it's neutral ground and I think that will help.'

Ross shrugs his shoulders. 'It's entirely up to you, it's your cottage and of course I'd make myself scarce.'

Aww… was that simply a slip of the tongue? 'Well, I like to think of it as *ours*, Ross.'

Ross's cheeky little grin is back. 'We won't be going for a prenuptial agreement then?'

My face drops. 'Is that what you did when you married Bailey?'

'It was the first thing she mentioned after I asked her to marry me.' He shrugs it off as if it's nothing.

'You thought that… uh… we'd be doing that too?'

Ross puts down his fork and reaches out across the table for my hand. As our fingers entwine, he shakes his head at me.

'Don't get me wrong, as far as I'm concerned whatever I have is yours, but you sold a successful business, and you might want to protect yourself. As for me, the next time I get married it's for good.'

Here we are, living together at last and we haven't even talked about money, or the long-term future.

'Well, I feel the exact same way and the truth is I'd have been horrified if that was what you wanted to do. Like it would jinx things between us. And Pedrevan is ours, Ross – I want you to be as happy here as I am. I know you have The Forge, but—'

'I am happy here because all I want is for us to be together. Just between you and me, Sy has already asked whether, when Tegan eventually sells her house, I would consider an offer for The Forge. As it's perfect for them how can I say no?'

His words come as a huge relief, because, as lovely as it is there, this is my forever home.

'Too many memories of old girlfriends?' I reply, looking amused.

'You know that's not the case. Pedrevan means too much to you to walk away from it and I can understand that.'

'In which case, we'd better make some more space for your things.' This is it – if Ross hesitates now my world will fall apart.

'The only items I have that mean anything to me are my books.' He narrows his eyes, questioningly. 'Won't that mess up the colour-coordinated country cottage vibe going on in here?'

'If I can find a man who is good at putting up bookshelves, I think a library would make the sitting area feel even cosier, don't you?'

Ross's expression softens. 'Now that's what I call true love. Any woman who is prepared to make a sacrifice like that is worth hanging on to!'

In the grand scheme of things, it's nothing – what's

important is that Ross starts to feel less like a guest and more invested in his new home. Without him in it, Pedrevan Cottage wouldn't be complete because this is obviously what fate had in store for us all along.

# 3

## Making Plans

After a quick breakfast, Ross leaves for work at six-thirty and as I'm about to shut the front door behind him, he half-turns to look back at me.

'Oh, by the way I've booked a table for two at The Lobster Pot tonight. You deserve to be wined and dined in style on a Friday evening to relax you ready for the weekend. After I've done a quick round of site inspections, I have some paperwork back at the office that requires my attention and then I'm done. Hopefully by four-thirty at the latest. Love you.'

It's unusual for Ross to leave work early so he's obviously feeling content. 'Missing you already,' I reply, making a sad face.

Suddenly the cottage feels empty and the thought of heading out to my office doesn't fill me with enthusiasm this morning. After a quick shower, I dress and head down to the cove.

Standing here watching the sun as it sits low in the sky,

its rays extending out across the dark blue water and a pink hue hovering in the sky above, how I wish Ross were standing alongside me enjoying this moment. As I gaze out to sea, I'm reminded just how stunning Penvennan Cove is at this time of the morning. The salty breeze being driven inland gusts a little, sending my hair in all directions and temporarily obscures my view. Suddenly, the sound of a dog barking makes me turn my head and I spot Bertie racing towards me.

'Hey little guy, you look excited to be up and out this morning,' I murmur to him as he launches himself up against me. I ruffle his head and he immediately sits, offering me his damp, sandy paw.

'Bertie couldn't believe his luck when he saw you,' Drew calls out, as he increases his pace to join us. It's a bright morning, if a little chilly and I notice that he too has his jacket zipped up to the neck.

'I know – it's early for me, but after Ross left for work the thought of a quiet walk along the beach was hard to resist.'

Drew pulls a soft ball out of his pocket and throws it for Bertie, whose little tail wags with excitement before he races off to fetch it. Miniature Schnauzers are energetic, intelligent and charming little dogs, with their bushy eyebrows and cute little whiskers. Bertie's wiry coat is mostly dark grey, with his front paws, chest and beard being white. Bertie may be small in size, but he's big on personality. He comes running back with the ball grasped in his mouth and his head and ears proudly erect. Bertie drops it at Drew's feet and seconds later he's skidding over the sand in hot pursuit once more.

'I'm glad that Bertie and Ripley are friends now,' I reflect.

'Me, too. It's quieter, for one thing. I haven't really seen you since Ross moved in three weeks ago. How's it going?'

That's the burning question on everyone's tongue.

Drew and I stroll in Bertie's direction as he's found something of interest on the beach, more interesting than his bright yellow ball.

'Really well, I think. I just feel that he's worried he'll clutter up the cottage with his things.'

Drew turns to look at me, frowning. 'I've got all this to come when Felicity finally moves in and we're on countdown now. Two weeks to go. If she delays it any longer, she'll be having the baby in Gloucestershire, and I'll end up driving them both back here.' He's disappointed that her departure has dragged on for so long. When you work for a family business handing in your notice is one thing, walking away is a different matter entirely.

'I feel for you both. It can't be easy.'

'It isn't. Felicity won't let me start on the nursery until she moves in, but it's cutting it rather fine. We've set a firm deadline and she's promised me it will happen.'

Poor Drew, he's been spending his weekends visiting Felicity to save her the long drive, but they should be at Tigry Cottage together preparing for the big event. One look at his face tells me he still has his doubts that she'll make the break away.

'Once Felicity is here, I'm sure that it will all be fine,' I reassure him. We exchange a quick glance and I grin at him as we approach Bertie, who is head down sniffing around what appears to be a small stone.

'Oh, it's a little crab. Come on Bertie, before you get your nose pinched – here you go!' This time Drew throws the ball high into the air and it travels a fair way before bouncing on the wet strip of sand left by the retreating tide.

Watching Bertie run off, I draw in a deep breath as my eyes stray over to the rocks beneath the promontory that rises up to Lanryon Church on the headland. It was on these rocks that Granddad Harry's two-man boat was smashed to pieces. An involuntary shiver runs down my spine. I was ten years old when Mum broke the news that he was now in heaven and that he was at peace. Naturally, I battled to accept the cruel way in which he was snatched away from us and the anger I felt left a wound that has never healed. Granddad taught me how to fish for mackerel using a handline from his boat; losing him to the sea like that cast a shadow over what should be some of the happiest memories from my childhood.

'Is it so very different – the big crossover? I mean, Ross stayed over a few times before he moved in permanently, didn't he? Albeit, slipping in after dark before Jago dropped the bombshell.'

Dragging myself away from my maudlin thoughts, I nod my head. 'Yes, and surprisingly it is. This is forever now and yet Ross only turned up with a carload of personal effects.'

'Ah. Right. The rest of his stuff is still at The Forge. Well, as it's rented out fully furnished that's understandable.'

'I know, but he's as good as admitted that when Sy and Tegan are ready he will sell it to them more or less as it stands. I just wish he'd do something to make his mark on Pedrevan.'

'You mean aside from his company having built the extension and erected your garden office?'

I roll my eyes. 'At least with your place Felicity had some input into the final finishes. I was simply Ross's client during the build. He had no input whatsoever when it came to the plans or the furnishings. And now he's… treading on eggshells, trying to fit in without causing any upset.'

Bertie has found another distraction, this time it's a large tangle of seaweed.

'And you're disappointed by his sensitivity?'

'No. I understand his hesitation, but I'd love it if he suggested a few changes to make it *ours*. Can you understand where I'm coming from?'

In sharp contrast to Tegan's response, Drew raises his eyebrows and it's clear he thinks I'm being paranoid. 'Well, Felicity will take over Tigry Cottage and I'll be glad to don my painting T-shirt again and follow instructions. Maybe Ross is happy with things as they are. The stuff we surround ourselves with doesn't always mean something, does it? In your case there's family history to the few bits you rescued and chose to keep, but everything else is either new, or recycled out of choice. All that really matters is that the two of you are together.'

It's funny how getting a man's perspective on things changes it slightly. He could be right and even Tegan said I should relax a little.

'It's a sensitive issue for me because I don't want to get it wrong, Drew. I can't believe where I am now as opposed to a year ago. I was struggling to keep up with a business I'd created from scratch that had outgrown me. The irony is that I came home to look after Dad and now we're not even on speaking terms.'

Drew draws to a halt and I turn to face him. 'Kerra, in my

opinion it's time to focus on the bigger picture. You brought Nettie Pentreath back into your dad's life because you knew he needed her. He no longer uses the house instead of the kennels for his canine borders – and that's down to you. Your mum would have scowled at that thought and you knew it, but he was struggling without her. Just remember that he knows you're safe and well. It's not your fault that he's stubborn at times, or that he's not convinced Ross is the man for you, but he'll get past that. I noticed the connection between you and Ross the moment I first saw you together. Give Eddie time to come around to the idea. He thinks he's protecting you from getting your heart broken, that's all.'

Drew is right, I knew exactly what I was doing that day Nettie arrived on my doorstep and I suggested we head over the road to say hello to Dad. Sadly, I'm the most impatient person on earth and when I see something that is broken which I truly believe I can fix, I want to make it happen. It's the stubborn streak that's in my genes and something I battle with all the time. Living each day agonising over whether I'm doing the right thing if I help someone is tough. Why can't I just go for the easy option and walk away like so many other people tend to do?

'Thanks, Drew. And if you get a chance to talk to Ross...' I tail off, not quite sure how to put this.

'If he has any problems he'll air them to me hoping it will filter back to you. He's no fool, Kerra. He knows how friendly we are.'

'Ah, my go-between. Thank you!' I lean forward to plant a kiss on Drew's cheek, and he smiles back at me. 'And I'm the go-between for you and Felicity. She loves you, Drew, truly she does, but allow her to make the move when the time is right. Believe me, she has no intention of having this baby anywhere other than in Tigry Cottage.'

Drew's face pales. 'I know. She keeps telling me that. Doctor Sharpe reassured me there will be a smooth handover between the midwives and Felicity's plans for a home birth are not in jeopardy.'

Drew is already turning into a nervous wreck, and it's been like this for the past three months. My problems begin to look small by comparison.

'Bertie, stop snuffling around in that smelly seaweed. It's time to put on your lead, little man.'

We're at the far end of the beach now, parallel with the gate that leads into the car park of The Lark and Lantern. It's owned by Sam Saunders and my other bestie from school, his daughter, Polly. She's Sam's second in command, but Polly recently started up a little business venture of her own on the side.

'How is Designed to Sell doing?' Drew enquires as he straightens, and Bertie dutifully waits for permission to start walking. 'Come on boy, that's a chilly wind this morning.'

'Really well, apparently. Polly is still managing to keep both jobs going, but reading between the lines I think she's already turning clients away.'

While IT is my chosen field, I was born an entrepreneur, or – as I like to think of it – a fixer. It's impossible for me not to spot opportunities and get excited about them. Even if they don't affect me, as was the case with Polly. It was a chance conversation with an estate agent looking for someone to make over houses going on the market, which made me think of Polly. I was buying Gwel Teg at the time, one of the old fishermen's cottages on the hill leading down to Penvennan Cove. The estate agent, Oliver Sinclair was new to the area, and I gave him a whole list of potential contacts. I was happy to put him in touch with Polly when he mentioned he was looking for someone with her skills. After studying interior design at college, she's wasted behind the bar and her dad, Sam, is equally aware of that fact.

'Until Sam decides whether he's going to sell up or stay, I should imagine that Polly is torn between what's best for her new business and what's best for him,' Drew reflects.

'She is and I do feel somewhat guilty about that. But Sam realises Polly has a life to live and at some point, in the not-too-distant future, she will probably want to move out and get a place of her own.'

'Change is daunting, no matter how young or how old we are. I hope Sam decides to stay, because The Lark and Lantern wouldn't be the same without him,' Drew acknowledges.

I think all the locals feels the same way. As we walk across the pub car park there's no one in sight at this time of the morning, but the lights are on upstairs. Polly fits her new business around pub hours and that means making the most of her mornings off and the couple of hours she has every afternoon after the lunchtime rush.

Bertie trots along quite happily as we exit the gate on the opposite side of the car park and circle back along the pavement in front of Pascoe's Café and Bakery. We round the corner, walking past the tiny newsagent's and sweet shop, run by Gryff, and climb the steep hill leading up to the High Street.

I smile to myself as we pass Gwel Teg. I love this little row of traditional, white-washed stonework fishermen's cottages that are so small it makes Pedrevan seem spacious. Originally, they were all two rooms up and two down, with a coal house on the back and a toilet at the end of the garden. Most, including the one I own, have been extended now. Only two are still homes for working fishermen, having been handed down from generation to generation.

'And how is your tenant settling in?' Drew asks, as our pace slows. My calf muscles are already starting to ache as the incline starts to bite. The breeze is really picking up now and blowing my hair all over the place. I bet my face is glowing, as my cheeks are beginning to sting from the salty breeze.

'He's loving it,' I reply, matter-of-factly.

James Hooper works for my business partner, Sissy Warren, who owns The Design Cave. After I invested some capital so that Sissy could move to larger premises a couple of miles away, she's now up and running, which means I can take a back seat. That's what good entrepreneurs do – they assess a situation, suggest improvements and once they're in place they don't micro-manage.

'He's a lucky young man, Kerra, to have you looking out for him.' Drew winks at me.

'I owe James and, besides, he's such a hard worker. He helped my dad out after Mum died and I was still in London. I don't forget kindnesses like that. James could easily have found himself a full-time job, but instead he worked at the kennels part-time.'

It's true and everyone knows that. James' parents – Tom and Georgia – are Dad's nearest neighbours. Tom has a car and boat repair business which is sadly in decline, and I fear its days are numbered. It abuts the council car park in the cove and there are rumblings as it's looking decidedly run-down these days.

'Well, it's nice to think you could do that for James. It's a pretty little cottage with an awesome view.'

We stop for a moment to let Bertie sniff around and find ourselves staring up at Treylya, standing proudly on the headland above the woods. Its modern design is iconic – mostly glass, given the marvellous views it looks out onto.

Ross, me, Drew, Felicity, Gawen and Yvonne had lunch together there back in the autumn. It was the first time Ross and I had entertained as a couple, although that fact was still a secret at the time and only our closest friends knew what was going on. Would it have been the smart thing to tell Dad back then? In all honesty, I doubt it would have made a difference.

'Ross has no regrets about selling the property to Jago?' Drew enquires.

I laugh, dismissively. 'None at all. Jago thought he'd pulled a fast one to beat the price down by getting someone he knew to view it and put in a ridiculously low offer. Ross saw through it and ended up settling for more than he'd originally planned. That's karma for you.'

Drew shrugs his shoulders. 'It's hard to believe they're father and son but what goes around comes around, as my mother says. Talking of parents, I suspect I'll be getting frequent visits from mine once the baby is here.'

'Does that bother you?'

'No. It'll save me the drive. I always pop in on my way up to Gloucestershire. But they've only met Felicity a handful of times and it will be nice for them to get to know her better while spending some time with their grandchild. Goodness, it's all beginning to feel very real now!'

Tigry Cottage is rather tranquil with only Bertie and Drew there at present, but the peace is about to be well and truly shattered.

Ross raises his glass as he looks at me across our table at The Lobster Pot, a playful smile creeping over his face. 'We should do this more often,' he reflects. 'I love it when you dress up.'

As our glasses touch, I can feel my cheeks warming under his gaze. It's not often I spend so much time getting ready, but when Ross arrived home with a bouquet of flowers and a spring in his step, I decided to make a special effort.

'I'm glad you approve,' I reply, thinking how wonderful it feels to be able to escape from Penvennan for a romantic dinner for two. Glancing around, I notice there isn't one familiar face in sight and, quite frankly, it's a relief.

Ross reaches across the table to grasp my hand in his as our waiter, Michael, reappears.

'Are you guys ready to order, or would you like some more time?' Michael asks hesitantly, picking up on the body language between Ross and me.

'No, it's fine. I think we've decided. Kerra?'

'We're going to share a starter – the butternut and sage risotto with amaretti crumb, please. And for my main course I'd like the roasted whole bream with charred gem hearts, lardons and the anchovy and caper dressing. Thank you.'

'Great choice, if I may say so.' Michael smiles at me as

he taps the device in his hand. 'And for you?' He turns to look at Ross.

'The slow roasted Cornish beef chuck, for me. Thanks, Michael.'

'No problem, Ross. It's good to see you both again. The last time was your friends' wedding, wasn't it?'

'Yes. End of November last year. It's been a busy time, but you can expect to see more of us from now on.' Ross flashes me a big, cheesy smile.

'That's good to hear. I'll get someone to pop over a dish of potato shavings with an artichoke and lemon dip on the house, it will go nicely with that champagne. Your starter won't be ready for about twenty minutes I'm afraid; evenings are getting busier and busier but I'm not complaining. See you in a bit, guys.'

If Ross and I are going to have a favourite restaurant, then The Lobster Pot is perfect. I love the ambience here, although it isn't always easy to get an evening reservation. However, Ross knows everyone of course, as a good builder is always in demand.

I'm struck by the interesting cross between a rustic and an industrial vibe going on here. The building itself is set back off the street leading down to the harbour, and off to the right-hand side, the tiny pebble beach. In the peak season parking is a nightmare as people flock here to see the tall ships in the harbour. It's a huge attraction.

The Lobster Pot is a purpose-built restaurant with a smart-looking café on the ground floor, but the modern structure doesn't look at all out of place. With its exterior made up of large expanses of glass, steelwork painted a bluish-grey and wooden cladding, it has a charm of its own. To me it looks like a modern-day beach hut on a much grander scale. Suddenly, I notice that Ross is watching me intently.

'What are you thinking?' he asks, smiling at me.

'How much I love this place. I like the exposed beams and although the industrial pipes overhead might be new, they look authentic. Plus, the fact that is has windows all round with extensive views out to sea is wonderful. I can even catch a glimpse of the tall ships moored up alongside the quay. Granddad would have loved it here.'

'Not all new builds are blots on the landscape,' Ross remarks, pointedly.

I shake my head at him, as I know exactly what he's referring to. 'Treylya is a stunning house, Ross. Looking up at the headland from Penvennan Cove the glass façade mirrors the landscape. Okay, maybe it's something you'd expect to see in some exotic location rather than Cornwall, but it's a dream house.'

'Well,' he says, raising his glass to his lips and taking a sip. 'At least this new project the other side of it won't stand out quite so starkly. I can't wait to break ground.'

It's wonderful to see him so excited and enthused about a project. Most of the new-build projects Treloar's are involved in are of a standard construction, from what I've gleaned from Ross. And a large part of their workload is building domestic extensions. Then there are the small jobs, like erecting my garden office, or taking out internal walls to create space in smaller properties. But it keeps an army of local tradesmen in employment and Ross doesn't like to turn work away. That's precisely why he wants nothing to do with the way his father is expanding the business. Ross is convinced that using contractors is the wrong way to go. The men who work for him now, and their families, depend upon a regular income and they are loyal. Plus, it's all about reputation and doing a good job is more important than cutting corners to increase profits.

'Did you always want to be in the building trade?' I ask, wondering why it's a question I've not thought to ask him before.

'No. Not at all, but I grew up getting hands-on experience on sites, helping out while I waited for my father to finish his inspections. I didn't really have a choice in the matter, as my education was steered in a particular way. At one point, when some of my peers couldn't find jobs locally and had to move away, I did count myself as lucky to be able to walk into the family business. But I was naïve in those days – I thought my father wanted the best for me, but I was simply a resource he could utilise and trust.'

'You have regrets?' I assumed Ross loves what he does, as he's so committed.

A young waitress approaches with a wooden platter and leans in to place it in the centre of the table.

'Michael said to enjoy, guys. Sorry for the wait tonight.'

'No problem at all.' Ross returns her smile as she walks away, but my eyes are lighting up at the sight and smell of the food.

'These remind me of the chips my mum used to make. Cooked in beef dripping and so crispy, who can resist?' I declare, as I pick one up and slather it in dip. 'A moment on the lips, a lifetime on the hips as they say but I don't care.' It tastes divine and tonight is all about relaxing and enjoying ourselves.

'And now you have a weird look on your face, Kerra. Like you're holding something back.'

I dive in for another crispy potato as Ross savours his first one, making an appreciate groan as he does. 'Oh,' he says, immediately picking up another the moment I move my hand away, 'these are seriously good.'

Leaning in a little closer and lowering my voice, as most of the tables around us are already full, I reward him with a heart-felt smile. 'Can I help it if being with you makes me happy? I know we have a few wrinkles to iron out in the plan going forward but I'm excited about the future, aren't you?'

Ross licks his fingers, wiping them on his napkin as he sits back in the chair.

'Look, I meant it when I said that the next time I get married it will be for keeps. It's all or nothing for me with you, Kerra. I'm going into this with my eyes wide open because I know in my heart it's the right thing for both of us. I can sense that buzz in you since I moved in permanently, even if it does feel a little strange. It was different before because I came and went. Now this is it and you're right, I need my books around me. I think it's time to talk bookshelves at Pedrevan Cottage, don't you?'

I know it's a silly little thing, but my eyes begin to smart. Determined not to turn this into a big deal, I continue dipping crispy potatoes but in truth my heart is pounding away nervously inside my chest. 'The options are endless for an experienced builder. Are we talking about a second floor on the extension?' I enquire boldly.

It's important to let Ross know that whatever he wants is fine by me.

'You'd go that far just to make me happy?' he jokes, but there's an intensity behind those dark brown eyes as they stare back at me.

'I'm being serious here,' I confirm, the warmth in my voice unmistakable. Ross stops, a potato chip halfway to his mouth as I continue. 'What woman wouldn't want Mr DIY as her other half? I mean, can you imagine how difficult it is to get hold of a plumber in an emergency, or find someone who is handy with a drill when the occasion arises?'

We burst out laughing in tandem.

'I sincerely hope I have a few more uses than that, but it's a valid point. I didn't realise quite what a catch I am!' He sits back, looking rather pleased with himself.

And that's the truth. Ross *is* a catch but not for the reasons I stated. He has no idea how wonderful he is and that's why I'm in love with him; he's happy being his natural self. You should only ever give your heart to someone you can trust implicitly, and I would trust Ross with my life. I fervently believe that he feels the exact same way about me. It's both scary and exhilarating at the same time.

# 4

## Counting the Victories

As we lie in bed talking, still buzzing from our romantic evening out, I'm surprised at how open Ross is as he talks about the long-term future.

'If my father does the right thing and forms two separate companies as he promised, I intend to negotiate a deal whereby I hold fifty-one per cent of the shares in the original business. It'll cost me but I've ear-marked the profit from the sale of Treylya for that. I don't think it will be much of a fight. My father has big plans for the new set-up and once its success is proved, he will use it as his future business model to expand even further afield – and good luck to him. At least it will keep him busy. But it's not for me.'

I wasn't aware Ross had a master plan. He hesitates for a second and when he starts talking again the tone in his voice is different. 'We've never talked about the possibility of having a family, Kerra. Do you see that as a part of our future?'

*Our future* – my heart skips a beat. Is it my imagination, or is Ross holding his breath, awaiting my reply?

Knowing that Drew and Felicity are about to start on their own journey into parenthood, I wish Ross was in on it – but I'm sworn to secrecy. I do want a family, but not quite yet. Maybe in a couple of years when we've had time to enjoy our new life together. And the bonus is that we'll get to witness someone else's experience first-hand.

'Well, having been an only child I'd want two, but the timing would have to be right for us both. I will be honest and say it's a scary thought for me because what do I know about children? It's a huge commitment and kids come first, always. We're both workaholics and that would have to change.'

There's no point in beating around the bush.

'You're worried that I'd leave you to shoulder most of the responsibility?' Ross sounds perturbed, maybe even a little disappointed.

'No, Ross. I know you'll make a wonderful dad and you'd be hands-on. But we'd need to be ready, because it will mean making a few sacrifices on both sides to make it work.'

Ross rolls into me, extending his arm to draw me even closer.

'I hear what you're saying Kerra, and everything we do going forward will be a joint decision, I promise you. Financial security is the top priority, but beyond that I don't intend to let work dominate my… I mean… *our* lives. And in case you're wondering, I won't be making the same mistakes my parents made. Each one of us is unique and children should be encouraged to be the best they can be, not the embodiment of someone else's dream.'

Ross's words touch my heart in a poignant way, and I can hear the determination in his voice. God willing, one day we'll go down that path, but in the meantime it'll be an eye-opener when Felicity arrives, heavily pregnant and not far off giving birth. The last time she made it down to Penvennan Cove she'd only put on a little weight, not enough to make it obvious. I can sympathise with Drew's obsession with not putting a jinx on their plans.

'If nothing else brings Dad around,' I reflect, 'it will be the thought of a new addition to the family. Oh, and talking about family, don't forget that Tegan and Trev are here tomorrow evening. Maybe Drew will be free and the two of you could head down to The Lark and Lantern.'

Ross groans. 'Don't worry, I'll disappear before either of them arrive. Even if it means heading back to the office. I hope it goes well, Kerra, but don't get your hopes up.'

As sleep begins to claim Ross, I'm content to snuggle up next to him, trying hard not to think about what might happen when Trev steps through the door of Pedrevan Cottage. He turned his back on Tegan because my cousin Alice repeated something that wasn't true and caused a major upset. It's only right I'm the one to try to get them together again. Will he be spoiling for a fight, or prepared to listen to what his estranged sister has to say? I wonder. And what will I do if it turns out to be a total disaster, because Tegan will be devastated. She's still hopeful about holding the party sometime in June.

It's time to switch off the negative thoughts. Today has been a stride forward for Ross and me, which is the reassurance I needed. And before too long he'll get to witness the joy and excitement when a new baby appears on the scene… that thought alone makes me smile. I hope Drew quickly brushes his anxiety aside and becomes our role model for perfect parenting. I mean, how hard can it be? Babies sleep a lot when they're small, don't they?

Popping across the road to The Penvennan Convenience Store to pick up a carton of milk, I wait around until the last shopper in the queue departs before approaching the counter.

'Good morning, Kerra. What a busy one it's been. Sorry for the wait.'

'No problem, Mrs Moyle. How's Arthur, today?'

I place the milk carton and a packet of cat treats next to the till, nestling the basket back into the stack at the end of the counter.

'He's not too bad, Kerra, thank you. I fancy he's not quite so reliant on the painkillers these days, which is a good sign. Besides, he's so busy running the Penvennan Community Link-Up that it keeps his mind off his back problems.'

'That's good to hear, Mrs Moyle. And the website is running smoothly?'

She glances up at me as I pass her some coins.

'Nothing to worry about there, Kerra. You did a brilliant job, and he nipped that little spate of gossiping in the bud.'

'I assumed no news was good news,' I respond, smiling. 'Have you… Has Dad been in recently?'

As I pick up the items off the counter Mrs Moyle lets out a low sigh. 'He has and he seems well. Nettie is keeping an eye on him, but he's not his usually jolly self. There's no doubt that he's missing you, Kerra.'

'I suppose the buzz is going around about Ross having moved into Pedrevan Cottage, now?'

'It has and you know that I won't put up with any of that careless chatter in here,' Mrs Moyle reassures me. The shop is the hub of Penvennan village, but she isn't a gossip-monger. If she passes on information, I know it's for a legitimate reason.

'Um... have you seen Alice recently? I've been wondering how she's doing.'

'We've had a few little chats and I think she's learnt a lesson or two, albeit the hard way. If there are any rumours about you and Ross circulating, they won't stem from Alice. Having been on the receiving end of careless talk about the trouble over her boyfriend Ian's brother, you'd be pleased how it's changed her. It's a real pity your dad is digging in his heels over Ross, but he'll come around, Kerra.'

'I know. It's tough though and I wish—' The sound of the door opening and a stream of cars driving by interrupts my flow. 'Thanks for getting in those new cat treats, Mrs Moyle. I'll let you know Ripley's verdict.'

She smiles back at me, genially. 'My pleasure, Kerra. And it's good to see you with a spring in your step.' The look we exchange is one of suppressed laughter. Mrs Moyle and Arthur are on my side and they both know that Ross and I are happy now that we're finally living under one roof.

I leave her to greet the next customer, knowing that nothing escapes her eye. Between them, Mrs Moyle and Arthur look out for anyone in need, no matter what their problem is. Arthur can now oversee that through the website, and it was such an easy thing for me to set up for him. No more hand-written messages passed via Mrs Moyle. Or phoning around when someone is taken into hospital at short notice, either because they have animals at home, or relatives who live a distance away and need contacting. Messaging takes seconds, neighbours can do it on behalf of someone else and each person who opts for the Action Aware scheme confirms the who, what, when, and where details that Arthur requires if an emergency situation arises. I foot the costs of the web hosting, as it seemed unfair that Arthur should pay that out of his own pocket.

Deep in thought, I step out onto the pavement. The first person I spot walking towards me is Dad. He's a little late going for his paper today and he stops in his tracks. Dad hesitates for a brief second then turns to cross the road, walking on as if he hasn't seen me. A gut-wrenching feeling hits me square in the stomach. My legs feel a little unsteady as I force myself to keep going, rather than standing to watch his back as he strides away from me.

I'm angry too, and I want to call out to him, *we're family and you always said family stick together, no matter what!* But the words are only in my head and remain unspoken. It's also unfair of me, because in his eyes he's only trying to save me making what he considers to be a huge mistake.

As I wait for the traffic to clear so I can cross over to Pedrevan Cottage, a quick glance is enough to confirm that Dad has crossed back over and is nearing the turning down to the cove. It's with a heavy heart that I approach my front gate. Without warning, Ripley jumps up onto the garden wall, startling me.

'Oh, Ripley! Were you asleep under the bushes? I have

some new treats for you to try.' She sits there staring at me and I'm sure she misses Dad too. 'Life isn't always perfect, Rippers,' I bemoan.

'Kerra!' Hearing my name, I turn around and see Nettie hurrying towards me.

We hug and when we step back, she stands there running her hands along Ripley's back, then tickles her behind the ears. *Miaow, miaow, miaoooooow.*

'We miss you too, Ripley. Eddie's just gone for his paper, and I was looking out the window wondering whether I should pop across for a quick chat. I was delighted when I spotted you.'

'I saw him, Nettie. I was directly in his path when I came out of the shop.' I indicate to the items in the crook of my arm. 'Dad crossed the road to avoid having to walk past me.'

Nettie gives me a sorrowful look. 'He'll regret this when he realises how wrong he is about Ross, Kerra.'

'But surely he can see for himself how happy we are? Well, even if he's going out of his way to avoid us, I'm sure other people are talking to him about us.'

There's an awkward moment as Nettie looks at me, a worried frown forming on her face. 'He… um… Eddie said something about Jago's big ideas costing money. He thinks you're going to get pulled into it, and he said you have a lot to lose. I told him that's silly – you're a businesswoman and you know what you're doing. Besides, I'm sure The Design Cave keeps you busy and having set up the Penvennan Community Link-Up, you're on hand to sort out Arthur's problems. There's only so many balls any one person can juggle.'

I shake my head in disbelief. Judging by Nettie's reaction, at least Dad hasn't told her that I sold my business for a seven-figure sum. My investment portfolio will continue to grow but Dad has it all wrong. 'Ross has nothing at all to do with Jago's new project. If you get a chance to slip that into the conversation, I'd be very grateful.'

'It would have to be on one of his good days. He blows hot and cold. Hang in there, Kerra – he'll come round to seeing the truth. He loves you way too much to cut you out of his life forever.'

'I do hope so. Patience wins the day but sadly that isn't one of my strengths. Is everything good at Green Acre?'

'Yes. The kennels are doing fine, busy in fact. Alice and Ian are being incredibly supportive to Eddie and Ian is enjoying helping out part-time in the kennels.'

Nettie still hasn't moved in permanently, but it's a comfort knowing that she spends most of her free time there.

'How is Ian coping? It can't be easy trying to keep both Dad and Polly happy.' Being Designed to Sell's only painter/decorator that must be quite a juggling act.

'Well enough, bless him. Most of the properties are empty and Polly is happy for Ian to come and go as and when he can, so he often works late into the evening. It's making Eddie see him in a different light. If only the same were true for your uncle Alistair. Anyway, I just wanted to say that I'm glad it's out in the open now about you and Ross. The couple of times I've spotted Ross getting into his van he always smiles and waves.'

'I'm glad, too, Nettie. It's nice not having to creep around and being able to go where we please without worrying someone will spot us. It's a huge relief.'

Nettie glances up, scanning the High Street. 'I'd better go as it will only inflame things if Eddie sees us talking. Is everything back to normal for Ross now at work?'

'Thankfully, yes. Ross is busy and it's going well. We're about to start making a few small alterations at Pedrevan.' I give Nettie a meaningful glance.

'Oh, I'm thrilled to hear that Kerra, as I know how much the cottage means to you,' Nettie replies, genuinely delighted for us. 'And it won't take long for Eddie to let go of his bias because when all is said and done, he respects your judgement, Kerra. Right, I'd better get back to it, or your dad will wonder what I've been doing. I'm on sweeping up duty this morning.'

Nettie bids Ripley goodbye and she immediately thrusts out her front paws, stretching to get that last lingering stroke.

'Thanks, Nettie, for everything. Dad is lucky to have you in his life and Mum would be grateful to know how much you care about him.'

As I watch her walk away, memories of the past fill my head. Nettie was Mum's best friend and her biggest supporter when the kennels were first set up, even though Nettie was working at the vet's surgery. Nestled on the edge of the village, it's literally a stone's throw away. Nettie was at Green Acre early in the morning for the first dog walking stint of the day, in the evenings on the way home from work and most weekends. She often stayed for dinner, and she was one of the family. But that was back when Dad worked with Uncle Alistair in the family carpentry and joinery business. Now he's carrying on Mum's dream, which was never his, but with Nettie stepping back into his life at least he's no longer lonely, albeit that for Nettie it's a bit of a sacrifice given that she also has a new career as a writer. It must be difficult at times, but somehow she manages to make it work. And she's happy, which is all that counts.

'Come on, Ripley. Let's go inside and you can try these new treats. It says they're for cats with a discerning taste and I think that sums you up perfectly, don't you?'

*Miaoooooow*.

'There's a reason I've been ignoring you, Tegan. Some things can't be forgiven.' Trev's opening remark the moment he sets eyes on Tegan doesn't bode well.

'I understand, Trev – really I do, but if we don't talk—'

'Talk? What is there to say? It was bad enough that people who didn't even know me were pointing the finger, let alone my own sister.' Trev raises his voice, unable to disguise his anger.

Tegan visibly flinches. The fact they're still standing isn't helping matters.

'Please, guys, take a seat. Raised voices won't achieve anything.'

Trev looks at me, apologetically. 'Sorry, Kerra. I'll tone it down, I promise.'

It's not me he should be apologising to, it's Tegan, who looks like she's in shock. She wasn't expecting him to rip into her from the first second he stepped through the door. Tegan glances at me, a look of desperation in her eyes.

Trev sits in one of the armchairs and I seat myself next to Tegan on the sofa. They are both looking at me as if I'm some sort of mediator. I swallow hard, conscious that if this meeting doesn't go well they may never reconcile.

'Maybe this is a mistake, but you're here now. It's time to talk about what happened because this might be the only chance you get.' It sounds dire, but it's true. 'I remember a time when you were the best of friends. I envied you having a brother, Tegan, because Trev idolised his big sister. And Trev, Tegan often stepped in to get you out of trouble when your constant joking around backfired. I'd have given anything to have had a sibling, someone to look out for me.'

At least they're sitting here looking more subdued. My words seem to have diffused the tension, at least for now. 'Before I leave you to it,' I continue, 'there's something that I need to say to you both and I hope you don't mind if I get it off my chest now.'

Trev merely shrugs his shoulders and Tegan simply nods her head.

'We're all well aware that it was my cousin Alice, whose comment caused the situation to escalate. Cassie knew exactly what she was doing and that was to use a young and naïve Alice to spread a rumour that wasn't true. Alice had no idea that Cassie was desperate to get you back at any cost Trev, following your break-up. When you and Ellie announced you were having a baby, Alice had been led to believe by Cassie that the two of you were still seeing each other in secret. Now I'm not condoning Alice's behaviour in any way. What she did was wrong as it was none of her business. But, at the time, Alice was repeating what she believed to be the truth. Ask yourself why Cassie didn't go straight to Tegan. Unless she knew that being face to face with her, your sister would instantly suss out that it was an outright lie. The best way to sow a tiny seed of doubt was to have everyone else talking about it and she set Alice up to kick it off.'

'I couldn't believe what I was hearing, Trev.' Tegan's voice is pained, her expression strained. 'I knew in my heart it wasn't true but what could I have said that would have changed anything?'

'Ellie, too, believed it for a while but mainly because you didn't instantly jump to my defence.' Trev stares at his sister, accusingly. 'You wavered, Tegan,' he says, bitterly. 'You weren't sure whether or not I was sleeping with both Cassie and Ellie. I would never have done that. Never in a million years and yet when it all blew up you said nothing. Not to begin with, anyway.'

Tegan bows her head, her hands fidgeting in her lap. 'And I can't forgive myself for that, Trev. When I came to you, you refused to speak to me but without hearing the truth from your lips what was I to do? I lost out on getting to see my nephew growing up first-hand; all I've seen are the photos. I made a big mistake and I've regretted it ever since.'

Easing myself up off the sofa, I decide it's time to leave them to it. I head upstairs to sit on the bed with Ripley. The first thing I do is to text Ross.

> They're downstairs talking now and at least they're calmer than they were to begin with. Why not head back for 9.30? They should be all talked out by then. Give Gawen and Yvonne my best regards. Ripley is snoring now and I'm lonely. I really hope Trev and Tegan can put the past behind them. See you soon. xx

I stare out the window to pass the time, feeling restless until my phone kicks into life and it's Ross; it's a comfort to hear his voice.

'I wish I'd stayed now. I don't like to think of you feeling lonely.' The tenderness in his voice gives me palpitations. If he was here he'd wrap his arms around me and my worries would melt away.

'I'm fine, really, just a little on edge.'

'Is there a reason why you've never told me the whole story, Kerra? I know it was something to do with Alice, but she was just a teenager at the time.'

My mouth goes dry, and I swallow hard. 'Ellie nearly turned her back on Trev when Alice repeated what Cassie had told her, believing it was all true. What if Ellie had decided not to have the baby? It was a truly horrendous experience with people treating rumour as fact and taking sides.'

'Believe me, Kerra, I had no idea how bad it was.' Ross's shock is tangible.

'You were living at the manor house by then, so how could you have known what was happening in the cove?'

'Yes, but it's been eating away at you and I should have made time to ask the question. I'm sorry I didn't, but I'm listening now.'

A lump rises up in my throat and I steel myself. It's not easy to acknowledge something we'd all rather forget.

'When Cassie eventually broke down and admitted that she had lied to Alice, Ellie and Trev kept to themselves for a while. The fallout had affected their families in ways no one could have foreseen. Some longstanding friendships were broken forever because Alice's careless words allowed

Cassie to make herself look like the victim for a while, suggesting that Ellie got pregnant to stop Trev leaving her. It should have been one of the happiest times in Trev and Ellie's lives and a part of me can totally understand why, to Trev, that was unforgiveable.'

'That's quite a burden you've been carrying around, Kerra. But it's not your fault.'

'I know, but that doesn't make it any easier. A test like that at the beginning of their relationship seems to have made Ellie and Trev even stronger as the years have passed. The chilling thought is how easily it could all have gone terribly, terribly wrong.'

The silence between us is heavy and I know he finally understands why tonight is so important to Tegan and, I freely admit, to me too.

# 5

## Confronting My Fears

Retrieving a tape measure from my bag, I hold it out to Ross who looks at me quizzically. It's the sort you buy at the supermarket checkout, not from a builder's merchants.

'I'm on breakfast duty this morning as you did it yesterday. I thought you might like to do a little measuring up while you're waiting?'

Ross raises an eyebrow, cagily. 'Measuring what, exactly?'

'Shelves.'

'Oh, right!' His face brightens perceptively. 'Why not?'

As I begin breaking eggs into the bowl, Ross disappears and returns just as I'm about to dish up, but he's scratching his head.

'It's going to be tight,' he mutters, mainly to himself as he slumps down onto one of the chairs. He has a piece of paper in his hands covered in what looks from here to be squiggles. 'The alcoves at The Forge are wider and I'm not sure we'll fit in my entire collection. I might have to weed out a few of my books.'

'That would be a shame. Why not extend the shelving around the corner and end it just short of the window opening?'

Ross taps the pencil against his pursed lips while he turns, scanning the wall as he considers my suggestion.

'You don't think the wrap-around would be too much?'

He's not entirely sure it's a good idea but I'm not giving up that easily. 'Or use the section of wall the other side of the window that shields the front door. It's a good run and should do the trick.'

'If you're sure you don't mind. It would make for a more balanced look. And I'd have a bit of shelf space to spare.' His face immediately brightens.

'Good, that means you can buy some more,' I reply, breezily. 'Please tell me that some of them are cookery books.'

'Why, are you thinking of learning?'

As I place the plate of French toast down in front of him I think it looks pretty good, aside from the burnt bit running along one edge. But hey, he can cut that off if he's being fussy.

'Maybe.' I try not to smile because I know anything I make doesn't quite go down as well as Ross's offerings.

But even so, he happily puts aside his pen and paper to grab a knife and fork, before grabbing the jug of maple syrup and pouring on a generous glug.

'The French are clever. There's not a lot you can do to spoil French toast and I'm impressed. But I don't have a problem cooking because I hate doing the dishes.' He beams at me as I watch him delicately cut off the blackened edge on one of the slices of brioche.

'As long as we share the food shopping, that's a deal.' Well, that was easy.

'I notice that you don't use the dishwasher very often. It's not broken, is it?' Ross looks at me questioningly.

'No. It's fine. I've used it once, or twice. It just seems a bit daft when there's only two of us. I hate having dirty dishes hanging around and it doesn't take long to clear them.'

'That's what fascinates me about you, Kerra. Expect the unexpected. You might be into IT but you're old school in other ways.'

I frown as I pop a piece of eggy bread into my mouth, wondering if that last remark is a compliment or a criticism.

'It's one of my strengths,' I confirm, proudly. 'I'm flexible, according to my peer reviews when I worked in London. And I've decided you and I need to walk more. If people get used to seeing us out and about together there'll be nothing to whisper about. We need to up our visibility.'

He looks at me and grimaces.

'Really?'

'There's no better time than the present. As soon as we finish, let's clear up and head down to the cove for a walk. Who knows, we might cross paths with a few people who haven't yet heard you've moved in with me.'

Ross looks disappointed. 'Do we have to do that today? I want to work out what wood and brackets I need to order.'

'Brackets? Hmm… invisible fixings would be better,' I point out.

'How about batons fixed to the wall and I'll paint them so that they don't stand out? A bookshelf takes a lot of weight, you know.'

'That sounds good to me – I'll be your assistant, fetching and carrying. But that's after our little trip down to the cove.'

'You are sure about this, are you?' Is he nervous about being seen together in public, or putting his stamp on the sitting room? I wonder.

'Yes, to both. And I'm looking forward to discovering some gems among your collection.'

Ross puts back his head and laughs as he reaches over to grab my plate and stack it onto his. 'Well, between eco-friendly building techniques, crop rotation and animal husbandry, and the memoirs of various historical figures, I'm sure you'll be spoilt for choice.'

Guess I'll be keeping my fingers crossed that he has a good collection of cookery books, then – but we're inching forward and that thought is enough to lift my spirits.

We don't have to go far before we bump into one of the main sources for Penvennan's grapevine – Zacky Carter. As he spends most of his evenings propping up the bar at The Lark and Lantern, everyone knows if you buy him a drink, he'll tell you whatever you want to know. And what he doesn't know, he's happy to put two and two together, but maths isn't his strong point.

'Hi Zacky, how are you?'

'Tickin' over, Kerra, ta very much. See there's been some further changes at Pedrevan,' he replies, lowering his eyes as he notices that Ross and I are holding hands. 'Big one fer you Ross, movin' out of Treylya.'

Both Ross and I have pleasant smiles on our faces as we watch Zacky's eyes stray to my left hand, which is ringless.

'It is, Zacky, but it's good to be living in the heart of the village,' Ross replies with enthusiasm.

'And yer makin' yerself at home in Pedrevan Cottage? I'd have thought it were a bit small for you.'

'No more glass boxes for me, Zacky. It's time I had a real home. I have a few bits and pieces still to move in, but we're doing good.' Ross turns to gaze at me adoringly and it's hard to suppress a giggle.

'I don't suppose the guy that's been hangin' around is anythin' to do with the thief who used to rent Pedrevan Cottage, is he?'

A sinking feeling makes my stomach turn over and Ross immediately responds.

'What guy?' His voice is insistent.

'Might be nothin' to worry about, but thought I'd mention it in case. Seen him a few times I 'ave, just walkin' up and down. Not a thug like the other men who turned up back last year, but smartish. The police got them all, didn't they?'

'Yes. Two of them are now serving time, but Kerra's tenant was let off with a suspended sentence. He was just a pawn in the scheme. But if you see this stranger again, Zacky, would you do me a favour and give me a call? Immediately.' Ross pulls out his wallet to grab one of his business cards and with it he extracts a ten-pound note, handing both to Zacky. 'Here's a drink for your troubles.'

'Thanks, Ross. Will do! And I don't know if you've 'eard

the latest but the police have yanked in Ian's brother, Fraser, again. Wriggled off the hook the first time, but there's a rumour goin' around they 'ave a witness. Bit of a worry there fer yer cousin, Kerra – I wonder what yer dad will make of that.' Zacky redirects his attention to me, obviously looking for some sort of reaction.

'Well, if that's true, then I'm sure that no one here in Penvennan Cove will think any the less of Ian,' I state, trying not to let my annoyance show. 'He isn't his brother's keeper, Zacky. Ian's a hard worker and he's certainly earnt my respect.'

Zacky looks a little startled at my robust response and shifts from one foot to the other, uneasily.

'I was thinkin' the same thing Kerra,' Zacky replies awkwardly. 'Just thought as it was linked to yer old tenant, Mr Mills, you'd want to know. Anyways, I'll leave you two love birds to get on with yer walk. I'm headin' to the shop to have a cup of tea with Arthur. Lucky man, he is – Mrs Moyle certainly knows how to look after him. Makes me miss me own wife, but there you go. Life gives and it also takes away.'

Ross and I exchange a worried look. Zacky might be, arguably, the biggest spreader of gossip in the village but some of that is probably due to loneliness. He's immediately on it whenever something out of the normal occurs because he doesn't have anything else to occupy his time.

'She was a fine woman, Zacky. She's missed by many around here, I'm sure.' A loss is a loss and I know from experience how deeply it cuts.

'Aye, she was that. I'd best get off as the tea will be stewin'. I'm glad you didn't hare off to Launceston, Ross, and that new office of yours. Chances are we'd have lost Kerra too, and that would 'ave been a shame.' With that he walks off.

My goodness, Zacky is feeling sentimental today. A sensation of guilt begins to flood through me, even though every single word we've exchanged will, I'm sure, be repeated verbatim in the pub this evening.

'I'm growing tired of people still talking about the burglary. I'm sure if what Zacky said is true, Sissy would have said something to me. After all, it was her old shop that was robbed,' I point out, keeping my voice low as we approach the turn down to the cove.

'If it's connected to the gang who trapped Mr Mills, you're right – I'm sure the police would have informed Sissy,' Ross reassures me.

Mr Mills was my last tenant at Pedrevan Cottage before I moved back for good. He was being blackmailed into driving stolen cars around the country. I assumed that following on from the court case, the entire gang was either behind bars or had received suspended sentences, and that all the loose ends were tied up.

'And what about this stranger poking around?' The mere thought of it sends an icy chill through my veins.

'Don't worry about this mystery man, Kerra. If this person reappears Zacky will let me know and I'll get straight onto it. Maybe it's someone looking to buy a shop here. What did strike me as strange, was how down Zacky sounded today.'

'I was thinking the same thing. Maybe I'll have a little word with Arthur next time I see him. It's not like Zacky to be maudlin. I wonder if something has upset him?'

Ross shrugs his shoulders. 'He's usually too busy talking

about other people, or gleaning whatever news he can, to give out anything about himself.'

I can't dispute that.

'Kerra, Ross!'

James is walking up to the gate of Gwel Teg as we approach, and he waits for us to catch up with him. A little smirk flashes over his face as he notices that Ross and I are arm in arm. I guess he wasn't sure the rumours were true, either.

'What a lovely day. Are you… two… off for a stroll along the beach?' He's such a pleasant young man and he seems to have settled into the cottage well.

'We are. There's nothing like a walk to work off a heavy breakfast – sorry, *hearty* breakfast,' Ross jests, as I playfully elbow him in the ribs.

'I'm giving up my Sunday to give Dad a hand. He's decided to start clearing out some of his *rusty gold*.' The look on James's face is priceless. The Salvager's Yard has several galvanised-roofed outbuildings filled with relics, mainly cars and boats, but the old ways of recycling spare parts is slowly dying out.

'I'm sure he really appreciates your help James,' I reply, thinking what a daunting task that is going to be.

'He can't stay locked in the past forever, can he? My granddad, Wally, is going to be working alongside Dad from now on. He gets bored and Grandma is thrilled to bits to get him out the house. Dad couldn't afford to do this on his own, so it's the perfect solution.'

'That's wonderful news,' Ross responds as I try to hide a look of total surprise.

'It was Sam at The Lark and Lantern who put the idea

in Dad's head. He said taking on a partner and an injection of cash opens up options. Dad wouldn't entertain working with a stranger, of course, but I think the two of them will be in their element. Anyway, I must go as I'm popping up to the shop to get a few supplies to keep them going.'

'Energy bars?' Ross quips, smiling.

'Nice one! I doubt either of them have had one before, but it's worth a try. Enjoy your day, guys!' James heads off up the hill as we continue our descent towards the cove.

'Well, that's the last thing I was expecting to hear. You do know that this is all down to you?' Ross comments, chuckling to himself.

'Me? I've never said a word to Tom.'

'No, it's your little business talks with Sam. He's passing on what's he's picked up. Georgia will be delighted that Tom is finally facing facts. If something doesn't change soon, he'll end up going bust and now it sounds like they aren't about to give up. Is Sam any closer to making a decision about selling up?'

Inwardly I groan. I hope that, too, doesn't become a hot topic of conversation as they stand around supping their pints at the bar. I can hear it now, *Kerra Shaw passing on her big ideas – she'll be taking over the entire cove next!* Well, it's not like it'll be something I haven't heard said before.

'Sam and I haven't spoken since – I don't know – late November, maybe? I hope he took my suggestion on board and called in a financial adviser. He's sitting on a valuable plot of land, in addition to the pub and the holiday lets he no longer uses.'

'I wonder if those tentative offers he's had in the past came to anything?'

It's such a dilemma for Sam. I'm sure there are some big deals on the table given the prime location, and it must be tempting when cash flow is a constant worry for him. But if he leaves the pub, his life instantly changes. He'd be starting all over again, albeit with a lot of money in the bank. Having been through that upheaval myself, I know how disorientating it can be and the problems it brings with it. The pub is his social life, too, and he's happy in his work surrounded by the folk who embraced him and Polly when they moved to the cove almost twenty-five years ago.

'Well, I see it as a good sign that he's taking his time to consider his options – unless he's done nothing at all, that is. But it's not for me to press him. At least you were able to give him firm figures for renovating the cottages, as that information might help him get a little more if he does sell up.'

'Yes, but let's hope that it's not to one of the big boys. It would be a real shame to lose the community feel at The Lark and Lantern. If the new owners turned it into one of those soulless places enticing people in with cheap meals and racking up the profits on the drinks, it would be devastating. Or, even worse, if it was turned into a wine bar. Can you see Tom, or Zacky, putting up with that?' Ross scoffs.

'Things move on, and people get used to change even if they don't like it. It throws up other opportunities,' I point out, truthfully.

Ross glances at me, looking somewhat amused as we step off the tarmac of the council car park and onto the pebbly sand.

'If that's the case, the only other option for the regular

old-timers is the bar at the village hall and I doubt they'd want to open during the week unless there's an event going on. The Lark and Lantern, Pascoe's Bakery and Café, and The Penvennan Convenience Store, are the heart of Penvennan. Major changes to any one of those would have a huge impact. If Gryff ever retires, I'm sure even the newsagents would get snapped up quickly. It's a little goldmine as it stands for a small investor. It's the only place within walking distance that sells newspapers.'

'And sweets!' I jump in, as I think back fondly to my childhood. But we both know that big business is all about profit. Unless someone was born and brought up in a small village, they wouldn't understand. It's the people who work and live here who uphold that quaint traditional family-style nostalgia. Ironically, today not all of them were born here, but it's what attracted them to the cove. And it's what brings the visitors back every year. Cornwall is full of little gems that can't be over-developed because of their location, but that doesn't mean we're not vulnerable.

'If Tom takes down some of those rickety old sheds, he'd have room for a modular building to create a bar, assuming he could get a licence to sell alcohol. After all, he's in the pub every night anyway. A bigger version of my garden office would be perfect. We could do some fund raising—'

Ross stops in his tracks, tugging on my hand to swing me around to face him. 'Stop with the ideas… we've enough to deal with for now simply putting ourselves on display.' And with that he draws me into him as I close my eyes and offer up my mouth to his.

When you are in the arms of the person you love, one kiss is never enough – one hug is never enough. I still feel like this could all be a dream and I'm praying that I won't wake up and discover that's exactly what it is and I'm still back in London.

'Listen, something is telling me that it's time you confronted your fears.'

I pull away, puzzled as I stare up into Ross's eyes. There's a hint of hesitation and his face reflects his concern.

'Look, Kerra – I know you feel a sense of guilt for not visiting your granddad's grave, but I'm here with you and we should go there together.'

Ross grasps both of my hands in his, willing me not to look away, but instinctively I turn towards the headland and Lanryon church.

'Come on,' he encourages as he moves forward. Reluctantly, I follow as he leads me by the hand.

From here it looks tiny but as we traverse the firm, wet strip of sand left by the retreating waves, little chills start to run up and down my spine.

'Can you see the face?' I half-whisper. We pass a family of four, two dogs running around them in circles while a group of young children screech at the tops of their voices.

Ross increases the grip he has on my hand, pulling it into him and pressing it against his body.

'The windows either side of the turret in the middle look like eyes,' I continue, my voice low. 'And the double doors are a gaping black hole – like a mouth. The day of Granddad's funeral, during the service I ran and hid behind one of the bushes because I felt it was going to devour us all.'

Ross lifts my hand to his mouth, tenderly kissing the back of it.

'Then let me prove to you that there's nothing to fear, except fear itself. Death is such a tough thing to come to terms with when you're so young and you would have been terrified at the time. Let's go and tell him our good news.'

We stroll along in silence, taking in the beautiful sky overhead, which makes the water look almost translucent this morning. There are lots of people out walking, ironically none of them locals to witness our first leisurely outing together. The closer we get to the rocks at the base of the cliff, the harder it is to control my erratic breathing.

The screeching, raucous call of the seagulls as they soar and swoop, some choosing to land on the jagged tips of the razor-sharp rocky outcrop, fill me with dread. Granddad once told me that the gulls' cries were said to be the souls of men calling out to be saved. As a child, the day that we all traipsed along the path up to the church to bury his ashes, I felt they were taunting me. It was overcast and the seagulls come inland when the sea is rough. To me it seemed they were letting me know they'd claimed another fisherman, as if they'd lured his boat to its doom on purpose. Doing my best to shake off the memories formed by an imaginative ten-year-old, Ross gives me an encouraging smile as we begin the climb.

All the local fishermen around here who die are buried at Lanryon church. The history of the place is that the land behind it was sold off a long time ago to raise much needed funds to repair the roof. It has a huge spire, in front of which the two turrets stand out imposingly. As there hasn't been any access by road for the last hundred or so years, the tradition is that the ashes are carried by hand. The funeral procession snakes its way up the long incline and the service is held at the graveside. It was a miserably grey day, the wind whipping around us and so many tears shed that it felt to me, way back then, like it was hell on earth. I didn't want it to be Granddad's resting place.

'The cowslips are pretty,' Ross remarks as we walk single file. 'It's rare to see so many of them.'

He's right – the clumps of coastal grass in between the outcrops of rock are interspersed with the raised stems giving a bright splash of vibrant yellow amidst a soft, feathery green. The natural beauty as the sheer drop begins to level off to my left and, either side of the path – where greener, more vibrant grasses take over – is stunning. As we step up onto the level, grassy expanse there are a whole variety of manicured shrubs and trees in between the ancient gravestone and the newer, marble headstones. Primroses abound, interspersed with little pockets of sweet violets, their soft, purply-blue hue a brilliant contrast and a total surprise. Tall stems of cow parsley run in swathes interspersed with clumps of crocuses, and it takes my breath away for a moment.

'It's not that bad up here, is it?' Ross prompts gently, as I wander closer to the church.

The dark, gaping hole that I perceived as a *mouth* is simply a pair of aged oak doors with metal studs and as for the windows high above it, the *eyes* are panes of leaded glass glinting in the sunlight.

I stop for a moment to scan around. All the earlier graves have solid headstones, with names chiselled into the lichen-covered stone. Some are now on a tilt, but the whole area is well-tended. Ross follows me as I try to make out the names, but the constant onslaught of the wind and rain have worn much of the lettering away.

Granddad's plot consists of a triangular black granite stone, which marks where his ashes lay. Much later, Mum had some of Grandma's ashes buried alongside his, the remainder were laid to rest at my great-grandparent's plot in the churchyard at Polreweek.

I kneel, running my fingers over the carved words, inset with gold.

Harry Pascoe
Beloved son, husband, father and grandfather.
In times of peril, firm and brave.

'You know why the fishermen still want their remains to come here, don't you?' Ross says, softly.

'Tradition,' I reply, letting out a low sigh.

'Partly. But here they rest among friends, with the church protecting them and all around the familiar sounds of the sea, the birds and elements they knew throughout their working lives.'

Ross crouches alongside me, slipping his hand into mine.

'It's a nice thought, Ross. One I hadn't considered before.'

Suddenly Lanryon doesn't look like that evil face constantly scanning the sea, eager to claim its next victim. It looks like a stout tower, a defender standing tall to guard the brave men laid to rest here, like an eternal protector. And it's surprisingly peaceful. I love the semi-wild feel of the colourful flower heads in among the neatly mown grass and it saddens me that I didn't make the trek before now.

'I'm back, Granddad,' I mutter, softly. 'Ross brought me up here today, but I will come again because I'm home now and I miss you and Grandma.'

As we walk away, hand in hand, Ross turns to look at me and catches me swiping a tear from my cheek.

'Always remember, Kerra, that the only thing to fear is fear itself. And now you're free of it.'

'Thank you for understanding and now I feel a little foolish. But a part of my fear is that Granddad Harry might have...' I hesitate, loath to say the words out loud. 'It might not have been an accident.'

The look of shock on Ross's face quickly turns to sadness, as if he can feel my pain.

'I can't prove it,' I add, hurriedly, 'but he was an experienced sailor, and he knew when a storm was brewing even before the clouds started rolling in. Maybe he wanted to give up on life, but if that was the case he was also giving up on his family. And me, because I idolised him.'

'Oh, Kerra. Have you ever talked to anyone about it?' The look of compassion in his eyes is touching.

'I couldn't get my head around why Granddad left it so late to start back to shore. Mum would become tearful if I tried to bring it up and Dad would always change the subject. I needed Granddad in my life. Not only were we the best of friends but he always made time to listen to me. And Grandma needed him too. He must have been very unhappy not to fight and to this day it still breaks my heart to think that we didn't see it.'

Finally speaking out loud the thoughts that I've been trying to ignore for so long is like ripping the scab off an old wound. Raw emotion is hard to handle, and it hurts.

'If that were true it would have come out at the time, Kerra.'

'Yes, but I was too young to be told the truth and then

as the years go by people think it doesn't matter anymore. But it does to me. It's easier to bury something forever than deal with the truth and, sadly, it seems that my family aren't any different.'

As we head back down to the beach in single file, I'm so grateful to Ross. I wonder how long he's been planning this, waiting for the opportunity to present itself.

'I love you, Ross – for understanding. And I'm glad you brought me up here.'

It has helped, but Granddad was a god-fearing man, and some believe that taking your own life is a sin. What if his ashes are at rest, but his soul is in torment? It's not something I know enough about to dismiss out of hand. If he died clinging onto that belief, then that thought crushes my heart into tiny little pieces because he was a genuinely good man. It's not fair. And it's not right.

# 6

## Good News Incoming

The last two weeks have flown by and so much has happened. Felicity arrived on Wednesday and Tigry Cottage is now her new home. Ross is taking his first Saturday off in a while, as we offered to help unload the small removal van when it arrives later this morning.

As Ross and I sit enjoying a leisurely coffee out on the deck, Bertie appears at our little pet window. We both give him a wave, and he sits there watching us with interest. His tail is wagging as if it's on fire and his head is tilted to one side.

'Hi Bertie,' I call out. 'Ripley's asleep, but she'll come out to see you later.'

Ross looks at me as if I'm mad. 'Bertie is extremely intelligent, but I think that's a step too far even for him to understand, Kerra,' he laughs.

'I don't agree,' I reply, sternly. 'I know that look of his and he wants to know where Ripley is.'

'So, you're an animal empath now, are you?' But Ross isn't mocking me this time, he's curious.

'Maybe I am. Or maybe Bertie and I have a special friendship, and he lets me know in his subtle ways. See how his head is to one side, but his ears are perky? That's him checking everything is all right this side of the fence.'

As if to prove it's safe to relax now, Bertie collapses down onto the deck, his head resting on his front paws.

'Hey, neighbours,' Drew calls over the fence and seconds later his face appears alongside Bertie's. They both look like they are grinning at us and it's comical.

'We need a bigger window,' Ross declares. 'I can't believe you are lying flat on the deck.'

'Kerra and I have managed, haven't we? It wasn't much fun in the depths of winter, bundled up in our coats, but we often lay here with Ripley and Bertie having a chat.'

Ross shakes his head, laughing. 'Perhaps we should take out that piece of fencing, cut it in half vertically and turn it into a gate. If we installed a plexiglass panel next to it you wouldn't have to lie down,' he suggests.

'I second that idea,' Felicity's voice looms up out of nowhere.

'Morning,' I call out. 'It's count down to the official moving-in process. Are you guys ready?'

'Just about,' Felicity replies, sounding far from convinced. 'It's mainly small boxes, but lots of them and just a couple of bigger items. We're made some space, but most of it is going up into the loft for now and I'll gradually sort through it when I have time.'

'We'll bring in a bottle of champagne to make a toast when the van arrives,' Ross joins in. Only three of us will be toasting with bubbles in our glasses today. He's in for a huge surprise and I can't wait to see his reaction.

'Right, we'd best get back to it. See you guys later,' Drew calls out. With that he disappears from view.

My phone rings and I snatch it up, my eyes on Ross as he lazes back in his seat to enjoy what is an unusually warm start to the day for mid-April.

'Hi, Tegan, how are you?'

With the phone held tightly to my ear, I listen in amazement as she tells me her good news.

'Oh, my goodness – that's incredible. I'm thrilled for you, really thrilled.'

Ross is now sitting forward in his seat, looking at me expectantly and I nod my head enthusiastically as Tegan babbles on quite happily.

'Thanks for letting me know. I'm delighted for you all. Please give Sy my love and we'll speak soon.'

As I click end call Ross looks at me impatiently.

'Tegan is at her parent's house and Sy is meeting Trev, Cassie, and their son, Daniel, for the first time. She sounded ecstatic and now they can finally fix a date for their big celebration – Saturday the nineteenth of June. I'm so relieved, Ross. There are three occasions that tend to bring a family together, even when they are distant – births, weddings, and funerals. Tegan didn't want to celebrate her and Sy's marriage without both sides of the family being there. How quickly the old wounds will heal is anybody's guess, but it's a great start.'

I assumed Ross would feel as positive as I am, but instead he looks pensive.

'Don't expect that sort of reaction from my family,' he

replies, soberly. 'My father isn't big on miracles, unless there's money to be made from them.'

Sadly, I fear that he's right and as for my dad, the thought of me becoming a Treloar is his worst nightmare, but he's going to have to get used to it.

Ripley appears just as the van draws up outside of Tigry Cottage. I hurry into the kitchen to get her some fresh food before heading out to join Ross, but the ever-curious Ripley insists on following me outside. She wants to poke her nose into everything that's happening, even though she's a little skittish around strangers. Especially when there's noise involved, and the tailgate makes the most awful sound. It's the grind of metal on metal and I fight hard not to wince as the young guy yanks it open.

'If you want to shift the boxes along to this end,' Ross informs him, 'we'll soon have this lot offloaded.'

'Great, thanks. And much appreciated. We're one guy down today and this was the smallest load, so I'm on my own.'

I leave Ross and the van driver chatting and head inside Tigry Cottage, calling out as I step through the open door.

'Felicity? It's Kerra.'

Her head pops into view. She's in the kitchen, standing at the sink, which is set back behind the open-plan staircase.

'Hi, Kerra, come on through. The van has arrived earlier than expected. I'm just finishing up and Drew's putting a paint brush in to soak.'

As I walk into the kitchen area Felicity turns around and a huge smile flashes over my face.

'Oh my, just look at you. You're positively glowing! The last time you were here was the middle of October and you were, what – nine weeks pregnant?'

'Yep, and now I only have five weeks to go,' she declares, sounding both excited and nervous.

I gingerly give her a hug, and she hugs me back with a fierceness which is touching. Today is a big step forward for Felicity and I understand that.

'It's still sinking in that once my things are offloaded then I really am here for good. It's all beginning to feel disconcertingly real. I'm sorry we've kept ourselves to ourselves since I arrived, but Drew and I needed a couple of days to unwind and adjust. He's been a star visiting me every weekend to save me the drive while I was getting everything sorted. And now it's time for me to pamper him for a change.'

Her eyes are bright as she draws back, taking a deep breath to compose herself.

'That's wonderful to hear, Felicity, and welcome to Penvennan Cove, your new home. I can't wait until word gets out that you and Drew are having a baby!'

It's been difficult for them both as for a long time the gossips referred to Felicity as the *phantom girlfriend* because she rarely came here at all. When her visits stopped completely, there really wasn't any point in them sharing their news. This is going to be a shocking revelation now that Felicity is here to stay.

'I'm anxious to see Ross's reaction,' she admits playfully, a twinkle in her eye.

'About what?' Ross's voice rises up from behind a stack of boxes obscuring his face. I hurry towards him to take off the top one. 'Thanks, Kerra, that's a light one and I was worried it would topple off.'

As he stoops to put them down on the floor and straightens, the moment he spots Felicity he looks dumbstruck.

'Surprise!' Felicity says, smiling broadly as she places her hands on her enormous baby bump.

He turns to me, accusingly. 'Did you know about this?'

The sound of footsteps announces Drew's arrival. He edges his way sideways through the door to accommodate the unwieldy box without scuffing the frame.

'What on earth have you got in here, Felicity? It weighs a ton,' he mumbles, not realising we're all staring at him. Dumping it down next to Ross's pile, he groans as he straightens.

'What? Oh…' When he looks at Ross, Drew's face breaks out into a mischievous grin. 'Sorry, mate. I was sworn to secrecy.'

'It's only taken him nearly eight months to get his head around the fact that we're going to be parents, but he's getting there – aren't you, darling?' Felicity teases, as Ross sticks out his hand to shake Drew's. Then he walks over to give Felicity a tentative kiss on her cheek.

'Well, you look radiant, Felicity. But, oh man… are you all geared up for this? I mean, when's the due date?'

'The twenty-first of May,' Drew confirms. 'We haven't even started turning the spare room into a nursery yet. And the big boxes at the back of the van are furniture that will need assembling. We've got a lot to do, that's for sure.'

'Well, now I'm here we can crack on with it,' Felicity adds, with great enthusiasm.

'You're going to be taking it easy,' Ross states, emphatically. 'You can supervise and keep the coffee coming, we're here to lend a hand.'

'If you're up for it,' I jump in. 'I was thinking it would be nice to organise a joint welcome-to-the-village and painting party. Maybe include Gawen and Yvonne, and Sy and Tegan?'

Three heads nod enthusiastically, and Felicity's eyes are shining again. There were times, I will admit, that I doubted this would ever happen – I mean, Felicity giving up her old life and settling here with Drew for good. She's not doing it just because of the baby, though. It was only her family ties and the responsibilities we all tend to shoulder out of duty that held her back. Her heart has always been here in Penvennan with Drew. But it's hard making that break.

'Great. Let me know when and I'll organise that, food included. You two have plenty to do finding a home for these boxes. Just make sure you have enough paint on hand.'

'How about next Saturday? We'll stock up on alcohol,' Drew declares, and Felicity fakes a cough, giving him a fixed look. 'Oh, and soft drinks, naturally. And thanks, Kerra, as we have a lot to do and I'd hate Tegan, Sy, Gawen or Yvonne, to hear our news via the grapevine.'

'Tell them it's my fault,' Felicity interjects. 'The truth is that Drew didn't want to jinx things in case I changed my mind, as if I would! Now I'm here we'll soon get things in order with the generous help of our friends.'

'I'll bring brushes, rollers and stuff like that,' Ross offers. 'Is it okay to ask whether you know if it's a boy or a girl?'

Felicity looks at Drew and he nods his head.

'It's a boy,' Felicity confirms, beaming at us. 'And we've spent the last few days designing the nursery.'

'Ah! How wonderful! I can't remember the last time I actually saw a baby up close,' I admit.

Ross shrugs his shoulders. 'Me neither!'

'Guess it's going to come as a bit of a surprise to us all, then,' Drew says, raising his eyebrows and looking a tad overwhelmed.

'Being a dad must be the most amazing thing in this world,' Ross mutters, more to himself than to us. My heart literally squishes up inside my chest. Ross might be ready, but I don't think I am – yet. My life seems to have a lot of loose ends to tie up first, and it's hard to imagine getting to the point where that's a real option for us.

'Hi, Arthur. It's Kerra. Is it okay to come up?' I shout out, after letting myself in with the key Mrs Moyle dropped into Pedrevan.

'I'm in the sittin' room,' he calls back to me and I head up the stairs.

It's rare for Mrs Moyle to go off and leave Arthur on his own, but when she rang me earlier this morning she asked if I minded popping in to see him this afternoon. It's something to do with the website. Sundays are leisurely at Pedrevan now Ross has moved in and today I'm glad of the break. Ross is putting up the shelves to house his collection of books and it's taking a lot longer than I thought, but he's enjoying himself.

Traversing the landing, I pop my head around the door and Arthur looks up, beckoning me inside.

'I hope I'm not bein' a nuisance, Kerra. I know how busy you are.'

'Oh, Arthur – I always have time for you and today I'm glad to have an excuse to pop out. Ross is drilling holes in the wall and my head is beginning to ache,' I confide. 'How can I help?'

I did wonder if the real reason Mrs Moyle asked me to call in was simply to check on him. She seemed preoccupied and that's unusual for her, as Arthur is the centre of her world. She's such a strong woman, purposeful is the word that comes to mind, but for the first time in memory she sounded a little unnerved to me. I hope nothing is wrong.

'Is everything all right? Mrs Moyle is well?'

Arthur nods his head, enthusiastically. 'She's fine. Off to visit an old friend and I think a couple of hours havin' a natter and catchin' up over a pot of tea will do her good.'

'How can I help? It's something to do with the website, I gather.'

'Yes.' He nods, frowning as he looks down at the laptop in front of him. 'I'd like to start sendin' out a Penvennan Community Link-Up newsletter and post copies on the website, but I don't know how to do that.'

I notice that his two walking sticks are in the usual position, hooked over the back of the chair, so nothing much has changed. Poor Arthur. Having caught him once on one of his good days, I saw him walking unaided from the kitchen to the sitting room with a hot mug of tea in one hand. At the time I startled him, and I guess I was unable to hide my surprise at seeing him so mobile. He explained that a good day is rare, as much of his life is spent hobbling around in dire pain. Unrelenting, sleepless nights cause Mrs Moyle a lot of anxiety over his condition but he's done with doctors, he told me firmly. So, I'm delighted to help him in any way I can, because having something worthwhile to do is what keeps him going.

'What a lovely idea and I have the perfect solution for you. There's a free digital marketing platform that's easy to use and allows you to create a newsletter with text and graphics. It's free if your circulation list has less than two thousand subscribers.'

'Free? I like the sound of that, Kerra. Is it easy enough for me to get my head around, do you think?'

'It's a piece of cake, I promise you. I'll get you set up and we'll create a template for you to use each time. Then you can save each newsletter and load it up to the website. I'll set up a new tab where you can post links to every issue.'

'Sounds amazin' and I'll enjoy playin' around with it. Folk are sendin' me all sorts of information and photos to share. I thought some of the housebound members might get a kick out of it.'

Arthur understands what an isolated world it can be if you can't get out and about. Especially for people on their own who don't have anyone to drop by regularly to brighten their day.

'Before we make a start, is Zacky okay? I bumped into him the other day and he seemed a bit down.'

Arthur pauses, his brow furrowed. 'He... uh... he's tryin'

to think of ways to get me down to the pub. It's kind of him, but I'm happy as I am. Besides, if I want a drink Mrs Moyle just pops downstairs – it's all on me doorstep.' He shrugs his shoulders, but we both know it's more about opening up his world a little and it would be company for Zacky. It's a pity, because everything is doable and Arthur has a lot of friends willing to help if he decides to give it a go.

'Zacky really misses his wife. Loneliness is an awful thing,' I reflect, sadly.

Arthur makes a dour face. 'She was his rock, not the other way around, although he'd do anythin' for her. He's going through a bit of a bad patch, that's for sure. Gettin' old, he told me, ain't easy.'

I didn't mean to lower Arthur's spirits and it's time to occupy his thoughts with something else. 'Right, 'Let's get on with it. I'll soon get you up to speed and I think you're going to have some fun with this, Arthur.'

His expression relaxes the moment we begin. Arthur is quick to pick things up and I brush off a niggling little sensation that I get whenever I'm with him. It's as if there's something he wants to tell me, but he's holding back. Is it something to do with what happened to my granddad? I often find myself wondering if Arthur knows anything. Considering he's housebound, not much misses his ears. He spends most of his time chatting to people on the phone. I can't imagine how his path would have crossed with Granddad though, who was an outdoors person. He was almost sixty when he died. Arthur would have been in his early forties, I reckon, as that was… what, twenty years ago. Goodness, that means Arthur has been stuck inside for what equates to two-thirds of my entire life. It's a sobering thought.

While we're waiting for an email confirmation to validate the free subscription to the newsletter platform, Arthur chatters away.

'I see your neighbour Drew is walkin' around with a big smile on his face. We noticed Felicity has filled out a bit since she was last here. Mrs Moyle has started knittin' already. She'll stick to white wool for now, but we're assumin' once Felicity is settled in properly there'll be an announcement. The missus can't wait until she pops into the shop to give our congratulations.'

'I'm sure that will be very soon, Arthur. In confidence, you can tell Mrs Moyle that with only five weeks to go we won't have long to wait to meet Penvennan's newest resident.'

His smile grows exponentially. Isn't life wonderful when someone else's good fortune spreads a little joy far and wide? I can imagine Arthur craning his neck to see Drew and Felicity out strolling with the baby in a pushchair; it will brighten his day, and put a huge smile on his face, which, in his isolated environment, is priceless.

# 7

## Focusing on the Positive

'Kerra, it's Oliver Sinclair from Property Professionals UK. Is it a convenient time to talk?'

'Oh, hi, Oliver. Yes, it's fine. I have that Monday morning feeling and I'm still savouring my first coffee of the day. How's business?'

'Good, thank you, and busy. Has your tenant moved into Gwel Teg?'

'Yes, and he's over the moon with it after Polly did a make-over for me. His parents live just off the High Street, and I've known them all my life.'

'That's good to hear. We're getting some great feedback from the clients we've passed on to Polly and Designed to Sell has a promising future. Let's hope she'll soon be in a position to expand her operation a little.'

Oliver knows Polly and I are great friends and I hope he isn't about to press me for information I can't share, even if I knew what Sam is planning to do – which I don't.

'The reason for this call,' he continues, 'is to ask if you'd be kind enough to keep an eye out for me. We really do need an outlet closer to Penvennan than Polreweek. As you know that's the nearest office we have, but given the huge number of visitors that come to the cove we'd be thrilled to have a small outlet there.'

'What type of outlet? There isn't any potential here for another shop. Do you mean slightly further afield?'

'Well, that's why I decided to approach you. We're keen to have a small presence in the cove itself. It's a part of our aim to link ourselves closely to the communities in the areas in which we sell and rent properties. Holidaymakers like to browse estate agents' windows and we feel that being in the heart of the community will strengthen our ties. And, as I mentioned when we first met, we're keen to give something back.'

From the moment I first met Oliver I was impressed by him. He's an astute businessman, working hard to set up a new network as his London-based company grows its presence in Cornwall. However, he understands that a corporate brand can only survive here if it genuinely respects the needs of the community.

'How?'

His laughter echoes down the line. 'That bit I haven't quite figured out yet, but I knew it would interest you. If you can come up with a workable solution for us to rent, or buy, space to accommodate a small operation I'd be most grateful. And any suggestions on how best to utilise a financial contribution for the benefit of the collective, would be extremely helpful.'

I chuckle. 'Oh, so find you a base *and* solve the

problem you haven't yet figured out in your desire to be philanthropic?' I jest.

'Spot on! We're not talking about paying for a few hanging baskets to pretty things up, but something that will add to the locality, benefiting locals and tourists alike. Who else would I approach, but you?'

I'm a sucker for getting pulled into things because I just can't say no. 'Well, it's a huge challenge. It's going to require some research and a great deal of thought but leave it with me and I'll get back to you.'

'If there are any other local businesses you feel we could support by using their flyers in the packs we give out to our clients, please just send them to me. Clean and Shine, too, has been a great resource for us and our clients. I can't thank you enough. Anyway, it's always a real pleasure talking with you, Kerra. Thanks for your time and I'll look forward to speaking with you again soon.'

'Same here, and no problem, Oliver. Cornwall needs new businesses and investment to make it thrive. And so does Penvennan. I'll be in touch when I've figured something out.'

Everything is do-able, right? It's time for some creative thinking.

Oliver's phone call derails my to-do list. I can't resist jotting down a few ideas when I suddenly realise that the video call I've scheduled with Tegan and Yvonne is about to start.

Settling myself back in my chair, I log on to my PC and wait impatiently while it loads. My mind is still in overdrive considering Oliver's dilemma and how it would be a real shame not to grab this opportunity and make the most of it. Eventually the app opens and within seconds two smiling faces stare back at me.

'Good morning, ladies. How are you both today?'

Tegan does a little wave. 'Tired. We had a late night binge-watching a boxed set and I ate way too much popcorn.'

'Lucky you!' Yvonne groans, enviously. 'What I'd give for a lie in. That's an impossibility when you live on a farm.'

'So, come on, Kerra – I'm intrigued. What's the big news you can't wait to share?' Tegan asks, unable to hide her curiosity.

I look back at them smugly. 'How do you fancy coming to a welcome party for Felicity on Saturday night at Tigry Cottage?'

'Ooh... count us in,' Tegan immediately responds.

'Me and Gawen, too. What should we bring?'

I burst out laughing and they both stare at me, frowning. 'It's a party with a difference. You'll need to wear some old clothes because it will involve rollers, brushes and paint.'

'What exactly are we painting?' Tegan enquires, her interest piqued.

'A nursery. Drew and Felicity are expecting a baby!'

Tegan's jaw drops and she puts her hand to her mouth.

Yvonne sits there beaming. 'Aww... a baby. How lovely!'

'That's a *yes*, then?'

Two heads nod, enthusiastically.

'When's it due?' Yvonne asks.

'The twenty-first of May.'

'You're j-joking,' Tegan splutters, sounding incredulous.

'And you knew all along, didn't you? Felicity must have

been pregnant the last time we saw her!' Yvonne declares, accusingly.

'Yes, but it was a bit of a surprise and Felicity was still getting her head around it. Anyway, I knew you'd be thrilled for them and want to join in. I've been told I can share the fact that they're having a boy. It's a mad dash to get the room sorted and assemble a mountain of boxes that arrived with Felicity's things at the weekend. They're prepping the woodwork in the nursery ready for the party.'

'It's going to be such fun. And we can turn it into a baby shower, too. Who doesn't love shopping for new-born babies? All those cute little booties and bonnets.' Tegan sounds wistful, which is a bit of a surprise. 'What else can we bring?'

'I said I'd handle the food and Drew said he'll sort the drinks. Ross is going to bring lots of rollers and brushes.'

'Why don't we all take a few plates along to make up a buffet? I'll go online and order one of those ready-made baby baskets as I don't have a clue what a new mum might need,' Yvonne admits. 'I still can't believe it – but I'm so thrilled for them.'

'Gosh, I hope it doesn't inspire Sy,' Tegan adds. 'Anyway, yes to food and I'll head into Polreweek as there's a wonderful baby boutique in the centre of town.'

Yvonne and I try to keep straight faces, but it's obvious that it won't be the first time Tegan has found a reason to wander in there.

'Right. Shall we say it will kick-off at five o'clock to give us plenty of time to paint, eat, celebrate and generally party?'

I get two thumbs up.

'Thank you, ladies. We can let our hair down and officially welcome Felicity to Penvennan Cove. Have a great start to your week.'

'You, too. Bye for now.' Tegan beams back at me.

'I'm off to feed the goats', Yvonne gives a wry smile. 'But when I'm done, I'll jump online and order that basket. Have a great day, both!'

There's something about the prospect of a new arrival that touches everyone's heart and it's just the little boost we need right now. But it's also going to be an eye-opener. I saw the reaction in Tegan's – and, surprisingly, Yvonne's – eyes too. I had the impression their lives were too full to think about having kids just yet but maybe I was wrong. Me, I'm worried, because if Felicity and Drew don't sail through this huge event with ease, it might put the rest of us off. Or am I the only one who fears that raising children isn't necessarily a set of skills we're all born with? I guess time will tell.

When Ross arrives home, he's on a high. Today was an anxious one for him, as the major works began on the site next to Treylya. Thankfully, the moment he walks through the door I can see he's had a good day.

'I'm shattered, but I'm hungry and whatever you're making smells good,' he declares, smiling at me.

'I'm guessing everything went well, then?'

'It did,' he replies and the positivity he's feeling radiates from him. 'I will admit that I'm still missing Will now that he's running the Launceston office. None of my other foreman have anywhere near his level of experience, so I will be spread thinly keeping an eye on everything, but you know me – I love a challenge.'

Those dark brown eyes glance over me, full of mischief and love. They shine with a passion that can not only light up a room, but also makes my heart soar. If you are lucky enough to find the one person you feel you were destined to be with, then you really can end up with the life you've always dreamt of having.

'It's going to be an amazing project,' he confirms, sidling up to rest his head against mine as I continue stirring the saucepan in front of me. 'And this is?'

'A peppercorn sauce. Gawen was passing and dropped in a couple of fillet steaks. Yvonne wrote out the recipe for the sauce for me and suggested I accompany it with some triple cooked chips.'

'This isn't some sort of special occasion, is it?' Ross frowns, worried that he's missing something.

'No. Nothing like that. I was chatting with Yvonne and Tegan making plans for the party on Saturday. Yvonne messaged afterwards to ask if I wanted anything, as Gawen was this way making a delivery. I thought I might as well order a few things as we're all mucking in to sort out the buffet. Off the top of my head, I ordered a leg of lamb and two chickens. Maybe I'll make wraps, or something like that, stuffed with cold meat and lots of salad.'

'A barbecue would be fun,' Ross suggests.

'Hmm… that's not a bad idea. Pity I don't barbecue,' I declare, batting my eyelashes at him.

'Leave it to your resident chef. I'll make sure I slope off early on Friday afternoon to start prepping. The lamb will be nice marinaded in yoghurt and mint, and the chickens can be cut up and skewered. I did a run to the builder's merchants on my way home, and we have enough painting supplies for everyone.'

He plants a kiss on my neck, snaking his arm around my waist.

'Go shower and change. You have ten minutes tops,' I warn him.

He looks sheepish as he heads upstairs. I don't think Ross likes me cooking for him; I think he prefers to do it himself, but he deserves a little pampering tonight.

I refer to Yvonne's hand-written instructions – she says the steaks are easy. They've been breathing at room temperature and I've hand-chopped a pile of fresh rosemary and thyme, added some pink Himalayan sea salt and a touch of black pepper. Now it says to lay the steaks on top of the mixture, coating both sides. Then I flash fry them for a couple of minutes, turning them once before placing the steaks on a tray and putting them in the oven for about eight minutes. Easy.

The chips have been a bit of a task, but after part-boiling them first and then cooking them in oil until a light coating is formed, all I need to do now is to pop them back into the fryer to heat them through and crisp them up.

Even so, I wipe my brow with the sleeve of my top thinking that while Yvonne means well, this is a lot of effort. But it is for the man I love, so a little sweat is justified.

By the time Ross reappears, smelling heavenly of something aromatic – there's a hint of amber and a fresh, citrussy note – I'm ready to carry the heated plates to the table.

'This looks amazing,' he replies, appreciatively.

'Well enjoy it, I probably won't be making this again. It's way too much effort,' I moan, but he's laughing at me.

'I appreciate it, really I do, Kerra. But I enjoy cooking, you know that. It's the perfect way for me to unwind after a day spent checking the depth of footings, sorting out delivery issues with my quantity surveyor, and helping to release a digger that was stuck in the mud. So, anything to report? No big scandal brewing to make us old news?'

His attention immediately returns to his plate, and he attacks his steak with relish. I love watching him eat. Our mealtimes are a high point in my day because he's relaxed and chatty.

'I haven't ventured out at all today, but I did have an interesting chat with Oliver first thing this morning.'

Ross pauses, his fork halfway to his mouth.

'Oliver? What did he want?'

'My help.'

He continues eating and I pretend not to notice his rather disdainful expression.

'You like him, don't you?' Ross puts down his knife and fork, reaching for his wine glass as he registers my reaction.

'I do,' I confirm, light-heartedly. 'He's genuine, proactive and is keen for Property Professionals UK to have a presence in Penvennan Cove.'

Ross raises his eyebrows. 'In the cove? Well, that's not going to happen.'

I watch as he carves off a large piece of steak as easily as if he's slicing into butter. When he pops it into his mouth, he utters an appreciative 'Hmm…' before focusing his attention back on me.

'You told him you're not a magician, right?'

Back last year when I tried to convince Ross to change estate agents as Treylya hadn't had any viewings at all, he did meet up with Oliver. He decided not to go with him, but to extend the contract he had for another three months. I felt Ross was a little unnerved that I made an instant connection with Oliver. As someone who was based in London, I could understand how different Oliver found it coming here to get things set up. Ross can sense that, but he shouldn't be worried about it because I only have eyes for him.

I give Ross a warm, loving smile. 'No. I said I'd give it some thought because I have an idea… or two. I'm not sure either will be appropriate, but I think some good could come out of this.'

'Really? You don't think he's taking advantage by tapping into your local connections, do you?'

It's funny how the green-eyed monster can put a rather jaded slant on things, and I reach out to place my hand on Ross's arm.

'Relax. Oliver isn't just a taker. His firm genuinely want to give back and I simply need to figure out the best plan to benefit everyone.'

'And you're doing all this for free, I suppose.' There it is, that little niggle because Oliver and I understand each other, even if it is purely business. It's almost amusing seeing Ross succumb to jealousy.

'Yes, and why not? He's already created links with Polly, and Sy and Tegan, and he's putting business their way. We need to stimulate the local economy and I can't see any harm in donating my time.'

Ross can't disagree with that, but he looks a tad

disappointed. 'You aren't going to share your thoughts with me, are you?'

'There's no point until I speak to a couple of people,' I point out, shrugging my shoulders. 'It might come to nothing, but you never know!'

'I thought you were supposed to be focusing on your next project?'

I remove my arm to let him begin eating again, but instead he raises his wine glass and I pick up mine to chink glasses.

'Oh, I've lots of ideas simmering away, don't you worry.'

'But I do worry because you usually go straight from one thing to the next and you're procrastinating. That's not the Kerra I know.'

'Procrastinating? No, I'm just being… cautious,' I declare, trying not to sound defensive.

'Until you've made it up with your dad you can't focus, can you? Although, you're happy to devote yourself to the common cause.'

Is there a hint of 'and what about me?' behind this? I wonder.

I pick up my fork and absentmindedly spear a chip, but these days my appetite isn't what it used to be. Stress affects every part of your life. And Ross is right. I spend a lot of time now wracking my brains for ideas to cross paths with Dad where he can't simply turn and walk away from me. But I'm coming up blank.

'It's a way of distracting myself, that's all. When it comes to Dad, the right moment will present itself and I'll be ready.' I'm trying to sound positive, but there's a sinking feeling in my stomach.

'It's a good job we have a party to go to on Saturday. I

mean, who doesn't love being among friends, lots of good food and drink, and helping to prepare for a happy event? Is there anything else you need me to pick up?'

'No. I've let Drew know that we're all bringing food, he's sorting the drinks and Yvonne, Tegan, and I have decided we're going to have a surprise baby shower, too.'

Ross pushes his plate away, as he looks at me with interest.

'A shower?'

'Not that sort of shower. It's to celebrate the upcoming arrival and we're all taking along presents for the baby. I've been online choosing some soft toys, as Tegan seems to be the expert on baby clothes and Yvonne is ordering a basket of all the bits and pieces a new baby requires.'

Ross's eyes open wide. 'That'll be interesting. What do any of us know about babies? You're all getting into the spirit of this, which is great, but I can't help wondering whether this is going to be catching. I'm not sure Penvennan is ready for a population explosion.'

I give him a knowing smile. 'All I can say is that if Felicity and Drew's baby happens to be a sleeper and a little gem, then who knows? The question is – who'll be next – Tegan, or Yvonne?'

Ross chuckles to himself. 'And I'm wondering how long it will be before Drew orders a garden office like yours to get away from the noise and is chasing me to get it erected in double-quick time.'

'Like *ours*,' I correct him and if I were a betting woman I'd say three months, tops.

# 8

## Perfect Timing

Ross leaves the house at five o'clock and Ripley isn't happy about it. He usually cuddles her on his lap while he's eating breakfast, but this morning he couldn't get out the door quickly enough as I handed him a thermal coffee mug.

'You must stop and grab something to eat,' I impress upon him as he leans in to give me a tantalising kiss. Although I'm still sleepy, I just want to drag him back into bed and snuggle up with Ripley next to us. But Ross's mind is firmly on the day ahead and he's off to the office before he begins his rounds. He'll end the day back up on the headland overlooking the cove as his new project is his baby. It's comforting to know he'll be close by, but it might as well be a million miles away because it's all-consuming for him. More and more when we're talking, I know his head is elsewhere and this project is one he finds both challenging and exciting.

Loving someone means not holding them back and Ross

has never stopped me, even when we both know there will be fallout. Like the endless gossip that is a direct result of even some relatively small changes. If this thing with Oliver comes to anything it will add to that, and Ross and I both know it, but my man is gracious enough not to point that out.

'Go careful. Don't get over-tired and don't forget to eat!' I command, as he snuggles me in his arms, rocking me back and forth on my feet.

'When we're married will you do me a lunch box?' Ross grins, mischievously. 'That's what wives do, isn't it?'

'Not this one. I have too much respect for your well-being. But there are companies who deliver healthy snacks to your door.' I wink at him, and he bursts out laughing.

'I wouldn't change a single thing about you, Kerra Shaw. You light up my life. Doesn't she, Ripley?' he asks, as we turn to look at her.

*Miaow, miaow, miaoooooow.*

'Go. She's not happy with you upsetting her routine so you're going to have to pander to her tonight. I hope today goes well, Ross. I love you more than you know.'

He places his fingers beneath my chin to tilt my head back and stare into my eyes.

'I need to do something that makes a difference. Whether that's employing local men, building something that will stand the test of time, or just being productive. I don't know how to be any different, but that's not to say that I'm not capable of change. We'll work out what sort of life we want together for the future, Kerra, but for now let's take it one day at a time.'

'Agreed. Thank you for reassuring me, Ross. I agree, but

I have this unsettled feeling I simply can't shake. The only time it eases is when we're together, which makes me sound needy.'

'Well,' he laughs, 'I'm here for you always. And Ripley's pretty good at alerting you when something is wrong, you know that. She certainly brought us together at a time when I was in your bad books.'

I tilt my head to look up into his eyes, questioningly. 'Oh yes… she kept visiting you at Treylya; heck, she ran away several times and you had to drive her back here. Ripley was trying to tell us something before even we knew that we were going to be together. She won't let us take a wrong step, will you, Rippers?'

Ripley turns tail and decides to slink slowly up the stairs while having a full-on conversation.

*Miaow, miaow, miaow, miaow miaoooooow. Miaoooooow!*

Talk about making a dramatic exit. She is the queen of this cottage, there is no doubt at all about that.

'See you tonight,' Ross murmurs, kissing my lips softly and lingering, even though he's eager to get on with his day. 'Love you!'

'Love you, too!' I say to his back as he turns to go.

'Love you, three!' He laughs as he pulls the door shut behind him.

An uneasiness swirls around me as if there's something in the air and it's getting stronger with each passing day. I'm pretty sure that Ross is feeling it, but all we can do is wait and see what happens.

*

As I hurry along the High Street, heading towards the turning down to the cove, I hear a frenzy of barking in the distance. Glancing up from my phone I see that it's Dad and Ian out dog walking. Two of the dogs are squabbling and, thankfully, they're too intent on addressing the problem to spot me as I speed up to take the right turn. My first conversation with Dad has to be just between the two of us.

I continue scanning my texts. Two are from Tegan, sending photos of adorable baby clothes and it's obvious she's enjoying herself. I respond with a few fun emojis. The other message is from Sissy.

*Kerra – I have news and this is HUGE. Can you give me a quick call please?*

As I begin the descent down to the beach, the ring tone in my ear seems to go on forever. When Sissy finally picks up, she's slightly breathless.

'Sorry, Kerra! I'm in a tizzy and I stepped out of the office without my phone. Seriously, you won't believe this, but I need your help!'

I hear yapping in the background and the sound of Sissy breathing heavily. 'Oh, Willow – I nearly stepped on you, poor thing. Come on, jump up onto my lap. I ought to sit down for this,' she declares, and I'm not sure whether she's talking to me, or to her adorable little Westland terrier.

'There's a new boutique hotel opening on the far side of Rosveth moor. It's an old hunting lodge that has just been refurbished. They want the contemporary, romantic country style throughout. It's totally empty and they've asked The Design Cave to go along and give them a price for furnishing it. The whole thing. There are eight bedrooms in the main lodge and a further twelve in an annexe attached to it, that is only ten years old but in a similar style. I don't even know where to start, Kerra.'

Sissy is panicking and, by the sound of it, she's in danger of hyperventilating.

'Right. First of all, take a deep breath to calm yourself down. How did they contact you?'

'By email. About an hour ago but we've been busy, and I've only just picked it up.'

'Okay. Reply, thanking them for getting in touch. Ask when it would be convenient to come along with your in-house designer to talk through their requirements and have a look around. Try your best to arrange a morning appointment and ask if we're talking furniture only, or the whole thing – including soft furnishings and window treatments etc. Also find out whether they have floor plans with room sizes they can let you have in advance of your meeting, as that will be a great help. Tell them that we use a 3D interior design programme and if they want to individualise each of the rooms that service is available free of charge.'

'A *what*? And who is our in-house designer?'

'Don't worry about it.' I giggle, as Sissy sounds truly bewildered. 'You can leave that to me. I'm heading down to have a quick chat with Sam, and I'll enlist Polly's help. I'm sure she'll be delighted to get onboard if you can pull this off. Don't worry – you'll have all the help you need. We're a team, remember, and that's the whole point of having a partner.'

I hear Willow come close to the phone and begin panting.

'Settle down,' Sissy croons to her, and I smile to myself.

'I'll phone you later. Do your magic – send a warm and welcoming response and then we'll put our heads together and take it from there.'

As I press end call and look up, I almost collide with Gryff, who is standing on the pavement outside his tiny newsagent's shop polishing the glass window. It's his pride and joy and the only thing obscuring his view across to the far side of the bay is the maroon-coloured decal that boldly advertises 'The Sweet Emporium'. The locals all refer to it as the newsagent's because it's the only place we can buy a newspaper or a magazine without jumping in the car.

'Oh, hi, Gryff. Sorry, I nearly kicked over your bucket then. That will teach me for not paying attention.'

He looks at me, nodding his head welcomingly as he chuckles. 'Always the busy bee, Kerra.'

'I know, Gryff, I'll never change.' I grin back at him.

'You were the same when you were a little 'un and yer grandparents used to walk you down to the cove. Always looking around and never where you was going. They loved showing you off, you were their pride and joy.'

'Granddad would always stop and buy me one of those sweet necklaces, they tasted like love hearts,' I recall, fondly.

'He did and he always had a bag of Everton mints, never without them in his pocket,' Gryff replies. 'Grand chap, he was.'

'Aww… good old days, for sure. Are you keeping well?'

'I am. The old emporium keeps me going, although the suppliers are getting fewer these days. They all want to sell sweets in plastic bags, but that's not my style.'

'Well, if ever there was a prize for the smallest, neatest,

most tantalising shop in Cornwall you'd win it. I still remember the smell from my childhood.'

His face lights up. 'Hang on a minute,' he says, turning and going back inside.

I gaze around, looking up at Treylya on the headland as the sun glints off the glass façade and then out to sea, where a small boat is bobbing up and down just metres from the shore.

''Ere you go, your favourites once upon a time,' Gryff says, pushing a paper bag into my hand.

'Oh, Gryff – that's so kind, thank you.'

'You're a breath of fresh air, Kerra. Ignore the folk who tattle. It makes me happy to see you and Ross together. I always said to your mum that all he needed was a good woman to rescue him.'

I start laughing. 'I think it's the other way around, Gryff, but that's just between you and me!'

Gryff tips back his head and laughs as I pop my little trove of sweets into the bag slung over my shoulder and give him a parting wave. During the peak season there is often quite a queue outside Gryff's shop. Visitors love to see the sweets all lined up in old-fashioned glass jars with black screw-on lids. He weighs them out on an old set of scales that have been there forever, and the young kids absolutely love walking off with a little paper bag clasped in their hands. No plastic bags or pre-formed packaging in sight.

As I turn the corner, Tom steps out of Pascoe's Bakery clutching a carrier bag. 'Morning, Kerra. Beautiful day for a walk.'

'It sure is, Tom. How's it going at The Salvager's Yard? It's all change, I hear.'

'Good, actually. Pop in and see for yourself if you've got a minute.'

I glance at my watch. 'I'm running a bit late I'm afraid, as I'm heading to The Lark and Lantern to see Sam.'

'Well, call in on the way back. I have a hevva cake in here with your name on it.' He holds up the bag in his hand knowing that's an offer I can't refuse.

'Guess I'll see you in a bit,' I reply, thinking how pleased he sounds with himself.

At this rate I'm going to need to go on a hike to work off all the sugar I'm likely to consume by the end of the day.

I step off the pavement as a group of children accompanied by three teachers come towards me. They have clipboards and pens, and the person in the lead points out some of the features that hark back to the past. Like the hand-carved stonework set above the bakery and café. Originally, half of it was a fishmonger's shop and there's a fine depiction of a crab with two leaping fish set above the spot where the old doorway would have been. Further along what was probably a breadbasket is worn away in places, but the bundle of wheat sticking up out of it is still easily distinguishable.

'The street is cobbled,' the woman with long dark hair informs the crocodile of excited children following on behind her. I'm not totally convinced it's the history that is enthralling them, or the fact that they're not in the classroom. 'These stones came from the cliffs over there.' She points to the headland. Most of her charges, I notice, seem to be looking longingly at the beach and she claps her hands to regain their attention.

'You're not heading for the pub, are you?' Polly's voice interrupts my observation as I step back onto the pavement.

'Oh, hi, Polly. I am. Sam is expecting me, but I was also hoping to have a quick word with you. Are you too busy to take on a project for The Design Cave?'

As I lean in to give her a hug, she chews her lip. 'Ian's fully booked for at least the next month, I'm afraid. Is it urgent?'

'Oh, it doesn't involve any decorating. Sissy's been asked to quote for kitting out a boutique hotel – twenty rooms in total. It's a huge job and while she's up to speed on what we can get our hands on at short notice, we need an interior designer on board.'

Polly's eyes light up. 'Count me in. Has Sissy been in to take a look around yet?'

'No. I've asked her to book a morning appointment and as soon as we know when I'll get her to give you a call. I thought you could go together and suss out exactly what they're expecting. I'll load up a 3D software package and while Sissy gets a handle on stock levels and prices, perhaps you and I could sit down together to design the rooms and produce a 3D video for them?'

Her eyes gleam with excitement.

'Perfect! I'd dearly love to stop and chat some more but I'm on my way to meet a new client. This sounds like an awesome opportunity though, and I can't wait to get involved. By the way, Dad's in an exceptionally good mood this morning. I don't know what's going on, but I think he's made a decision about the pub. Is that why you're calling in?'

'Oh... I... no. Your dad didn't contact me, I got in touch with him. This is about another matter entirely.' Goodness, I don't want Polly to think that Sam is talking to me about the future of The Lark and Lantern behind her back. Sam has always said from the start that Polly is a part of his decision-making process.

'It's okay, Kerra. Whatever Dad decides is fine by me, I'm simply relieved to see him smiling again instead of frowning. When he's ready I'm sure he'll take me through it step by step. Anyway,' she says, her voice full of enthusiasm, 'my other job is calling, and I can't be late. We'll catch up soon!'

I watch her stride off and there's a definite swagger to her walk these days. Polly is utilising her skills and it's about time.

Finally, I make my way around to the rear door of The Lark and Lantern, tapping on it as loud as I can in case Sam is upstairs, but seconds later the door flies open.

'I was just mopping the corridor. Come on in, Kerra, mind you don't slip.'

The smell of lemon floor cleaner fills the air with a pleasant aroma, but the minute we step through into the bar it's obvious someone is busy in the kitchen. It's a bit early to be accosted by the smell of lasagnes baking and Sam leads me out into the annexe. The double French doors are open and as I gaze out at the sea view it's heavenly and tranquil without the usual buzz of the customers.

'I envy you that view,' I say, without thinking. If Sam decides to sell up, he'll be leaving this behind for good.

'It's impossible to tire of it. No matter what the weather it's spectacular. Granted, most of the day and evening I don't get time to stop and look out, but often enough to know how lucky we are to be here. Anyway, take a seat, Kerra. Can I get you a drink? Tea, coffee… it's a bit early for a tipple,' Sam teases.

'Just a bit, but I'm fine, thank you. I promised Tom I'd pop in on the way back. He's been hard at it, I hear.'

Sam pulls out a chair for me and walks around the table to sit on one of the padded and buttoned bench seats.

'He has and I'm amazed. Tom and his old man have really got stuck in. They've had two big skips already and filled them to the brim. And there's a scrapyard near Trevethan that has taken away over a dozen old cars, as well. To be honest it's not just the fact that it had become a rusty-looking eyesore, but it spoilt the natural beauty of the cove. There's been a lot of muttering and moaning for a long time now and I think word finally got back to Tom. It wouldn't have been long before someone filed a complaint with the local council.'

'It's hard to see a business in decline, isn't it? And without much money coming in, Tom partnering up with his dad is a great idea.'

'To be honest it's a case of rather the devil you know, than the one you don't. If he sold up and they levelled the yard who knows what might have sprung up. You can't tell with planning rules these days and it's not always in the best interests of the community, as we know. Anyway, it's nice to catch up but I'm assuming there's something on your mind.'

I like Sam. He's what Granddad would refer to as a salt-of-the-earth type of man.

'The reason I popped in is a bit of a long shot, really. I'd appreciate it if this could stay just between the two of us as it's commercial in confidence, but… uh…' I pause, wondering if mentioning Oliver's name will upset Sam. After all, he's the one keeping Polly busy in her free time. 'Oliver Sinclair is very keen to set up a small office here in the cove.'

Sam does a bit of double take, scratching his head as he peers at me and narrows his eyes. 'Where?'

'Look, I'm just throwing out ideas here, because Property Professionals UK also has a budget set aside to give back to the communities in which they're based. Now, I don't know how much we're talking about, but I know it could be put to good use if I can just find them some space.'

'I can't see how. They're not thinking of buying up a bit of land and building something, are they?' Now he's frowning.

I shake my head, emphatically. 'No. But I was wondering whether… well, you have the three holiday lets that aren't in use. Would you consider renting one of them out as a shop? Subject to approval for change of use, naturally. It could be an extra source of income for you if it fits in with your future plans.'

Sam raises an eyebrow, deep in thought. 'It's a good idea, Kerra, and I appreciate you coming to me with it, but I've already decided what I'm going to do. Funnily enough, as soon as I get up the courage to talk it through with Polly, you'll be the first person I call.'

'Me?'

'I'd rather not say any more until I've sat down with my girl, as there's a bit of a delicate matter I need to raise with her at the same time. I don't know what Polly's reaction is going to be and if she isn't happy, then the plan might require a bit of tweaking before I begin to move it forward.'

'Oh, of course, I fully understand, Sam.'

'And I won't mention a word about this to anyone, Kerra. It's a shame really, as I like the idea, but my plan is better.' He beams at me, pressing his lips together tightly as if he's sorely tempted to blurt it out.

'I'm sure Polly will be on board with whatever you decide is best. She's a strong woman and resilient, and if you're content with it, then I'm sure she'll be happy, too.'

'I do hope so, Kerra. Our lives are about to change forever, and it signals the end of an era.'

Hearing that tinge of sadness in his voice as I stand makes my smile fade a little.

'Well, thanks for your time, Sam, and I'm glad you know where you're heading now as that's half the battle. Don't leave it too long to have that chat with Polly. She knows something is up and even I can see the change in you.'

As Sam walks me to the door, he pauses for a second before pushing it open and I hang back a little.

'I will be in touch, Kerra, and soon. It's a crazy plan, but somehow I think you'll understand the reasoning behind it.'

With that I take my leave. As I make my way to The Salvager's Yard my curiosity is now in overdrive. Sam has a lot of options, only one involved me and that wasn't anything out of the ordinary. It certainly wasn't crazy, that's for sure.

# 9

## Food for Thought

I stroll back along the beach, deep in thought. The group of school children I passed earlier are playing ball, while others sit writing on their clipboards. It's busy today and Pascoe's bakery is packed, a snaking queue inside is now right up to the door and spilling out onto the pavement.

There are several people out walking dogs and it would be nice to bump into Drew and Bertie, but I can't see either of them. Overhead the sunshine is glorious and it's going to be a hot one come noon. The sun on my skin is so welcome, though, and it certainly lifts the spirits.

As I approach the far end of the beach where it butts up against the headland, I instinctively gaze up at Treylya. From this vantage point it's a shiny object that draws the eye. The huge glass panels reflect the sky, the sun, and the wide expanse of water that today shimmers like liquid silver. It's not the blot on the landscape Ross fears it to be, it's the negative emotions it reminds him of that means he's unable to look at it objectively. I wish I could say the same for The Salvager's Yard, but the outline of the dilapidated metal sheds rearing up in the background are ugly and out of place. It's simply something you don't expect to glimpse so close to such a stunning setting.

I follow the low stone wall that divides Tom's workshops from the hillocks of sand, pebbles and wild grasses. The wall itself is robust, but most of the fencing panels above it are in a terrible state. Tom has made some repairs here and there using wood from old pallets, but there are gaps and it's getting to a point where safety must be a real concern for him. I can't see anyone wanting to break in, but a small child could wiggle through. It's a shame because it spoils a lovely, quiet stretch of the beach. People tend to congregate down at the other end nearer the bakery and the pub and I'm sure the dilapidated yard puts people off.

'Here she is,' Tom calls out the moment he spots me. I walk around a lorry in the process of loading up a skip. It's so full that the driver has tied a tarpaulin over the top of it and the lorry's engine is groaning at the weight as it swings erratically in the air.

'Come on inside, Kerra. I'll put the kettle on.'

As kids we were always warned that the yard was a dangerous place and not a playground; at one time I remember Tom had a problem with rats and that was enough to put most of us off. But never having stepped inside the gates before, I'm shocked. One of the two sheds has been taken down and sheets of weather-beaten corrugated metal are stacked high. The other remaining one is barely standing. I should imagine it's only the piles of rusting metal inside that stop it from being blown over. The original unit housing the garage looks tired but seems structurally sound.

The rest of the site is now clear of small pockets of debris and there's a lot more space here than I'd realised.

'This is my dad, Wally. Dad, do you remember Kerra Shaw?'

Wally steps forward, proffering his hand and grinning at me as we shake.

'Course I do, and I know your uncle Alistair, he's a drinking buddy of mine. We crossed paths several times when you were a nipper, Kerra, but I doubt you'll remember. Ain't often people return and make their mark as you seem to be doing. That Community Link-Up idea is going to prove to be a lifesaver, you mark my words.'

What a lovely man, so warm and sincere. 'Thank you, Wally. I figure what benefits Penvennan is good for us all and Arthur is doing a wonderful job. You've both been hard at work I see – what a difference!'

Tom's back is facing me as he pours the tea, but Wally nods appreciatively. 'It was the wife's idea. She said our savings aren't earning much sitting in the bank and that money could do a lot of good now for the family. Tom here has worked hard, but we all know the world is changing fast. It's time to get rid of the junk before the council comes knocking on the door. We have plans, you see. Expanding the forge for one thing, as that gives Tom a steady income. But there's a lot of history in those old sheds – cars, boats, fishing nets, lobster pots – you name it. Seems like things the kids today don't often get to see and maybe they should.'

Wally indicates for me to take a seat at the old Formica-topped table, which probably graced someone's kitchen back in the 1980s, as Tom carries over a tray of tea and cakes.

'Help yourself, Kerra. Busy folk need the right kind of fuel to keep 'em going.'

Wally offers me the plate of hevva cakes and I'm more than happy to take one. Made with copious amounts of milk, sugar, lard and raisins, who can resist?

'See now, this here is another example of what I mean,' Wally continues, pointing at the bun in my hand.

'Really?'

'Yep. I'm sure your granddad, being a fisherman, would have told you the story of how the women out spotting up on the headland would call out "hevva, hevva" to warn the menfolk the fish were coming. Then it was all hands on deck, as they pushed out the boats and the women would wait on the beach to help offload the pilchards into their baskets for salting. After the work was done, in celebration of their bounty, they'd have a good bake up. I remember watching it myself as a young boy when we first moved down to Cornwall,' Wally explains. 'But how many visitors eat one of these, not knowing it's a part of the history of the cove?'

I never tire of hearing the old stories and seeing the pleasure people take in recounting them. But these days there are fewer and fewer folk alive to tell the tales. 'It's a real shame, isn't it?' I reply, in total agreement.

'It'd be a crying shame to just dump everything because it's not all junk. And while Tom will be busy expanding his range of ironwork once we've cleared the site, I've all the time in the world to rescue a few things for posterity.'

'My granddad would love that idea, Wally. Did you know him well?' I enquire, casually.

'Not as well as Tom, here. But whenever we visited,

we always stopped by to see Rosenwyn and Harry. They were good to Tom and Georgia when they first arrived in Penvennan. The missus and I would have preferred them to have been a bit closer to us in Falmouth, as it's a good forty-minute drive, especially after James was born, but this was where they settled and this place has done them well.'

As we sit eating and sipping our tea, the lorry driver suddenly pops his head around the door.

'All loaded up, Tom. When you're ready for the next one you have my number.'

'Do you have time for a cuppa before you go?' Wally offers.

'Wish I did, but I'm running late. That was a bit on the heavy side, but it's all strapped down now. Have a good one!'

As the door closes, I look at Tom. It's a question I've longed to ask but feared I might not like the answer.

'Do you remember seeing my granddad on the day he died, Tom?'

'I did that, Kerra. Sad day, my dear, for us all.'

I take a deep breath. 'It wasn't like him to take a risk,' I state, my voice belying the way my heart is pounding in my chest.

'But it weren't risky you see, Kerra,' Tom reflects, sadly. 'We knew a storm was coming, but not until the afternoon. Harry popped in here as usual, and I helped him trolley out his boat. It was too much for him on his own and he appreciated having a bit of extra muscle behind it. We laid the boards on the beach and got it into the water. Harry said to give him an hour and a half, and he'd be back with enough of a catch for Rose to make one of her big pots of stew and for me to take home some fish for Georgia to freeze.' Tom stares into the distance as if he's re-living the moment.

'He didn't intend to stay out for long that day?'

'No. When the squall started it descended all of a sudden like. I ran out when the wind began to rattle the windows. At first, I couldn't see him. I was frantic, scanning the bay as the waves rose to heights that made my stomach churn. Panic set in as I made my way along the beach wondering if he'd been carried on the current and was hauled up somewhere beyond the headland. And then I saw…' Tom stops, his voice wavering and his eyes glassy. 'It were just bad luck, Kerra. The storm changed direction and he got caught up in it as he were coming back in. The current was going one way and the wind pushing against him. The boat was hardly moving at one point until a wave scooped it up and… and…'

And smashed it onto the rocks.

'Oh, Tom – please forgive me. I had no idea you were there to witness it. What a horrible memory for you and I'm sorry for mentioning it.'

He clears his throat and then stops to drain his mug of tea. 'It were a waste of a good man, taken before his time—'

My stomach is churning as images spring into my head triggered by Tom's graphic description. To my surprise, Wally interrupts.

'Only him upstairs,' he says pointing his finger towards the heavens, 'determines when our time is up, Tom. No one was to blame, least of all Harry. Ask any fisherman – there's a reason why they're superstitious. When you're up against the elements it tests you. I've seen it in the faces of the men who came back to shore having been caught in a storm, convinced it was all over. And yet they were spared for a reason. It was Harry's time, that's all.'

Wally's expression reflects both awe, and respect.

'He was a good man and the loss hit us all hard,' Tom declares, heaving a deep sigh.

'It was a sad day, for sure,' Wally continues. 'But Harry would have been so proud to see Kerra back at the cove. Some people only think of themselves, but you're different Kerra, and you always were. You're a part of his legacy.'

I force down a lump in my throat as Tom and I exchange a touching glance hearing Wally speaking from the heart. Wally doesn't come across as an overly sentimental man and I'm grateful for his honesty, as he isn't merely trying to ease my pain.

'It warms my heart to think about it in that way Wally, thank you so much. And it's a real treat to sit and chat like this. I love how peaceful it is down at this end of the beach.'

'It's a great spot and about time we tidied up this old relic of a place. We have a few ideas to maybe give the visitors something different to look around, don't we, Dad?' Tom says, raising an eyebrow and looking pleased with himself.

'Actually, while I'm here,' I speak up, making a huge effort to hide the emotions still swirling around inside my head. 'There is something I'd like to talk to you both about. It's a little unusual, but the timing could be perfect. I'm guessing that a boost to the budget might really help kick-start your plans, am I right?'

'Sounds interesting,' Tom says, sitting forward earnestly in his chair.

It's funny, I thought the solution for Oliver would lie with

Sam. If I hadn't found myself sitting here now, I might never have considered The Salvager's Yard as a potential option.

An hour later, I say goodbye and Wally escorts me to the gate. Once we're out of earshot of Tom, I turn to look at him.

'No one has ever talked to me about what actually happened the day Granddad died. I didn't mean to upset Tom and I wouldn't have asked him if I'd realised how painful the memory still is.'

Wally's expression is sombre.

'My son was the last person to see him alive, Kerra. I didn't realise how heavily that weighed upon him 'til just now. It's only natural to think "what if?" I've only ever heard him mention it once before and that was to your grandma, Rosenwyn. Now I know why, and I feel I've let him down because I should have raised the subject.'

'Every time I tried to talk to Mum or Dad about it over the years they cut me off, saying there was no point in dwelling on the past. But I couldn't understand how it could have happened. Granddad's days on the trawler were the hardest, but the happiest of his life and he was too experienced to make a mistake like that. As I grew older I feared the reason no one would talk about it was because he chose to end his life and that hurt. I felt he'd abandoned us. It was a big part of why I left Penvennan Cove. Every time I visit the beach it's all I think about and now...' My voice grows quiet.

Wally places his hand gently on my shoulder, giving it a comforting squeeze.

'It's tough to understand, Kerra. It's a different world

today but it's only the oldies who can really appreciate that. For the likes of me and your granddad Harry, we were born during a world war. The aftermath was just as tough, and the only way families could get through it was not to dwell on what they'd lost but pull together to rebuild their lives. Stiff upper lip as they say, and we didn't talk about emotional stuff. When it came to raising Tom, his mum and me tried our best to work through the gut-wrenching moments and the disappointments together. No secrets, we thought, but Tom kept this one buried deep.'

The empathy between us is humbling. 'Regrets are hard to live with, no matter which side of the line you're on, Wally, aren't they? I battled with alternating anger and sorrow. All I could think about was *my loss*. Now I need to start letting go of my fears.'

'Just know that Harry is happy where he's resting, Kerra,' Wally adds. 'Next time you take a wander up to the headland, listen to the sound of the wind when it's in an easterly direction. It whistles as it blows around the side of Lanryon church and it's the sound you hear when you hold a seashell to your ear. It's the quiet roar of the waves as they crash upon a distant beach and it's soothing to the souls who rest there. It was Harry himself who pointed that out to me once, many years ago.'

It truly was an accident and Granddad can rest in peace. If I hadn't bumped into Tom this morning, I might never have known the truth. As a child it was heart-breaking to lose someone I adored, and with whom I had so many adventures. I found it hard to forgive him for taking a risk and at one point even wondered if he loved the sea more than he loved me. It sounds silly, but I was bereft. Even as an adult, it made trips back here a bitter-sweet experience.

'Please tell Tom how grateful I am to him, Wally.'

'I surely will, Kerra. Your grandma was a strong woman, but out of respect for her wishes your mum and dad never talked about it. I don't know if this helps, but Tom once told me that after the accident Rosenwyn would often wander along the beach when the weather was closing in. He said she'd stop to gaze out at the waves as they came crashing in and maybe in her heart that made her feel closer to Harry. A fisherman's wife is used to long periods apart but now they're together again.'

A single tear escapes, trickling down my cheek and I swipe it away. 'That's comforting, Wally. Thank you.'

'Hey, Drew, how is the unpacking going?' Walking and talking on the phone at the same time isn't easy and I pace myself on the long uphill climb as I head back to the High Street.

A groan filters down the line. 'Considering Felicity wasn't going to bring much with her, the loft is now rammed full of boxes. We're trying to get the things she wants unpacked and put away, so that it's all clear for the party. How are things with you? Ross has been leaving earlier and earlier, I see.'

'Sorry, he'll be gutted to think he's disturbing anyone. This big project means he'll be on site up at Renweneth, the other side of Treylya, for at least half of his time and that means he's spreading himself thin elsewhere. But he's been talking about getting his foremen to debrief him at the start of each day. That should cut down on the number of site visits and allow him to make sure things run smoothly in the office. It's time he loosened the reins a little and his men understand it all helps to guarantee their future.'

'That's a lot of pressure on his shoulders, but he'll pull it off. It's not Ross waking me up though, it's the thoughts constantly going around and around inside my head. I have a couple of trips away coming up and, uh,' he pauses, lowering his voice. 'I haven't told Felicity yet. One of them will involve what is likely to be a two-day trip to Bristol to meet with a new client. He has a couple of properties there he wants to convert into boutique hotels.'

My breath is now a little laboured as the incline begins to take a toll. 'Sorry… I'm walking back from the cove and I'm not as fit as I think I am,' I explain. 'That's… great news, Drew!'

'I know. We're going to need the money, but the timing isn't the best. He's one of those men who are hard to get hold of and then, when he's ready to talk, he expects everyone to drop everything and go at a moment's notice.'

'Look, there are plenty of people around to make sure Felicity is fine.'

The line goes quiet for a moment. 'You know, Kerra, that's what I love about living here. I know at times it's frustrating that everyone knows everyone else's business, but no one is ever alone if they need help, are they?'

I laugh. 'It's one of the perks. The other is the beautiful walks. I'm sure there must be more benefits but ask me again after I've made up with my dad. Anyway, I'm calling to pick your brains. I need an interior design software package that isn't too difficult for someone who needs to get up to speed quickly. One that will deliver a professional 3D output for the client. Is there any particular package you can recommend?'

'Of course, I'll send you a link. Probably the best one for a first-time user is one where your plans are created in 2D, but the actual design takes place in a 3D environment. That's extremely helpful if you don't have an architectural background. You can also add digital photos to the design, so you can create your own catalogue of furniture. The customer gets to see a truer representation that way.'

'Awesome! You are a star. You've probably saved me a day's work sifting through what's available and I need to get onto this fast. Sissy has a great lead for furnishing a newly refurbished hotel and this could take the business in yet another direction.'

'That's good to hear, Kerra. The two of you have worked hard and that bodes well for the future.'

'Thanks, I have a good feeling about it. And we're all looking forward to Saturday, it's just the lift we need.'

'What, working for your supper when you're all bringing it with you anyway?' He chuckles.

'It's the start of the next generation in Penvennan Cove. That's a big deal.'

'The start? If we don't get a baby that sleeps and responds well to two paranoid parents who are reading every book and article they can on how to raise children, we might be stopping at just the one.'

'Oh, I think you might not have to wait too long to have a playmate for your new arrival. Both Tegan and Yvonne went all dewy-eyed at your news.'

'Not you?' He sounds surprised.

'I'll reserve judgement until I've seen how the two of you cope,' I admit, sounding a little hesitant.

'Felicity will be fine, I'm the one who is going to be panicking all the time, believe me.'

The problem is that Drew isn't exaggerating. Fortunately for him, Felicity is the sort of person you want on your side when the going gets tough. She will be his tower of strength and ground him.

'You'll be fine once you get the hang of it. I must go. I need to pop into the convenience store. And thanks for your advice, I'll wait for that link.'

Popping the phone into my pocket, I head straight for The Penvennan Convenience Store and as soon and as I swing open the door to the shop, the first thing I notice is a stranger standing behind the counter. After piling a few things into the basket, I wait until there's no one in the queue.

'Is Mrs Moyle around?' I ask, tentatively.

'She's in the kitchen having a cup of tea.' The young woman smiles at me.

'I'm Kerra Shaw, I live in one of the cottages opposite. Is she tied up, or can I pop in for a quick word?'

'Oh, Mrs Moyle is just tidying up, I'm sure it will be fine.'

'If you could put these into a bag for me please, I'll only be a couple of minutes.' I pull out a ten-pound note and hand it over, then make my way around the counter.

Heading along the corridor I tap on the downstairs kitchen door before easing it open, popping my head tentatively around it to check that Mrs Moyle is happy to have a visitor.

'Oh, Kerra – how lovely to see you. Come in. I'm just having a sort out.'

The contents of one of the cupboards is strewn over the worktop.

'Spring cleaning?'

Mrs Moyle frowns, which is unusual for her. 'I decided it was time to get some help in the shop. I don't mind baking in the evenings when Arthur is busy online, but... um, it's good to have a bit of time off occasionally.'

'Arthur was fine when I popped in while you were visiting your friend,' I remind her, with an encouraging smile.

She looks away, avoiding eye contact. 'Barbara is the wife of the man who delivers our fruit and veg. She's happy to work part-time to help me and I do need a break.' There's an edge to Mrs Moyle's voice, as if she feels the need to justify herself.

'Oh, of course you do, Mrs Moyle. I just thought I'd call in to check everything is okay and that Arthur doesn't need a hand with anything.'

'He can figure out most things and it's not as if he doesn't have time on his hands, is it?'

My goodness. I take a step backwards, wishing I hadn't popped in. I'm not sure if this frosty reaction is aimed at me, or Arthur. Maybe they've had cross words and I unwittingly picked the wrong moment to barge in.

'As long as everything is ticking over nicely, I'll leave you in peace. Just ring if you need anything.' And with that I make a hasty retreat.

Ross is cooking tonight, but when he eventually arrives home, he has a carrier bag from the Chinese takeaway in one hand.

'Sorry,' he says, the moment he steps through the door. 'It's been a long day and I knew you'd be starving. I meant to leave work an hour ago, but things just dragged on.'

'Was it a tough day?' I ask, taking the bag from him and walking through to the kitchen.

'Not really, just hectic. There's so much going on and I'm still doing some handholding. It's a confidence-building thing for two of the foremen who have only been with Treloar's for a year. Some decisions cost money and that's a big responsibility when they're used to getting me on site to make the ultimate call. Now I'm expecting them to weigh up the odds and decide for themselves unless it's a major problem, but even small over-runs add up. We don't work under a blame culture, and I must accept that there will be a few mistakes made along the way. Hopefully, not expensive ones but even I've been caught out on occasion in the past. On the whole I'm pretty happy with the way they're stepping up.'

After a quick kiss, Ross heads upstairs to shower and change, while I lay the table and place the contents of the bag on a tray. Ripley isn't around and that can only mean she's stalking prey. It's been a while since she brought any presents to lay on the decking and I'm hoping she doesn't suddenly appear with something in her mouth. As if he's mirroring my thoughts Ross pads across the kitchen in bare feet, staring out of the glass wall of doors as he looks for Ripley.

'She's still out,' I confirm.

He's wearing jogging bottoms and a loose t-shirt, looking chilled-out. His hair is towel-dried and the top flops down over his forehead, touching his eyelashes. I watch as he scoops it back with his hand, noticing how brown his arms are already. By comparison, I still look quite pale as I spend so much time in my office.

'Have you been hanging around long just waiting for your man to come home?' he asks, turning down the corners of his mouth, apologetically.

'No, I'm fresh out of the shower myself. Time ran away from me today, as I'm learning how to use a new software package. Sissy has been asked to quote for what could be the biggest single order of her working life so far. It came out of the blue, so I have a week to become an expert user, as there are twenty rooms to furnish.'

'Twenty? My goodness, go Sissy!'

We settle ourselves down at the table and Ross eases the lids off the assortment of plastic boxes.

'It's not quite as nice as home-cooked, but it's the thought that counts,' Ross says, passing me a serving spoon.

'It's fine. We've both had a busy day and I was fully prepared to scramble some eggs and toast some bread.'

'You sound tired,' he remarks, his eyes scanning my face.

'It was a bit of a weird day, I will admit.'

'Weird?'

'I went to talk to Sam and ended up sitting with Tom and his dad, Wally, drinking tea and eating cake. They're doing an amazing job of sorting out The Salvager's Yard… and we talked about Granddad.'

Ross stops ladling egg fried rice onto his plate to stare at me with concern reflected in his eyes. 'And?'

'And everything is just fine.'

He lets out a long, slow breath before he continues

scooping more rice onto his plate. 'I told you so,' he gloats, shamelessly.

'You did. And taking me up to Lanryon allowed me to face up to whatever truth there was to tell if the chance arose for me to ask the question.'

Ross is obviously hungry, but he sits back and what I see is a look of relief on his face. 'I'm glad Tom was the one who could give you the resolution you were seeking, Kerra. If it had been your dad, there's a chance you'd always have wondered if he was simply telling you what you wanted to hear. It's human nature to protect the people we love from being hurt, isn't it?'

'Hmm,' I remark, making a concerted effort to sound positive. 'Anyway, as it turned out it might have solved two of my dilemmas. Come on, let's eat. It's been quite a day all round.'

I don't know how I feel, to be honest. Relieved on the one hand and let down by Dad on the other. I can understand Mum and Grandma Rose not wanting to talk about it in detail. But at some point over the years, he should have answered my questions. Just because I was young when it happened doesn't mean the horror of it hasn't stayed with me and it left its mark.

# 10

## Party Time!

Felicity is sitting in one of the glacier-white designer chairs that complement the black marble-topped dining table in Tigry Cottage. In front of her is a mound of presents and she gazes back at us all, her eyes glistening.

'You guys, I don't know what to say… except thank you, because… well, I wasn't expecting this and it's terribly kind of you.'

Drew is beaming from ear to ear as he stares lovingly at the woman the Penvennan grapevine once thought was a figment of his imagination.

I point to the toy box as a good place to begin. Ross and I wrapped each item individually and as Felicity rips off the paper, she starts grinning. 'Oh my! Soft toys – ahh, what cute little birds. They're simply adorable and it's perfect for the design we've chosen for the baby's room!'

'Squeeze them and they sing.' I nod encouragingly, and Felicity chooses the blue bird. A blast of birdsong has everyone smiling and we watch as all ten of the palm-sized packages are unwrapped.

Next, Yvonne slides forward her and Gawen's gift. Six helium-filled balloons attached to a beautifully presented trio of three mini suitcases in a soft grey colour, decorated with the cutest little bees. Felicity loosens the blue bow holding the balloons and hands them to Drew. As she opens each case there are a whole variety of items – everything from creams and lotions to mini hand towels and flannels in a soft baby-blue, with a bee embroidered in one corner.

It isn't long before we're looking in amazement at the tiny clothes Tegan carefully wrapped in tissue paper decorated with little blue hearts.

'Oh, this is adorable!' Felicity gushes, as she holds up a white all-in-one sleep suit decorated with the outline of fluffy clouds in pale blue and a similar one with tiny little blue tractors. Next is a pair of navy-blue dungarees and a short-sleeved navy and white striped t-shirt with an anchor motif.

Tegan slides forward the final package and as Felicity rips off the outer paper, we all mutter an 'ah!'

'I love the hopping bunnies,' I declare.

Felicity reads from the card insert.

'One long sleeve zipped grow suit, one sleepsuit, a rib singlet, a bunny rug, a knot hat, a bib and some mittens. Aww… look at this!' Felicity exclaims, as she holds up the hat and the mittens.

'And that will fit a baby? It looks like something you'd put on a doll,' Sy comments, looking at Tegan as if this can't be right.

'It's standard size for a new-born, Sy,' Tegan confirms.

'If a baby comes early, they do a special premature range, which is even smaller.'

Drew pales as he listens to their interaction. 'We have a couple of parenting classes to attend and I'm hoping they go through the basics. I can't imagine how to pick up anything small enough to fit into that. Anything smaller, then I'm panicking big-time,' he declares, looking concerned.

'Anything? You mean our little boy,' Felicity laughs. 'Don't worry, Drew, I think he's extremely comfortable where he is and I'm not expecting him to put in an early appearance. If he takes after you, he'll let us know when he's good and ready, and he won't be in a hurry.'

We all burst out laughing and Drew joins in, looking slightly awkward as he stands there clutching the balloons. But Drew isn't one to be hurried in anything he does, and I guess when it comes to having a baby it's a good gene to inherit.

'I need a glass of wine,' he says, turning to find something to tie the balloon strings onto and as Tegan, Yvonne and I sit down, the men head over to the island in the kitchen.

'I think we're traumatising them,' Felicity says, her voice lowered and her eyes sparkling. 'But aren't these outfits teeny? Even I'm beginning to wonder what I've let myself in for! Seriously, though, I can't thank you enough ladies. It's so thoughtful of you. The reality of what's about to happen is really beginning to kick in now. This is the life I dreamt about, and I keep wanting to pinch myself to check it's for real.'

I can't help but cast my mind back to the last time Felicity was here and the conversation we had. Then it was all about the practical things – untangling her links to the family business and setting up on her own to guarantee some sort of income for the future to reassure Drew the financial burden doesn't fall solely on his shoulders. I guess a lot has happened in the interim and they've found a happy medium. For now, it means she can focus on becoming a mum.

'Drinks are over here, help yourselves. There's a jug of apple and elderflower cordial laced with sliced strawberries and mint.' Drew, bless him, is making a real effort to make sure Felicity doesn't feel left out.

There's a knock on the door and we're all delighted to see Polly follow Drew into the kitchen.

'It's a flying visit, I'm afraid, as I have to sort Ian out. He's working on a project for me this evening and then I'm manning the bar for the last two hours.'

'Polly has designed a mural for us,' Drew explains.

'Right. I think it's time you unveiled the plan.' Ross smiles, raring to go.

Tegan and I help Felicity to clear the table, piling the presents onto one of the armchairs. Then Drew sets up his PC to talk us through the vision.

'The ceiling and the paintwork are done, and Felicity and I have already given the entire room a coat of white emulsion. There are three walls to be painted in what is called *a shimmer of white*. It's pearlescent and will require at least two coats to get the full effect as it's very subtle.'

The 3D image looks amazing as we all lean in to get a closer look.

'Is that a hand-painted mural on the back wall?' Ross queries.

'It is, but it's not freehand,' Polly assures us. 'There is a lot of masking up involved, but the painting bit is surprisingly quick and easy, I promise you.'

We're all a little bemused as what we're seeing are two silver birch trees, which fill the entire wall. The background is white and everything else is in a soft grey, even the leaves. It's gorgeous but gazing around at the others none of us look confident enough to take on the challenge. I certainly wouldn't want to mess anything up.

'It will take two people to work on it,' Felicity explains. 'I'll also need a willing pair of hands from someone who isn't afraid to climb a ladder.'

'It's easier than it looks to get the outline and it's all done with a roll of low tack tape,' Polly confirms.

They all turn to look directly at me.

'Guess I'm volunteering,' I reply, nervously.

'Don't worry, you'll be fine,' Polly assures me, her eyes full of amusement.

'The rest of us need to arm up with paint rollers,' Drew states, 'but we will need one person to do the tricky cutting in at the top of the other three walls and along the skirtings. Who has the steadiest hand?'

'I'm up for that,' Tegan offers. 'Brushes I can handle, but I tend to overload a roller. I hope you have dust sheets down.'

'We do. Let's make our way upstairs. Do you want a hand with anything, Ross?' Drew asks. 'The paint is already upstairs.'

As the guys sort out the boxes of supplies Ross brought with him, we follow Felicity upstairs. She talks to us excitedly, over her shoulder.

'This is so great of you all to do this. We can't assemble any of the baby's furniture until the painting is done. The boxes are stacked up in the main bedroom and there's hardly any space to move.' Her voice is full of gratitude.

'And here we are.' Felicity swings open the door to the second bedroom, which is literally a large, white canvas. 'Drew knocked through into the third bedroom to turn it into an en suite. I think you did the same with Pedrevan, Kerra, and it's a good use of what was a tiny room anyway.'

'Oh, this is lovely, Felicity,' Tegan enthuses. We take it in turns to pop our heads inside and I glance around at the white marble tiles and the strips of tiny little beads of coloured glass that run around about a foot up from the floor and the same height down from the ceiling. The pale blue, lilac and soft green tints are a perfect lift to brighten the well laid out en suite.

As soon as the guys appear, Polly shows me and Felicity what to do while the others decide on their strategy. I can hear Ross already directing operations, as he suggests Tegan is sorted out first so she can get that top couple of inches of the walls painted. Drew is prising the lid off the paint while Gawen sorts a small tray and a brush for her.

'It's time to make a start, ladies!' Polly grins, as Felicity and I look at each other and pull a face.

'I hope we can do this justice. It's rather ambitious,' I remark.

'You'll be fine. Here's a bag of tape, most of it is an inch thick, but there are two rolls of narrower stuff for the smaller detail. You'll need a set of steps while you outline the branches,' Polly informs me, but Tegan is already halfway up the tall step ladders with a brush in her hand.

'There's a second, smaller set of steps in the master bedroom,' Felicity confirms.

'I'll fetch them,' I reply, springing into action.

'Sorry, there's not much room to move around in there and they're on the far side by the window.'

As I pass Ross on my way back into the room, he waylays me to plant a quick kiss on my lips. He lingers and I can see how happy he is to be a part of this.

'Behave yourself,' I warn, laughing as I manoeuvre the surprisingly lightweight steps past him.

Standing back in front of the wall it's hard to believe we're about to turn a plain white expanse into a woodland scene.

'The thing with trees,' Polly informs us, 'is that nothing is perfectly straight and it's all about proportion. First off we're masking up the trunk and the branches.'

Felicity produces a print of the overall look we're trying to achieve, while Polly hands us both a roll of green tape. 'Tree trunks are broad at the bottom and graduate up before they widen out at the point where the branches grow.' Polly rips off a small piece of tape and presses it onto the wall. 'We only want the branches to fill out the top third of the scene, so this marks the height of the tree trunks.'

Polly places another small piece of tape further along the wall as a marker for the second tree trunk and we stand back to get a feel for the overall proportions.

'Are we in agreement that the trees are equally spaced? The branches need to run in both directions and there will be a little crossover, but that will be covered by the leaves.'

'How on earth are we going to paint leaves? That'll take forever,' I comment, hesitantly.

'I've already made up some templates – that's the easy

part, trust me! Right, I'll do one trunk, then you two can paint the other.'

Felicity gingerly lowers herself down, sitting back on her heels. I sit next to her as we watch Polly. Polly peels back the end of the tape on the roll and presses it next to the marker on the wall, gradually easing it down in an increasing curve. 'Nature produces knots and bumps, so I'm just going to create a little detour here, see? You simply deviate a little in a couple of places and then continue down to the skirting board. Then do something similar on the other side. It should be about nine inches wide at the top and double that at the bottom. Then place a small piece across the top of the skirting board to cover the gap between so you don't get paint on the woodwork at the bottom.'

I'm surprised at how quick and easy it is to do, and when Felicity and I have finished creating our outline, I help her up and we stand back to give it a quick check.

'Looking good over there.' Drew glances across at us as he grabs a tray and a roller from Gawen. Ross is straightening the dust sheet the other side of the tall stepladder, on which Tegan is crouched at the top, her head bent. She's already halfway along one wall, the small band of shimmery paint forming a perfectly straight line with the ceiling.

'Ooh, that's pretty. Great job, Tegan,' I congratulate her.

'Sorry, I can't turn around. I'm on a run and I daren't stop.' She chuckles.

Conscious that Polly doesn't have a lot of time, Felicity and I return our attention to the job at hand.

'Now all we need to do is create a little interest on the trunks themselves before we paint them. You'll be applying the paint lightly with a sponge and it dries really quickly.'

Polly demonstrates how to cut thin, tapering slivers of the tape placing three together, slightly staggered at several points along the tree trunk, two sets on one side and three on the other.

'This replicates how the bark peels away in places on birch trees. Together with the curves on the sides, these lines soften the look and then you do the branches, which is the same process. Add some little bumps here and there along the way. Remember that the leaves will cover sections of the branches anyway, and I think you'll be surprised how effective it will look afterwards.'

'It seems relatively easy, but we won't know until after we pull off the tape, will we?' I point out.

'The worst-case scenario will mean lightly sanding an area, flashing it over with some white emulsion and then re-doing a section. Seriously, you can't really go wrong.'

We then have a masterclass in how to paint using a small sponge the size of a kitchen scouring pad. It's very clever. Polly shows us how to pull off small pieces so that the flat surface of the sponge is irregular. She hands out disposable gloves, donning a pair herself.

'This is how you achieve a softer, more muted finish. If it was painted with a brush, it wouldn't have any depth to it. Simply put a little paint in a tray, like this.' She scoops a couple of tablespoonsful of paint into the tray and gently dabs at it with the sponge.

'Don't overload it and take off some of the surplus by pressing it onto a piece of card first.' She pulls out a stack of recycled cardboard from the carrier bag at her feet to demonstrate. 'You don't need much paint and then you begin dabbing.'

Within seconds she's working her way down the entire tree trunk, creating a mottled effect with surprisingly little effort. 'See how quick it is to do? Try not to go over the same place twice, but there will be some overlap and if that happens, as long as you aren't too heavy-handed it simply gives a little more depth in places. There, it's done! Now you have a go.'

Felicity goes first and then halfway down she hands the sponge to me.

'Wow – it really is a doddle,' I agree.

As I work my way down, Polly begins to pull the tape off the first tree trunk and Felicity watches in amazement.

'It looks pretty good to me,' she enthuses.

'Usually, I'd let it dry first,' Polly comments, 'so the tape isn't quite so messy when you roll it up into a ball.' I glance across and see that her gloves are no longer pristine. 'But the paint is so thin that five minutes is enough drying time. Now let's take a look at the second tree.'

It took minutes to finish it off and Felicity indicates for me to do the honours. As I peel off the tape I'm conscious that everyone is watching now with interest.

'Well, that's not bad. And I like the fact that the two trees look a little different,' Felicity says, giving me a high five as I join her.

'Lesson over,' Polly concludes.

Everyone returns to what they're doing.

'In this bag are the stencils for the leaves,' she tells Felicity and me as we peek inside. 'There's a dozen of them and they're all different layouts because you want variety. Mask up the branches in the same way, have some thicker ones and then spindly twigs coming off as you go further up the wall. Once they're dry, you simply tape the different templates on a section of the wall and dab the leaves with the sponge. Once they're dry, peel them off and place them randomly on another section. I suggest you vary the shades of grey by adding a little white to some of the paint in the tray. And why not add some of the pearlescent white, too? It would be fun to have a couple of areas with that wonderful lustre to break it up.'

'Oh, Polly,' Felicity declares, throwing her arms around Polly's shoulders – rather awkwardly because of her bump. 'This is amazing, truly amazing. You are a real star. Now off you go – get Ian sorted so you can make your client happy. We owe you big time.'

'My pleasure entirely, Felicity. Drew was a great help when I was talking Dad into letting me make-over the interior of the pub. It was a battle I wouldn't have won if Drew hadn't been on my side, believe me.'

Isn't it funny how good deeds rarely go unrewarded? I bet Drew would never in a million years have envisaged the payback would be a hand-painted mural on a nursery wall.

'Who would have thought a painting party could be this much fun,' Yvonne declares, as we sit out on the deck watching the guys gathered around the barbecue.

It's true, we've had a great time. 'Polly really knows her stuff, doesn't she? She turned us into artists!'

Felicity looks tired but happy, as she sits with one hand gently massaging her bump. 'I do hope Polly's new business is a success. It would be such a shame to waste a talent like that. Ooh… he's kicking – do you want to feel?' she offers. Both Yvonne and I lean forward, eagerly.

'You don't mind?' Yvonne asks, tentatively.

'Not at all. Here, give me your hand. This is his foot, wait a second until he kicks again.'

Suddenly something happens and Yvonne jumps, instantly pulling away. 'That's amazing!' she declares, the look on her face one of almost disbelief. 'That was one solid kick. Doesn't it hurt?'

'It gets a little sore at times. He's kicking the same spot repeatedly now that there isn't enough room for him to turn around. He's head down and ready to go, apparently. Do you want to feel, Kerra, or will it freak you out?'

'I'd love to,' I admit, leaning even closer and Felicity indicates for me to place my hand on her tummy.

Moments later something sharp and pointed literally pushes against my hand. 'That's not a foot, I think that was a knee!' I exclaim.

'It was, he's adjusting his position. Hopefully, he'll settle down a bit before we start eating. I'm ravenous. But what a result. Seriously, I was beginning to panic and now the room is ready for the furniture to go in. You have no idea what a relief this is for me and Drew. We're trying to stay calm and take one day at a time, but everything is a first for us. And the baby will be here before we know it.'

Her voice is low and I'm sure there are moments when Felicity thinks about how far away her family are now.

'If you ever need some company, you know where to turn,' I tell her, firmly. 'I'm just next door.'

'And I'm only half an hour away, Felicity. Being

self-employed has some perks and one of them is being able to drop everything if necessary,' Yvonne adds.

'All for one, and one for all,' I say, and we raise our glasses of apple and elderflower infusion to toast exactly that.

'The first batch is ready. Only another five minutes, ladies, and the chicken skewers will be cooked to perfection,' Drew calls out.

Ross walks towards us with a tray stacked with sizzling lamb and my stomach begins to rumble. 'Are there any more serving platters?' he asks. I jump up, excusing myself to head inside to find one for him.

As I make room on the kitchen island, moving plates around to accommodate the hot food, Ross gives me one of his wicked smiles. It's wonderful to see him enjoying himself.

'What?' I ask, staring at him and wondering what he's thinking.

'This is a glimpse of the future, hopefully for us all.' Ross turns to face me, his eyes searching mine. 'When good things happen it restores one's faith in human nature, doesn't it? Things haven't gone smoothly for us from day one, Kerra, have they? Some of the problems weren't of our making, but we've been so caught up in trying not to make ripples, the irony is that we ended up making waves.'

I can't disagree with that. 'It's different for us, Ross, we were both born in Penvennan – we're not incomers like Sy, Drew and Felicity. Tegan had a rough time losing Pete, and people respect her privacy. But we're fair game because we're different and always have been. Now that we're no longer living our relationship in the shadows it's freeing though, isn't it?'

Ross's eyes search mine, the look on his face making my heart skip a beat. 'All that remains is to make peace with your dad and quite frankly, I don't give a damn about what anyone else thinks. When we're among friends, life is simpler and that's our aim from here on in.'

'If only...' My voice tails off, wondering if anything can be that easy.

'Settling down in Pedrevan Cottage feels right and I won't always have to work long hours, I promise you. Once my father's new endeavour takes off, it will keep him occupied and he'll be off my back. I have a team of good men, willing to be trained up to take on a lot more responsibility, but I'm hampered because of my father. He doesn't believe in rewarding people when they step up, he says they should simply be grateful to have a job. If things go well, I can change all that and then I'll become Mister Nine-to-Five.'

Ross is poised, ready to spring into action. It's obvious that a part of him envies the adventure Drew and Felicity are about to embark upon. I hope it doesn't unsettle him, because it's going to be quite a while until we'll be in a position to even consider starting a family.

# 11

## A Guessing Game

After a very enjoyable weekend and a good start to the week, by eleven o'clock on Wednesday morning I'm on my third cup of coffee as I sit alongside Polly in Pedrevan's garden office.

'Three rooms down,' she groans, 'and seventeen to go. But you'll succeed in turning me into an expert before we've finished.'

'That's the general idea. It's a tool that will be invaluable to you in the future and between us we're finally getting the hang of it, aren't we? We'll soon be flying through them.' Personally, I think we're doing a great job as we've only be at it for just over three hours. It takes a while to become familiar with any new software package and loading up the catalogue of photos Sissy and her assistant, Sienna, diligently pulled together wiped out the first hour. But Polly is our official interior designer on this project and it's her call on what photos work best.

'We have half-an-hour left until Sam is expecting you

back at the pub to get ready for the lunchtime rush,' I point out.

'Sorry if I'm being a little fussy but—'

'Not at all. The detail matters, Polly, and that's the expertise you bring to the table.'

'But you're spending time on this and that's my job, Kerra. Now I've seen how the software works, I'll purchase a copy myself and if you email me the files, I'll take it from there.'

It's funny how some people are content to sit back and have everything done for them, but others see an opportunity and grab it, gratefully.

'That's a great idea, Polly. Sissy is already forewarning our suppliers as if we get this job then we need everything to happen very quickly indeed. What sort of impression did you get when the two of you were at Easterton Lodge?'

Her mouth twitches. 'Like they want it done yesterday and as long as the price is competitive it will be full steam ahead.'

'That's good to know. The other problem is going to be getting it all assembled, of course. We're going to need a team and, uh, hmm... without your expert eye there to oversee it, someone who can make sure everything is set up correctly according to the individual plans.'

Polly drains the last dregs of her coffee and sits back, frowning. 'Let me have a word with Dad. This is a one-off project and sorry, but I really do need to be there in person. It would be unfair to expect someone to step in for me.'

'But it means five full days onsite, Polly. I'll also be around to help out wherever I can, but I'd hate this job to cause any friction between you and your dad.'

Polly starts laughing. 'Oh, I think he'll be amenable in this particular case,' she replies, with a meaningful smile.

'Why's that?'

'I have a feeling, that's all. He's revealing his big plan to me tonight after we close up.'

'Are you feeling nervous about it?'

'No, but it could signal big changes all round. He's been talking about this for a couple of years now and he's accepted that at some point I want to follow my own career path. If Dad decides to sell up, it means he'll have to find a house somewhere. I can't afford a place of my own right now and I wouldn't want to go too far afield as most of my work is local. But I know someone who lives a five-minute drive away who has a spare room. It might be fun to house share.'

Fun is one word for it, but what other choice does Polly have right now?

'Change is never easy, but I agree with you that it's time. When I spoke to Sam last week he seemed happier. It must be a big relief to get to this stage, but he did say if you weren't happy with his plan it might need a little tweaking.'

Polly's expression is giving nothing away. 'I just hope that Dad's decision isn't based around what he feels is best for me. He can't continue living his life putting me first as if I'm still his responsibility. Dad has a life of his own too and it's about time he started focusing on his future happiness.'

In all honesty I'm a little surprised by Polly's response. I can't help wondering whether she's met someone, hence the house share, and doesn't quite know how to break the news to Sam. That would be ironic, because a few months ago Sam mentioned to me that he'd met someone online but it doesn't sound like that has gone anywhere, which is a pity. It will be easier for Polly to go off and do her own thing if she knew she wasn't leaving Sam on his own.

'I'll be thinking of you – both, and hoping it goes well.'

'Thanks for making this work, Kerra. You could have found another designer to bring in for this job and I really do appreciate your support. If it weren't for you, I'd still be a barmaid dreaming of being her own boss.'

I can't help but smirk at that thought. 'You were never just a barmaid, Polly. You and your dad are a successful team running a business together, but he'll reinvent himself, if that's what's called for. Sam has no intention of holding you back, of that I'm very sure.'

Polly looks down at her hands, intertwining her fingers nervously as they lay in her lap. 'I just don't want him to have any regrets going forward, Kerra. Dad made a life for us – a good life, and I feel as if I'm deserting him.'

'You know that's not the case, Polly. Overheads go up year on year, and if the profits don't mirror that trend, then something is very wrong. He's well aware of the problems, and the potential solutions – doing nothing is no longer an option and he knows it. But more importantly, he's proud of you and what you're doing. Sam wants you to grab the chance to live your dream – don't spoil it by putting yourself on a needless guilt trip. That would disappoint him.'

When she looks up her eyes are teary, but she pushes her shoulders back in a concerted effort before we return to the task in hand.

'You're right. Dad is no fool, whatever his plans are it's enough to have him whistling when he thinks he's out of earshot. That's something he hasn't done in a long while. Now, are you ready to set up room number four?'

'Go for it!'

'Hi, Kerra. I just dropped some fabric swatches down to Polly and as I was passing, I thought I'd… um… pop in. I hope I'm not bothering you.'

Sissy is standing on my doorstep looking decidedly awkward. She shifts from one foot to the other, uneasily.

'No. Of course not! Come in. Do you have time for a tea, or a coffee?'

I indicate for Sissy to step inside, and as she does her face immediately brightens. 'It's such a lovely cottage, you did a great job with the renovations. Unfortunately, it can only be a flying visit as James is waiting for me to return so he can grab some lunch.'

As I shut the door and follow Sissy through to the kitchen, we take a seat at the dining table, and she smiles.

'It's perfect for this space, isn't it?' she muses, rubbing her hand over the top of the pine table. I fondly remember her driving me to the storage unit to check it out. With a bit of a sand and a paint, we both knew it would look amazing in here – and it does.

'Is there a problem?'

'No,' she replies, rather cagily. 'But there might be, and I thought it was only fair to give you a heads-up.'

Sissy is well known for her almost permanent smile, but today she looks uncharacteristically anxious.

'That sounds ominous.'

The silence is unsettling as Sissy sits fidgeting in her seat for a few moments. 'It's probably best to just blurt it out,' she states, her face colouring up. 'I've been seeing Sam for a little while now and we've been discussing the future.'

Trying my best not to look totally shocked, I focus on smiling. 'That's... um... great news, Sissy. Is Polly aware of this?'

'No. But she will be tonight because Sam is going to sit her down and share the news.'

If I'm reeling, then Polly will be too. It's good news, but totally unexpected.

'That's wonderful, Sissy. I had no idea—'

'No one knows, Kerra. You, better than most, understand what it's like with all the tittle tattle that goes on around here. Sam and I began talking online after he joined a Facebook group run by The Shanty Men. Nettie and I have been fans of their seafaring songs for a long time, and we often enjoy an evening out to see them perform.'

'I didn't know that. Mum was a great fan, too.'

She's nervous and it shows. 'Yes, she was. I saw Sam's name pop up on a comment and then he turned up one Sunday morning when they were doing a fund-raiser at Drakestown. The Lobster Pot held a special breakfast afterwards and Sam and I happened to sit next to each other.'

'Does Nettie know about the two of you?'

'No, not at all. She was at the kennels as usual that day, helping Eddie. The thing is that Sam says Polly knows he's holding something back from her. She'll no doubt think he's going to sell up and I told him straight that it's unfair to let the situation continue. I said that first and foremost, he should do what's right for them both. It's just been the two of them for so long. Sam simply told me it was time to get everything out in the open.'

'That's a good thing, isn't it?' I ask hesitantly, not sure what's going on inside Sissy's head.

'Sam thinks Polly will love his idea and I've come to realise that Sam is a bit of a dreamer. Oh, not in a bad way, but he wants that elusive happily-ever-after and from my experience that's a rare thing to attain. I'm just not sure he needs to complicate matters by talking about us at the same time.'

It wasn't until my return that I crossed paths with Sissy, who is probably fifteen years older than me. She lives the other side of Polreweek, and I don't really know very much about her past. Tegan told me that Sissy's grandma used to own Leath's Farm, but I didn't know the family.

'You're really worried about this big reveal, aren't you?'

'Yes. It's been awkward being around Polly recently given the situation. It just felt wrong, if you can understand that.'

'All I can say is that if she's anything like me, I don't want my dad to spend whatever years he has left on his own. If Sam's happy with the decision he's made, why not be guided by him?'

Sissy gives me a grateful smile and eases herself upright. 'That's reassuring to know, thank you, Kerra. I must go, as James will be wondering where I am. He's such a lovely guy and it was good of you to offer Gwel Teg to him. He knows you could have got a much higher rent for it, but it's not always about the money, is it?'

When we part at the door Sissy leans in to give me a hug. 'That's twice you've saved me, now. You got me back on my feet after the robbery and now I know that I need to be there tonight to reassure Polly. Thank you, Kerra.'

Polly said that it was time her dad began to focus on his own future. However, being confronted by the reality of it might be another thing entirely. You can never tell for sure how someone is going to take unexpected news, can you?

'You're very quiet tonight.' Ross's voice breaks my chain of thought as he nestles closer to me in the darkness.

'Sam told me he was going to talk to Polly this evening about the future of the pub.'

'Oh, I see. Well, I'm sure whatever he decides will be right for them both.'

Ross sounds sleepy and I know he's had a long, hard day. It wouldn't be fair of me to share the reason why I'm so on edge, so it's best to change the subject.

'I'm glad things are going well on the new build up on the headland. Being a stone's throw from Treylya, I did wonder if it would unsettle you. You know, memories from when you were up to your eyes in that build.' And maybe even thinking about Bailey.

'Nope. That's done and dusted as far as I'm concerned. You know me, I don't look back – only forwards. And I'm working with a great architect and project manager. He reminds me a lot of Drew, to be honest. Whenever there's a problem, he's as eager to solve it as I am. We put our heads together to come up with a workable solution. A good architect who understands the importance of compromise saves the client money in the long run. Never mind that, why do I get the feeling you're lying there deep in thought – what's up?'

'I've arranged a meeting with Oliver, Tom and Wally tomorrow. It should be interesting.'

'Hmm... that's the last thing I was expecting you to say.' He yawns, then rests his head against mine, as we gaze out at the starry sky. 'But I'm used to the way you operate now. You're always thinking outside the box and I'm sure something good will come out of it.'

Ross lapses into silence and just as I suspect that he's fallen asleep his body suddenly jerks. 'I just tripped over a cable and trod in some wet cement.' He laughs, softly. 'Oh, I forgot to mention that I bumped into Zacky yesterday and he had news about the stranger who was hanging around.'

My interest is sparked. 'And?'

'Zacky found out that the guy went into Pascoe's café for a coffee. One of the women remembered him because he questioned her as she was wiping down his table.'

Ross pauses, taking a deep breath and I wait rather impatiently as he yawns again. 'Sorry, I'm shattered and it's a fight to stay awake. He was asking questions about Mrs Moyle and Arthur.'

'What sort of questions?'

'How long they'd live here and whether they had any family. She didn't know anything about them, other than they'd been here a long time.'

'I was almost five when they took over the shop and that was back in 1995.'

'How old do you reckon Arthur is?'

'Early sixties. He was probably in his mid-thirties way back then.'

'Well,' Ross replies sleepily. 'Someone's interested enough to pay this guy to gather some information about them. It's hard to imagine why because they're such a quiet couple, aren't they? Perhaps Arthur robbed a bank.' The bed begins to shake as Ross starts laughing, but it doesn't last long as his breathing soon deepens.

No, Arthur isn't the sort to rob a bank. He's harmless, as is Mrs Moyle. Perhaps they owe someone some money – who knows? It's hard to imagine, as it's not as if they lead a lavish lifestyle and I can't imagine Arthur is a gambling man. What if a distant family member has passed on and someone is tracking the Moyles down to tell them they've inherited a small fortune? But good news usually travels fast, and Mrs Moyle is looking a little tense these days.

Ross's gentle snoring makes me sigh, dejectedly.

'Thanks, Ross,' I whisper as I reach across to move a lock of hair that has fallen over one eye. 'Now I'm wide awake and I have two issues going around and around inside my head.'

Still, I reflect, I might know the outcome of one of them as early as tomorrow.

# 12

## Change Happens One Step at a Time

As Oliver and I stand outside The Salvager's Yard he furrows his brow, looking at me as if I'm crazy.

'The local scrapyard wasn't quite what I had in mind, Kerra. Quite frankly this lot needs levelling.'

'But it's probably the only chance you have of getting a presence in Penvennan Cove, Oliver. Think about it. This former garage and boat repair shop is in decline and if it didn't have a working forge the business would have folded a long time ago. Given its proximity to the beach, obviously there are rumblings because it's been an eyesore now for quite a few years. It's in the process of being tidied and there's still a lot of work to be done, but it's a potential opportunity.'

'It does dominate this end of the beach and in the state it's in, it's not exactly good for the other businesses,' he agrees.

'No, and that's why the owner, Tom, has partnered up with his dad to start the clear up. My fear is that the local authority will put a compulsory purchase order on the lot and commandeer it as a second council parking area. There were rumours about that going back about a year ago, but the fact they've done nothing about it yet probably means that the council don't have the budget for it. They also won't want a big developer coming in here because it will increase the traffic flow on the High Street, which isn't wide enough to accommodate a significant increase in volume. I know this for a fact because Tom and I went to the council offices to have a chat with one of the planners.'

Oliver gives me a beaming smile. 'I would expect no less, Kerra. Do you want to enlighten me about the part my company is going to play in your master plan?'

'Oliver!' I exclaim, but I can't keep a straight face. 'It's one step at a time. Let me introduce you to the owners first. Turning this site around on a shoestring budget isn't going to be easy, but Tom and Wally have an idea to open it up to the community. Which is where you come in. We've come up with a plan that could be mutually beneficial.'

Oliver takes a second to scan around, his eyes coming to a resting point far out to sea. It's a beautiful day and the water is calm. This is a slice of heaven, especially for someone who has always lived and worked in London. I remember the effect the cove always had on me every time I came home to visit. Yes, London is an exciting place to be – with the dazzling shops, museums, shows and fabulous restaurants – but I can see that Oliver connects with the Cornish vibe.

'I wish my wife felt the same way that I do. She's paid a few visits since I've been staying here, but she won't consider relocating.'

I'm shocked by his words. 'Is that a real option for you?'

'It is. I've been offered the chance to set up a new sub-office in the region and expand our operations across the whole of the south-west of England. However, Naomi works at the British Museum and I'm afraid... Well, let's just say that her job comes first.'

Ooh... I can tell by the pained expression on Oliver's face that he's struggling with a potentially life-changing decision. I give him a sympathetic smile and change the subject as we walk through the gates of The Salvager's Yard. After giving him a quick rundown on the overall size of the plot, I point out two further areas that are due to be levelled very soon. His interest is growing, and his face brightens. Maybe my idea wasn't quite so whacky after all.

It's going to be a busy morning, as I'm heading straight to The Design Cave afterwards. Sissy texted me first thing and asked if I could pop in. Last night was a big deal for her, Sam and Polly, so fingers crossed she'll be wearing a happy smile when I catch up with her.

The moment I walk into Sissy's office I can tell that something is wrong.

'Thanks for calling in at such short notice, Kerra. Everything is fine here, but I have some rather shocking news and I wanted you to hear it as it was told to me.'

Willow comes running up to say hello, intent on distracting me. I ruffle her ears affectionately, but I can see that Sissy is put out by the interruption. She opens her drawer and pulls out a doggy treat for Willow, who immediately takes it back to her doggy bed as I take a seat.

'The police rang to let me know that Ian's brother, Fraser,

has been charged in connection with the robbery at my old shop.'

'Oh.' I feel my body slump and now I understand why Sissy is so subdued.

'Just when I thought all of that was behind us, but apparently a witness has come forward with some new evidence.'

'But I thought they dismissed the charges against Fraser and let him off with a warning?' I question, convinced that I'm right.

'They did. There wasn't any evidence that he knew he was committing a crime. Fraser was simply approached by a friend of a friend to help your former tenant, Mr Mills, move some stock from my old shop in Polreweek to a warehouse. Fraser was given a key and as far as he and Mr Mills were concerned, it was all above board. As we know, the ringleaders went on to blackmail Mr Mills and he ended up driving stolen cars around the country for them.'

'It's hard to imagine what new evidence they have to incriminate Fraser.'

'Apparently, after Mr Mills dropped him home Fraser jumped in his car and drove straight back to the shop. The scoundrels had paid him to make it look like a break-in – so he knowingly framed Mr Mills.'

'And we thought it was one of the men who ended up behind bars who did the deed. Why on earth didn't Fraser own up to that when the police originally questioned him?'

'He was probably scared. Apparently, a guy who was staying with a relative in one of the flats over the shops was out dog walking that night. He saw something suspicious and took a few photos. Enough to identify Fraser's car and a side shot of him wearing a distinctive hoodie.'

'But why wait all this time before coming forward?'

'The guy was only staying here for a couple of days. It was a chance reference to the break-in by his sister-in-law a couple of weeks ago that made the guy check out his photos. When he realised what he had, he got straight onto the police.' She grimaces. 'I really hate to be the bringer of bad news. Just when Alice and Ian are settling in so well at your dad's.'

'Oh, Sissy – you have nothing at all to apologise for. You were the victim in all this. It nearly destroyed your business before you had a chance to get it off the ground. Most people in your position would feel nothing but anger.' I let out an exasperated sigh as Sissy continues.

'It is what it is, Kerra. The financial loss was down to me dropping the ball and not confirming the start date of the insurance policy. And I suspect that Fraser is about to learn that whatever those rogues paid him for the part he played that night wasn't worth the price he'll end up paying. It's Ian I feel sorry for, as none of this has anything at all to do with him but you know what people are like.'

Fraser's stupidity makes me shake my head in dismay. 'I do. Uncle Alistair is already upset with Dad for taking Alice and Ian in. Ian wasn't sacked because his work was below standard as his employers levelled at him, but because customers weren't happy to have a painter/decorator in their homes whose father is known to be a petty thief.'

'It's unfair, isn't it? That's why I wanted you to hear it direct from me, before the garbled version hits the grapevine.

Things get twisted very easily when people don't have the full story.'

'I really appreciate the heads-up and I'll call in and break the news to Dad next.'

When Ross and I bumped into Zacky and he told us that the police were talking to Fraser, I'd hoped he was wrong. But if he knew something was up, I'm guessing that Sissy is right, it won't be long before it's general knowledge.

'I don't envy you that conversation, Kerra but if your dad hears a whisper about it in the pub he might go off on one of his rants. It's likely that word will get around in advance of it appearing in the local paper.' Sissy's kindness reflects the sort of lady she is, a very private person who understands the impact of speculation. Shortly after the robbery there were some horrible rumours about it being an inside job. No one knew Sissy didn't have a valid insurance policy at the time; but then some people don't wait for the facts to come out.

'Yes, well, let's hope he lets me over the threshold. Anyway, how did it go last night… with Sam and Polly?'

Finally, Sissy's face crumples up into a smug smile. 'You'll find out soon enough because Sam will be getting in touch with you shortly. Let's just say that the future is looking rosy.'

I stand and walk around to give Sissy a congratulatory hug.

'Come on,' she says, giving my back a positive pat. 'Come and take a look at our newest display.'

We take our time, leisurely walking around as Sissy is constantly refreshing the displays and much of the stock is new to me.

'The shop floor is looking amazing,' I comment, waving out to James as he trollies a stack of boxes over to one of the room set-ups. Sienna is updating the display and making up the double-bed with a gorgeous, vivid green and white patterned duvet cover.

'What do you think of the new rainforest range, Kerra?' Sienna asks, her eyes sparkling.

'Fresh, inviting and now I want to re-do my bedroom,' I exclaim, laughing.

'But I think your bedroom is lovely, very calming,' Sissy remarks.

'Oh, I'm using the bedroom at the rear as the master now. It's easier with the en suite.' Well, ever since the first time Ross slept over and now it's *our* bedroom, because he loves the views. 'This would really suit the room.'

'It's not too feminine, is it?' Sissy laughs.

'No. And Ross will love it, he's so into nature. I'll email across an order. It does work seeing the room layouts. What other bits and pieces have you got to complement it?'

I watch as James unpacks a box and carefully holds up a bedside lamp. It's a cluster of leaves reminiscent of the exotic castor oil plant, sprayed in a soft green. They have been cleverly intertwined to look like a vase. The light will be diffused as it seeps between the gaps and I wish I had time to stop and watch them complete the makeover. However, I have a daunting task to perform that can't wait. 'I'll be in touch this afternoon,' I confirm as I bid them both goodbye.

I'm nervous as I undo the latch on the gated entrance to Home from Home and pause. I can hear a metallic scraping sound coming from the other side of the kennels and I hesitate, not sure whether to head towards the house first. It's a crushing feeling knowing that I'm not welcome in a place that was my home for so many years. My feet take me in the direction of the sound, but my nerves are jangling, and anxiety is giving me an adrenalin rush.

The dogs start barking and the shovelling sound stops. I freeze, scanning around. It seems there are only three of the runs in use today which is unusually quiet, and I don't recognise any of Dad's doggy guests.

I spot a movement out of the side of my eye and Dad appears from behind one of the sheds. He has a spade in one hand and a bucket of weeds in the other. The moment he spots me his expression hardens. 'What do you want, Kerra? I'm busy,' he snaps.

'Hi, Dad,' I reply, softly.

He stares at me, narrowing his eyes. 'What's wrong?' His tone is curt, but his frown reflects concern.

As I'm relaying the news Sissy shared with me, he lowers the bucket to the floor and leans on his spade. His face shows no emotion whatsoever and I wonder if he's already heard a whisper of it. A sound behind me makes me turn around and Nettie is walking towards us, looking every bit as anxious as I feel. I give her a weak smile as she joins us.

'...the chances are it will be in the local paper. I think a few people are already aware that Fraser was arrested, so there will be some rumours going around before the facts come out,' I conclude.

When I mention Fraser's name Nettie momentarily closes her eyes, her shoulders visibly sagging. Dad, on the other hand, hasn't moved a muscle. There's an awkward silence before he begins speaking.

'It's one thing after another with that family, which is a shame. Me brother will be knocking on the door, no doubt, accusing me of not looking after Alice's best interests in letting Ian stay here too. The lad hasn't done anything wrong, and I have no intention of throwing the pair of them out. You can tell anyone who asks that's my take on it. Is there anything else?'

I knew this wasn't going to be easy but he's treating me like I'm no longer family.

'No, but I'm glad you're standing up for Ian. When someone is wronged, it takes courage to side with them no matter what other people think. I, more than most, know what that feels like.'

With that, I turn and walk away. I know hypocrisy when I see it, but I didn't expect it from Dad. Like Ian, Ross has done nothing wrong, but Dad's hatred of Jago colours his judgement. Tears well up in my eyes as I increase my pace, but Nettie shouts out for me to hang on and I can't ignore her.

'Wait, Kerra – don't go. Eddie,' she calls over her shoulder. 'I'm putting the kettle on and I'll expect you inside in five minutes.'

With that, Nettie indicates for me to join her as she makes her way into the house. She leads me into the kitchen, a pinched expression on her face.

'That was unnecessarily rude of your dad, Kerra. It wasn't easy for you to come here to pass that on and you were only thinking of him. Alistair won't take this well, but at least when he does turn up at the door your dad will be prepared.'

I swipe away my tears with my hand. 'Really, there's no need to try to get us to sit around the table and talk, Nettie. It won't work.'

She looks at me pointedly, pulls out a chair and inclines her head. I've never seen her like this before and as she presses her lips tightly together, I can tell how angry she is. I sit quietly as she makes the tea and carries the tray over. By the time she's ready to pour, Dad appears looking distinctly subdued as he takes the seat opposite me.

'If you think I'm going to let the two of you part like that, then you don't know me,' Nettie states, firmly. 'I think it's time you both said what's on your minds. Goodness knows you've had enough time to stew on it, and life moves on. So, let's get it over and done with.'

We're all avoiding eye contact and I don't know who is feeling the guiltiest, Dad or me. Neither of us say a word.

'Eddie, Kerra needn't have bothered coming here to forewarn you, knowing what sort of reception she'd get, and there's no excuse for rudeness.'

That's brave of her.

'Fine!' Dad shifts uneasily in his seat. 'Thank you, Kerra, for setting me straight.' He replies, begrudgingly. His words lack both warmth and enthusiasm.

Nettie means well and it would be wrong of me not to acknowledge my sniping, parting remark.

'And I'm sorry for what I said.' At least my apology is real.

Nettie lets out a huge sigh. 'And that's the best the pair of you can do? I'm beyond disappointed, I'm appalled.'

Dad sits there looking like thunder. His jaw is firmly set, and he drums his fingertips on the table until Nettie gives him a thunderous look. There are things I want to get off my chest and now's my chance.

'The reason I wanted you to hear word for word what the police told Sissy, is because I believe you really don't want to fall out with Uncle Alistair. At least if the two of you cross paths you know the truth.'

'Alistair's a fool if he can't see how happy Alice is with Ian,' Dad scoffs. 'Or how hard the lad has worked to pick himself back up. If it means we end up not speaking to each other that'll be me brother's doing, not mine.'

Nettie looks like her blood pressure is about to go through the roof. Her cheeks are flaming. 'You're going to end up alienating everyone you love because of your stubbornness, Eddie? They either agree with you, or you cut them off like you did with your own daughter?'

Dad looks shocked as Nettie's role in this has always been to try to calm things down, in the hope that as time passes relationships will be mended. She's losing it and even Dad is getting worried as he shifts his glance to me.

'I wouldn't be much of a brother, or a dad, if I stood idly by and saw people making mistakes that could ruin their lives. I'll willingly tell my brother, as I will my daughter.'

I can hardly believe what I'm hearing.

'What exactly is Ross guilty of – other than being Jago's son?' Now I sound bitter and Dad instantly bites.

'It won't be long before Ross tries to get his hands on your hard-earned cash. Once his own funds are exhausted from the sale of Treylya, he'll have nowhere else to turn. His greedy father will push him and push him, and Ross's pride won't let him fail. That's what will bring him down, and you too, Kerra.'

'No, Dad,' I reply indignantly, holding his gaze. 'You have no idea what you're talking about. Ross wants nothing at all to do with Jago's expansion plans. He's fighting to protect the part of the business he's spent his entire working life building into something worthwhile and I'm going to support Ross every step of the way. That's what you do when you love someone.'

'Then you'll end up with nothing.' Dad's words aren't filled with anger now, but a pained acceptance.

'If that's the case then we'd start over again and accept that at least we gave it our best shot. Nothing is ever a sure bet.'

Dad sits back, sipping his tea and avoiding eye contact. Nettie might even be wishing she hadn't invited me inside, although when I glance at her she appears calmer. However, she widens her eyes urging me to continue.

'I think it's time you faced up to the truth, Dad. You're angry and it's eating away at you. That anger is directed at Ross, but this isn't about him. Not really. It was Jago who succeeded in winding you up when he was here by saying a lot of things that weren't true. And now he's no longer around you're aiming your pent-up aggression at Ross.'

He lets out a disparaging laugh. 'Really? This isn't about not liking the fact that me daughter is being taken for a ride?'

Do I say what I'm thinking and risk him never speaking to me ever again? Or do I take the coward's way out and back down?

'Every day at the kennels is a struggle for you, Dad.' I'm

talking from the heart and if he can't see that, then all is lost anyway. 'You miss working with Uncle Alistair and you're cross with yourself for not having the courage to admit that. Mum never intended for you to make the kennels a shrine to her, and she'd be gutted to see you going through the motions out of a sense of… misplaced duty.'

'You know better than me what's going on inside my head now, do you, Kerra? I got myself and this place back on an even keel and it wasn't easy. It's been a sacrifice, and now it's clear you don't think I'm doing a good enough job. Should I go cap in hand to beg me brother to take me back into the family business? Because that's what he wants.'

Nettie jumps straight in. 'It was tough, Eddie; we all knew that. But things only changed for the better here once Kerra returned home. You can't ignore the part she played in supporting you.'

'Oh, so now I should be grateful!' He bangs his mug of tea down on the table, slopping it everywhere and Nettie jumps up to get a cloth.

He's lit my fuse and there's no turning back. 'I'm trying to explain why you're so explosive all the time. Every little thing is the last straw, why can't you admit that? You miss working with your hands, the feel of the wood and building something that will stand the test of time. Looking after animals was never your thing. What is so annoying is that you're too stubborn to accept the truth – even from your own daughter. I promised Mum I'd be here for you, but all you do is push me away. It's like you feel guilty for moving on to the next chapter of your life. But working here is making you miserable, Dad. That's why it's easier to keep me at arms' length because I know you, I can see how confused and frustrated you feel. But I'm the only one who can say that to you.'

I don't know if Nettie is shocked by what I've said, however it's abundantly clear that Dad is.

'In me best interests, of course! So, can you tell me why you were carrying on with Ross behind me back?'

I'm fighting not to lose it and my words come out in a rush. 'Because what was the point of upsetting you over a couple of dates that might have come to nothing? In hindsight maybe it was a mistake and I should have said something, but I didn't want to upset you unnecessarily.'

'Oh, so Jago just happened to announce it to everyone in the pub before you had a chance to sit me down and tell me what was going on.'

'It wasn't just that. I'm sick and tired of having every little thing I do become a topic of general conversation. Can you really blame me for wanting a little privacy?'

'They might call it privacy in London, but here in Cornwall we don't hide things unless something's wrong.'

I roll my eyes at him. 'You haven't always been honest with me, Dad.'

He flings his hand down on the table, making me jump. 'Honest? What does that mean?'

'I grew up thinking Granddad took his own life. Have you any idea what goes through my mind when I look at those rocks below Lanryon Church? Well, until I got up the courage to ask someone the question and they told me the truth. That person should have been you, Dad. And that was a mistake, a big one. Living in the belief that Granddad had gone out that day knowing he wouldn't come back, was a thought I simply couldn't bear.'

Nettie's expression makes my heart sink and it's time for me to leave.

It's strange because I've spent my life puzzling over why families fall out. Logic told me that everything can be solved by sitting down and talking honestly to each other. It's up to me and Dad to sit back now and consider where we go from here. I wish I could say I'm walking away feeling optimistic, but I'm not. Nettie knows that Mum wouldn't have wanted Dad to live out the rest of his life feeling lonely and sad. She would have been touched to see how, in their grief, her best friend and her bereaved husband eventually sought comfort in each other. It simply demonstrates the massive hole her passing left in all our lives. I brought Nettie and Dad back together because it felt like the right thing to do. But I fear that Dad feels he's betrayed Mum's memory and that breaks my heart.

I didn't mean to make it any worse by mentioning Granddad, but Dad I are both guilty of holding things back for the wrong reasons. If we can't forgive each other, I'm not sure this rift between us can be mended.

# 13

## Never a Dull Moment

It takes a lot to knock the wind out of my sails, but that's how I'm feeling this afternoon. When my mobile rings I'm tempted to switch it off without even checking who it is, but curiosity gets the better of me. When I see that it's Ross, I eagerly raise it to my ear.

'Kerra, can you do me a favour and pop in to check on Mrs Moyle?' Even though it's an odd request, just the sound of Ross's voice lifts my spirits.

'Of course, what's up?'

'That guy who was nosing around is back. Zacky happened to spot him driving up from the cove, as he turned left into the High Street. Good old Zacky jumped into his car and followed the man to a pub on the outskirts of Renweneth. I'm heading over there now but I was at Rosveth, and the traffic is slow moving.'

'You think this man might have paid Mrs Moyle a visit?'

'Zacky couldn't say for sure. It could be nothing. He

might be a sales rep, but I want to check it out if I can catch him in time.'

'Ross, you will take care, won't you?'

'Of course! Text me when you've spoken to Mrs Moyle. I don't want to go wading in making accusations if Zacky has got this all wrong.'

'I'm on it. Love you!'

'Now that put a smile on my face. I sincerely hope you're having a better day than me.'

I'm glad he can't see the expression on my face. 'I'm fine. Just drive carefully.'

I ease Ripley off my lap, and she isn't happy to be disturbed.

*Miaow, miaoooooow.*

'I know and I'm sorry. I won't be long.'

As I rush out the door, Ripley slinks upstairs, miaowing unhappily as she goes. Less than a minute later I'm pushing open the door to the convenience store and everything looks quiet. But it's Barbara who is behind the counter again today and she's serving a customer. I loiter in the aisle until she's free.

'Is Mrs Moyle about?' I enquire, casually.

'She's in the kitchen baking, I think. Either that, or you'll find her upstairs making a pot of tea for Arthur.'

I make my way behind the counter and along the passageway, listening out as I go. I can hear some sounds coming from the sitting room above, but I might as well check the kitchen first. Giving the door a gentle tap, I open it slowly. Mrs Moyle is sitting at the table, a mug of tea in front of her. Inwardly I give a sigh of relief – at least she's fine. But when she looks up, I can see she's upset. Closing the door gently behind me, I hurry over to her.

'What's wrong?'

'Oh Kerra – I don't know what's real and what's make believe any more,' she blurts out.

'Make believe?'

She pulls a tissue from her pocket to dry her eyes. 'I've been living a lie and I had no idea!'

I ease myself down onto the seat next to her and wait while she blows her nose. 'This man came into the shop, he said he's a private investigator. He was asking me questions, but I didn't answer him. I asked him to leave; he refused to budge so I wheeled the stack of baskets in his direction and he bolted. I locked the door and put up the closed sign until Barbara arrived. I didn't know what else to do.'

'You should have called the police,' I point out, but Mrs Moyle turns to me looking distraught.

'I can't,' she whispers, although we're out of earshot of anyone. 'He said he's working for Mrs Helen Moyle, Arthur's wife.'

Trying not to look as horrified as I feel, I reach out and place a hand on Mrs Moyle's arm to comfort her. 'He might be a con man,' I reply gently, but she shakes her head.

'He told me that he's seen the marriage certificate,' Mrs Moyle says, her voice not much louder than a whisper and I notice that her hands are trembling. 'I don't know what I'm going to do, Kerra, because she wrote to me a couple of weeks ago. I burnt the letter because I didn't believe it.'

'Did you mention it to Arthur?'

'No.'

My mind is whirling, so I pop on the kettle and make Mrs Moyle a fresh mug of tea.

'Can you take one out to Barbara? It was very kind of her to step in at such short notice.' Even in her darkest hour, Mrs Moyle is thinking of someone other than herself.

Barbara gives me a grateful smile, totally oblivious to what's going on. Loitering in the passageway for a few seconds I quickly text Ross. Whether what this man says is true, is anybody's guess. The letter might have been a part of his plan, who knows? But Mrs Moyle is in such a state of shock that when I return to the kitchen I offer to stay with her while she decides what she's going to do next.

Half an hour later it's all arranged. She calmly walks upstairs, and I watch from the passageway as she stands in the doorway of the sitting room talking to Arthur. She tells him that her friend, Iris, called asking for help and she'll be gone for two days. Barbara and her sister will look after the shop while she's away. I can't hear his response, although he must be a little surprised. Mrs Moyle disappears into another room, and I go back to the kitchen to wait for her.

Ten minutes later her bag is packed, and I'm driving her to Polreweek. Throughout the entire journey Mrs Moyle doesn't utter a single word. My mind keeps straying as I think of Arthur, sitting in his chair looking out of the window and totally unaware of what's really going on.

When my phone rings I pull over, thinking that maybe it's Arthur to say Mrs Moyle has forgotten something, but it's Drew. I pull into a lay-by, willing myself to sound upbeat.

'Hey Drew, how's it going?'

'Good thanks. Are you around tomorrow?'

'Yes. Why?'

'I've just received an email about a meeting I need to attend in Bristol. My client said he'll make sure it's all wrapped up in one day, which is a huge relief, and Felicity says she'll be fine, but I'd feel better heading out at the crack of dawn if I knew you were definitely going to be around. You know, just in case…'

'It's not a problem, really. If I have to pop out for any reason, I'll make sure my phone is next to me. I'm not likely to go far, anyway.'

'That's good of you, Kerra. Felicity says I fuss too much, but it's going to be a long day. I probably won't get back until seven in the evening.'

'If I don't hear anything, I'll find an excuse to knock on the door mid-afternoon to check on her. She might appreciate some company by then.'

'Thanks. Felicity is still adjusting to online working. It's not quite the same as turning up at the office every day and mingling with colleagues and clients.'

'I've been there myself, so don't worry. How's Bertie?' I venture.

'He's much more relaxed for sure and loving having Felicity around to fuss over him.'

'That's good to hear. And don't worry about her tomorrow. I'm just a phone call away.'

'You're telling me that this private investigator is convinced that Arthur really is a bigamist?' I exclaim, as I flop down next to Ross on the sofa.

He yanks off his socks, wiggling his toes, which always makes me smile and I reach out to pull up a footstool so he can stretch his legs.

'That seems to be the case. He wasn't very communicative at first, until I pointed out that accosting Mrs Moyle on her own premises could be construed as harassment. I said she was poised to call the police and lodge a complaint unless he was able to show me some form of identification and proof that he wasn't an opportunist thief casing the joint. He showed me his driver's licence and a couple of documents from a file he had with him. One was a letter from his client, Mrs Helen Moyle.'

'She does exist then. It's almost too incredible to believe.'

'I said that if he turned up again, the police would be called without further warning. He was flippant and said he had enough evidence to satisfy his client.'

I stare at Ross, horrified. 'What does that mean? Does this woman want him back? Arthur has lived with Mrs Moyle in Penvennan Cove for twenty-three years. If he does have a first wife, why is she suddenly looking for him?'

Ross shrugs his shoulders. 'It's anyone's guess. What did she say when you dropped Mrs Moyle off at her friend's house?'

'Not much. I suggested she contact a solicitor, just to find out where she stands. But she needs to talk to Arthur sooner, rather than later. She was dazed – it's a lot to take in, isn't it?' I leave out the bit about the letter Mrs Moyle received from Arthur's first wife, as I don't feel at liberty to share that.

'Arthur is the last person anyone would suspect of something like this, so no wonder she's in shock. Barbara didn't get wind of what was going on, did she?' Ross's frown deepens.

'No. Give Mrs Moyle her due, she walked out of that shop with her shoulders back and her head held high. I think Barbara assumed Mrs Moyle's friend wasn't very well.'

Ross raises his arm so I can snuggle into him, and he plants a tender, loving kiss on my cheek. Pulling back, he looks down at me intently.

'There has to be a perfectly good explanation, as there is no way Arthur could be called a womaniser, is there? I mean, the man has been housebound for years.'

That's true. Arthur hasn't been able to get out and about since he hurt his back and that was before they moved to Penvennan Cove.

'Oh dear. Poor Mrs Moyle. I told her to give me a call if she needs anything at all. Arthur is expecting her back the day after tomorrow.'

Ross grimaces. 'If it's true, I can't even imagine living with a secret like that for all these years. Having one wife is a lot to handle, let alone two.'

Maybe some wives are more trouble than others, I reflect but that would be a mean thing to say out loud.

'Ross, this isn't a laughing matter. Arthur could go to prison, couldn't he?'

His face falls. 'Sorry, that was a bit thoughtless of me, but it makes no sense at all. The question is how on earth did Arthur get himself into a mess like this? And why? Because you're probably right – he must realise that it's a serious offence. He's obviously very happy with Mrs Moyle, I mean… the second Mrs Moyle. I don't even know her Christian name.'

'It's Daphne,' I reply, only ever having heard Arthur use it on the odd occasion. I wonder if that's because in the early days he was worried he might slip up and call her Helen? I start laughing and it's my turn to look apologetic because it's so far-fetched.

I lie back thinking what a shocking day it's been. When I tell Ross about Fraser, I skate over the heated exchange I had with Dad. He's better off not knowing and I've decided that for my own sanity the next move must come from Dad. And as Ross isn't exactly Oliver's biggest fan, I skip that part of my day, too. Then I let Ross tell me about his big meeting up at Renweneth on the new site. He goes on to talk about his visit to Rosveth where they're about to start clearing a large plot of land to build three new bungalows. It's wonderful to see him so animated as he shares the details of what sounds like an extremely productive day.

Will living in Pedrevan Cottage be enough for Ross in the future? There's not much he can do here to put his stamp on it. But I push away my niggling little doubts as I glance across at his book collection and find myself smiling. This isn't just a cottage that's been in my family for several generations, it's our home. And I can't wait to surprise Ross with the new look for our bedroom – he's going to love it.

I'm up bright and early the next morning to make sure Ross has a hearty breakfast before he heads out for what he says is going to be a long day. I was rather hoping he'd get in the Friday mood and aim to get home a little earlier, but no such luck.

When the doorbell rings, my hands are in the kitchen

sink as I wash the last of the dishes and I assume Ross has forgotten something. Including his key.

But when I swing open the door, I'm caught off-guard. 'Oh, Sam, this is a surprise. Come in.'

'I was going to call you a bit later, but after a stroll along the beach I found myself heading up to the shop. When I saw Ross getting into his van I asked if you were up and he said to come straight over before you head down to the garden office.'

'I'm just clearing up the breakfast things,' I reply, peeling off my rubber gloves and leading Sam through to the kitchen.

'Please, take a seat. Is there anything I can get you?'

'No. I'm fine, Kerra, thank you. I… um, well, Sissy said she spoke to you yesterday and I want to get things moving.' Sam slips off his backpack and places it on the floor next to his feet as Ripley comes to investigate.

'Here, Ripley, come and have some treats,' I call to her. Grabbing a tube of dried chicken pieces out of the cupboard, I slide open the glass doors and place a few out on the deck. 'She's very vocal Sam. And Bengals think that everything revolves around them first and foremost. She'll soon spot something lurking in the bushes and leave us to talk in peace.'

Leaving the doors ajar, I join Sam at the table. After such a long period of deliberation over whether to sell up and move away or stay, it must be a huge relief to have finally made the decision.

'My life is here in Penvennan Cove, Kerra. It always was and I can't imagine myself anywhere else. And now that Sissy and I are making plans for a future together, I want to have a life away from the business. Naturally, Polly was surprised when we told her, but she was pleased about it. Her new business is going off in a totally different direction and she can follow that now without having to worry about me. Which is strange, because parents are supposed to worry about their kids, not the other way around, aren't they?'

'It doesn't always work out like that, Sam.' I grin at him. 'But I'm glad you've decided to stay.'

'I know you and I kicked around a lot of different options, but what I'm proposing is a little different. I wanted to run it past you as it might not make investing in the pub such an attractive option.'

Hmm… I like that Sam has really invested his time and energy into making the plan his. 'Fire away.'

Sam unzips his backpack and pulls out a sheaf of papers. 'I loved the idea of doing up the three holiday cottages, but instead of running them as lettings I want them converted into two properties.'

'Into two?'

'Yes. Polly will live in the first of the rank of three cottages. On the ground floor it will be knocked through into the middle cottage so that she has a proper office.'

Wow. I'm impressed.

'The cottage at the other end will be home for Sissy, me and Willow. We'll be knocking through into the middle cottage at first floor level because we want to make the most of the marvellous views. It'll be an upside-down house, with the bedrooms on the ground floor and an open plan sitting room, kitchen and dining space above it.'

As we study his rough sketches for the proposed new layouts, I can see it's quirky but it works.

'This is going to cost a fair bit Sam.'

'I know. Probably more than Ross's initial estimate to simply get them back up to spec as holiday lets. I'm going to sell the strip of land that abuts the lane at the end of the rank of shops, to Pascoe's Café and Bakery. They'll be able to widen the entrance around to the rear of their premises, which will mean deliveries won't have to go through the shop. And it will create at least a dozen car parking spaces for their staff.'

'But it cuts the pub garden on the side in half,' I point out. It's very popular in the summer as there's a children's climbing frame with two slides and a big wooden fort.

'We'll put up some fencing to make it private and plant a hedge. In a couple of years' time it will be a nice secluded little spot. The kiddies play area will be relocated to the other side of the pub. It's a big area we don't use, mainly grass with a couple of borders, so it will need a total rethink. We could also fit in at least a dozen wooden tables and benches making it a real family area with the benefit of some unobstructed views out to sea.'

It's a great solution as that means the land behind the cottages, which back onto the gravelled lane running in front of the pub itself, can be turned into private gardens with views directly out over the beach.

'Why don't you turn what's left of the former play area into a cosy and tranquil little tea garden? Plant some roses and climbers and advertise traditional Cornish cream teas.'

'Hmm… that's a great idea. And as we won't be using the accommodation above the pub, I think your suggestion to change the layout and add another restaurant area plus a sizeable function room, will up our profits. If you're still interested in coming on board to put The Lark and Lantern on the map as a top venue to visit, I'm up for the challenge.'

What a result. I thrust out my hand and we shake.

'I feel we should be cracking open a bottle, but it's not even eight o'clock.' I laugh. 'I'm thrilled you found the right solution for you all Sam. I bet Polly was blown away when you revealed it to her.'

'She was, Kerra, and she deserves it.'

'It's not just the fact that you'll still be living and working in the heart of the cove, but that you're acknowledging her success.'

'She's done well my girl. Working two jobs around the clock while she got her business set up is no mean feat. And I've never heard her moan once, no matter how tired she's been or how many hours she's had to work. We're really going to do this then – you and me?'

'We are. I'll talk to my solicitor, and he'll send over some papers for you to check over. I'm in for the long haul, Sam, so I'm not expecting a quick return on my investment. But I'd say a year – maybe eighteen months – down the road we'll be celebrating.'

'Fingers crossed, Kerra, and thank you! If you can ask Ross to give me a call to arrange a meeting, I'd like him to do a revised quote based on my rough drawings of the new layouts for the cottages. Maybe he could point out anything that might fall foul of planning and building regs. Then I'll ask Drew to draw the plans up properly and get them submitted. I've been told that a change of use for the cottages shouldn't be a problem, but I want to do everything by the book. And I'm keeping it just between us for now.'

'I'll let Ross know and my lips are sealed.'

When word finally gets out, this is going to make Sam's regulars smile after a period of uncertainty. No one wants the hub of the village turned into an over-priced wine bar, or one of those cheap eateries selling beer at half price and attracting all-day drinkers. It's always been a place for families and people who enjoy the simple things in life. A visit to Penvennan Cove is the perfect place to relax, walk along the beach or the headland and reconnect with nature. Sam is making sure that tradition will continue, and the locals will always have a place to meet up, chat and be among friends.

# 14

## Stepping Up

'Kerra, it's Mrs Moyle.'

'I'm glad you rang. I was wondering how you were doing.'

She exhales softly and it's such a sad sound that I hold my breath, expecting the worst.

'I've been to see a solicitor.'

At least she took my advice. 'Was it… um… helpful?'

'I wanted to know what the implications were, Kerra, and now I know chapter and verse. I'm going back up north to stay with my cousin for a few days. I need you to do me a favour and the reason I'm asking you is that it will reassure Arthur.'

Reassure him?

'Obviously, whatever I can do to help, I will.'

Mrs Moyle is the innocent party here, so how can I refuse her?

'I told him a lie, that it's a family emergency. It doesn't sit well with me, Kerra, but I'm trying my best to protect him while I get to the bottom of this nightmare. He's packed a bag for me, and I'd be very grateful indeed if you could collect it.' Her voice dips suddenly and I can tell how distraught she is – it must be taking an enormous toll on her and yet her first thoughts are to protect Arthur. 'I've told him you're meeting me at St Austell railway station to hand it over. If it's not convenient I'll get a taxi to come and pick it up from your cottage, if you don't mind.'

'It's no problem at all for me to meet you at the station, Mrs Moyle. Really it isn't.'

'Oh, thank you, Kerra. It means a lot to have a good friend like you. I'm aiming to be at the station by three o'clock at the latest. I've booked a taxi and it doesn't matter which train I catch. You're the only person I can trust to… you see, Arthur feels comfortable around you.'

'I know and I'll make sure he's okay, don't you worry.'

'If you can just… oh, how can I ask you to pretend you don't know what's really going on? And yet, if you tell Arthur it will break him. If I'm right, that man has sacrificed leading a normal life because of me. A problem that could have been fixed and saved him from a lot of unnecessary suffering wasn't corrected because of a vindictive woman who wanted to destroy any chance he had of future happiness. How can I not fight for him now? He's a proud man and Arthur wouldn't hurt a fly, so I refuse to believe…' A solitary sob echoes down the line before she pulls herself together.

I'm not sure I understand what she's saying, but it doesn't matter. This woman comforted my dad when my mum was dying. And with Arthur by her side, they have helped so many elderly and disabled people in the community to keep ticking over. I'm going to be here for her – for them both – by making sure no one, including Arthur, suspects anything is wrong. Mrs Moyle is a gentle, meek and mild woman, but she has the heart of a lion.

'I'll pop in and collect the bag now. Text me when you're about to leave and I'll meet you by the ticket office. And don't worry. No one will be any the wiser.'

Ross rewarded Zacky handsomely yesterday while making it clear that when he pays someone for their time and inconvenience he expects loyalty in return. Zacky got the message loud and clear. I didn't ask how generous Ross was, but he said I didn't need to worry on that score. Suffice to say that no one here will hear a whisper about the man who has been asking questions about Arthur.

Mrs Moyle begins sobbing. 'Oh, thank you for understanding, Kerra.' She pauses to blow her nose. 'Arthur is no criminal, but I have no idea how long it will take me to prove that.'

Having texted Felicity to let her know I was running an errand and would be back in an hour, I'm surprised she hasn't responded. After parking, I head straight for Tigry Cottage, in two minds whether to pop into the shop first to grab something to go with a cuppa. However, when I knock there's no reply. Yanking the phone out of my bag, I give her a call. After a dozen rings it goes to voicemail, and now I'm not quite sure what to do. Maybe Drew didn't mention the fact he'd asked me to keep an eye on her and she's gone for a stroll.

Staring at the screen, half expecting it to kick into life, there's nothing. I pop into Pedrevan and grab Drew's spare key. I don't want to scare Felicity if she's napping, so I open the door quietly and step inside.

'Felicity? It's Kerra,' I call out rather gingerly, thinking that I'm being totally paranoid.

And then I hear a load moaning sound. I rush upstairs and notice that the bathroom door is ajar. Pushing it open, I find Felicity sitting on the floor with her back up against the tiled wall and a bath towel scrunched up around her. She's panting.

'Kerra,' she moans, in between taking some very shallow breaths. 'My waters have broken. The baby is coming… now!'

'Who can I ring. The midwife?' I blurt out, trying not to panic.

'It's too late for that…' She pauses before letting out an agonising groan. 'I want to push. Call 999 – ugh… ugh…'

I freeze. I don't know how to deliver a baby. What if I do something wrong?

'Kerra – 999, now! And grab some clean towels from the airing cupboard but be quick.'

'Kerra, where are you? I managed to finish earlier than expected.' Ross is munching on something, probably crisps. He's always ravenous when he arrives home from work.

'I'm next door. You'd better pop round, as I can't leave Felicity until Drew gets back.'

'Okay. Shall I bring anything?'

'No. We're fine.' All three of us.

When I let him in, he's carrying a bottle of red wine, and an elderflower pressé for Felicity.

'I'm full of the Friday feeling – it's been a good day. I can grab us all a takeaway if you like,' he offers, ambling through to the kitchen without a care in the world and placing the bottles on the countertop.

I look at him and then burst out laughing.

'What?' he demands.

'Felicity is upstairs with the midwife.'

His jaw drops and he gawps at me before whispering, 'Oh… will Drew get here in time?'

'No. Baby Ethan arrived an hour ago, but mother and baby are doing well.'

Ross looks startled. 'The baby is here?'

'Yes, and I delivered him.'

Felicity is upstairs cuddling her new-born bundle of joy. Me? I'm still in shock, even after downing two very strong mugs of tea. I don't know who was yelling the loudest at one point, but my voice is hoarse now. When I rang for an ambulance Felicity was yelling out in pain and the poor man on the other end of the line could hardly hear me speaking. He was brilliant. He calmed me down, so that I could reassure Felicity and together the three of us got through it. When I shrieked out that I could see the top of the baby's head, I stared at Felicity and said, 'We can do this. Push!'

And push, she did. Within less than a minute the head was out and I followed the instructions I was given to the letter. I had to check the cord wasn't around Ethan's neck before the final push and having given the okay, I was shocked when he came out in a sudden gush. As Ethan lay on the towel I'd strategically placed, Felicity and I stared at him in awe. The voice on the other end of the phoneline was calm and collected, but he was as elated as we were.

'Well done, ladies. We just need to get that cord tied off, but I'll talk you through it. The ambulance car is on its way, and it'll be there in about five minutes.'

It was a life-changing moment. And an experience I will never, ever forget.

'Nothing could prepare me for what I saw when I pushed open that bathroom door,' I reply as Drew quizzes me.

Felicity starts laughing. 'You looked like you were going to faint, Kerra.'

'I thought so too, until you started barking orders.' I grin at her.

'Sorry. I was intermittently cursing and then panting as each pain reached a peak and poor Kerra was on speakerphone talking to the paramedic. When she suddenly yelled out that she could see the top of the baby's head, things got very serious indeed. Who has something in their bathroom cabinet to tie off an umbilical cord?'

I look at Ross as he makes a face. 'Don't ask...'

Drew is sitting back in the bedroom chair cuddling his son, who is swathed in a white blanket with a beehive and some cute little bees embroidered on one corner. Drew's face is almost the same colour as the blanket.

'This is unreal,' he blurts out. 'Felicity was fine when I left this morning.' He keeps staring down at the tiny little face of the babe in his arms. Ethan is sound asleep, but the rest of us are still feeling traumatised – Ross included.

'Is it natural for things to happen so quickly?' he checks.

'The midwife arrived shortly after the ambulance car. She said I'd been mistaking real contractions for practising ones,' Felicity admits. 'They're referred to as Braxton Hicks contractions. It wasn't that bad, until suddenly it was and when I heard Kerra call out, I can't tell you what a relief it was. If I hadn't been in so much pain, I would have burst into tears of joy, but things were about to happen fast and furious. I don't mind admitting that I was feeling pretty scared by then, but Kerra was brilliant. She kept up a constant dialogue with the paramedic, telling him exactly what was happening. And shouting over the top of my moaning when I was letting rip.'

'Well, he's here now and he's beautiful,' Ross replies, his voice full of emotion. 'Congratulations, guys.'

'And a massive thank you to Kerra,' Drew adds. 'You saved the day – and what a day it turned out to be!'

Felicity is tired, Drew is overwhelmed and it's time to leave them to it. As Ross unlocks the front door to Pedrevan he's smiling to himself.

'It's crazy,' he mumbles.

'What is?'

'This morning they were just a couple, now they're a family. Just like that! Shouldn't they have whipped Felicity and the baby off to hospital to check them both out? I mean he wasn't due until… what, the twenty-first of May?'

'Dates are just indicative. He's a healthy six pounds nine ounces, Ross, and the midwife is happy that both mother and baby are doing just fine. Felicity wanted a home birth and I'm pleased for her, even though it didn't quite go according to plan.'

Ross makes a face as he stands back, ushering me inside. The second the door is closed he wraps me in his arms, pulling me close and placing his lips on mine. When, eventually, he pulls away to look at me his eyes are twinkling. 'Was it really that awful?'

'Between you and me I was terrified. Felicity kept calm in between the contractions but they were coming so fast. I'm going to need something a little stronger than a glass of wine to wind down this evening.'

'Me, too!' he exclaims. 'And poor Drew. I mean, suddenly they have this tiny little thing to take care of – no matter how many books he's read he's going to be in for a bit of a rude awakening.'

I can't argue with that. Drew didn't seem at all disappointed to have missed the actual birth and I half-wondered whether even Felicity was a little relieved. Drew has a tendency to panic whenever he feels out of his depth.

'How about a glass of Treeve Perran Cornish bramble whisky?'

'If that doesn't hit the spot, nothing will.' I laugh. 'But first I need to shower and grab a change of clothes.'

'Right. I'll pop some nibbles in the oven and meet you in the garden when you're ready.'

All I can think about is that if it had been Ross and me going through that today, how would we be feeling right now? And judging by the way Ross is acting, he's thinking the exact same thing. Get a grip, Kerra, I tell myself. You have an engagement and a wedding to come first. By the time you get to the stage of even considering the possibility of having a baby the memory of today will have dimmed. Just remember the look on Felicity's face when you wrapped baby Ethan in that towel and placed him in her arms. It was a truly magical moment.

'Morning, Barbara. Is Arthur up and about?' I enquire, as I place a loaf of bread and two packets of cat treats down on the counter.

'Yes. I called up when I arrived first thing and he said he was fine, but he might appreciate a little company. I'm only here until one o'clock then my sister will open up again after lunch and will be here until six this evening. I thought I'd pop back a bit beforehand to check whether there's anything Arthur needs before I lock up.'

'Mrs Moyle will appreciate that. I'll see if Arthur would like me to make him a pot of tea. It always tastes better when someone brews it for you, doesn't it?'

'Yes, it does, and he'll be missing Mrs Moyle,' she adds.

As I hold my card against the reader, Barbara pops the shopping into my carrier bag. 'I'll put it behind the counter for you Kerra.'

'Thanks. I won't be long.'

The passageway is eerily silent, and I stop at the foot of the stairs to listen. After a couple of minutes, I hear the sound of Arthur tapping away on his keyboard. He's rather heavy-handed and prefers to have a wired one.

'Arthur, it's Kerra. Is it okay to come up?'

'I'm on me own, please do!' he calls out, cheerfully.

The stairs creak, which is a good thing especially as it

warns Arthur when anyone is coming. I wonder if he's been sleeping in his chair while Mrs Moyle is away. It's a recliner and he told me once that he spends many a twilight hour gazing out at the High Street when he's in too much pain to get a proper night's rest.

'You're a sight for sore eyes, Kerra,' he welcomes me warmly.

'I thought I'd pop in to say sorry that yesterday was a flying visit, but I didn't want Mrs Moyle to miss her train.'

'Oh, that's no bother. I'm only too glad you could help her out. She's a worrier, my missus.'

'And I've come to share some good news,' I inform him as he indicates for me to take a seat.

'Yesterday at four-fifty-seven in the afternoon Drew and Felicity welcomed the arrival of baby Ethan. He weighed in at six pounds nine ounces and he's a handsome little chap.'

Arthur beams at me. 'Oh, that's wonderful news, Kerra. I saw the commotion and thought somethin' was up. Mrs Moyle will be cross with me if I don't dig out the present that she has all wrapped up ready and waiting. Give me a minute, as I'm sure she'll have left it somewhere even I couldn't fail to find it.'

Arthur grabs his sticks off the back of the chair and heaves himself up rather awkwardly. It takes him a couple of steps to find his stride, but once he gets going it's a little easier for him. There's an empty mug on the small table next to his chair and a TV handset. His worktable is always within arms' reach and he's very organised. I suppose that's out of necessity because Mrs Moyle spends most of her day downstairs serving.

'Here you go.' Arthur grins as he drops a rather bulky

parcel wedged between his arm and his torso, down onto the sofa next to me. 'She's been knittin' like crazy ever since she heard the news. It's excitin' havin' a baby on our doorstep. It's been a fair old while.'

It's poignant hearing him so cheerful, given what I know. But he's better off being in the dark for now. The Moyles are happy here in their own little world, with their set routines and it's enough for him to contend with while his wife... while Daphne, is away. I stand, giving him an encouraging smile.

'It won't be long before Felicity is popping across the road to introduce you and Mrs Moyle to little Ethan.'

'And the population of Penvennan Cove grows by one.' He chuckles.

'Would you like me to make you a mug of tea before I get back to work?'

'No. I'm good, ta. There's lots to do as I'm about to put out another community newsletter. Sam's asked me to put the word out that there's a bit of a meetin' planned at The Lark and Lantern on Wednesday week. It's not official or anythin', but I gather there are changes afoot at the pub.'

'Oh, perhaps I'll pop along.' I thought Sam was going to hold off a while longer before making his news common knowledge. But the constant rumour-mongering about the site being turned into a holiday camp, or the latest one – that the pub is being knocked down to make way for a caravan park, must really annoy him at times.

'I'd best leave you to get on, Arthur. If you need anything at all just give me a call.'

'I will, and thanks, Kerra. When the missus rings, I'll tell her the good news. It'll make her day.'

*Oh, Arthur. You're such a genuinely kind man*, I reflect,

as I make my way downstairs. *If you had a secret life before you came here, there must be a jolly good reason why you walked away from it*. I prefer to think that it's all a huge misunderstanding and before long Mrs Moyle will be back where she belongs.

# 15

## A Leisurely Sunday Barbecue with Friends

The atmosphere in the garden of Tigry Cottage on a sunny Sunday in May is one of celebration. The sound of laughter and bantering from Ross and Gawen momentarily distracts me. They've misjudged the ferocity of the heat from the barbecue coals and are trying to rescue the first batch of sausages from burning. But even that is a part of the fun.

My eyes return to rest on Tegan, who is gazing down at ten-day-old baby Ethan as Sy holds him very gingerly in his arms.

'He's still so tiny,' Sy remarks softly, for fear of waking Ethan up.

'They lose a little weight after they're born but he's already putting it back on. The midwife says he's doing great,' Drew informs us proudly.

'Yes, he's our little star,' Felicity muses, sidling up to Drew. 'We're in the hands of the health visitor from tomorrow.'

'Well, I can't believe how well you're looking Felicity,' Tegan replies, and I agree that she does.

Felicity starts laughing. 'Oh, I'm doing fine because as soon as this little one drops off, I do too. But it's poor Drew who's suffering.'

The shadows under Drew's eyes are a bit of a giveaway.

'I've got a lot of work on and it's hard getting back into a routine,' he admits. 'Even in the early hours, every time Ethan wakes up the two of them often get back to sleep before I do.'

Felicity leans into Drew, affectionately. 'That's because you insist on getting up with Bertie when he's more than happy to curl up under my chair in the nursery. I keep telling you that you need ear plugs. You can't function without sleep, can you? I have a couple of months to enjoy being a new mum and find out what works best for Ethan before I ease myself back into work. You don't have that luxury, Drew. We need to find a solution and quickly.'

'A solution for what?' Ross enquires as he joins us, leaving Gawen to it as the barbecue is now under control.

'Lack of sleep, but it's not Ethan's fault. I'm a light sleeper and um… I'm just not used to the distractions during the day,' Drew explains.

'Why don't you use my garden office to work? It's not a problem for me to work from the kitchen table,' I offer.

Felicity's face brightens. 'Oh Drew, it would certainly take the pressure off and get you through this peak in your workload. Although for the longer-term what we need is a permanent solution, isn't it?'

He nods his head, unable to disagree because she's right.

'Why not soundproof the loft and put in some dormer

windows to extend the height? It would make a generously sized office and save digging up the garden again to lay a base,' Ross suggests.

Drew immediately perks up. 'Now why didn't I think of that?'

Felicity snakes her arm around Drew's waist. 'Because you're over-tired, stressed and worrying way too much about me, the baby and Bertie.'

'I can't throw you out of your own office, Kerra.' Drew does look drained and by comparison Felicity simply looks content.

'The sausages are ready and I'm about to put on the fish,' Gawen calls out.

'Think about it, Drew. It's really not a problem,' I reassure him, and I can see he's wavering.

'There's plenty of room in there for two desks,' Ross confirms.

'It's a kind gesture, thank you guys, and I'd be delighted to accept the offer. You can throw me out at any time, but I'll also turn my attention to designing a loft conversion. Anyway, those sausages need eating before they're over-cooked. Shall I take Ethan, Sy, while you grab something to eat?'

I step in between them.

'I think it's my turn to grab a cuddle,' I declare and Sy very carefully places that little bundle into my arms.

'He doesn't weigh much and yet you feel it when you hand him over,' Sy says with a smile.

'Tell me about it,' Felicity groans. 'My back isn't too happy, and I can't wait to take a trip to the local chiropractor. It's just been so busy what with two sets of parents coming to visit and we've had several video calls as everyone wants to see him. At some point before too long we're going to take a trip to Gloucestershire and try to organise a bit of a family get together. Right, shall I take him while you grab something to eat, Kerra?'

'No, you go ahead. We'll take Ethan for a stroll around the garden.' I grin at her.

She gives me a knowing smile and leaves Ross and I to enjoy some time with Penvennan's newest resident.

'I never realised babies had a distinct smell, but they do,' Ross half-whispers to me. As our eyes meet, his face lights up. 'Drew is finding it hard to adjust, isn't he? Do you think I'd be the same?'

As I snuggle Ethan even closer, I realise that there's something so wonderful about nestling a tiny baby in the crook of your arm. Is this my maternal instinct kicking in? I wonder.

'Yes, Drew is struggling and no, I think you're used to drama going on around you and you'd simply take it in your stride.'

'Do you trust me enough to have a hold of the little 'un?'

I'm reluctant to pass Ethan over, but it's obvious that Ross is eagerly waiting his turn. 'Of course. Look at his darling eyelashes. And the way he curls his fingers as if he's making a fist. Maybe he's going to be a fighter,' I reflect, thinking out loud.

As Ross takes Ethan from me, I'm surprised how confident he is and the look on Ross's face makes my heart melt. 'Hey there, little dude. As soon as you're big enough I'm going to teach you how to use a hammer.'

I start laughing as Drew walks over to us, munching as he

walks, then wiping his mouth on a paper napkin, which he shoves into his pocket.

'Come on, you two, it's time to grab something to eat. The fish is almost ready, but the sausages are good, you won't want to miss out. They're Treeve Perran Farm's own pork, sage and onion – a real treat.'

'We're coming. And I just remembered that we have a second desk and a rather comfortable chair in boxes under the stairs waiting to go into the garden office. I ordered them for Ross ages ago.'

I give Ross a pointed stare. 'Um… yes, it's a back-up… in case we get snowed in and I, um, can't make it to the office. Kerra's been on at me for ages to assemble it. I'll dig it out this evening and get it set up.'

Ross is thinking on his feet, and I almost burst out laughing. Snowed in? But Drew simply looks relieved.

'There you go, Drew. I'll pop a key in for you and one for the side gate so you can come and go as you please.'

Drew's expression is rather hesitant.

'Look, you'll get through your work a heck of a lot faster if you can do that in peace and quiet. All you'll hear down there are the birds, and Bertie when he's chasing his ball around the garden.'

Drew gives Ross a grateful smile, before turning to me. 'I'll owe you big time. I will be honest and say that it would be a lifesaver for me right now. I have several projects on the go and with Sam eager to press ahead with his planning application, until the drawings are done and the two of us can meet with the local authorities, I'm stopping you scheduling a start date for the work,' Drew confides to Ross.

I look down at baby Ethan as he lies in Ross's arms,

thinking that he has no idea how he has turned his parent's lives completely upside down.

'I keep thinking I should have been more prepared,' Drew continues. 'But now that our boy is here, I realise that's not how it works. It's not real until you experience it hands-on. But Ethan is worth every second of the worry and the time I spend staring up at the ceiling at night thinking about the future.' Drew's anxiety is touching but understandable. 'Here, I'll take him inside. He might sleep for another hour if we're lucky, bless him.'

'He's all yours,' Ross says, reluctantly handing over his charge.

'I see that Mrs Moyle is back, Kerra,' Drew remarks. 'I bet Arthur is relieved now that she's home.'

'Yes. I've popped in a few times while she was away to check on—'

Ethan stirs and I raise a finger to my lips as Drew slowly turns and heads back inside.

Lying next to Ross as we stare out the window at the starlit sky, I reflect that this is a million miles away from the life I had before I came home to Penvennan Cove. It's the same for Ross. Being on your own is easy, even if it is lonely at times. You leave the house in the morning and when you return home at night it's exactly as you left it. It was the same for Drew. His house was so neat and tidy; a place for everything and everything in its place. Now there are baby products everywhere, admittedly in neat little baskets because Felicity is very organised. It made me smile today because in a way Tigry Cottage now looks lived in, rather than a pristine, glossy-surfaced show home. But it does change everything.

'Mmm...' Ross rolls into me, murmuring before he lets out a huge yawn. 'Aren't you sleepy?'

'Yes, but my mind won't shut off.'

As he wraps his arms around me, I think of all the years I had a bed to myself, feeling a sense of pride that I didn't need a man in my life. I could go on a date and say goodbye at the door without hesitation. Why invite someone in if it's merely a distraction? And now Gawen, Yvonne, Tegan, Sy, Ross and I all spent the afternoon and evening fighting over who was going to hold Ethan. How does that transition happen? And then the answer jumps into my head. Because you find the one.

Ross starts chuckling to himself.

'What's funny?'

'Remember when Drew told us Felicity was going to move in? I vividly recall saying that I wondered how long it would be before Drew wished he had an office in the garden. When we laid the concrete and put in the wiring for your wonderful getaway, I suggested he think about it too. He thought he'd always have a spare bedroom. Life is full of surprises, isn't it?'

'It sure is.'

'Talking about surprises, is there any further news from Mrs Moyle?'

'No. All she said when she returned was that her solicitor is looking into it. The lady who calls herself Helen Moyle refused to meet up with her in person. Something isn't right, but Arthur is still totally unaware of what's going on. If there's any truth to it, of course, the solicitor will have no choice but to involve the police. Personally, I think Mrs Moyle is making a big mistake not telling Arthur what's going on.'

Ross expels a huge breath. 'Well, thank goodness Zacky is behaving himself as I haven't heard a whisper about it. But something else is brewing, so no doubt his mind is on that. I think we should pop along to that meeting at The Lark and Lantern on Wednesday evening, what do you think?'

'I thought maybe I should, but Sam hasn't asked me to attend. I think he just wants to put an end to the rumours. Mrs Moyle said in passing that it would be awful if they do knock down the pub and turn the whole lot into a caravan park. Even though it would mean extra trade for the shop.'

'What did you say to that?'

'I pointed out there would be grounds for objection as the High Street just isn't wide enough to take cars parked both sides and passing caravans. With only two lay-byes along the whole stretch, in the peak season things would grind to a halt.'

'I know Sam had interest from a budget hotel group and a restaurant chain, but the caravan park is news to me.'

'Me, too. I don't know how these rumours start but they do the rounds, and it unsettles people.'

'Is Arthur still monitoring the threads on the Penvennan Community Link-Up?'

That's a good point. 'Yes, but he usually only calls me in if there's an IT problem. Why?'

'Hmm… I'm just thinking out loud. You know, after that little incident last year.'

'He shut the culprits down as going off topic is in breach

of the rules. Maybe I'll have a quick word with him before Wednesday. I think we should show our support, just in case.'

'Today was great, wasn't it?' he mumbles, sleepily.

'Yes. And Sy and Tegan are getting really excited about their summer party. They're about to send out the invites to confirm that it's going to be on Saturday the nineteenth of June. I volunteered us to help with the setting up,' I inform him. 'Gawen and Yvonne want everything to be perfect for them on the day.'

'Well, considering it's what... a little over six months after the ceremony, it'll be the first time both families will be together in one place. I hope it goes smoothly on the day.'

I give him a stern look. 'Think positively. Tegan and Trev are talking to each other again at long last, so fingers crossed everything will be fine.'

'Is it a smart do? I mean, Treeve Perran is a farm, after all.'

'I have no idea. All will be revealed nearer to the day, apparently.'

Ross gives another huge yawn. 'I'm beat. Did you hear a noise just then?'

I roll away from him, lying on my back and then I hear it too. 'It's Ethan.' I smile to myself in the gloom. 'Aww... he is so cute.'

I'm about to suggest to Ross that maybe I'd better close the window when I hear a gentle snore. Raising myself up on my elbow I stare down at him. Those dark eyelashes against his tanned skin and that tousled hair flopping down over his eyebrows making me want to stoop over and kiss him. *I've always loved you, Ross*, that little voice in my head can't deny. *Every man I ever dated I compared to you and none of them came close.*

As I lie back down, I remember Sy asking me once what I was looking for in a man. We were in a smart new wine bar that had just opened close to the office. It was packed and I was avoiding eye contact, which amused him as there were two guys he said were checking me out. I remember giving him a disinterested look, but he insisted on pointing them out to me. A discreet scan around took seconds and while they looked fine, I distinctly remember rejecting them out of hand. It puzzled him. Wind the clock forwards several years. Shortly after my return to Pedrevan Cottage, the day I opened the front door to find Ross standing there with a clipboard in his hand, my legs almost gave way. That's how you know; it's not something I can put into words... it was instant.

Snuggling into Ross once more, I marvel that every day he surprises me in some small way or other, but he never, ever disappoints.

'Morning, Arthur. I hope I'm not interrupting anything?'

'No. Not at all. Although it was an excitin' start to the day. Felicity popped in with the baby about half an hour ago, to say thank you for the present. He's a grand little chap, isn't he? Mrs Moyle was overjoyed, and she brought them straight upstairs to see me.'

'He most certainly is,' I remark, pleased that Felicity remembered them. 'The reason I'm calling is to check that everything is going smoothly with the Penvennan

Community Link-Up website. The plugins all update automatically, as does the theme, but if you ever need me to tweak anything you only have to say.'

'It's all tickin' over well, Kerra, thanks. I get an email every time there's somethin' goin' on in the background and there's never anythin' in the alert box on the email. Guess I haven't managed to break it yet!' He laughs.

'Ah, you're more IT savvy than you give yourself credit for, Arthur. No more problems with people posting off topic comments on the various chat boards?'

'They've grown considerably, and I can hardly keep up with it. I do scan the comments every few days and I took your advice. I just delete any that stand out as bein' tittle-tattle.'

Hmm… the problem is that it's set to auto post so even though Arthur eventually takes them down, they're being read. 'Is there any chatter about this meeting at the pub on Wednesday?' I casually enquire.

'There was a "Save Our Pub" topic set up and I let it run for a bit before I put up a reminder of the community site rules, then it died off. That's not to say the conversations have stopped of course. They just have 'em somewhere else. Are you goin' along to it?'

'Yes, Ross and I thought we'd wander down.'

'Well, if Sam is goin' then it could get a bit raucous. Folk don't like change, do they?'

'No, but I'm sure it will all be fine. Is Mrs Moyle there?'

'She left about ten minutes ago to take one of her apple pies down to Tom and Wally. By all accounts they've done a grand job of tidyin' up the scrapyard and she thought they'd appreciate it.'

'I'm sure they'll be delighted, Arthur. Right, I'd best leave you to it. Enjoy the rest of your day.'

'You too, Kerra and… and thanks for everythin' you've done for me and the missus. It means a lot.'

As I put the phone down, I wonder what triggered Arthur's parting comment, but he's a man who appreciates every little thing. It's that very quality which makes him the backbone of the little support network he runs. I'm just being paranoid, wondering whether he suspects something is going on in the background. But why would he if Mrs Moyle won't broach the subject with him?

Right, I'd best get back to unpacking the boxes James delivered first thing this morning. It's time to turn the master bedroom into a little sanctuary to surprise Ross. It's a decadent way to spend a couple of hours as I should be working, but when I looked out the window first thing I noticed the light was on in the garden office. I want to let Drew settle in for a bit before I join him.

# 16

## Is This the Calm Before the Storm?

'Good morning, Drew. It's good to see you hard at it. What time did you start?' I enquire, giving him a sympathetic smile as I slide back the folding glass doors to the garden office.

'I crossed paths with Ross as he was getting into his van. It's a bit of a late one for you. Are you sure it isn't putting you out me being here?' Drew checks, as I head straight over to the coffee machine.

'Not at all. I've been unboxing a new look for our bedroom. Ironing isn't my favourite job, but it didn't take long to freshen up the room. That's the problem with popping into The Design Cave for a meeting, I end up spending a fortune. Can I make you a coffee?'

Having a coffee machine really does make this feel like home.

Drew nods his head. 'Please, a double espresso would be great. I nodded off at the keyboard just now for a split second. Woke myself up with a jolt and nearly got whiplash,' he groans. 'I'm glad you weren't here to witness it, but… um, if you ever need the office to yourself just let me know. For now, when it comes to work I'm grabbing a few hours here and there, as I don't want Felicity to feel I'm not doing my bit.'

I pass the cup to Drew and walk behind my desk, sliding out the chair. 'It's actually rather nice to have a little company. Not that you'll hear a peep out of me once I start work. Focusing to the extent that I'm oblivious to anything going on around me has never been my problem, it's knowing when to break off is the struggle I constantly battle with.'

Drew sits back, sipping his coffee appreciatively. 'Me too. I love what I do, but it needs one hundred per cent of my attention and once I'm in the zone I just want to keep going. It used to stress me out when Bertie was going through his barking phase, but that was nothing compared to a baby's cry. Ethan gets terrible wind, and he goes red in the face, pulling up his legs and screaming. It's awful. I'm sure you must hear it at times, even though the walls are thick.'

'Only if the bedroom window is open. I wouldn't have a clue what to do, it must be a steep learning curve.'

'Oh, it is. Felicity seems to just get on with it, although she does jump online a lot and we have one book that has become our daily go-to for advice. It's scary at times. I mean, how do you know if it's wind or something else?'

I shrug my shoulders. 'I guess it'll get easier as each day passes.'

'I hope so. Felicity says if I panic, then Ethan will pick up on that and he'll panic too. But honestly, he's so little and all we can do is keep rubbing his back until he does an almighty burp. It's funny, because sometimes it's so loud it makes him jump and he extends his arms and his legs, like he's freefalling. Except that he's propped up on your knee, or lying over your shoulder while you keep rubbing and patting.'

It's obvious Drew is finding his first steps into the world of parenting a scary process and my heart goes out to him.

'The only thing I know about babies,' I reply, 'is that eventually they grow up.'

He starts laughing. 'Thank goodness. Let's hope in the meantime we do the least harm, poor little chap. But already he makes it clear when he's not happy and I'm getting to differentiate between his different tones when he cries. The *I'm hungry* one is unmistakable. Anyway, here's to a productive couple of hours until lunchtime.'

Drew raises his cup and I do the same. I have a lot of paperwork to deal with this morning as Sam and I move our partnership forward. It's an exciting time all round, that's for sure.

After a quick sandwich I'm just about to return to the office when Tegan rings.

'Hey, you – how's it going?'

'Good. Busy. There's hardly time to stop and think, and Sy keeps pressing me to finalise the details for the party. I think Gawen had a quiet word with him on Sunday, as until we figure out what overall feel we're aiming for they can't come up with the suggestions for the buffet. And they need to start placing orders for things they can't supply themselves.'

I'm surprised by this admission because Tegan is usually so organised.

'I thought the new Clean and Shine operation was running smoothly now?' Sy spent months streamlining the business to make it more profitable.

'Oh, it's working well having contractors rather than employees, but it's the sheer volume we're dealing with. It's exhausting at times.'

I did notice she didn't have her usual sparkle when we were at Tigry Cottage. Well, until she held Ethan in her arms and then she was all smiles.

'Everything is all right with you, isn't it?' I check, tentatively.

'Yes, I'm fine, just tired. I have a long list of things I need to get sorted today. I guess I didn't think this party would go ahead, and it's just hit me that there's just over five weeks to go. It's no wonder that Sy, Gawen and Yvonne are beginning to panic as I have some major decisions to make in a short space of time.'

Tegan has always been a workaholic, but now she has Sy to rely on I'd hoped things would get a little easier for her. Sometimes success has a downside, but few appreciate that.

'Anyhow…' She sighs. 'Sy is still pressing to make it a celebration of our wedding for those who weren't in attendance. I get that, but I managed to persuade him we should call it a summer party, as I don't want people fussing over presents. I was right, wasn't I?'

I did wonder about the change of emphasis when Ross and I received our invite. Back in November, on Tegan's thirty-first birthday, Ross and I were the witnesses when Sy and Tegan tied the knot at the local registry office.

'Look, Tegan, it's your party and you can make it anything you want.'

'Hmm.' The sound echoes down the line. 'I guess you're right, but I don't want to disappoint Sy.'

A thought pops into my head. 'How about a ring blessing ceremony? You can do it yourself if you don't want to get someone to officiate, like a vicar. Someone I worked with a while ago moved to Italy. For her fifteenth wedding anniversary that's what they did, as they realised none of their new circle of friends were at their wedding. It was simple, but it was rather special.'

'Ooh, I like that idea, what does it entail?'

'It was simple; they put the rings on a cushion, both said a few words and then took it in turns slipping on the rings as if it were the first time. I'll find the link to the video they made and put up online.'

'That could be the perfect solution. The thought of making a huge thing of it is just too daunting.' She sounds enthusiastic. 'I simply want to give the party a flavour of summer elegance and make it as relaxed as possible.'

'You've waited a long time to bring together both families and your friends. It's important that you can enjoy yourself, without feeling any pressure.'

'Oh, Kerra – that's exactly what I needed to hear. I didn't know if people would have expectations… you know, because Sy and I did our own thing and told them after the fact. But you know me, I don't really like being the centre of attention anyway.'

'Treeve Perran farm is a wonderful setting, Tegan. Yvonne was telling me that they have a three metre by nine metre, white party gazebo to house the buffet if you'd prefer to have it in the field rather than in the brick-built barn they've recently cleared out.'

'I know and that's one of the decisions I'm supposed to be making today, but I love the barn and it'll be cooler.'

'Well, for what it's worth, bear in mind that there's no guarantee even in the middle of June that we won't get a shower and the barn has a solid floor. And don't go overboard on things like flowers. I'll give you a hand on the day and there's a lot the countryside can offer for free that will give it a natural, romantic vibe. Ross and I will be there early to lend a hand with setting it all up and you know that Gawen and Yvonne won't let your guests go hungry.'

'Thanks, Kerra. I was on the verge of having a meltdown.' She does sound perkier.

'Deep breaths and I'll email you shortly. I'm here if you want to talk anything through. Take care, Tegan!'

The sound of Ripley padding down the stairs is followed by a tirade of miaows.

'Good afternoon, Ripley. Did you have a nice sleep?'

*Miaow, miaow, miaoooooow.*

'I'm thinking that's a yes. Right, let's get you some food before you go out to see what Bertie is up to.'

I empty a sachet into her bowl, but she walks up to sniff it and then promptly sits back expectantly.

'It's your favourite!' I stress, as she stares at me disdainfully. 'It's not time for treats.'

Ripley continues to sit there gazing around as if she's bored waiting for me to do her bidding. When she realises that I'm serious, she walks over to take a drink from her water fountain before idly making her way over to the sliding glass doors.

*Miaow, miaow, miaoooooow.*

'I'm coming.' When I ease them back, I can see Bertie through the little pet window in the fencing. He's laid out sunning himself on Drew and Felicity's decking.

'Hi, Bertie,' I call out.

*Woof.*

He's such a cutie and I go over and sit down cross-legged, to soak up a few rays myself. Ripley comes to sit alongside me, and the two of them look at each other for a little while. Then Bertie rolls over onto his back, waving his paws in the air. Ah, he wants to play but doesn't understand cats are very different to dogs.

It's not that long ago Ripley would have jumped straight up onto the fence and sat there hissing at him. As I smooth Ripley's back, she begins to purr and it's a sound that I find quite comforting. Then I feel guilty for not having given her any treats, so I go back inside and return with a tube of dried chicken and a doggie biscuit. Sliding Bertie's bone-shaped snack under the fence he immediately jumps up and begins wagging his tail, then, taking it in his mouth, off he trots out of view.

I pour a little pile of chicken pieces in front of Ripley and it's no surprise when she immediately begins to tuck in, being the little diva that she is. Next door it's all quiet and I wonder if Felicity and Drew have taken Ethan for a walk as it's such a lovely afternoon. Just as I'm pondering whether to grab my sunglasses, a book and a cold drink while I wait for Ross to get back, the doorbell rings and I hurry back inside.

'Mrs Moyle, this is a lovely surprise!'

'I can't stop, but I just wanted to drop these in. I know how you and Ross enjoy my saffron buns.'

'Ah, thank you so much, that's very kind of you.'

She doesn't turn to go, and I indicate for her to step inside but she's in two minds.

'I um… oh, well, just for a minute. I've um…'

Shutting the door behind her, it's obvious she has something to tell me but is having second thoughts about sharing it.

'Please, take a seat.'

'No, no, I can't stop. There's a bit of trouble brewing for Tom by the looks of it. You know I don't pay any heed to rumours, but I hear it all. It's got something to do with what's going on at The Salvager's Yard. Two of my customers were talking about it earlier on. Something to do with a goodwill gesture and they were saying it would be better spent on buying some benches. Now I have no idea what it's all about, but Arthur mentioned you're going to Sam's meeting. I've no doubt Tom will be there, so you might want to warn him.'

Oh no. Nothing has been tied up with Oliver yet, so I can't even begin to imagine how word has got out already.

'I appreciate the heads-up, Mrs Moyle. As usual they have the wrong end of the stick, so the quicker they're put right, the better.'

She looks at me for a brief second and I can see there's something else on her mind.

'Is everything all right with you?' I check.

'The solicitor rang and… Arthur is still legally married to that woman. I had no choice other than to break the news to him and it was the hardest thing I've ever done. The look in his eyes will haunt me forever. There'll be an investigation and it's hit us both like a ton of bricks, Kerra.

My head is still all over the place at present. The next step is for the solicitor to interview Arthur and get his side of the story.'

'I don't quite know what to say. It's no wonder you're reeling though.'

Mrs Moyle draws in a long, slow breath and as she begins talking her voice falters. 'My Arthur… he's in shock and I should have been straight with him from the start. He rambled on about his wife having left him several years before we even met. If only he'd sought legal advice at the time it wouldn't have come to this, but he didn't and at the minute we're not entirely sure what's going to happen.'

Clearly, Mrs Moyle can't bring herself to utter the word *bigamy* but it's obvious that she understands the gravity of the situation.

'Oh, Mrs Moyle. I'm so terribly sorry to hear that. What a worry for you both.'

'It all makes sense now, his rush to move down south. Arthur just wanted a fresh start. He said the weather was milder and it would be better for his back. The truth is that when he married me, he genuinely believed his first marriage was no longer valid. It wasn't something he planned, Kerra, being married to two women at the same time. It takes a cunning and deceitful man indeed, and that isn't Arthur. But what if the police don't believe him?'

Mrs Moyle is struggling to take it all in and I can't even imagine what Arthur is going through. Not least because they're only at the beginning of what could be a lengthy process, one with no guarantees what the outcome will be until the facts are established.

'All you can do now is take it one day at a time and

support each other through it. If Arthur needs to go to see the solicitor in person, then just let me know and I'll drive you both there. Don't go getting a taxi. Promise me?'

'I'm hoping the man will come here, but if that isn't possible then I may well take you up on your offer, Kerra. Arthur will be a bag of nerves. We're hoping to keep this quiet, but when the police get involved who knows what will happen. We'll cross that bridge when we get to it.'

As I see her out, I sincerely hope it doesn't come to that. There's nothing people like better than a good scandal. Jago gave them that when he was here and outed Ross and me as a couple. We've both laughed at times and said we can't wait to be old news, but I'd willingly wait a while longer if it saves Arthur and Mrs Moyle the problem of being the next distraction.

As soon as Ross has slipped out of his work boots, I walk straight up to him, throwing my arms around his shoulders. 'I have a surprise for you,' I reveal in my best beguiling tone.

'That's worth a special kiss then.' He grins at me.

This is the part of the day I love the most, welcoming my man home. The urgency of his kiss tells me that he's in a good mood and he lingers, letting out a satisfied 'mmm' as I relinquish my grasp on him.

'Do I take it you've had a good day?'

'Yes, I did. The best bit of the job is when you invest time in people and start to see them come into their own. I have a couple of site managers now that I can rely upon to sort out the day-to-day problems and shout if they can't find an economical solution. It'll mean more time in the office for me and less in the car doing the endless rounds of daily inspections.'

'That's brilliant news.' When Jago persuaded Ross's leading foreman, Will, to manage the new depot in Launceston, his father knew it would cause a major headache. Unable to replace Will, Ross had to take that role on himself in addition to everything else he does. Mistakes on site cost money, so Ross had no other option, as Will was the trouble-shooter.

'Does that mean you'll be able to scale down to a five-day working week?' I ask, hopefully.

'It looks like it. I'm also thinking of taking on an extra admin person to become my personal assistant, screening my phone calls and emails. Once the new person is trained up a lot of it is standard stuff and doesn't need any input from me. I won't mention that to my father, as all he monitors is the bottom line and business is brisk. But it means that I'll only deal with the big issues, so I'll have fewer interruptions. I'm eager to put my focus back onto chasing new business and then I'll use the promise of bigger profits as leverage to increase my share of the business to fifty-one percent. That's crucial.'

I wasn't expecting him to make a move so quickly, but he has money to invest, so why not?

'Do you think they'll go for it?'

'He's backed right off and I'm assuming that means the new business in Launceston is proving to be worth his time and effort. As long as he's guaranteed a good return for minimal input, it's a win–win situation. He's well aware that he went too far, and I can't see him trusting anyone else to manage the business. No one would put up with the aggravation I get from him and he knows that. Anyway, what's this surprise you were talking about?'

'Come with me!'

Ripley appears and Ross stops to pick her up, smoothing her as we walk. When I push open the door to the bedroom his eyes widen.

'Wow – I wasn't expecting this!'

Admittedly I didn't put the new blind up, but the vibrant green duvet cover and pillow slips against the white walls is a real burst of colour. I've teamed it with half a dozen scatter cushions, three in a soft green and three in a vibrant orange.

'That's a lot of cushions on the bed,' he notes, but I can see he's thrilled with it. 'Ooh, nice side lights.' Then he chuckles. 'I guess I'd better go get my drill and put that blind up.'

I did leave it out in plain view.

'And as a reward,' I tease him, 'I'll make you a drink. What do you fancy?'

'I'm feeling chilled this evening. Let's have a glass of wine down on the lower decking area. This won't take me five minutes.' He lowers Ripley to the floor, stroking her ears. 'I'm surprised you haven't thought about some sort of mural after Polly's masterclass next door,' he adds, cheekily.

I give him a knowing look. 'I already have a few pots of paint I've picked out. I just need to make up some stencils. I was thinking of the headboard wall. And I know this pale cream carpet sort of goes, but I've seen a soft fern green that would be amazing.'

He stands, walking over to move a few stray hairs off my cheek, before kissing it softly. 'You did this for me. I wasn't fazed by the flowers you know, but I love the vibrancy of the colours. It's like bringing the garden inside and it's perfect.'

By the time I carry the tray down to the bottom corner of the garden, Ross has pulled two of the sun loungers out of the shed and is lying back with his eyes closed.

'I'm not asleep,' he murmurs, 'I'm just resting my eyes as you were taking so long.'

'Sorry, Tegan rang about some info I sent her earlier on. She's in full-on party planning mode.'

'I'm looking forward to it. Gawen was telling me that they're turning one of their open barns alongside the courtyard into a venue space. It will be ready if Tegan goes with that option rather than the marquee. It's a part of Gawen and Yvonne's longer-term plan. So even if it rains, nothing will stop the festivities.'

I pass him a glass of wine, thinking how the moment he's home with me, everything in my little world is just fine.

'White?' he queries.

'Red doesn't really go with saffron buns, does it?' I muse as I pass him one in a napkin.

'Goodness… what have I done to deserve this?'

'Oh, Mrs Moyle brought them over to say thank you.'

'Ah, I see. And uh… did she say anything about Arthur?'

He leans over to place his wine glass on the floor and then starts eating as if it's the first thing he's had all day.

Ross shakes his head in total disbelief when I repeat what Mrs Moyle told me. It's the first time I've ever seen him speechless. I move on quickly because it's not something either of us wants to dwell on. I tell him all about my day and when I recount the latest whispers going around the frown on his face deepens.

'That's the trouble with calling an unofficial meeting. I'm not sure Sam's doing the right thing.'

'I had a word with him, and he said it'll quash the rumours about the pub once and for all. I do sympathise with Sam, as it must be galling with Zacky and the usual lot propping up the bar every night mumbling away about things that aren't even true.'

'Yes,' Ross agrees, 'but let's hope it doesn't get out of hand. And what's this about a goodwill gesture and Tom?'

'Oh, it's nothing. Crossed wires, that's all.'

'Hmm… tread wearily, Kerra.'

'What's that supposed to mean, Ross?' I peer at him, narrowing my eyes.

'Hey, don't shoot the messenger. All I'm saying is that little things can get blown up out of all proportion – you know that. Sometimes you're a little too… enthusiastic for your own good.' His smile is playful, but I can't help wondering if there's a more serious undertone going on here.

'Is that a criticism?'

He rolls his eyes. 'Only if you choose to take it that way.'

'We both know that the only way to make things happen is to keep going until it's done. That's the difference between success and failure.'

I'm puzzled by his reaction. Does he think I'm pushing too hard? But his method of operation is exactly the same. His drive has helped to build an empire. I assumed that he'd understand because what I'm trying to do will benefit the whole community. Ross and I are alike. Or am I wrong? It's easy to assume you know someone, but even I have things

I haven't shared with Ross. Like my growing resentment towards Dad for not talking about Granddad's death, and the fear I have of missing an opportunity that could make a real difference here in Penvennan Cove. For whatever reason life has given me a set of skills and it would be wrong of me to use them solely for my own benefit.

Then I think of Mrs Moyle and Arthur. Who could have guessed what secrets lay hidden in his past?

'We're good, aren't we, Ross? If something was wrong you would be honest with me, wouldn't you?'

'Like I could hide anything at all from you. Sometimes I think you can read my mind,' he jests.

We lapse into silence, enjoying the sound of the babbling stream less than fifteen feet from the back fence. Looking towards the two cottages, I think again of my *if only* moment. At one point, when Drew and Felicity looked like they were never going to live together as a couple, he was thinking of going back to Gloucestershire. I asked him to give me first refusal if he decided to sell up. As one property, this would more than satisfy all our space requirements. But then Ross and I wouldn't have two wonderful friends on our doorstep and baby Ethan to watch as he grows up.

'This really is a little oasis.' Ross sighs happily, as he wipes his mouth on the napkin. 'Are there any more buns in that tin?'

'There are. But do you deserve it?' I banter, playfully, holding it tantalisingly just beyond his reach.

'Yes, I do. I didn't mean to upset you, really I didn't. I'm sorry. I was simply trying to suggest a cautious approach. Plus, you have a working blind now, that must count for something. And I filled in the holes where you took the curtain rail down.' He raises his eyebrows as if he's proved his point.

'Here you go. But save one for Drew for tomorrow morning. I'll leave the tin next to the coffee machine in the garden office with a note for him.'

'Ah yes, it seems he's up with the lark these days. We crossed paths this morning and he said he's drawing up plans for a loft conversion. I wondered whether it might be a good idea to think about it for Pedrevan too.'

Finally! Oh, how good it is to hear Ross talking about how to make the most of what we have here.

'It's a brilliant idea.'

'Then I'll have a word with him, as it will give us all more scope if there's a big dormer extension across the entire width of both roofs. We're talking a generously sized bedroom or study, an en suite and plenty of storage space.'

'It's fine by me. Now all we have to do is to find a really good builder.'

'I think this deserves a bit of a toast.' Ross raises his glass and leans across.

'Here's to exciting things to come!' I beam at him as our glasses touch to seal the deal.

# 17

## A Few Home Truths

Twenty-six people filter into the conservatory at The Lark and Lantern as Sam unlocks the doors and pins up a 'Meeting in Progress' sign.

While there are some local people still out in the bar and restaurant area, the vast majority responded to Sam's call informing us the meeting is about to begin.

Ross leans into me, whispering in my ear as we bring up the tail end. 'It's a good turnout for an informal meeting.'

I raise my eyebrows ominously, as I was thinking the exact same thing.

'Right. Ross, do you mind closing the doors behind you? Polly will pop in if she can, but we're a bit short-staffed tonight. However,' Sam pauses for effect, 'the good news is that is all about to change. And that's why we're here tonight, to get the facts straight.'

It's a robust start and Sam even has some notes in his hand as he waits a few seconds for people to settle down. Ross and I join Sissy, who is on her own. Dad and Nettie are here, of course, but kept well away from us as we stood in the bar chatting earlier on. Mrs Williams is here with her son, Logan. She lives a few doors along from Gwel Teg, in one of the fishermen's cottages and Logan, an old schoolfriend of mine, is married to Sienna who works at The Design Cave. It's good to see some friendly faces.

Tom and Wally are here too, and the manager of Pascoe's bakery, Davy. He's one of Zacky's mates, the posse who hang out in the bar most nights. Jared is here with Neil, but I don't really know either of them very well, only that they worked together on the trawlers with Granddad at one point. I spot the man who owns the vet's surgery and his wife, and several of our neighbours from further along the High Street.

'Okay, I don't intend to commandeer much of your time this evening. What prompted this is some worrying rumours, which seem to have resulted in a few folk bandying about the slogan *Save Our Pub*.'

Apart from the low rumble in the background from the bar, in here the silence is unnerving. I glance over at Zacky, and his expression is fixed. He's learnt a few lessons this last year, enough to be eager to disassociate himself from anything that could be perceived as needlessly stirring things up.

'You can't blame us for bein' concerned,' Neil replies sharply, and Sam invites him to stand up.

'The floor is yours, Neil.' Ooh, Sam isn't going to let them sit in their seats and grumble and mumble. Either stand up and be heard or shut up. I like it.

Neil is thrown off-guard, but he'll look foolish now if he doesn't say something.

'No one wants a caravan park here on this land. And if the pub goes, the nearest one is a car ride away. It's the heart of the community, is the pub.' The moment he finishes speaking he sits back down, looking rather pleased with himself.

'And where did you get your information from, I'd like to know?' Sam asks, accusingly, and Neil just sits there not moving a muscle.

There's an awkward silence before Sam continues. 'I've lived here with my daughter, Polly, ever since she was a little 'un. Selling up was an option, but this is our home and there's nowhere else we'd rather be. So, whatever you're hearing, I'm telling you that we're going nowhere.'

'That's comforting news, Sam,' Davy confirms, as he rises out of his seat. 'I've been drinking in here for over twenty years and it's good to know that will continue. I'm sure everyone is aware that Pascoe's Bakery has purchased a strip of land from Sam. It will allow the delivery vans to drive around the back, avoiding the problem of blocking the road down to the car park next to the beach. I'm here on behalf of my boss, who wanted to confirm that we aren't expanding the café and bakery, just trying to ease congestion and make sure our staff can park at the rear of the premises. That takes the pressure off the limited parking in the High Street.'

The news is well received as Davy sits back down.

'Thank you for making that clear, Davy,' Sam continues. 'I gather there were no objections logged with the local authority and it's heartening when locals realise that change is a necessity.'

There's a rumble of overall agreement.

'It costs a lot to run this pub. We open all year round, even in the middle of winter when there's only a handful of our regular customers in the building. To guarantee the future of The Lark and Lantern there will be some big changes. Plans have been submitted to turn the holiday lets into residential accommodation so that Polly and I can continue to live on site. Further plans will be lodged very soon to turn the first floor of the pub into a function room and a second restaurant.'

The general muttering falls silent.

'Yer not goin' upmarket, Sam, are you?' Zacky responds without thinking, and quickly waves away Sam's invitation to stand up and say his piece.

'What I'm doing, Zacky, is realising that if I can't grow my clientele the pub won't survive. But I also won't be bought off by one of those big chains who kept upping their offer. So, the aim now that I have a new partner onboard, is to expand what The Lark and Lantern can offer. That will include a programme of evening events, as well as hiring out the new function room for parties. And with the addition of a second restaurant, we're aiming to start up a Gourmet Evening Experience for lovers of fine dining. But the bar will still be here, and the downstairs restaurant will continue to serve traditional Cornish pub grub to keep our regular customers happy.'

Glancing around I think Sam has done the right thing, but I feel for Sissy who is so nervous on Sam's behalf and looking rather anxious. Suddenly the door opens and Polly walks in. All eyes turn to face her and I'm sure she's surprised to feel an atmosphere in the room.

'Sorry,' she murmurs, making her way over to sit with Ross, Sissy and me. We exchange a worried glance.

Betty Williams puts up her hand and Sam gives her an affirming smile to ask her question. She's a quiet woman by nature and has lived in Penvennan Cove all her life.

'Your partner is going to be replacing Polly?'

'Not really. Polly's new business is taking off and I'm excited for her, but what The Lark and Lantern needs is investment. And that has now been secured. Once planning confirm we can go ahead, we'll commission the building works and there will be a period of disruption. However, our doors will remain open.'

Betty seems satisfied with the answer, but Jared pushes back on his chair to stand, surprising us all. He's another one who usually doesn't speak his mind, but he's a known grumbler.

'Everyone has to make a living, Sam, and there's no one in their right mind would fault you for that, or the hard work you've put in over the years. But the truth is that what's got folk upset is hearing about outsiders wanting to muscle in on the cove and putting their hands in their pockets to get what they want. Business is business, we all understand that, but when you bring in an outsider, they'll likely look out for their own interests first. Once they creep in anything can happen.'

Sam glances across at me and inwardly I feel myself sag. I'm not sure it will do him any favours bringing my name into this. Before either of us can react, Tom takes to his feet.

'It's not easy running a business these days. The big companies can pretty much do what they want, but for most of us independents it's a constant struggle to make ends meet. I'm not ashamed to admit that The Salvager's Yard was on its last legs, but with some family backing and – like Sam – a bit of outside help, I'm not done yet. Re-thinking the business is not selling out, Jared. Selling out is handing over your land to the person willing to pay the highest price and not giving a damn what they do with it.' Tom never gets angry and it's clear he's annoyed.

'Oh, so back-handers don't count even when those handing them out want something in return?' Jared replies, clear enough for us all to hear and people begin talking among themselves.

'Settle down, everyone,' Sam calls and the talking dies down. 'Tom, I'm very grateful to you for having the courage to stand up and say what was on your mind. People are often quick to judge and wrong to do so when they aren't privy to the facts.' Sam pauses and as our eyes meet, I nod my head. 'It's true that outsiders don't always understand the impact they have on the community. We all know that. My new business partner is Kerra Shaw.' With that, all heads turn in my direction, and I plaster on a pleasant smile as Ross reaches for my hand to give it a reassuring squeeze. 'Kerra never forgot her roots and returning to Penvennan after a successful career in London, she's very aware that if we do nothing then it won't be long before businesses begin to fail. As Tom is the perfect testament to that, none of us want to give up.'

It's obvious Sam expects me to say something, and I ease myself upright. Now is not the time to be reticent.

'Change isn't easy to accept,' I begin, making eye contact as I scan around the room. 'But it's a reality of life that nothing stands still. People come to the cove because it hasn't been spoilt over the years. There are no arcades with slot machines, no loud music playing out into the early hours of the morning. It's a sedate place, a destination for people who come back here year after year because they value the peace and quiet of a beautiful beach, stunning views and some marvellous walks. The pub, the bakery, the newsagent's and our local convenience store are what keeps our little community going. It's up to us to support them in whatever way we can to ensure they're always owned and run by local people. A part of that is reliant upon a constant influx of visitors and if trade increases everyone benefits.'

As I reclaim my seat, Ross snakes his arm around my waist, giving me a squeeze.

'There's no truth in the rumour that you and Oliver Sinclair are doing some sort of business together here in the cove?' Jared levels at me.

If Tom joins in now, he might say something he'll regret, so once again I get to my feet.

'With all due respect, Jared, if you're interested in making an investment in the future of the cove, I doubt that anyone would turn you away. Without ongoing capital investment what happens is that businesses fall behind, or worse – fall into disrepair. I'm sure Tom won't mind me labouring the point that creating parking spaces on both sides of the High Street killed his boat repair business. Recovery vehicles were no longer able to get through and he lost that contract, too. I commend Tom and his father, Wally, for what they're doing to improve the site and bring it back to life. Anyone interested in getting involved, I'm sure Tom would be only too delighted to talk to you.'

One glance at Ross and I can see he's stifling a smile. As I sit back down, Polly stands.

'I think that has probably answered most people's questions and hopefully will put an end to the speculation and uncertainty. Can I just add that I'm proud Dad has chosen to stay and make it work, having turned down some very enticing offers, some he felt wouldn't benefit Penvennan Cove in the longer term. With that said, I'm heading back behind the bar, and I will be delighted to take your orders.'

As some follow hot on Polly's heels, Sissy pulls me to one side as Sam walks over to join us. Dad and Nettie have already disappeared, and Ross is talking to Tom.

'That was hairy,' Sam says, his voice low. 'Nice one though, Kerra, and sorry I had to pull you in.'

'Oh, it wasn't your fault, Sam. I took Oliver to The Salvager's Yard and obviously people take notice of something like that. What makes me cross is that Jared seemed to have an axe to grind. I always smile and say "hello" if I see him in the shop, but he's never once acknowledged me back. Maybe I did something to upset him without realising it, who knows?'

'Oh, he's a miserable so-and-so, and I think someone set him up. It's not like him to speak out,' Sissy remarks. 'Anyway, I just wanted to tell you both that you handled that really well. And Tom, bless him, he's got a good heart, that man, and he wasn't going to put up with any nonsense, either.'

It's funny how the people who complain the loudest are often those who aren't prepared to rise to the occasion, even to help themselves. Ross agrees with me as we wander home together along the beach that is virtually deserted.

'Some people just can't see it, can they?' he states, sounding annoyed. 'I mean, what was the purpose of Jared standing up when he didn't have anything constructive to say?'

The meeting has left me feeling a little jaded and it's time to change the subject. 'We don't get to walk the shoreline as often as we should,' I say, linking arms.

'Some Bengals love having a lead and going for a walk,' Ross informs me. 'If we had a dog, we'd be down here twice a day.'

I burst out laughing. 'Can you see Ripley welcoming anyone into her domain? Let alone a dog. And good luck getting a collar and a lead on Ripley, she's a tiger.'

'We could borrow Bertie to give Drew and Felicity a break,' Ross jests.

'How about we borrow Ethan, too, so they can both catch up on some sleep?'

'Ooh, I'm not sure we could handle a baby and an animal. But having seen you in action this evening, you're a much stronger woman than even I imagined. No one's going to mess with you, Kerra Shaw, that's for sure.'

As we make our way back to start the long climb up the hill, I remember the old days. After school we'd get the bus to the stop in the High Street and then a group of us would head down to the beach. At that time Ross's family lived a stone's throw away from the High Street, in the poshest house around here. We'd all be jostling around, and I rarely got to walk next to Ross, but I remember one day he hung back and waited for me to catch up. The look he gave me stayed with me forever; it's the look I see in his eyes in quiet moments when I turn around unexpectedly and catch him watching me. There's a connection between us that's always been there, but as young teenagers, when it's all about the fear of rejection, neither of us was confident enough to explore our hidden feelings. Now we both understand that the time we had apart allowed us to discover who we are.

I'm no longer the shy, IT geek desperate to blend in with the gang and Ross is… My thoughts suddenly grind to an abrupt halt as I cast around for the right words. A man who knows what he wants; the right woman by his side and, having earnt the respect of a lot of people despite living in the shadow of his father's questionable dealings, an honest living. Soon he'll be totally free of any constraints because Jago is all about the money. He knows that Ross would never take orders from anyone else, it's all or nothing.

# 18

## Cast Adrift

I'm going to surprise Ross tonight by cooking traditional Cornish pasties. But for the last hour Ripley has been an absolute nightmare, refusing to settle herself down and distracting me when I'm trying hard to concentrate.

I'm using Grandma Rosenwyn's recipe. Mum wrote it out for me just before I left home in the hope that I wouldn't live on takeaways alone. Seeing her handwriting is a bit of a comfort thing for me and today, for whatever reason, I was drawn to step away from my PC early. Equally as unusual for me, I had the urge to roll up my sleeves and get hands-on in the kitchen.

Admittedly, I did pop to the shop to buy a couple of packets of ready-made shortcrust pastry, but I also wanted to check on Arthur.

'What is it, Ripley? I can't keep stopping to give you a stroke every couple of minutes. Why don't you go outside and see if Bertie is about?'

For the umpteenth time I wash and dry my hands,

leading her over to the glass doors and sliding them back a few feet. She sits there as if she isn't sure what she wants to do and, eager to get the first batch of pasties in the oven before Ross appears, I return to the island, determined to get this done.

I have some chunks of cooking apple lightly poaching in a honey and cinnamon infused liquid and they're probably ready. While they cool, I roll out four circles of pastry on the marble slab.

Carefully scooping up a small handful of the diced beef skirt steak, waxy potatoes, and white onions, I place the filling to cover two thirds of the lower half of each pastry circle. I'm following Mum's note in the margin and am adding a little swede. A small sprinkling of salt and pepper, a couple of small dots of Cornish butter, and I'm ready to add the dessert. Traditionally, the miners' wives would make the savoury pasties with a sweet portion at the end. The thick crusts would be discarded and left as a bribe for *the knockers*, the little sprites believed to live in the mines causing havoc and misfortune. I remember Granddad telling me that story and it always makes me smile.

Carefully lifting out a few chunks of apple and using a sieve to drain off the excess liquid, I place them at one end. Now for the tricky bit. Wetting the edge of the pastry with a little water on my fingertips, I ease the top half over the contents. My crimping is freestyle, but it doesn't look too bad. Then it's time to wash a little beaten egg over the top.

'Right,' I inform Ripley who turns to gaze at me, tilting her head. 'Ten minutes on high and then fifty minutes on a lower heat and fingers crossed they'll hit the spot. They've turned out much better than I thought,' I add, proudly.

Smug is a more apt description, I chuckle to myself as I slide the baking tray into the oven and make up another four. I've been promising Drew a homemade pasty ever since the day that I returned to Penvennan Cove.

As I wash the countertops down to finish up, Ripley is still sitting there with her two front paws resting on the deck and I find myself frowning. It's not like her to be undecided – she's either out, or in. Then the sound of Bertie barking is enough to rouse her and out she trots.

When it's time to turn down the oven, the kitchen is sparkling, and I pop on the kettle for a well-deserved drink. A noise at the front door makes me turn around and to my utter surprise Ross walks in carrying a large cardboard box. It's only just after four o'clock, which is unheard of for a weekday, but I can also tell from his overall demeanour that something isn't right. He places the box down next to the stairs and, in total silence, walks straight over to me. Instinctively I wrap my arms around him, and we stand hugging each other tightly for a few seconds.

'What is it, Ross? What's happened?' I enquire softly, my voice wavering. He looks haggard.

'I've been sacked, Kerra. My father has won, and I didn't even see it coming.'

I lead Ross over to the table and pull out a chair. He slumps down into it, as if he's in a trance.

'You didn't drive home in this state, did you?'

'No, the van is a company vehicle and I had to hand over my keys. My personal items are all in that box. One of the guys gave me a lift home.'

'Jago is back?' I'm confused.

'No. You remember that guy who shadowed me for three

days when my father was here setting up the new office in Launceston?'

'Quentin Armstrong-Jones?'

'Yes. I was told he was a consultant, an old friend of my father's brought in to help Will generate new business to kick-start the Launceston depot. It turns out that my father is about to sell Treloar's Building Limited to him. In the meantime, Quentin has been visiting my sites and collecting evidence to prove that I'm in breach of company policy, which is cause for instant dismissal.'

'But… but you're one of the shareholders, Ross. There must be something you can do about it if the sale hasn't gone through?'

'It's smoke and mirrors, Kerra. There's no point in spending time and money fighting this as Quentin will end up with two-thirds of the shares. He's not a man I could work for anyway, and he made it crystal clear that I won't be needed. It's clever, as ostensibly this stems from some clauses that were inserted into my contract when I became the general manager. Like getting written approval from the other two shareholders if the company spending goes above a certain limit. Obviously, as the business has grown that limit has been breached but my father never once pulled me up on it. Unfortunately, it didn't occur to me that could be used as ammunition to push me out the door. I'll end up owning twenty-five per cent of a company I have nothing at all to do with. That won't work for me.'

I'm stunned by Ross's revelation and horrified at Jago's underhanded tactics. But am I surprised? It's sad to admit that I'm not.

'All I've ever known is working for the family business.

I'm devastated that my mother didn't have the courtesy to warn me about my father's intentions, when she obviously knew exactly what was going on behind the scenes. Quentin said that financially I'd do well out of it when I sell him my shares and, in her naivety, she probably thought that was justification enough. Quentin's veiled threat is that if I don't go quietly, he might have to axe a few jobs – you know, weeding out guys who have stood by me over the years – and I can't let that happen.'

I flop down onto the chair next to him, feeling gutted that Jago has won.

'It's really over?'

'Yes, and this is going to sound pathetic, Kerra, but I don't know what to do next. I'm numb. This can't be happening and yet I know it is. I was so close, or at least that's what he allowed me—'

*Miaow, miaow, miaoooooow.*

Ripley reappears, heading straight for Ross and jumps up onto his lap. He begins stroking her and the way Ripley settles down, without any fuss whatsoever, tells me that she understands he's hurting. It's a poignant moment and my emotions are threatening to overwhelm me. I get up and busy myself making a drink as I battle to keep my composure and not speak my mind about his father. What Ross needs now is a show of strength, not empty words that won't change a single thing.

By the time I carry the mugs across and sit down again, his face has a little more colour to it.

'Have you ever stopped to ask yourself what you want out of life?' Ross asks, his eyes searching mine.

I pause for thought, knowing that now is the time to be

totally honest. 'From my experience it doesn't quite work like that,' I reply, thinking of the way life still catches me unawares at times. 'You start out on a path and you follow it, but it doesn't necessarily take you where you thought it might. Things go wrong, or opportunities you couldn't possibly have foreseen crop up and suddenly there's a fork in the road. You make a choice and off you go again, hoping that you haven't made a huge mistake.'

'Are you saying that if you could start afresh you wouldn't change a thing? Or you'd change everything?' His expression is troubled as he stares back at me.

'After almost a decade dedicating my life to building The Happy Hive, Mum's passing led me back here and no one could foresee that happening. It was a huge wrench, but now I'm with you and I've never been happier, Ross. Did I ever see myself as the woman in your life? The answer to that is *no*, quite frankly. Not even in my wildest dreams, but that's just the way things have panned out for me.'

'So, you think I should just wait and see what life throws at me next?' Now he's beginning to sound depressed.

'I accepted that one's first love – which happened to be you – is a treasured memory to keep locked away. No one can take it from you and every now and again you think of it fondly. It warms your heart and gives you hope you'll feel that same intensity again at some point in the future. So, no – I don't regret the twists and turns that got me here, as painful as they were to get through. In hindsight, even Mum's wish that I come back to help Dad find his feet might not have been solely for that reason. All I know is that I didn't arrive with a master plan, I just take each day as it comes. But what's going through your head?'

'I would never have worked for my father, that's for sure.'

I could be totally wrong, but that sounds like a normal gut reaction considering how badly he's been treated by his own family. What worries me is that Ross sounds pragmatic and he's unbelievably calm considering what's happened.

'What would you be doing now if things had been different from the start?' I ask, encouragingly.

Ross stares dully out across the garden. His emotionless state is beginning to scare me. Just when I thought things were about to get easier for us as a couple, to see him looking so defeated is heart-breaking.

'I don't know, but it's time to find out. The world is a big place and maybe I've been so focused on one thing, I've lost sight of that fact.'

*Miaow, miaow, miaoooooow.*

Ripley too is lending her support, but she hasn't moved an inch. She knows when someone needs comfort. As I reach for the mug, my hands are trembling as I'm fearful for what's to come. I've never heard Ross talk like this before and it's unnerving to see him looking so drained and... defeated. It's obvious to me now that Ripley could sense that change was coming and that's what unsettled her today. Was I feeling it too, hence the desperate search for something to divert my attention? Ross is a part of me now and without any warning at all his working life has been snatched away from him. He doesn't deserve this – he's a good man and an honest, hard-working one. He's a man who loves a challenge and how will he feel waking up tomorrow morning knowing that the very thing he put all his energy into building up is now in the hands of a total stranger?

*

The second half of May flies by and as we hit the first of June my nerves are frazzled. I've been treating Ross like he's recovering from an illness, giving him space when he needs it and downing tools to suit his mood. We've avoided talking about his future and anything to do with the past, which makes conversation difficult to say the least. I wasn't sure what to do about Sam, who was liaising with Ross and Drew almost daily over the proposed renovation works to the cottages and The Lark and Lantern. I had no choice but to tell Drew what happened. He was shocked, obviously, and said I wasn't to worry. They're nowhere near ready to put the work out to tender and by the time they are Drew was sure that Ross would be back in *the game*. It seems everyone I bump into assumes Ross is taking a bit of a break before launching his own building company. What they don't know is that it's become obvious to me nothing could be further from the truth.

Tonight, I've arranged for Gawen to meet up with Ross and go for a pint down at The Lark and Lantern. Not least because it's about time Ross showed his face among the locals. The initial reactions I've had since word got around is a huge wave of support for Ross. Jago has upset so many people over the years, and his *better than you attitude* didn't fool anyone. He got where he is by paying backhanders and everyone knows that. At least Gawen can chat for hours about the farm, which will be a pleasant distraction for Ross.

As I knock on the door to The Forge, Sy opens it and seconds later I step into his arms.

'You look tired.' He sighs, hugging me a little bit tighter before letting me go.

'Don't keep Kerra standing in the hallway, Sy,' Tegan calls out. 'Come on in. There's a glass of wine with your name on it in the kitchen, Kerra.'

When I enter the sitting room Tegan's expression turns into an upside-down smile as the strain of what Ross is going through is clearly visible on my face. Catching sight of myself in a mirror these days sometimes stops even me in my tracks. I feel worn out with worry.

'Oh, Kerra. I'm guessing that Ross is still wandering around like a lost soul?'

I nod my head, unable to speak as Tegan and I sit down on the sofa while Sy disappears into the kitchen.

'It must be hard starting over again, but he has garnered a lot of goodwill.'

'I know and I've pointed that out to him,' I reply, sounding as jaded as I'm feeling. 'Ross is adamant that he wants nothing at all to do with the building industry. It's crazy because he has all that experience. Drew suggested project management would be a great opportunity while he firms up his long-term plans and even gave Ross a couple of contact numbers to ring. But instead, Ross decided we don't need the deck down at the bottom of the garden and he's turning it into a vegetable patch. I mean, is that avoidance, or what?'

'Everyone has a different coping technique and maybe that's his,' she replies, gently.

'I know, but it's hard to hide my anxiety. I'm feeling frustrated; there doesn't seem to be anything I can do to help Ross through this because he seems to have switched off from everything.'

Sy appears carrying a tray with three glasses of wine on it. 'Ross and Gawen got off for their pint at The Lark and Lantern then?' He exchanges a concerned glance with Tegan, as he lowers himself down onto the sofa facing us.

'I had to apply a little pressure to get Ross to say yes. He said he didn't want to spoil the mood by accompanying me here tonight, but I needed a little break. I didn't have the heart to leave him on his own, though. I hope that a chat with Gawen will do him good.'

'Is Ross suffering from depression, do you think?' Tegan asks, a sorrowful look reflected in her eyes.

'I don't think that's the problem. He was stunned at first, numb even and then this constant need to keep himself busy. That's when he suddenly decided to get stuck into some gardening. He spends several hours on it each day while I'm working in the office. In the evenings all he ever wants to do is to read and another thing he insisted on is taking over the chores.'

I roll my eyes and Sy shakes his head sadly.

'Anything to avoid making a decision. It's understandable given the circumstances but that's so out of character for Ross. We're gutted on his behalf,' Sy commiserates.

'That business won't be anywhere near as successful without Ross,' Tegan continues, angrily. 'He's the one who grew the company's reputation for reliability and quality workmanship. For all the gossip that has surrounded him over the years, both his men and his customers respect him. It wasn't easy to shake off the bad feeling his father's manipulative dealings left behind, but Ross did it. And now this throws years of dedication and effort in his face, as if it counts for nothing. Bloody typical of Jago, isn't it – but this is his son he's doing it to this time and not a stranger. Has the man no conscience whatsoever?'

Tegan never swears and Sy and I both look at her in surprise.

'Jago won't see it that way. Ross has benefited financially from the sale of the business, and this was obviously his father's plan all along. He thinks money is the solution to everything but Treloar's Building Limited was Ross's life's work. His father saw to that.'

'It's awful to think that he worked endless hours in good faith, never dreaming he'd end up being treated this way. You don't expect family to turn on you like that, but it happens.' Sy's disgruntled remark resonates with both Tegan, and me. I'm sure it's bringing up painful memories of past battles with his own father.

'It's taken the wind out of his sails,' I confirm. 'As my granddad was often heard to say, without that you lack direction. Life hasn't come to a complete standstill for Ross. I try to find little things that will make him laugh and he enjoys cooking dinner every evening. But when he goes shopping for ingredients it's obvious that he's been into town and not popped across the road. Anything to fill his time and avoid bumping into people he knows. He's also waiting on me hand, foot and finger, which is driving me mad.'

I sound ungrateful, but I just want the old Ross back, not this man who is hiding his pain and scared to show how vulnerable he's feeling.

'We've been wanting to ask if there's anything at all we can do to help, Kerra. You only have to say, and it's done.'

Sy nods in agreement at Tegan's offer.

'Thank you, guys and it's really appreciated. I wish there was, but even I don't know what to do for the best any more. Drew has tried to coax Ross out of the house, but to no avail. In a way it would be easier if we needed him to work, but we don't and that's what's making this even worse. Without any sort of deadline to motivate Ross, this is the only way he can cope for now; but how long do I let it continue before I point out that he can't live in limbo forever?'

Tegan reaches out to touch my arm.

'It depends on how you're dealing with it too, Kerra. This affects you both.'

Tegan is right and I know it. 'I'm constantly having to hold my tongue for fear of saying the wrong thing. But how long can we go on pretending everything is fine when it isn't?'

The eye contact between Sy and Tegan shows how concerned they are, not just for Ross.

'The strain must be awful, Kerra. You can't keep bottling it up.'

'I feel like I'm betraying him even talking openly to you two, but if it gets it out of my system then anything is better than upsetting Ross. And I can't thank you both enough for this excuse to get out of the house tonight.'

'Are you still sharing your office with Drew?'

'Yes, and the fact that he's around stops Ross appearing every half an hour to check on me, but I'm not getting much work done. There are a couple of new business opportunities that have come my way, but I'm hanging back in case Ross does decide to go it alone. If that happens, we'll need every penny we can rake up between us.'

'So, you're in limbo, too?' Sy interjects.

'Yes. I don't mention my work at all in case he takes it the wrong way, thinking I'm trying to make a point. On the other hand, a part of me wonders if that's what he needs. I just want him to feel relaxed being at home, it's his only comfort zone right now.'

'Tricky,' Sy agrees. 'As long as he's not depressed, maybe all he needs is a little more time. I can empathise with that. I never thought I'd quit a job on the spot, and even though it was my decision, the fallout afterwards was devastating. It must be even worse when it's inflicted upon you. Coming here and meeting Tegan helped me piece my new life together and I had you, Kerra, as my listening ear. But it was a fresh start and maybe that's the problem for Ross.'

An icy chill begins to course through my veins, because Sy has just voiced the exact same thought that has been going around and around inside my head for the last twenty-four hours.

'Eddie would never forgive Ross if he took you away from Penvennan Cove, Kerra,' Tegan declares, her voice wavering.

How could I not support Ross if the only way he can get through this is to turn his back on memories that are too painful to live with and start anew somewhere else? Why is life doing this to us now, when there is so much to lose?

And then it dawns on me. Jago knew exactly what he was doing when he bought Treylya from Ross – he doesn't want him to have anything to keep him here. Together with the money Ross has from the sale of his shares, if Sy and Tegan end up buying The Forge, he'd have a sizeable amount of capital to invest. Maybe not enough to set up his own building company, but I bet his father has connections in Spain that would present a great opportunity. Having seen Jago's true colours, there would be money in it for him too I suspect.

My head is reeling. If that's the case and I try to convince Ross that our life is here, will he end up resenting me?

'Kerra, talk to me. Tell me what you're thinking.' Tegan is staring at me, concern written all over her face.

'What if Ross is meant to be with someone like Bailey, and not me? Someone who wouldn't bat an eyelid at moving away to begin an exciting new journey. I did that and ended up longing to return home, but Ross might want to spread his wings.' With that, I burst into tears. My mind conjures up memories of watching the girls fawning over Ross, while I stood back feeling that I wasn't... I don't know, attractive enough? Witty enough? I often felt like a hanger-on; I never sought attention. I'm a homely girl, not the sort who turns heads.

Sy shakes his head sadly. 'Don't worry, Kerra. Ross has made his mistakes and he won't repeat them again. Just give him some space to sort himself out and trust in your gut instincts. You wouldn't have chosen him if you'd had any doubts whatsoever, but sometimes people need to fix things for themselves. That's the tough bit to accept, isn't it?'

Sy understands, as that's exactly what happened when he hit rock bottom. As his main source of support, all I could do was stand back and wait for him to reach out to me. Turning his back on London was something he'd never considered. It was a massive leap of faith for this city dweller to embrace a quieter life in Cornwall. What if Ross comes through this wanting to make as drastic a change? Could I cope with that?

# 19

## A Distress Call

'Dad, it's Kerra. Please... please don't hang up on me.' My voice wavers as I continue to dab at the tears cascading down over my cheeks with a wad of tissues. 'Everything is falling apart and... and I don't know what to do!'

Pride is a luxury I can't afford because I'm desperate and I'm fighting for the only thing that matters to me right now.

'Whatever has happened?'

'Ross is gone, Dad. He woke early and I didn't hear him. He left me a note to say he needs some time on his own to sort himself out and I'm scared he'll never come home.'

'You'd best come round, my girl. That's an awful shock and he must be desperate. I'm sorry to hear you so distressed. I'm on me own, so there's no one to overhear us. If the kennels weren't full, I'd pop over to Pedrevan.'

'It's not a problem, I'm on my way.' Ending the call, I rush out to the kitchen to scoop some cold water onto my face. It's no doubt red and blotchy, but I don't care. Ripley makes no sound as she sits with her tail wrapped around her paws, watching every move I make. She's been like this for the past half an hour, while I've been pacing around, my head in a whirl. Usually, she'd be up on the bed sound asleep at this time, and I hope she'll settle down before I get back.

Crossing the road and walking down to the five-bar gate to Green Acre, I try not to think about the last time I was here and the angry exchange of words. The minute I close the gate behind me and begin treading the path up to the front door it swings open and Dad stands there, a pained expression on his face.

'My poor girl. Come on in. The kettle is on. As your old mum would have said, the best thing when someone's in shock is a strong cup of tea. I'm just sad it's come to that for you.'

His tone is gentle as I step over the threshold and he wraps his arms around me, hugging so tightly that I begin to sob. 'I've missed this, Dad. I never meant to hurt or disappoint you.'

'And the truth is that I've missed you, my lovely. It's my fault this argument went on for so long. This has all been a bit of a nightmare for us both and your mum would be disappointed with the way I've handled things, I realise that now. The minute I heard Ross's news I should have come across and knocked on your door to lend my support.'

'Oh, Dad – it's been a horrible time and now this. Jago knew exactly what to say to drive you and me apart. But I've always loved Ross, and you probably suspected that – you just wished it wasn't true.'

As Dad releases me, he stands back holding my arms

quite firmly and staring into my eyes. 'The fault doesn't lie with you, lovely. I got on me high horse, as your mum would have said, and lost me perspective. Jago played me for a fool, and I fell for it. This weren't Ross's doin', he's a victim and I haven't treated him right.'

My tears flow unabated until I feel empty and desolate.

'The man I turned my back on when I left Penvennan is the only man who has ever succeeded in touching my heart, Dad. And now Ross is on a journey I can't share with him because Jago has taken everything away. In his note Ross asked me to forgive him, he said he'd let me down and I deserve better. Better than what? His love means everything to me.'

'Come on, dry those tears. The kettle's on.'

I follow Dad into the kitchen and I'm glad we're alone, even though Nettie has tried her best to bring us back together.

'Ross thinks he's being kind,' I continue, as I plonk myself down onto a chair. 'He said his future is uncertain as he struggles to reinvent himself. He fears he'll end up hurting me in the long run. Ross can't see a way forward for himself and now he's gone off somewhere to mull it over. I don't know if I can go on without him by my side.'

Two cups of strong tea later, there are no tears left in me to shed and Dad is looking shellshocked. 'I thought they were tarred with the same brush, Jago and Ross. That was my foolhardy, obstinate pride preventing me from seeing the truth, Kerra,' Dad admits. 'You don't have any idea where he might be?'

'His phone is switched off and he never does that. He doesn't want me to look for him, Dad.'

'Ross has been wronged, but Jago isn't the only culprit, Kerra. I guess I'm more like me own brother than I thought because I didn't give Ross a chance, did I? Look, Ian and Nettie will be back soon from dog walkin' and it's best we keep this to ourselves for now. Trust your old dad to see what I can find out, as you're in no fit state to deal with this. Go home, snuggle up with Ripley on the sofa and watch a film or somethin' to lift your spirits. You're stressed and at the end of your tether. You can't function properly when you're so het up, so your job today is to relax and calm yourself down.'

I look at Dad, the sense of determination and positivity in his voice brings fresh tears to my eyes.

'Mum knew,' I mutter, softly.

'She always had a soft spot for Ross; she weren't like me. The name Treloar is like a red rag to a bull in my case, but I'm not such a silly old fool that I don't know when I'm wrong. I was glad when you got away from here because I saw how you caught his eye. You were different, lovely, always were and always will be. But I've come to realise that he's different too. Nettie and I had a few words yesterday when Ross's name cropped up. Nettie pointed out that Ross has had a rough deal all his life. You're no fool, Kerra, and you wouldn't be with him if it weren't the real thing. Anyway, you get off now and I'll keep my ear to the ground. There are people in and out all the time, and if he's staying somewhere local, the chances are someone will mention having seen him. I'll let you know as soon as I hear something.'

I nod my head, knowing there is nothing at all I can do anyway.

'Good. This is no one's business but yours and Ross's. Once you're back on an even keel, keep yourself busy and act as if everything is fine. You don't have to explain anything to anyone.'

'There is one other thing that's been bothering me, Dad. I'm sorry for what I said... about Granddad's accident. I know how tough it was for you supporting Mum and Grandma through that period. I was angry about everything and I took it out on you that day.'

'Oh, my darling girl. You have no idea how that ripped my heart to shreds because what you said shocked me. I just thought if your mum walked in on us... it was easier to brush it off, but I never really stopped to think about what was going on inside your head. If for one second I'd have thought it was... He'd never have taken his own life. He loved you way too much for that, Kerra. You were the sunshine in his day.'

We stand and Dad steps forward to throw his arms around me once more. As we cling to each other for comfort words are unnecessary.

The twisted irony of the situation is that all it took to bring me and Dad back together, was for Ross to leave me. Dad forewarned me this would happen, but it's not quite the scenario he envisaged. That doesn't mean it hurts any less, because I have no idea what the outcome will be.

The only way I'm going to get through this next period is to do more or less what Dad suggested, although I've never been one to laze around. Instead, I spend the rest of the day cleaning the cottage. Then, after a night of constant tossing and turning, even Ripley is glad when I head down to the garden office this morning so she can get some undisturbed rest. By the time Drew joins me I've been hard at work for almost two hours.

'Morning, early bird. Ross must have been up with the lark, too. I usually hear his van kick into life.'

'He was parked further down as he left super early. He's away for a few days visiting a couple of contacts. Mainly gathering some information; next steps that sort of thing.' It's not exactly a lie.

Drew pulls some files out of his backpack before sitting down.

'Ah, it's good to hear he's over the slump. Although he was enjoying working in the garden. But it never was going to keep him occupied for long, was it?'

I shake my head, giving a dismissive laugh. 'How are things going in Tigry Cottage?'

'Good. Ethan slept for a solid five hours between feeds, last night. Things are looking up!' He grins at me.

The worst bit is over and now I can relax. Drew accepted my explanation, so other people will too. And now it's a waiting game. In the meantime, I spend the next three hours tidying up Tom's business plan and checking his figures. When my phone rings and I see that it's Dad, I simply say 'Hello', indicating to Drew that I'm heading up to the house for lunch.

'I've just come back from a trip up to Treeve Perran farm to buy some eggs. Gawen was nowhere to be seen and when I asked if he was about, Yvonne said she wasn't sure where he was. She was a bit on edge and kept looking at the door, as if expecting someone to walk through it at any moment. Normally we have a bit of a chat, but she didn't encourage me to hang around. If I were a betting man I'd say Ross is staying at the farm, but they're keeping it quiet.'

I let out a huge sigh of relief. 'Oh Dad, I hope that's the case. At least he's with good friends. This won't be easy for them as they know I'll be worried.'

'Hmm… I was thinking the same thing. She was feeling very uncomfortable, I can tell you that, but we must respect his wishes. You do understand that, Kerra, don't you?'

'Yes, Dad.'

'As for Nettie, I told her we talked. She thinks I contacted you to say I was sorry to hear about Ross's troubles. We don't need to say any more than that. How're you doing?'

'Okay. The cottage is sparkling, and I've been at my desk since six o'clock.'

'Good. Don't go stewing over what's happening. Gawen and Yvonne have their heads screwed on right and if they have any worries, they'd be on the phone to you. Of that I have no doubt.'

'It was really good of you to head up there. It helps to know he's only a half an hour drive away and it's far enough that he doesn't have to worry too much about being seen. Although Clean and Shine do service the holiday cottages, thankfully Sy and Tegan rarely visit the properties now. It's only if there's a problem with one of their contractors. Hopefully it won't be someone who knows Ross by sight.'

'You gotta leave him to it now, Kerra. He can look after himself. It's a great place to be for a man who has some serious thinking to do. If you need anything, whatever time of the day or night, just give me a call.'

'It's like old times,' I reply, touched by his concern.

'Well, I've some making up to do. And when he gets back, I'll be letting Ross know how much I regret the way I treated him. Right, I'm off to walk the dogs. Take care of yourself, lovely, and we'll speak soon.'

Standing in the kitchen, knowing that I'm cooking for one tonight, makes me realise how quickly Ross became a part of my life. Even when he was at work all day there was that little buzz counting down the hours until he was home. I walk over to the bookshelves and run my fingers lightly over the spines of some of Ross's favourite titles. Many of the cookery books are well-thumbed and I pull one out, hugging it close to me.

'Hurry back, Ross,' I whisper. 'I've forgotten how to be alone. Nothing is the same without you beside me.'

Most of the afternoon I have the office to myself as Drew takes charge of Ethan while Felicity has a nap. As often happens when I get stuck into something, the hours just fly by. After Polly and Sissy successfully furnished the rooms at Easterton Lodge, Sissy sent me a link to a folder of before and after photos. They've given The Design Cave their consent for us to upload them to our website as it's a good marketing opportunity for them as well as us. It's work I love doing. Cropping, enlarging and making collages is a wonderful way to while away my time while being productive. It blots out everything else going on around me and calms my mind.

When it's time to quit for the day I don't feel much like cooking, so I head over to the shop. I've noticed that Mrs Moyle is spending less time behind the counter since her trip away. As I walk past Barbara, who is serving a customer, I give her a wave before heading over to the fridge section. Ross would roll his eyes at me as I pick up a packet of fresh linguine and a ready-made tomato and red pepper sauce. Walking past the bakery section I notice there are still some saffron buns and a couple of home-made apple pies left.

'We can't tempt you with a dessert?' Barbara banters, as I lift the items in my basket onto the counter and lean over to place it on the stack.

'You have no idea how hard it is to walk past the shelves but I'm going to be good,' I reply. I doubt I'll enjoy the pasta either, as everything I do when I'm on my own in the cottage feels mechanical. I'm going through the motions because my life is on hold. 'It's unusual to see anything left at the end of the day.'

'Oh, Mrs Moyle did a double batch today in between spending time with Arthur. I think he appreciates the fact that she's taking it a little easier now my sister and I have worked out a rota.'

'Oh, I didn't realise.'

'It's great for me, as my kids are in their teens and they come and go as they please these days. It's a couple of minutes in the car to get here, which is perfect and the extra money comes in handy.'

'Arthur is all right, isn't he?' I query, putting the groceries in my bag and then flashing my card in front of the reader.

'All done!' Barbara confirms, handing me a receipt. 'I

think so, Mrs Moyle hasn't said anything to me. They're upstairs having a cup of tea I think, why don't you pop up?'

I'm in two minds, as I'm not really in the mood to make polite conversation but Arthur will have noticed Ross's second-hand 4x4 pickup wasn't there last night.

'I might as well as I'm here, thanks, Barbara.'

As I walk through into the hallway, the kitchen door is open but the only noises I can hear are coming from upstairs. I call out, 'It's Kerra. Am I interrupting you?'

Mrs Moyle appears on the landing. 'Well, isn't that a coincidence, we were just talking about you! Come on up.'

'You were?' I smile at her, determined to be upbeat.

'Yes, Arthur was saying things must be looking up as Ross hasn't been about.'

Everyone is assuming he's off planning his next venture.

'Hey there, Kerra. I was saying to Daphne he'll be showin' his dad he can go it alone and he'll have the backin' of a lot of folk around here.'

Oh Arthur, if only you knew.

'Ah, that's kind of you to say so. It's certainly the start of a new chapter but everything takes time.' I manage to make it sound positive, even though inside I'm filled with dread. Pushing my thoughts aside there is something I've been meaning to ask Arthur and now's my chance. 'The meeting at The Lark and Lantern didn't go quite as smoothly as Sam had hoped. I wondered if you've noticed any grumbles on the Penvennan Community Link-Up chat boards since, Arthur?'

'Funny you should say that, Kerra. A couple of things did pop up, but I just post a link to the rules and advise them all that a repeat after a warnin' will get them banned. Was there anythin' in particular you want me to keep an eye out for?'

'Jared was all fired up and although his question was answered I just felt that maybe it wasn't the end of it.'

Arthur shakes his head, looking dubious. 'Well, he got the shove from the website a while ago. He came in the shop and had a good old moan afterwards, but Mrs Moyle put him in his place. He's always had a chip on his shoulder, Kerra. I don't like bannin' people, but he goes off on one and some of the stuff he says doesn't go down well. I need to think of the majority. Sounds like it might not be a good time to give him a second chance, though?'

'Don't let me influence you, Arthur, it's your project. It just grates on me when someone purposely tries to stir up trouble and he was aiming it at Tom. Tom and Wally are doing a great job down at The Salvager's Yard and they should be commended, not criticised.'

'Jared is a bit like Zacky, Kerra,' Mrs Moyle joins in. 'The pair of them spend too much time sitting around moaning about the state of the world and winding each other up. If they had some proper work to do they'd be too busy to invent new rumours.'

'You're probably right, but it's a sad state of affairs. Anyway, how are you two doing?'

Arthur looks at Mrs Moyle as she indicates for me to take a seat.

'I'm feelin' like a bit of a fool to be honest with you, Kerra.' Arthur sounds gutted.

I swallow uncomfortably. I'm not sure I can handle this right now given how fragile I'm feeling.

'We had one of those video calls with the solicitor this

morning,' Mrs Moyle explains. I notice that she reaches out to pat Arthur's hand as it lies on the arm of his reclining chair.

'I've proof of what happened,' Arthur continues. 'He says if I'd just got some advice at the very beginnin' and lodged the right forms, me first marriage would have been over on the grounds of desertion. It was stupid of me to think that just because Helen chose to disappear, even after eight years I could start afresh when I met Daphne. Now our marriage is void and Daphne doesn't deserve that, or the worry about what's to come.'

I'm rendered speechless. Arthur really is a bigamist.

'Solicitors don't speculate,' Mrs Moyle takes over. 'He told us what was what, according to the law and laid out the steps we need to take next. He's a nice man, didn't make us feel uncomfortable. He knows his stuff but afterwards we jumped online. There's no point burying our heads in the sand and thinking it's all going to be fine if it isn't. We found a newspaper article where one man had two wives on the go at the same time. How he managed to live two completely separate lives, goodness knows. We were disgusted, weren't we, Arthur?'

'We were, Daphne. He only got three months in prison and had to pay each of his wives a thousand pounds. Now any normal person will know that ain't right.'

This is a bizarre conversation and I remain silent.

'Those poor women… Anyway, the thing is that the solicitor thinks Arthur has a good case if it does end up in court. His first wife left him and never made contact again until she tracked him down quite recently and sent me that letter.'

Curiosity gets the better of me. 'But why make contact after all these years… and why write to you, and not Arthur?'

Mrs Moyle sighs. 'I wish I hadn't burnt that letter, but I did. I thought… I thought maybe it was someone Arthur used to know from years back thinking we had lots of money.'

'Blackmail?'

She shrugs her shoulder. 'The letter simply said she was Arthur's wife, and she has the marriage certificate to prove it. Then, when I went up to see her, she panicked and refused to see me. The solicitor sent her a letter and now she's claiming that Arthur is the father of her daughter. She says that the birth of her daughter's first grandchild made her realise Arthur had a right to know, but she's worried what his reaction will be.'

My jaw drops and I can see from their own expressions that Arthur and Mrs Moyle are conflicted.

'When I first read the letter I thought if I acknowledged it, the next one would demand money. But, as it turns out I was wrong. The solicitor suggests we get a DNA test done and don't take her word for it. In the meantime, he says the police will contact Arthur, as he'll be required to make a formal statement now that his wrongdoing has come to light.' Mrs Moyle is trying to stay strong for Arthur, but I can see the toll it's taking.

'It's a right old mess, Kerra, and it'll take months to sort out. We're still reelin' because if what Helen is sayin' is true… well, that's a big thing to keep hidden all these years. I don't even know what to think, to be honest with you.' Arthur's frown is deep.

Mrs Moyle pats his hand affectionately.

'Helen was right not to turn up here sayin' somethin' like that,' Arthur says, forcefully. 'I wouldn't have handled it well. I've lived all these years worryin' about what happened to her. If she knew she was havin' a baby when she left, why not tell me? I would have supported her no matter what. Still, I've been a silly man in more ways than one and I needn't have put you through this, Daphne. The truth is that Helen didn't want to be found and if I'd sought advice, I'd have kept on the right side of the law.'

'You're not a criminal, Arthur, not in the real sense of the word. We'll get through it together whatever the outcome.' Mrs Moyle smiles at him encouragingly. 'As far as we're concerned, Kerra, we plough on like normal.'

'That's good to hear. If you need anything, like help filling out forms or just someone to drive you both somewhere, please do call on me. It sounds like you've found the right help at the right time.'

'Only because you mentioned it to me, Kerra. I doubt I'd have thought of it so soon. Anyway, that's enough about us and our antics, how's little Ethan doing? We hear him crying sometimes when Drew and Felicity take him for a walk in the pram, but the little lad settles down quickly. He seems to like the movement.'

'He does,' I reply, laughing as I think about some of the things Drew has shared with me. 'When Ethan won't settle, sometimes they put him in the car seat and go for a short drive. It doesn't take long to get him off to sleep, apparently.'

'Oh,' Arthur exclaims. 'I've noticed Felicity behind the wheel and she's seldom gone for long. That explains it!' Arthur begins to chuckle.

Goodness… if it turns out that Arthur does have a daughter, he also has a grandchild. This could really change their lives forever. And while Arthur did break the law, the fact he waited eight years to marry again must surely demonstrate that his first wife had abandoned him. So, isn't some of the onus on her, too?

# 20

## Back to Nature

I can't remember the last time I was home alone on a Sunday and I'm feeling maudlin. Ripley keeps wandering around as if she's expecting Ross to suddenly appear and I have to admit every time I hear a noise my heart turns over.

'I know, Rippers, I know. He'll be home soon.' I stoop to smooth her back and she flicks her tail appreciatively. Her night-time pursuits have stopped, and she's taken to curling up in a ball on Ross's side of the bed. In the end, I laid out her favourite blanket as I thought it might comfort her.

Shortly after I finish breakfast the doorbell goes and my heart sinks. Ross would let himself in, but when I see Nettie standing there her smile is enough to lift my spirits. She quickly produces a beautiful bouquet of flowers from behind her back.

'This is from your dad and me,' she says, holding them out.

As I take them in my arms I give her a quivery smile. 'Aww… thank you. Come on through, I'll just put them in water.'

I'm touched and while I grab a vase and fill it, Nettie hovers.

'I didn't know if you were busy, but I wanted to come over to say how glad I am that the two of you have made up. Eddie is like a different man, but he's worried about Ross.'

'That makes two of us.' I sigh.

'Ross isn't a man who cares what people think, Kerra, but he cares about what you think.'

'Then why can't he talk to me, Nettie? Why hide himself away instead of talking it through with me? Doesn't he understand that if he's not happy, I'm not happy either?'

Nettie pulls out a chair at the table and sits down, watching me as I automatically nip off half an inch on each of the stems before arranging them.

'In a way I can sympathise with the way Ross has reacted. I avoided your dad for a long time, and he did the exact same thing with me. Losing Meryn changed everything. I'd lost my best friend and your dad had lost the love of his life. Oh, I know we're close and I want to impress upon you that I'm not trying to replace her in his affection. But I'd like to think that there's a little room in his heart for me too. The point is, that life goes on no matter how tough it gets and your dad and I take comfort from each other. Eventually, you and Ross will get to a place where you realise you are better together, than apart.' Her voice is full of tenderness, and I'm touched that Nettie is prepared to open up to me like that.

'I do hope so. And for what it's worth, Mum would be happy to see the two of you together. You know Dad so well that you sense exactly when to challenge him for his own good. He struggles being on his own, Nettie, even I can see that.'

Her smile is wistful. 'And I don't think you or Ross are good on your own either, that's why you finally got together after a decade apart. However, Ross sees himself as a strong man, a provider. He's not a dreamer and yet he finds himself at a crossroads in his life. What if the reason he's taking his time isn't because he's not sure what his next step should be, but for fear of losing you because of it?'

I stop clipping stems and stare at Nettie. That's my fear, too.

'But if he won't talk about it, where do we go from here?'

'Eddie is convinced he'll set up in competition with his father just to prove a point. But I think your dad, and lots of people around here, don't know Ross, not in the way that you do. I've come to know Ross quite well since he started making the scenery for the drama club. In my humble opinion, he's not a man who would waste his time just to exact revenge.'

My instincts have been telling me loud and clear he isn't interested in the building trade. His only problem is finding something he can connect with, which will also satisfy that need to be successful at what he does.

'Ross and I are very alike, aren't we?' I reflect, soulfully. 'I wanted to be successful, and I was, but when I got to that stage it turned out to be a hollow victory rather than a fulfilling moment in my life.'

It's the first time I've ever acknowledged that because I didn't think anyone would understand. Money equals success, right? The truth is that it doesn't.

'Just be ready to support Ross in whatever he decides to do next. Change is scary; failure is always a very real option. It takes courage to go after what really fires you up. I know. I love working with animals, but I've always longed to write. Now that I've set aside time to do that I'm in for the long haul because nothing happens overnight. It means I can't give your dad as much time being hands-on at the kennels as I'd like, but he understands. That shows me how much he cares. And in return, I try to keep him on the straight and narrow. It isn't easy', she smirks. 'But he listens to me… well, sometimes. What warms my heart is the difference I see in him already now the two of you have made up. He's even whistling again as he works.'

'Thank you, Nettie. And the flowers are beautiful. Just the lift I need today. I'm off to The Forge shortly to spend the day with Tegan doing some prep work for the party.'

'Oh, it's the weekend after next, isn't it? I bet she's in a flap,' Nettie replies, conspiratorially.

'It sneaked up on her and yes, she is in a bit of a panic. But I hope today we can pull together some of the finishing touches, which should help to reassure her everything will be just fine. Great food, champagne, dancing and – hopefully – a glorious summer's day spent in the middle of the countryside is a recipe for success.'

'Well, I hope you both have a fun day. Before I go, did you say anything to your dad about your uncle?'

A sense of unease washes over me. What didn't I say? I was so upset I can't really remember.

'Probably. Why?'

'He rang Alistair and invited him and your Auntie Marge over for a chat tonight. It's probably to make his peace over the situation with Alice and Tom, who aren't due back until gone ten. I'm cooking a special supper, which should hopefully help to ease the tension. Let's hope Eddie and Alistair can keep their cool and talk things through calmly.'

I pucker up my face. 'Good luck with that.'

'Thanks. Wanting to make up is one thing, being man enough to do it civilly, respecting the other person's viewpoint is another.' She rolls her eyes as she stands.

'Something tells me that with you and Auntie Marge there they'll behave themselves.'

She laughs. 'There's a time to be supportive and a time to speak up. I think Marge and I will find we have a lot in common. Anyway, say "hi" to Tegan from me and I hope things go well today. Those two deserve to have a lovely party with no hiccoughs.'

'Thirteen days to go until the big day!' I bustle through the front door of The Forge, cradling a large black bin liner in my arms. 'I raided the beach and even braved jumping over the stream at the back of the house to fill this sack,' I inform her.

Tegan beams back at me. 'Ooh, thank you, Kerra. Let me take that.'

Grateful to have a hand free, I turn to shut the door and slip off my walking boots. The banks of the stream were a little muddy in places, but I think Tegan will be pleased with what I managed to forage.

'I've spent every single evening for this last week candle making,' she calls over her shoulder as I follow her through to the kitchen.

'No Sy?'

She pauses. 'No… um… he… he's um… running a few errands. He won't be back until late this evening, so we have the place to ourselves.'

Which probably means that he didn't want to get in our way. Which is fair enough. The kitchen table has been covered with an old sheet and there must be thirty tall pillar candles lined-up and a stack of offcuts of wood. Alongside are some old cloths and a pile of pre-cut greaseproof paper.

'Right, where do we start?'

I slip off my white cotton shirt and place it on the back of one of the chairs. I've come wearing an old t-shirt and prepared to get messy.

Tegan picks up a stack of wrinkly photocopying paper from the dresser and carries it across to the table.

'What have we got here?'

'I picked these leaves about ten days ago and they've been under a stack of heavy books ever since. They should be dried enough to use. I just hope they don't adhere to the paper. Can you start separating them while I grab some spoons and a couple of jugs of hot water?'

I'm intrigued.

'It's a bit fiddly, I hope I don't break any of them,' I warn her, as I ease back the top sheet. After a bit of gentle persuasion, four beautifully dried little clusters of leaves are exposed. 'These look good. We might need a craft knife to tease them off.'

'There's a box on the seat of one of the chairs. Help yourself.'

Tegan seems to know what she's doing and when she sits down, she does a demonstration.

'Right. Lay a candle down on one of the clean rags then choose some leaves. Place one on the wax and wrap a piece of the greaseproof paper over the top. Then you grab one of the spoons from the jug of hot water and hold the back of it against the leaf for about ten seconds. The aim is to melt the wax just enough to anchor the greenery, so you need to keep replacing the spoon for a hot one and move onto the next part of the leaf. The test is when you peel off the greaseproof paper.'

I watch in awe, and it only takes a few minutes to complete the process. The effect is simply lovely.

'That's gorgeous, Tegan. What a great idea.'

'My mum cut out an article for me on how to make candles from natural soya wax. I bought this special fragrance called white grapefruit. It's grapefruit, pineapple, apple wood and orange blossom. But I want to make the table decorations feel bountiful, you know – lots of greenery and twigs. I thought about your suggestion not to go overboard on the flowers. We can add some colour on the day.'

'Clever you. I think you'll be pleased with what I managed to collect.'

It's fiddly, but great fun and in between we drink coffee, reminisce about old times and get creative with our designs.

'Sy is dreading coming face to face with his father again, but at least his family will be there and that means something. My lot, well, it's going surprisingly well. There's only so long you can hold a grudge, isn't there?'

I burst out laughing. 'That's very true. Dad and I have made up.'

Tegan's jaw drops.

'That's not a good look on you.' I giggle, and she quickly closes her mouth. .

'I'm so glad to hear that, Kerra. We're all gutted for Ross.' She furrows her brow, rooting around in the box to pull out a metal spike on a disc. 'Sy thinks he should go with his gut instincts and forget about what people expect him to do next.' The minute she finishes speaking she looks at me in horror.

'You've seen him?'

'Um… no. Um. Oh dear…'

My eyes don't move from her face.

'I haven't seen him, but Sy has. Gawen, Sy and Ross are up at Treeve Perran today picking elderflowers to make a cordial for the party. I wasn't supposed to say anything. You won't go chasing up there, will you?'

I let out an exasperated sigh. 'I already know where he is, I just don't know what he's going through.'

'Oh, don't feel down. Sy joined them for a drink last night at the farm and that's when they enlisted his help for today. He said Ross is full of guilt.'

'Guilt?'

'Yes. Sy said it was sad to see him being so hard on himself.'

'It's not like he's on his own in this, Tegan,' I reply. 'If only he'd talk to me, together we'd figure out what to do next. We're in a good position, it's not like he needs to borrow money to start over again.'

A worried look flashes over her face.

'What? Sy said something, didn't he?'

'The only thing he knows for sure is that Ross doesn't want to work in the building trade any more. I think that's the problem, Kerra. He wants to do something completely different, but Ross isn't really a risk-taker, is he?'

'No, he isn't.'

'Just be happy knowing that he's safe and in good company. And he's promised Sy that he'll be at the party.'

The depressing thought is what if Ross doesn't come home before then? That's a long time to be apart, not knowing what's running through his mind.

'Before we start gluing the spikes to the bases and assembling the table decorations, I think we deserve a glass of wine, don't you?' Tegan checks, her voice unnaturally bright and breezy as I nod my head.

I don't know about *deserve*, but I certainly need one.

It's just gone six when we hear the front door opening and Sy calls out.

'It's only me. I brought takeaway. I hope you ladies are in the mood for crispy duck and pancakes,' he calls out.

Tegan raises her eyebrows. She wasn't expecting him back until much later.

'We're just about to pack up,' she replies as he comes bustling in.

He pops the carrier bag next to the hob and comes over to kiss Tegan, then gives me a hug and a peck on the cheek. 'It's good to see you, Kerra. And look at this – you've been hard at it.'

Judging by the note of approval in his voice we've done a

good job. The candles are now firmly fixed to their various bases, and each has a unique look. Some are surrounded by twigs, others with dried seed pods and pinecones I gathered this morning. The two large pieces of wood make up the centrepiece for the buffet table. With some weathered driftwood gracing a line of four candles, it won't take much on the day to add some fresh, vibrant greenery and Tegan has ordered a large delivery of white hydrangeas and stems of eucalyptus to arrive on the day.

Anyone can buy table decorations off the shelf, but these involved getting hands-on and it's the small touches like this that will make the day more meaningful. 'I think it's going to look lovely once we add the final embellishments,' I remark.

'It's just as well because everyone has RSVP'd. They're all coming. Let's just hope the only fireworks going off are the ones Gawen will be lighting up at the end of the day.'

What can possibly go wrong? Two families meeting up for the first time. One has only just healed a big rift and the other hasn't seen their son for a couple of years. Tegan grabs the carrier bag and begins to decant the contents onto a tray.

'We'd better eat this in the sitting room. We can carry that lot upstairs a bit later, just in case the glue isn't fully set. Was, um, everything all right up at the farm?' Tegan enquires.

Sy's face instantly colours up, bless him. 'Fine. Good. Right... I'm starving, let's eat. I'll grab some plates and cutlery.'

When Sy reports back to Ross later, I wonder what he'll say; that it's obvious I'm not my usual bubbly self, or the fact that I used Ripley as an excuse and left early? It seems like it's going to be just the two of us for a while, as Ross digs deep to discover what will make him truly happy. I can only hope that Ripley and I are an integral part of that.

# 21

## Teamwork

'This is a great workspace you have here, Kerra.' Tom remarks. Wally and Oliver follow close on his heels as they step through the opened doors to my garden office. It's a bright and sunny Monday morning and it feels like a good omen.

I've pushed both desks back against one wall to accommodate four of the patio chairs so that we can sit around in a circle quite comfortably.

'It's great to be able to open up the glass doors,' Oliver joins in. 'All the benefits of being in the shade and having everything you need to hand while enjoying the fresh air.'

Wally is quiet, but we exchange friendly smiles. He's nervous about today but there's absolutely no need for that. He's among friends.

'Did Treloar's build the extensions on both cottages, too?' Oliver enquires.

'They did.'

'Well, they made a beautiful job of it. It's a great blend of the old and the new. If you ever want to sell up you know where to come.' Oliver gives me a cheeky grin.

'It's been in my family for three generations, so I won't be going anywhere. Anyway, let's go through the final version of the plans in preparation for your meeting with the planning officer.'

'Thanks for all your hard work, Kerra, in getting it to this stage,' Tom replies. 'I'm nervous, but with Oliver there I'm sure he'll jump in if I run out of steam or get stuck.'

'We're going to be just fine,' Oliver reassures him.

I'm concerned at how quiet Wally is because he's Tom's partner and a big part of this going forward. I hope I'll find a way to get him talking.

'Oliver, I sent you Tom's final version of the business plan in case you were able to spot anything we missed. If you find any mistakes just drop me an email and I'll get it updated and forward everyone the final version.'

'Will do. I have everything ready to go at my end and signed off by head office. It's just a case now of getting this meeting with the council out of the way to see if there's anything we need to tweak. Then Tom and Wally can submit the formal application. Hopefully by the end of August we'll be able to get things rolling.'

'Right. Let's run through Tom and Wally's master plan then. Tom, do you want to take the lead?'

He passes each of us a document folder. 'Thanks for printing them out, Kerra. I'll be getting my new kit for the office soon and it'll make things a lot easier. If we look at the revised site plan the new structure to house the forge will be moved to the far end. The whole area at the front will be tarmacked and just inside the gate there will be a dozen car parking spaces on the left. Dad, could you talk us through the set up for the new History of Penvennan Cove Centre?'

Wally shifts in his seat, but I give him an encouraging nod.

'Now then, let me see... um... okay. Visitors will be directed to the smart new building, maybe not quite as posh as this one, Kerra, but it's gonna be big. There'll be various displays, hopefully a few volunteers as well as me to regale them with stories of the past. We'll organise the walking tours from there, too. Then they can head over to The Salvager's Retreat, as we're now calling the old industrial unit. The bare bones of it are sound and we'll be cladding it with some new facia board to smarten it up. We've already cleared out most of the stuff in there that needs dumping. It'll give us plenty of room to display the interesting old relics that still tell a story. And the kids will be able to get up close to the exhibits so we can show them how things work.'

'That's great news, Wally. It's a brilliant idea moving the forge,' I comment. 'That's another skill that is fascinating to watch. Obviously, a lot of people will be walk-ins, but do you think twelve parking spaces will be enough?'

Tom takes over. 'We've decided to go with pre-booked tours only and will be limiting it to a head count of thirty for each tour. Maybe a few more if it's a school party.'

'That sounds very reasonable to me as it's family-orientated.'

Oliver joins in. 'Don't forget that there will be three additional designated spaces alongside the estate agency office. One for the member of staff and two for visitors.

We think it's enough to satisfy the local authority. Oh, Tom – have you mentioned our little bit of good news to Kerra, which should help to keep the locals happy in the interim?'

Tom's face brightens as I look at him expectantly.

'Ahead of planning approval, we're getting a new sign courtesy of Property Professionals UK and we'll be adding their logo to it as a bit of advertising. And that ain't all. They've stumped up fifteen thousand pounds in total, which Dad and I reckon will allow us to replace the dilapidated fencing panels with feather board. The stone walls and pillars are sound and just need a jet wash, so in less than a month it could all be looking neat and tidy if we keep the old gates shut. Once we get to that stage, I'll be designing some special ones incorporating a sea-related theme.'

I look at Oliver as I break out into a huge beaming smile. 'You are a miracle worker. Seriously, Oliver, you have no idea how the timing of this is going to be instrumental in getting the locals on our side.' When I confided in Oliver about the grumblings at Sam's meeting, it was really just to forewarn him. I had no idea he'd go away and come up with a perfect solution for the donation that no one will challenge.

'It's just a goodwill gesture, Kerra, and you know that the company I work for is keen to do something meaningful. Nothing is guaranteed until we've gone through the planning process, but it's looking good on paper. Actually, I'm really excited and rather proud to be involved with this project.'

'Dad and I will be ordering that wood and getting it up as quickly as we can,' Tom confirms.

A thought jumps into my head. 'You know, Tom, if you

want a little help why not mention what you're doing to Zacky and Jared?'

Wally rubs his chin, his brain whirling. 'Now there's a thought. And they're both ex-fishermen.'

He turns to look at Tom, who immediately raises his eyebrows. 'Well, those two like telling their stories about life on a trawler, don't they? Maybe Kerra's on to something there.'

That moment of satisfaction when you make a purposeful, but throwaway comment and someone picks up on it and can immediately see the opportunity is so satisfying. My job is done. This team of three are more than capable of making this happen.

'Oh, it was just a thought,' I reply breezily. 'Anyway, um… would anyone like a cup of coffee? And I have some of Mrs Moyle's saffron buns to go with it.'

I love it when a plan comes together, and I know it's almost time for me to step back.

Since Ross left I've been taking extended lunch breaks. Ripley just isn't settling, and I feel guilty. She won't join me down in the office. It's as if she's expecting him to return at any minute and is keeping watch. I even jumped online and bought a cat-calming plugin. It's not quite the purpose it's designed for, but I figured it might help a little. After I've eaten – well… toyed with my food – we snuggle on the sofa. She loves to curl up on my lap now, whereas before Ross was the one who got the most cuddles.

I've taken to looking through some of Ross's books while she catnaps, as once she's asleep I don't have the heart to disturb her. I don't read the books, but glance through the pages. I'm trying to understand what makes him tick and it's quite telling. None of the books are about the building industry, although a few of them are what I call coffee table books featuring innovative architectural design. There are a few local history and geography books, but the rest are mostly cookery books and, I'm discovering, lots of gardening books. Every day I water what I call Ross's windowsill herb garden and the kitchen garden he planted not that long ago. Everything is suddenly looking abundant because he isn't here to harvest anything. I've told Dad to help himself rather than waste the results of Ross's hard work. I don't have the know-how to turn a few simple ingredients into a taste explosion. Sadly, for me eating has become a necessary chore.

As I'm wondering why a book on soil management induced Ross to pay twenty-three pounds and ninety-nine pence to purchase it, the doorbell rings.

Ripley opens one eye. 'Sorry, Rippers. I'm going to have to lift you off my lap.'

When I swing open the door Alice is standing there.

'Hi, Alice, how are you?'

'You aren't working, are you?' she asks, tentatively.

'No. Just relaxing after lunch. Come on in.'

It's been a while since I bumped into Alice, and I can't believe the change. Not just in her physical appearance, although she's wearing hardly any make-up. She's such a pretty girl she doesn't really need it anyway. But in general, she looks content.

'I've been meaning to call in, but I didn't want to upset Uncle Eddie. I hoped you'd understand that. It's not that

I wasn't worried about you, but I know Nettie has been keeping in touch. It's just that Uncle Eddie has been so good to me and Ian.'

I can see she means what she says. 'Of course, Alice. Have you got time to sit and chat, or are you rushing back to work at the salon?'

'I have a few days off. Polly is giving me some training this afternoon and I'm going to be helping Ian on his next job.'

'Doing what?'

'Painting, of course.'

I glance at Alice's nails and am shocked to see they look natural. She's always worn acrylic nails and I've often envied how elegant they make her hands look. For me, bashing away at a keyboard all day, it just wouldn't be practical.

'Ian talked her into it. I think together we'd make a great team and it's kind of Polly to let me have a go. Ian will be watching me like a hawk because he's such a perfectionist, but I'm looking forward to it. Anyway, I can't stay long, but I wanted to thank you for whatever you said to Uncle Eddie.'

Now I'm at a loss. 'About what?'

'Well, I'm assuming it was you. Nettie and Uncle Eddie invited Mum and Dad to Green Acre for supper. Ian and I made ourselves scarce when Nettie dropped the hint. In fairness, Ian was going to work late anyway on this empty property he was finishing off and I went with him. He had me masking up walls, as Polly wanted a few pops of colour.'

'Ah, yes, Nettie did mention something about that. Did it go okay?'

'Dad texted me this morning and Ian and I going over to have Sunday lunch with them this weekend.'

'That's amazing, Alice! I'm so delighted to hear that.'

She looks at me, smiling. 'I know… it's hard to believe, isn't it? Especially given the news about Fraser. We both know how close you are with Sissy and wondered whether you might be upset about—'

'All of that is nothing at all to do with Ian. Polly is always singing his praises and I'm delighted to see how well the two of you are getting on.'

Alice chews her lip, a habit she's had since childhood. 'Nettie and Uncle Eddie had an invite to Tegan and Sy's party. Ian wondered if we didn't get one because of his family.'

Awkward!

'I haven't heard anyone talk badly of Ian.'

'Oh… so this is about Trev and me. I knew it!' Her cheeks immediately colour up.

'He's finally made his peace with Tegan and one day he'll make his peace with you, Alice.'

She accepts that with good grace. There was a time when Alice would have responded very differently indeed. She was fiery when she was younger, but aren't we all? She never lied, she just repeated something she was told and had no reason to believe it wasn't the truth. Now she has experienced some of life's hard knocks herself, she understands what it's like to be on the receiving end.

'I appreciate you being honest with me, Kerra. I don't want Ian to think it's his fault and now I can tell him that it isn't. I hope Sy and Tegan have a wonderful day, and I wouldn't want to spoil it for them.'

'Ian and you have a lot of support, Alice. And now Dad is talking to Uncle Alistair they both have a reason to regret some of the things they've done in the past. Don't we all?'

She looks down at her hands, an ironic smile tweaking at her lips.

'I know. And I just wanted to say that Ian and I are grateful to you, Kerra. Polly has been a lifesaver taking Ian on. Even if she only allows me to help him out from time to time, it means a lot to us as the salon have cut my hours. We're hoping to rent a little place of our own soon.'

That's a bit of a shock. What will Dad do when they move out? I wonder. I hope it doesn't put pressure on Nettie to spend more time working at the kennels, time she doesn't have. My mind begins to tick over. Dad is going to need some help, but off the top of my head I can't think of anyone local who would be ready to step in to fill the void.

As I give Alice an affectionate hug goodbye, it seems that the moment one problem is resolved another one raises its head. Dad will be back to square one and he'll struggle if Ian and Alice do end up moving out of Green Acre.

The sound of my phone pinging wakes me from an unsettling dream. I rub my eyes, glad to snap out of it. A glance at the bedside clock reveals it's just after two in the morning and the noise has stirred Ripley.

*Miaow, miaoooooow*, she wails, clearly not happy.

'Shush,' I croon, 'settle down.'

When I see it's a message from Ross, I'm not sure what to do.

*Are you awake? I wanted to check that you're okay. x*

I need to hear his voice so badly that I instinctively press the call button. Ripley eases herself upright to have a stretch and I smooth her as she comes to headbutt me, it's what she does when she's in need of comfort.

'Yes, I'm… fine. You?'

'I can't sleep. Did I wake you?'

'I wasn't having a very nice dream, so you did me a favour.'

He sounds tired. It's stressful when your mind refuses to switch off and all you seem to do is drift in and out of a light, troubled sleep that isn't restful at all.

'I'm staying over at Treeve Perran Farm.'

'I know.'

There's a brief pause. 'I didn't mean to worry you, Kerra. Switching off my phone was a silly thing to do, but I just…' He tails off, his voice deadpan.

'You need time to think. I get that, Ross. But I don't know why you can't do that here with me. Pedrevan is our home, it's supposed to be the place you can shut out the world. Somewhere you feel safe, knowing that Ripley and I are here for you. I don't understand why you just up and left like that.'

'I don't want to hurt you, Kerra.'

'Then come home.'

'I can't, not until I'm able to stand in front of you with a clear picture of what I think the future will hold. I want you, and I miss you and Ripley more than you can know, but I'm a… I'm a mess. When Gawen and I were at The

Lark and Lantern that night, a steady stream of people came up to wish me well. Most said how disgusted they were about what happened. Everyone thinks I'm going to set up in business and, as Jared put it "get yer own back". Do I really want to leave one battle and start a new one?'

It's tough hearing how defeated he sounds. 'Don't let people wind you up, Ross. Anyone with your best interests at heart wouldn't say something like that. I certainly wouldn't. All I want is for you to be happy.'

The silence as Ross considers my words is poignant. His mind is usually crystal clear and now he's struggling. It does help a little to understand why he left so suddenly. On the other hand, it crushes me to think that he was lying next to me in the early hours of that morning going over and over things that were said to him at the pub. No wonder he took himself off to Treeve Perran; Gawen and Yvonne helped him through his divorce and now they're helping him through another life-changing event. But that's what hurts the most. It should be me he's turning to now.

'I'm leaving you alone Ross,' I continue, 'because that's what you want from me right now. But it isn't easy.'

*Miaow, miaow*. Ripley is unsettled, desperate to nestle up close to me but I think she can hear Ross's voice and she keeps readjusting her position.

'I'm no good to you like this. I'll end up saying what you want to hear just to fill the gaping hole in my life, but that isn't the answer.' Ross is angry with himself, not Jago as I would expect.

'If I wait... when will you be ready?'

He groans. 'I don't know. Soon, hopefully.'

'You will be at Sy and Tegan's party... won't you? They're expecting you to be there.'

The pause this time seems to go on and on.

'It wouldn't be fair to spoil their day of celebration if I'm still in this frame of mind. I don't know... I might make myself absent if I'm not in a good place.'

'But do you think you'll be ready to talk to me by then?'

'Maybe.'

'I love you, Ross. Whatever you decide is fine by me – you know that, don't you? I can't even imagine a future without you by my side.'

The guttural sound I hear escaping from his lips reminds me of Ripley when she limped home once with a bad paw. I think she'd been in a fight. She was traumatised, in shock and hurting. She hid under the bed for twenty-four hours before I could tempt her out. She wouldn't eat and all she did was take a little water from a bowl I put next to her. The noise she made sounded equally as heart-wrenching. Like a soft moaning sound.

'I messed up, Kerra. Now I can't seem to get my act together. What if this isn't just a temporary state? What if—'

This is too painful to bear. 'Just know that I'm here whenever you're ready to talk, Ross. I'm not expecting everything to be the same from this point onwards. Life is going to be different. But I'm in limbo until you come back to me. My fear is that you underestimate how much I'm prepared to give up just to be with you.'

Another yawning silence that tears at my heart.

'My dream is gone, Kerra. There are moments when I hate myself for falling into my father's trap. What does that say about me, other than I'm easily fooled? And does that mean I could talk myself into doing something and end up losing everything? Where would that leave us?'

A solitary tear tracks its way down my cheek. 'It would leave me still longing to be with you, convinced that eventually we'd find a future together that was right for us both.'

*Miaow, miaow, miaooooow.* I reach out to comfort Ripley, but she isn't in the mood to settle down.

'Sort out our girl. I just wanted you to know I'm thinking of you day and night, Kerra. If you need me my phone will be on but I won't ring until I have something to say. I love you, always did and always will.'

The sound when he hits the end call button makes me burst into tears. 'Oh Ripley,' I moan, scooping her up into my arms. 'I don't know what I can do to bring Ross back to us. Doing nothing feels like I'm giving up, but if I press him before he's ready I think he'll crumble.'

## 22

### A Reality Check

'Morning, Kerra, how are you doing?'

'I'm hanging in there, Nettie. Is everything okay at your end?' I hold the phone tighter to my ear, tempted to cross my fingers. It's unusual for her to call and not just pop in.

'All's good but we have a little problem. I have a deadline to get this manuscript off today and I'm still tinkering with it. I'm supposed to be driving over to Green Acre to do the lunchtime dog walking with your dad. Usually, it wouldn't be a problem as Ian would step in, but he and Alice are working on a job for Polly today.'

'Ah, Alice called in to see me and mentioned Polly was going to give her a trial. I can certainly head over to give Dad a hand a bit later. I'm not in the mood to work this morning as I had a restless night. In fact, I'm popping in to give Felicity a bit of a break as Drew has been hard at work in the garden office since early this morning.'

'If you're sure it's not putting you out, that would be

amazing. I could ask for a day's extension, but I pride myself on always delivering on time. I think it looks bad, otherwise.'

'It's fine, really. And in a way a nice chance to have a natter with Dad. I was shocked there were only three dogs in the other day. Is business quiet?'

'No. He's purposely limiting the number of bookings he's taking at the moment so Ian can work full days for Polly as she has a rush job on. Plus, Alice has taken this week as leave to be Ian's assistant.' She chuckles. 'He bought her a pair of white painter's overalls. Honestly, those two were definitely made for each other. He really boosts her confidence.'

Ah, that's lovely to hear.

'I've noticed some huge changes in Alice since I've been back. I'm glad she's found someone like Ian. He's very considerate. Anyway, you'd best get back to work and I'm off to cuddle baby Ethan. I hope he's not asleep!'

Nettie laughs. 'Don't say that within earshot of Drew or Felicity, I suspect the quiet moments are like gold dust right now. Have a fun walk with your dad. There are six canines in today and one of them is Rufus. He'll be so happy to see you, Kerra. Enjoy your time with the baby.'

'You have no idea how good this feels,' Felicity declares. She flops back onto the sofa as I rock Ethan gently in my arms. Felicity is in her dressing gown, her hair up in a towel as she sports a mud face pack. 'That was the most decadent bath ever… and I mean *ever*!'

'Well, this little one certainly likes movement, doesn't he?'

'He does. Poor Arthur opposite must wonder what's

going on. One of us has to jump in the car at least half a dozen times a day to do a trip around the block to get Ethan off to sleep. It does the trick though, so it's worth it.'

'Do you feel you have some sort of routine now?' I ask, genuinely interested.

'At first Ethan had anywhere from six to eight feeds a day, which was exhausting. He'd just take his time and then fall asleep. Now he seems to have the hang of it, or maybe I'm more relaxed and it's down to four now. That really helps, because I feed him just before bedtime and he's starting to sleep through until about two or three in the morning.'

Ethan's eyes have been shut for a little while, his dark lashes stark against his cheeks. I gently lower him down into the rocking crib in the sitting area, covering his bare little legs with a tiny cotton sheet.

'Mm… this face pack is beginning to tighten,' Felicity mumbles, trying hard not to move her face muscles too much and crack it. 'Thanks so much for letting Drew use your office. It gives him a break and that's important. He kept everything pristine and now he's getting used to a little baby clutter, but he really does need to push that loft conversion.'

It's difficult as I know why he's dragging his feet.

'We were talking about this earlier this morning. I told Drew to go ahead with submitting the plans for both cottages. I can't bother Ross with it, but the problem is which builder to use.'

Felicity puts up her hand, pointing to her face and rushes upstairs. While I wait for her to return, I wander over to look out onto Tigry Cottage's garden. It's not as big as my plot next door, as the bottom right-hand corner slopes off at a sharp angle. Over a third of the entire area is taken up with Drew's precious vegetable garden and a shed. The rest is made up of a tidy little lawn, some flowering borders and the large deck that mirrors mine. Tucked away in a little island of shrubs is Bertie's kennel. Drew said he's spending more time in there now that the weather is so mild. He said that Bertie finds Ethan's crying rather stressful and I had the distinct impression that it still panics Drew a little at times, too.

'Right, I'm back and I'm invigorated!' Felicity flounces into the room dressed in a pair of leggings and a baggy t-shirt. Her damp hair is pinned up on top of her head and her face is pink, her skin glowing. 'Right… where were we? Oh, yes. I hadn't thought about that. Naturally we can't use Treloar's Building Limited. And it must be weird for Ross having nothing to do with a company that still bears his family name. Oh gosh, no wonder he needs time to think.'

I'm guessing that Felicity knows he's at Treeve Perran. 'I said I don't really care who does the job. Ross wouldn't want Drew holding back when it's so important for you guys.'

'If they do a good job of soundproofing it, we'll get a day bed to go in the study. I was thinking Drew and I could take turns using it to catch up on a little sleep if we need it.'

Felicity pops the kettle on and we sit at the breakfast bar.

'You're adjusting really well,' I remark.

'To be honest I can't really remember what it was like before Ethan. He consumes every second of my time when he's not sleeping. When he is asleep, I'm catching up on the mountain of washing, ironing and tidying up, but I can't imagine life without him. Drew now does a lot of the endless walking up and down and winding Ethan. This phase won't last forever.'

And then, in that split second, I understand exactly what Felicity is talking about. That's how I feel about the situation between me and Ross. It won't last forever, but he can't see past it. When he does, I'll know he's turned the corner.

'That's not to say I don't have moments of sheer panic, or when I'm so tired I pass Ethan over to Drew and say, "I'm off to bed, it's your turn". I'm scared I'll fall asleep with Ethan in my arms and end up dropping him!'

And if Ross and I were to have a baby, we'd get through it just as Felicity and Drew are doing. 'Ethan is certainly gaining weight. He looks a lot more robust now and I feel more confident picking him up, but doesn't it make your back ache after a while?' The kettle clicks off. 'You sit and relax; I'll make some tea.'

Felicity points me in the direction of the right cupboards to open, and I envy the general vibe of contentment radiating from her.

'It is a constant physical strain just because Ethan only wants to go in his crib when he's literally tired out. Other than that, we do a lot of pacing back and forth, but that's mainly down to the fact he suffers from colic. The health visitor said that should start to ease soon. I've already been to the chiropractor in Polreweek once. But I'm determined that we should enjoy this time. The prenatal class I attended was mostly mums for the second time around and they all said the same thing.'

As I carry the tray across to the breakfast bar, I try to second-guess what that was.

'Grab whatever sleep you can?'

Felicity does a belly laugh this time. 'No, they all accepted it's a given that sleep is a luxury. Expect to nod off while singing nursery rhymes or reading a bedtime story, as that's the new normal. What they said was wait until you get to the terrible twos. Lifting a heavy child off the floor in the middle of a supermarket really does your back in. All those times you looked scornfully at a parent out in public with what you assumed was a problem child, will come back to haunt you. Even the most angelic child will have meltdowns at the most inconvenient of moments. But they do, eventually, grow of it.'

I raise my eyebrows, pulling a face. 'Thank goodness for that.'

She smiles at me, shaking her head. 'It's only the start of a very long, but incredibly rewarding journey. We have the "why?" stage to come, apparently, which is totally draining. And the stamping of feet with the "no, I won't!" phase. Then there's…' She draws to a halt as Ethan starts to wail.

When Felicity returns, she looks down lovingly at the little bundle in her arms. 'But isn't he gorgeous? I even see his face in my dreams when I fall asleep.'

Oh, I wish I had my phone with me as I'd take a picture. That look on Felicity's face says it all. And that's why despite the pain, the worry, and the lack of sleep so many mothers are willing to go through it more than once.

Any fears I had of being put off are beginning to fade… quicker than I'd like. The only person I could see myself making this sort of commitment with is Ross and now the last thing on his mind is a marriage proposal and having a family.

*

'Rufus, you are one crazy red setter, but I've missed you!' I say affectionately, as I ruffle his ears and unhook his lead.

He knows these woods as if they're his second home, and he never strays very far. The other three dogs I'm juggling are all small, two terriers and a beagle named Barker, who doesn't seem to bark much at all. We're standing in the woods at the bottom of the cliff and above us the house that Ross built, Treylya, stands proud.

'Does Ross have any regrets selling it to Jago?' Dad asks, as he gazes upwards.

'No. It represents a time in his life he wants to forget. Even in that transaction his father used underhanded tactics. But Ross sussed out what was happening, and he ended up making a reasonable profit on it.'

That evokes a wry smile. 'That's good to hear. Any father who puts money before his kids is a disgrace in my book,' Dad states, adamantly.

Rufus comes bounding back, almost pushing me over in his enthusiasm to get me to throw something for him. I put all three of the other leads into one hand and pick up a stick. Off he goes in hot pursuit.

Dad's canine charges are trying to pull him in two different directions. I took charge of the small dogs and he's dealing with an energetic labrador retriever, and a powerful boxer dog who is a softie, but constantly yanks on the lead. He steers them over to a stout oak tree. They'll sniff around the base quite happily while he lets out their leads so they can roam a little.

Rufus is already back with his stick. He drops it at my feet, and I throw it again.

'Are you coping all right?' Dad enquires, tentatively.

'Now I know that Ross is with friends, it's easier to bear. But Ripley is lost without Ross and it's the same for me. I'm just going through the motions and life doesn't feel real anymore.'

He heaves a heavy sigh. 'I'm sorry to hear you say that Kerra. I'm proud of the way you get things done – you know, putting people together and the like. It's a way of making things happen. I had a pint with Wally Hooper the other night. He was singing your praises. Him and his wife knew they didn't have enough money to bail Tom out, but they had enough to put in to motivate Tom to do something. Tom and Georgia, like Sam, couldn't imagine living anywhere else but here and word is that his parents will be joining them. Nothing stays the same forever. However, safeguarding the future takes courage and action.'

That's quite telling coming from Dad.

'Some people think I'm interfering, others think I'm trying to bring in outsiders. I don't think it will be long before Oliver Sinclair settles here. We need people like him and Drew. They'll always be emmets, but they aren't just here to profit.'

'I hear what you're saying, Kerra. Some of the things you've done have created a stir, that's for sure. See, when everything has ticked over for a very long time, people don't notice the decay and the way things don't quite operate as they should. Like Sam always being short-handed behind the bar. And Tom's eyesore, getting worse by the day. They fear change and, if truth be told, I'm no different. I get up each day and keep going, it's what we do.'

Two of the dogs I'm walking have tangled their leads and I head over to Dad so he can help me sort it out. With three dog leads in one hand, I'm not prepared when Rufus gallops towards me from behind, knocking me down onto my knees. I accidentally drop one of the leads and a little Scottie dog named Bettie-Boo hares off into the woods.

'Grab these!' I yell to Dad. Seconds later I'm chasing her up the steep incline to the rear entrance of Treylya.

Considering she has such little legs she doesn't hang around. It doesn't take that long before I'm within a few feet of her trailing lead and I take a flying leap, landing on what I thought was a pile of old leaves, but they were simply floating on a muddy puddle. Splosh! Mud flies everywhere, covering Bettie-Boo's off-white coat, my hair and the front of my pale blue cotton shirt. Yuk!

'Got her,' I call out, as I stoop to pick her up. I'm muddy anyway and she's looking bewildered.

Dad's face when we appear between the trees is a picture and he bursts out laughing.

'I remember when you invited Sy here to give me a hand at the kennels. If he so much as got a tiny speck of mud on his wellie boots he was horrified. I never thought you'd entice him here for good, but you did.'

'No, Dad. He stayed for Tegan, not me. And now he's fitted in, hasn't he?'

'Yes. He has.'

'People like Drew, Felicity and Oliver, they see how a small community works and have decided it's the life for them. I was born here, and I took it for granted and couldn't wait to get away. I came back and for the very same reasons. People do care about each other, and the pace of life is different. Okay, some people also talk behind your back because anything new, or different is unsettling. I get that. But Arthur isn't a Cornishman, and yet he is the local support hub. It's time people started embracing change if it means Penvennan Cove will continue to thrive.'

As we sort out our little and not so little charges, Dad grins at me.

'You need a shower and I need to give Bettie-Boo a doggy bath. She's looking mightily sorry for herself. And thanks for coming to save me doubling up me walks today. It's quiet without Nettie and Ian around. And I still can't believe Alice is rolling up her sleeves and wielding a paint brush today.'

'Me neither, but that's what loves does for you, isn't it?' I give him a pointed look.

'What you're hinting at is that Nettie's running late with her deadline because I've been commandeering her time.' It's not a question, it's a statement.

I wasn't going to say anything and yet, here I am on our first real chance to talk in a relaxed manner, sticking my oar in. But it's the truth.

'She's waited a long time to do her own thing. If you need help just let me know. I can break off for a walk any time of the day. For me it's a welcome bit of exercise.'

A group of walkers are heading towards us and as we stop to let them pass, they all smile, wishing us a good afternoon. As they walk on, I hear someone giggling.

'I don't look that bad Dad, do I?' I ask and he chuckles.

'You look just fine, lovely. A bit of mud is good for you.'

It certainly worked a treat for Felicity this morning as her skin looked radiant afterwards. Maybe it will add a bit of a shine to my hair, who knows? But I really don't care and I guess it's because I'll always be a country girl at heart.

# 23

## Pulling Together

As Drew pulls into the car park at Treeve Perran, he glances across at me. It's obvious that I'm on edge.

'Hey, relax, Kerra. It's a big day for Sy and Tegan. Just focus on that.'

I draw in a deep breath, but my heart is pounding in my chest. Will Ross put in an appearance? I wonder. Or has he taken himself off, not ready to face the world, or even me?

'I know. I'm not going to ask the big question whether Ross is around. I don't want to make anyone feel uncomfortable, but my emotions are all over the place.'

'Then it's time to get them under control. If it becomes too much, just shout and I'll drop you back to Penvennan.'

The thought of letting Sy and Tegan down would be too much to bear. It's time to grit my teeth and plaster on a smile. It won't be the first time I've had to do that and it probably won't be the last.

As the engine dies Drew turns to look at me, placing a hand lightly on my shoulder.

'You can do it,' he reassures me. 'Right, let's go. Do you want to leave your things in the car and collect them later?'

'Yes. Tegan and I are going foraging first thing.'

'I said I'd give Gawen a hand setting up the rotisserie and the campfire. I'm heading back to Tigry Cottage later to change and collect Felicity and Ethan.'

As we walk over to the farmhouse Drew continues to natter away, but I'm only half-listening to him. My eyes are scanning around, hoping I'll spot Ross. If he's staying in one of the holiday cottages they're not visible from here, but I'm thinking it's more likely he's staying in the house.

'Morning, guys! You're both nice and early,' Sy calls out, hurrying over to us. He gives Drew a fist-pump and then throws his arms around me. He whispers in my ear, 'The coast is clear – for now, anyway.'

'You certainly picked a good day for it,' Drew remarks.

'Tegan ordered a blue sky and no rain. Nothing is going to spoil our day; we've waited far too long for this.' He calls out, 'Tegan, Kerra is here.' Leaning closer he gives me a grimace. 'She hardly slept a wink last night but she's raring to go. Tegan will feel a whole lot better once the barn is all trimmed up.'

I give him a nod. He's looking to me to be a calming influence when the reality is that my nerves are jangling. When Tegan appears a look of relief passes over her face, as she bustles towards us carrying several jute sacks and with a wicker basket dangling from her arm. 'It's great to see you both. I'm all prepared.' She grins at me.

Tegan stops to give Sy a quick kiss. 'We'll be gone a while. I can relax now Drew is here. Gawen is tied up in the kitchen for an hour or two, so at least one of you will know how to assemble a barbecue.' She chuckles, looking straight at Drew. 'Good luck.'

With that, Tegan and I set off. I put out my hand to take the basket from her. When we're out of earshot Tegan confides in me.

'Sy is better off not being in the kitchen. It's hectic in there as they have two extra people giving a hand and he'd only be in the way. There's more than enough outside work to keep Sy and Drew busy. It's a bit daunting, given that there's so much to do.'

The fact that Tegan hasn't mentioned Ross means he's not around. My spirits take a dive, but maybe it's for the best.

'Don't worry. It's surprising how quickly things will come together. We're better off taking back more than we need. I see you have six sacks, but I doubt we'll be able to manage them all once they're full.'

'Oh, we're taking a detour first. Gawen says there are several wheelbarrows in the big shed. He said to take the plastic ones as they're lighter and the ground is a bit uneven.'

It doesn't take long before we're trundling across an expanse of pastureland, turning it into a race. Ahead of us is a swathe of trees and a mass of overgrown bushes, delineating the edge of the farm on its farthest side.

'This is called "no-man's land", Gawen told me. It's where he and his neighbour come to gather mistletoe at Christmas.'

It's perfect, although glancing in the basket nestled up against the empty sacks in my wheelbarrow, all I can see are two pairs of secateurs and some protective gloves. But when we stop, on further investigation there's a folding hacksaw/ come knife that looks like it can do some serious damage.

'Right, let's grab what we need and as we fill the sacks we'll bring them back here, shall we?' Tegan suggests.

We don't really have a choice because the ground rises up evenly. Some of the trees are so large, the roots growing above the ground are a tripping hazard.

'Those laurel bushes could do with a haircut,' I point out. 'If we lop off some large branches that will give us a lot of greenery to play with.'

We don gloves and Tegan is keen to get out the hacksaw. Her first attempt at sawing isn't very successful. 'The branch keeps wobbling and I can't keep it in the same groove,' she complains.

'Here, I'll hold the branch steady, and you saw.'

Before long we have a huge pile of greenery and in all honesty the bushes look a lot better for it. But they're too big to put into the sacks and we carry them over to fill one of the wheelbarrows.

'I'll pop these back. They'll be better off in the shade of the barn. On the next trip I'm hoping that we can manage to take three sacks each.'

'Shall I start cutting some long stems of ivy?'

'Good idea. I'll be back in a bit.' Tegan is in her stride now we're actually doing something.

Slipping a pair of secateurs into my back pocket, I head further into the forest-like area, where the ground is literally covered with ivy. Some is a luscious dark green, but there is also a lighter green variety and a huge mass attached to an old stone wall with a golden yellow centre to each leaf. I'm so busy yanking up a large tendril, which seems to have rooted itself to the ground every few feet, that I'm in a world of my own. Suddenly, there's a movement and I turn my head sharply. It can't be Tegan as she's only been gone a couple of minutes.

Ross steps into view.

'I didn't mean to startle you. I saw Tegan trundling a wheelbarrow back in the direction of the barn.'

He walks towards me and suddenly I'm in his arms as I drop everything. Ross starts to kiss me hungrily, moving his hands up to hold my face as he pulls back to stare into my eyes.

'It's been hell without you,' he murmurs, as a solitary tear tracks its way down my cheek. He groans, wiping it away with his finger. 'I decided it was best if I leave everyone to it. But when I spotted you getting out of the car I knew I couldn't just go without telling you how sorry I am for letting you down.'

'You'll only be letting me down if you go, Ross. Please don't leave me here on my own.'

He smiles softly. 'You're among friends, good friends and later your dad and Nettie will be here. You're not alone; I'd never do that to you.'

'But without you nothing is the same. It will spoil the memory of today for us all.'

Ross's smile turns into a frown. He drops his hands down, taking a step back and looking undecisive. I don't want to make him feel guilty if it's not the right thing to do, but I think he'll regret leaving.

'People will ask questions, questions I can't answer right now. And if I could, you'd be the first one to know anyway.'

'So, tell them you're thinking through some different

options and you're here helping on the farm while you fathom it out. It's no one's business but yours, Ross. If you hide yourself away people will start to speculate. That's worse, isn't it?'

He reaches out to grab my hands in his. 'If you're okay with that, then I am, too. I don't want to make you feel awkward.'

'Sy and Tegan will be so disappointed if you're not here to be a part of it. After all, we were their witnesses on the big day and that means something.'

'You think I don't know that? I thought you wouldn't want me here… that you'd be angry with me.'

'Angry for what?'

'For needing some space. And now, well, the answer isn't quite what I was expecting. Look, Tegan will be back soon. The choice is yours. I'll stay, but only if you want me to.'

'Then stay. Head back and just get stuck in. They need help in the kitchen, I hear. And when you get a minute, seek me out and we'll act as if nothing is amiss. Everyone will take their lead from us.'

Ross gives me a heart-felt smile and as he turns I stop him, throwing my arms around his neck. Moulding myself up against him, my lips on his tell Ross just how much I need him here with me today.

'You always surprise me, Kerra. You make everything seem easy when we know it isn't. I'll catch up with you very shortly. Don't hang around here too long.' He grins at me. One final kiss and he strides off, leaving me with a glimmer of hope but an aching heart.

Tegan has obviously been waylaid, because by the time

she gets back I have a mountainous pile of ivy, some pieces are a good twelve-foot long.

'Oh, this is amazing, Kerra. Sorry for the delay, one of the farmhands asked me what sort of ladders we needed to put the greenery up. We can manage most of it with a tall pair of stepladders, but he's going to find another solution for the central beam. It's way too high for normal ladders. It would be wonderful to hang some sort of garland overhead.'

The gathering of greenery was supposed to take about an hour. I'm thinking now that it's going to take twice as long but my spirits are beginning to soar at the thought of spending some time with Ross and suddenly I'm full of energy.

'And I brought more sacks!' Tegan enthuses, her eyes gleaming.

I'd better get cutting and hope we can pile them high without losing any on the way back.

'Lunch is… wow, ladies. What a transformation!' Sy blurts out. 'I came to say it's being served in the barbecue area. They want everyone to eat now so we can start getting the rotisserie in place ready for later. But, my goodness, you've done an amazing job here; this is something very special indeed.'

Tegan sidles over to wrap her arms around Sy's waist and he smiles down at her tenderly. 'It's good to see you smiling again and not frowning.'

'This is exactly the look I was hoping to achieve. Kerra and I have worked without stopping and even then, it's taken twice as long as we'd hoped. But it's worth it.'

This old three-sided, brick-built barn is one cavernous space right up to the rafters. With a level, concrete floor it's very useable. At some point the fourth side was equipped with huge, sliding wooden doors but they no longer work. They probably haven't been closed for many, many years and the shabby-chic look of the weathered wood is beautiful. We decorated each one with a circle of laurel leaves, some of the smaller pieces of trailing ivy, and a huge wicker heart sprayed white. The final touches will be added at the last-minute. Behind us the delivery of flowers stands in buckets of water in the shade of the rear wall.

Overhead, the main beam has little swags hanging down at regular intervals. It would have taken us all day to dress it completely, so we made short garlands by twisting the ivy around some old lengths of rope. We threaded through some bushy stems of mock orange blossom which hang like lanterns, providing a blast of colour. Two of the farmhands erected a scaffolding tower on wheels so we could get up close and it worked a treat.

The long buffet and drinks table has been covered in a thick white cotton fabric and Tegan and I pinned a narrow tape around the edge. From that we draped more ivy and clusters of viburnum leaves. They're a paler green than the laurel leaves, with a satin look and tiny blue-black berries.

With the candle and driftwood table display that Tegan and I put together and the addition of a little greenery, it's just awaiting some glorious white mop head hydrangeas. With their wide, bright green leaves it will add a little opulence; keeping the theme of green and white is simple but natural-looking against the rusty-red bricks of the barn.

'Come on, Ross has been helping out in the kitchen for

the last two hours,' Sy encourages us to stop what we're doing. 'And everyone is waiting.'

'He has?' Tegan responds, surprised.

She turns to quiz me. 'Did you know that, Kerra?'

'I did.'

She beams back at me. 'It wouldn't have been the same without him here,' Tegan acknowledges. It's one small step, but at least it's going in the right direction.

It's a scramble for everyone to shower and change before people start arriving. Thankfully, Ross has been staying in one of the holiday cottages and both Tegan and I use it to get ready.

When I'm in the bathroom I recognise his things, running my fingers over his hairbrush and picking up his favourite cologne to sniff it. I'm instantly transported back to the night of Sy and Tegan's wedding. After the registry office and a wonderful meal at The Lobster Pot, Ross and I eventually made our way back to Pedrevan Cottage in high spirits. We talked until the early hours of the morning and then ended up having an impromptu picnic on a blanket in front of the wall of glass doors.

It was then, without any warning whatsoever, Ross asked me a theoretical question. He said that he wasn't actually proposing to me, but if he were what would my answer be. I gave him a teasingly theoretical yes, but laughingly told him that there are no guarantees because it pays to keep a man on his toes. Little did I know there would come a time when I would long for him to be ready to ask me properly. Now, the likelihood of that seems even further away. He isn't a man to commit if everything isn't just right. How do I convince him that nothing matters if you love each other – and we do.

'Are you okay in there?' Tegan calls out.

'Yes, I'm about done.' One quick glance in the mirror and all that registers is a hint of sadness in my eyes. Or is uncertainty? I'd taken getting married for granted and in my head I was already moving on to the next stage – having a family. And now I wonder if Ross is lagging way behind, thinking that until he's found his next challenge and proven himself, everything is on hold. That would be the gut punch for me.

'Is there anything I can do to help?' Tegan prompts me and I make my way back out into the bedroom.

'Oh, you look wonderful in that dress, simply wonderful, Kerra,' Tegan remarks.

I wish I felt it, but I don't.

'Thanks. But you are truly the belle of the ball!' I remark, wistfully.

Tegan isn't a girly-girl, she's more jeans and t-shirt, a bit like me really. But she looks divine in a soft blue floaty floral print midi dress, with fabric-covered buttons. Paired with pale blue heeled sandals and silver drop earrings, she looks elegant. It has short, semi-sheer sleeves, but the body of the dress is lined, which gives it enough weight to move independently as she walks.

'Well, you will melt Ross's heart the moment he casts his eyes on you,' Tegan exclaims. 'You know what they say… absence makes the heart grow fonder!'

My dress is a little fussier than I usually go for, with a tie wrap front in a pale, almost silver grey with tiny white polka dots. The top is body-hugging, but has a deep frill around the neckline, which complements the fact that it's sleeveless. The tie-waist is flattering, and the skirt hugs my hips, falling in gentle folds to just below above the knee in the front, but lower at the back. Even now I'm not sure whether it's really me, but I wasn't in the mood for shopping the day I bought it. I got to the point where I no longer had the heart, or the energy, to keep going in and out of the dressing room.

'Let's go. It's time for the party to begin.' At least I'll have my man by my side and that's all I need to have a great time.

# 24

## Romance is in the Air

'You look amazing!' The glint in Ross's eyes as he grasps my hand makes me feel like I'm a teenager again – full of hope and expectation. That wonder of realising anything is possible and dreams can be turned into reality. But having lived through that, what I found was that destiny sent me far away. What did I learn? Well, how to be true to myself I suppose and the fact that money doesn't buy happiness. Love is the only thing that matters, and you should never take it for granted.

'It's not too much?' I ask, tentatively.

'No. And we're colour-coordinated. Everyone is going to think you picked out my shirt to match your shoes.'

I look down at my silvery-grey strappy shoes and laugh. Ross is wearing a matching linen shirt and slim fit dark grey trousers. He looks wickedly handsome, without even trying. The top of his hair is as unruly as ever, but he's been to his barber's I notice, because the back is super short, and the lines are pristine. But that's more than one day's growth on his chin. When I saw him this morning, I'd assume he'd shave but he hasn't. It suits him and I like it.

We wander around hand in hand, trying our best to avoid groups of people. The candles have now been lit inside the barn and the scent wafts on the air, mixing with the freshness of the greenery. It's such a romantic vibe. Gawen has hung long strings of white fairy lights around the walls, and it makes everything sparkle. On the buffet table, the soft flickering light from the pillar candles add a glow to the shady interior, in sharp contrast to the brilliant sunshine outside. In here it's pleasantly cool and it's the little touches that have turned Sy and Tegan's celebration into a romantic, and charming summer party.

I have no idea if their two families are mingling, but everyone we pass is smiling. The music isn't too loud, just a pleasing sound in the background and most people are deep in conversation. As Ross and I leave the barn and walk across the expanse of patio at the rear of the farmhouse, the smell wafting over from the firepit, and the rotisserie is mouth-watering.

'Kerra, Ross!'

We stop and turn around. Dad and Nettie make a beeline for us, all smiles.

'Doesn't everything look lovely?' Bless her, Nettie doesn't point out the obvious, that she wasn't expecting to see us both here.

Dad puts out his hand. 'It's good to see you, Ross.'

As I give Nettie a hug, Dad and Ross shake hands, but I

can see Ross isn't sure what to say. 'Thanks, Eddie. I've been um, helping Gawen on the farm for a few days.'

I lean in to put my arms around Dad and he kisses my cheek. 'You look gorgeous, lovely!'

'Thanks. And look at the two of you looking very stylish indeed!'

Nettie gives Ross a hug and she gives him a beaming smile. 'There's nothing like some fresh country air to recharge the batteries, is there?'

I notice that Ross rewards her with a cheeky grin.

'The barn is just the perfect setting, isn't it?' Nettie observes, when suddenly Gawen's voice bellows out.

'Can everyone gather around please!'

There must be fifty people here at the very least and we fill the patio and spill out into the opening of the barn.

Sy isn't one for speeches but having quietened everyone down, Gawen hands over to him.

'First of all, Tegan and I would like to thank you all for coming. It means an awful lot to us both to get everyone together. Our decision not to have a big wedding was simply because we were working flat out making sure Clean and Shine had a profitable future. It was hard work, but that's behind us now. We've invited you here this evening to share a very special moment with you all. We would love you to witness and be a part of our ring blessing ceremony. Kerra is going to do the honours.'

Tegan looks in my direction and I give Ross a quick kiss on his cheek before pulling away from him. He looks on, intrigued, as I walk over to the happy couple.

'Sy and Tegan can you please place your rings in this bag.' Everyone is hushed.

They slip off their rings and I place them in the pale blue velvet pouch.

'Can I ask everyone to gather around and kindly form an inner and an outer circle? The pouch will pass from one person to the next. Hold it in your hand for a moment and warm it with your love. Make a silent wish for Sy and Tegan, one that will carry them into a bright and happy future full of joy and happiness.'

Everyone seems caught up in the moment, there are even a few who mumble a heartfelt 'ah' as people shuffle around. It takes a few minutes and what is rather lovely is that everyone seems to be taking it seriously. I watch Sy when the pouch reaches his father's hands and while he doesn't say anything, his father holds on to it for several seconds longer than anyone else.

When the pouch eventually makes its way back to me, I pull open the drawstring and offer it to Tegan. She pulls out a ring and it's her own. She laughs and hands it to Sy. The sound of a baby crying fills the air and as Felicity makes a shushing sound, I look up. To my surprise, Ross offers to take Ethan and wanders off, leaving Felicity and Drew to clasp hands as they watch the little ceremony. As it grows quieter once more, Sy clears his throat.

'Tegan. My wife, the keeper of my heart. I place this on your finger as a reminder of the depth of my love for you. Always and forever, babe.'

Even the birds are quiet as Sy pulls his ring from the pouch next and hands it to Tegan.

'Sy, you came into my life at a time when I was struggling. You rescued me and made me see that life is what you make it. And together we've overcome so many obstacles. You are my rock, but it's more than that. Every day I wake up with a smile on my face and it's because of you. I love you more than words can convey.'

As they exchange a tender kiss, everyone is touched.

'And with that,' Gawen says, his voice unusually gruff with emotion, 'the hot food is now being served!'

I make my way over to Ross and he stands there grinning at me, holding a sleeping Ethan in his arms. 'That was lovely. I bet it was your idea. I don't stand much of a chance surprising you with a romantic gesture, do I? You set the bar high.'

That makes me laugh, as we make room for people to walk past. Everyone is following Gawen, tempted by the smell of roast chicken and baked potatoes cooked in the fire pit. Drew comes ambling over.

'Our little lad is asleep. Well done, Ross. I'll put him down in his carrycot in the farmhouse. If you see Felicity, let her know where I am and that I'm mightily hungry.'

Ross gazes down at Ethan, reluctant to hand him over. 'He's certainly an armful now, Drew. You must be doing something right.'

As he very gently transfers his little charge into Drew's arms, I reflect on the fact that everyone gets that certain look on their face when they're holding a baby. And it tugs on my heartstrings to see it on Ross's face now.

Drew makes his way slowly into the house and Ross asks me to hang back as he rushes over to catch up with Felicity and pass on Drew's message. They chat for several minutes and it's wonderful to see them both so animated. She puts her head back and laughs, and Ross looks happy. He's not a man who is meant to spend too much time on his own; he's too serious, too much of a thinker. He strides back to me, a broad smile on his face. Catching up my hand in his, to my surprise he pulls me off in another direction entirely.

'Where are you taking me?'

'I figure we have an hour before we're missed. What do you think?'

Some offers are simply too good to refuse.

Wrapped in Ross's arms, I'm conscious that we've been absent from the party for way too long.

'We should get dressed,' I murmur, but make no attempt to move. I track my fingers down his arm, feeling the solidness of his muscle and then the tiny little hairs on his forearm. I always feel so safe when I'm with Ross. I don't have to worry about anything because he can handle it, even if I can't. It's ironic, as I've spent so many years striving to be self-sufficient and prove myself and yet when I'm with him I become a different version of me.

The sound of a disco beat filters in through the open window. 'They'll all be up on their feet dancing and if anyone is worried about us our phones would be ringing by now.'

'I feel guilty though, don't you?'

'No. We were there for the important bit, and we rolled up our sleeves to make sure everything was ready. Sy and Tegan won't be worrying, believe me.'

'Is my hair sticking up?'

Ross laughs. 'It's not quite as sleek as it was earlier on. But to me you always look gorgeous. You don't have to head back to Pedrevan tonight, do you? Why not ask Drew to pop in and sort out Ripley? She'll cope for one night. I doubt they'll stay much later, as the music will be too loud for Ethan.'

I think of Ripley. 'She misses you Ross and if I'm not there she might think we've abandoned her.'

He pushes himself up on one elbow, shaking his head at me and laughing.

'So, you're going to drag us both out of bed to get dressed and sneak out because our girl might, or might not, be missing us?'

'Yep, that's about it. I'll text our hosts to thank them, naturally.'

'Okay. Let's do this.'

My heart leaps in my chest. Ross is coming back to Pedrevan with me tonight. Everything in my little world is suddenly bright and happy again. Who knows – perhaps I can even convince him to stay.

It's a little after three in the morning and after insisting on lying across both of Ross's legs for the last five hours, Ripley has finally gone out for her usual night-time jaunt. She's been so out of sorts lately and yet, in no time at all, it's like everything is back to normal for her. Maybe that's thc way I should act now, as I lie here wide awake.

'I'm hungry,' I state, emphatically.

'You're always hungry at unearthly hours.'

'But we missed the rotisserie and the baked potatoes done in the giant fire pit. I bet it was wonderful.'

Ross makes a groaning sound. 'Don't talk about food. I'm enjoying being in my own bed again.'

Even in the gloom that puts a smile on my face that I'm sure he can see.

'I could make us some French toast,' I offer.

'Hmm...' He pauses, probably thinking of the last time I made it and burnt the edges. 'How about scrambled eggs and some finely chopped chives?'

I'd eat anything as long as Ross is the one cooking it for me. It's just like old times.

'Sounds perfect!' I whisper, vaulting out of bed and searching around for my silky, rose print kimono.

'Well, are you going to keep me waiting?' I demand, as I pull my hair up on top, twisting it around several times and securing it with a scrunchie.

'Would I dare!' Ross sits up, sliding his legs over the side of the bed and reaching for his shorts. He pulls a t-shirt over his head and as he pads around in bare feet my heart is overjoyed. As I follow him downstairs, he tramps off into the kitchen and I walk over to stare out at the garden.

'What did Drew say when you told him you didn't need a lift?'

'He assumed I'd come back with Dad and Nettie, I think.'

'Ethan surprised me. He's grown a fair bit in such a short time. He's much more interesting now. I'm sure he smiled at me.'

I turn, watching Ross's back as he pops the frying pan on the hob and grabs some eggs from the fridge.

'Yes, he's adorable. Ross, something tells me you've made your decision, but you're waiting for the right moment to share it.'

He half-turns. 'I can't hide anything from you, can I?'

Taking a seat at the table, I remain silent. This is his chance and I'll be disappointed if he doesn't take it.

'Pedrevan Cottage is lovely,' he begins and I'm waiting for the but. 'Your mum was born here, and you have so many childhood memories of your grandparents.' He's choosing his words carefully, which is a bad sign.

'I waited a long time to make it mine,' I admit.

As he begins whisking the eggs, I notice the way his shoulders have slumped a little.

'Did you know Leath's Farm is up for sale? Well, the farmhouse, a couple of barns and some pastureland. They've already sold off the organic ice cream business to one of their competitors and the equipment is being moved to a big factory the other side of Rosveth.'

A farm? Ross wants to buy a farm?

'No. I didn't.'

'It's something I've been considering.' His voice is hesitant, as if he's waiting to see my reaction.

'But what do you know about farming?'

'Not a lot, but I'd learn as I went along as they already have farmhands who've worked there for almost ten years. I'm more interested in making the move to organic vegetables and herbs. It's a big step, obviously, as I'd have to sink in every penny I have. There are a lot of hoops to jump through, but Gawen is very knowledgeable, so he'd point me in the right direction.'

Is Ross trying to get me on board, or is he telling me this is what he's going to do?

'It's... it's...' I let out an unbidden sigh. 'It's a surprise, that's all.'

He turns off the heat beneath the pan. 'This has turned

into more of an omelette than scrambled eggs, I'm afraid.' Ross carries two plates across and then goes back for the forks. 'I forgot to stir when we were talking.'

He's on edge. He didn't intend telling me this now.

'Are you confident you could jump into something so different and make it work?' There's no point in glossing over the fact that a bit of mucking in at Treeve Perran Farm over the years doesn't really count as experience.

'I could if we built the business together.'

And there's the catch. It's Ross, or a peaceful life at Pedrevan and I can't have both.

The money doesn't mean anything to me, but Pedrevan does. I blended the old with the new to make it my forever home and then Ross came into my life. I thought it was going to be our home and for a while it was. I can't rent it out now. It's too personal. Every single item in here is something I felt an attachment to. All those trips with Tegan to antique fairs and car boot sales. The thrill of the chase to do what my grandma did – make this a refuge from the world. Which it was for me as a child, and still is now as an adult.

'How are the eggs?' Ross interrupts my thoughts, and I hadn't even realised I was eating.

'Perfect,' I mumble. *Just like you, Ross*, I find myself thinking as I stare across at him. *Perfect.*

'I have this great idea, you see,' he continues. 'I've been looking into hydroponics. It's a way of growing plants without using soil, by feeding them on mineral nutrient salts dissolved in water. Basically, it involves the use of polytunnels and grow lights. Obviously, there's quite an investment upfront to buy the necessary kit, but it's a fast-growing market, Kerra. The produce is healthier because it's not grown in depleted soil. The plants are fed exactly the right combination of nutrients to make the end product better for the consumer.'

It's only half past three and we're talking about a subject I know absolutely nothing about. It sounds like laboratory stuff to me and that's supposed to be a good thing, is it? Ross looks animated, caught up in the moment. I continue eating and listening.

'Some plants are ready to harvest up to fifty per cent faster than if they were grown traditionally. Herbs do particularly well. Aside from their use in cooking, lots of herbs have healing properties – think essential oils. And they're used in making soap, shampoos, hand lotions and candles. This could be a great opportunity if we can find the right place at the right price.'

I love Ross, I love this house, I love my neighbours, I love living opposite the kennels and the shop, and now Dad is back in my life things could return to normal. But I'm talking about the old normal and I have to let go of that now. Ross is sitting here, his ideas coming thick and fast as he looks at me expectantly.

'It sounds interesting,' I reply, trying to match his level of excitement.

He throws down his fork and jumps to his feet, scooping me up off my chair and waltzing me around the semi-lit room.

I hope I'll feel a little more enthusiastic after a few hours solid sleep. Just having Ross back home reminds me how bleak it felt when he wasn't here and a part of me is thinking what choice do I have? The fear is that I'll end up so far outside of my comfort zone in the pursuit of his dream, that I'll lose all sense of me. Is that too high a price to pay – blindly following the person you love, in the hope that everything will come good in the end? I don't know, I just don't know.

# 25

## The Cold Light of Day

After a leisurely breakfast, during which Ross is careful not to talk about anything to do with his early morning revelation, we head back to Treeve Perran Farm. We volunteered to be a part of the clean-up crew and afterwards Gawen and Yvonne are putting on a picnic lunch.

I've never known Ross to be so hyped-up and he's trying to play it down. Mainly to stop himself from raising the unmentionable subject, he quizzes me about what I've been up to while he's been away.

'After several informal meetings between Tom, Oliver, Drew and one of the planning officers, the application is now under way. Behind the scenes everything is set up and ready to go at The Salvager's Yard. Their new sign goes up this coming week and work to replace the fencing, which will go a long way to reassuring the locals, will start tomorrow.'

Ross purses his lips. 'That's quite something. Tom's totally happy with what he's getting in return for letting Property Professionals UK erect an office on his site?'

'Yes. They're footing the bill for the two new wooden buildings that will be erected; one will be a ticket office, shop and display the history of the cove. In return, they'll be granted a ten-year lease for the space their office will sit on and three dedicated car parking spaces alongside it. They'll make an annual contribution to the upkeep of the site. Both Tom and Wally are delighted. Wally has put in enough to cover the cost of clearing the remainder of the scrap and cladding the old industrial unit that was the former garage. It will become a museum and be a part of a walking tour, which will take visitors around the cove and up along the cliff path.'

'Oliver wasn't all hot air, then?' Ross muses, trying hard to mask a smile. Before I get a chance to reply, he jumps straight in. 'I'm only teasing you. It's not that I don't like the guy, but you never know if there's a hidden agenda.'

'Ross! That's so unfair of you. Oliver is genuinely interested in getting involved in community projects. Plus, he's about to take up a new position in the company and will be moving to Cornwall permanently.'

'Really?' There's a note of surprise in Ross's voice.

'Yes, sadly he's splitting up with his wife.'

Ross is no longer smiling. 'It's not a sob story to get you on his side, is it?'

I start chuckling. 'Ross, I can't believe Oliver makes you so uncomfortable. He's a really nice man and we're just friends. Okay, I've seen quite a bit of him recently as we pulled the deal together with Tom, but he's harmless.'

There's still a frown on his face. 'You're not a part of this deal going forward, are you?' he checks.

'No, of course not. For now, it's just The Design Cave and the new project with Sam, which will unfold over the coming months.'

Argh. The moment I mention Sam's name I could kick myself.

'I feel bad that what's happened to me has thrown a spanner in the works,' Ross admits, dejectedly.

'It's not a problem. Drew got another company in to do a quote and they came in a little under, so Sam was pleased. Poor Drew has been kept busy and he's back and forth to the council offices but at least it's on his doorstep.'

'Your dad caught up with me last night when I wandered off with little Ethan.'

'He did? What did he say?'

'That when I disappeared he was shocked by how devastated you were. He said he was sorry he never really gave me a chance back last year when we were working together on the scenery for the pantomime. He really meant it, too and I understood. My father said some awful things that night in The Lark and Lantern that weren't even true. Your dad did go on to say something that made me stop and think though.'

'He did?' It doesn't sound like it was an outright apology as I hoped, but it seems to have cheered Ross up.

'Eddie said that he's watched you reinvent yourself since you've returned home. He admitted that he had his doubts you were doing the right thing as you were walking away from a successful business, but you found your niche.

I would too, he told me. He said anger is a waste of time and energy. He learnt that truth the hard way.'

'You're no longer angry with your father?'

'No, because it won't change anything. And I'm not jealous of the way Oliver feels comfortable sharing his troubles with you.'

Ross's expression belies his words. Which means he's extremely uncomfortable and for some odd reason I find that incredibly reassuring. If I'm going to give up everything for Ross, at least I know he loves me enough to be jealous.

I wasn't expecting Dad and Nettie to be here at the farm today, but it's nice that Alice and Ian have a little alone time. It's a shame they weren't invited, but it was too big a risk in case Tegan's brother, Trev, isn't quite ready to forgive and forget her part in the whole debacle.

There are fourteen of us and Nettie and I volunteer to help Tegan dismantle the flowers and the greenery. It's all still very fresh looking and we make up small hand-tied bouquets to distribute to their neighbours.

'They're much too pretty to waste,' Nettie remarks, as she snips off the ends of the hydrangea stalks. I concentrate on cutting down some of the larger greenery into more manageable pieces.

'Are you two happy to make a dent in what's here, while I start carrying some of the other things over to the car?' Tegan checks.

'Yes, this little lot is going to take a while.'

Tegan loads up a low-level trolley and trundles it across

the patio. The rumbling of the wheels makes me turn to watch her. 'I think it might have been best to pack it all up first. She's having to go slowly as the riven patio stones make it a bumpy ride,' I remark.

'Hmm... you're probably right. It was a lovely party though, wasn't it? And no arguments, thank goodness.' Nettie mirrors my own thoughts.

'I was just thinking the same thing. It was perfect. I admire the fact that they had the quiet wedding they wanted, although it was a shame that they had to delay the party for so long.'

Nettie glances at me. 'I know but holding it outdoors on such a glorious day made it easier. When two families, who haven't met before, come together for the first time it can be a little awkward. However, with people able to wander around at will and the lovely setting, it all felt very relaxed and natural.'

'I saw Sy talking to his dad, albeit briefly. Old wounds can sometimes run deep and take a long time to heal. He was more comfortable around his mother, I thought. It's still sad though.'

'Some families are supportive, and some aren't,' Nettie says pragmatically. 'That's life. I was delighted to see you and Ross here together, so was your dad.'

A little smile creeps over my face. 'He came back to Pedrevan with me.'

'I know. We saw his car parked up. Is he back for good?'

'Yes, but there's a lot we need to talk through.' My smile fades a little and Nettie instantly reacts.

'That sounds troubling.'

I turn to check that no one is within earshot, as people are coming and going from the farmhouse to the car park.

'He's talking about buying a farm.'

Her eyes open wide. 'A farm?'

'That was my exact same response. He says together we'd make it work.'

Nettie looks as concerned as I am.

'And how do you feel about it?' she asks, hesitantly.

'I'm still in shock. I'd assumed he'd set up some sort of business, but farming was the furthest thing from my mind. Apparently, Leath's farm is up for sale.'

'Yes, they had financial problems. They sold off a parcel of land and the ice cream factory, which was all that was making money for them really.'

'Well, that doesn't bode well then does it?'

'I suppose they'd overcommitted themselves and what's left is a more manageable lot. It was profitable when Sissy's family owned it and now it's been pared back to make it more of an attractive option. There's the farmhouse, a few outbuildings that could be converted into holiday lets and a big herd of cows. It's a steady income based on that alone,' Nettie points out.

'Yes, but what do Ross or I know about looking after animals?' I wrinkle my nose. 'Let's just say I wouldn't want to get hands on.'

'No, but you have a business head and that's the key to keeping a going concern in profit. Ross could then spend his time learning all about animal husbandry.'

Nettie is trying to remain positive, but it doesn't make any sense to me at all.

'Oh, he's not really interested in that side of things. He sort of brushed it off, saying they have men who have worked on the farm for years. No, Ross has this idea to grow herbs and vegetables in big polytunnels.'

'I see. Well, he's such good friends with Gawen and Yvonne that he'll know the pitfalls of farming life. So, it's not as if he's going in blinkered. Has he been up to take a look around Leath's Farm?'

'He didn't say, but I suspect he has and probably took Gawen with him.'

'It sounds like he's serious about this. As you said, it'll take some talking through. It's a huge step for both of you.'

I can tell by the seriousness of her tone that I'm not the only one who thinks it's a bit of a stretch.

'I'm not averse to taking a risk and I know Ross can probably fund this himself. If it all went wrong and we had to start over again, we'd be okay. No investment is cast iron, but I've spread my money and kept enough cash in the bank as a failsafe.'

'But?' Nettie asks, pointedly.

'Ross said that together we could make it work. But I'm no farmer's wife. Gawen is so reliant upon Yvonne. She works on the land, feeds the animals, bakes, makes chutney and jam… the list is endless. I burn a toasted cheese sandwich. I'm just not qualified for the job.'

The look we exchange says what neither of us are prepared to voice out loud. Some dreams can become a reality but there's also the chance it could turn into a nightmare.

'You're going to back him, aren't you?'

'Yes. But the day I sell Pedrevan a piece of me will feel broken.'

'Oh, Kerra. Love hurts, doesn't it? I've felt the same way with the trouble we've had at Green Acre. Eddie still feels guilty about us being together, which is why I haven't moved in. I do stay over, but not very often. I'm glad Alice and Ian are staying there, as it's a big house and the company does Eddie good. However, if Polly gives Alice the chance to work alongside Ian permanently, I have a feeling it won't be long before they'll be looking to rent a little place of their own.'

That's exactly what Polly said when she called in to see me for a chat.

'Mum always said that when one door closes, another opens. Let's hope it's true and Dad quickly finds someone in need of a part-time job.'

Poor Nettie. I understand how she feels. Sy was the same when he got together with Tegan. Living in the home Tegan had bought with her first husband, Pete, was a constant reminder of the past. Renting the place out and moving into The Forge meant leaving behind a house full of old memories and allowed them to focus on creating new ones together. I do hope the pair of them end up buying it from Ross, even though it's where he wined and dined me, before getting me into bed. I burst out laughing.

'What's so funny?' Nettie enquires, bemused.

'Life has a funny way of making the impossible seem possible. Maybe I was destined to be mucking out cow sheds, who knows?'

It's Nettie's turn to start laughing. 'Sorry, Kerra, but I just can't visualise that. You're a woman of many talents and quite artistic, but I think that's where you'd draw the line.'

'Okay, so I will be supervising people mucking out the cow sheds.'

'Hmm…' she replies, not sounding convinced. 'Maybe I'll stand corrected, but I fear it's a long shot.'

'What have you been up to?' I enquire, after enlightening Ross on how Nettie and I spent our morning. We're tramping across the field, our arms full of folded blankets in preparation for the delayed picnic lunch. It's nearly three o'clock and everyone is starving.

'Your dad and I were given the task of emptying out the fire pit and dissembling the rotisserie ready for a deep clean.'

I grimace. 'Sorry. Was it awkward making conversation?'

'No. Not at all. We had a nice chat.'

They did? I give Ross a quizzical look.

'Don't worry. Eddie and I might not agree on everything, but it's like a switch has been flicked. It's ironic that it was the way my own father treated me so deplorably that made Eddie see I simply don't have those family traits. I saw what went on in the past and it taught me a thing or two about right and wrong.'

Dad always says that respect has to be earnt, and finally he's no longer blinded by his bias.

'It's funny how things work out, isn't it? I mean, we couldn't have engineered you having a little quiet time with Dad like that. Nettie and I had a bit of a heart-to-heart, too. It made me realise that when I blurted out some rather harsh comments to Dad a little while ago, I went too far. It's easy to judge and that was wrong of me.'

We stop, turning around to survey the view, in silent agreement that this is the spot. As we lay out the blankets the sound of chatter on the breeze signals that the others are on their way.

'Eddie knows that whatever you say is said with love and his best interests at heart, Kerra. And the same is true for him. He thought he was protecting you. Eddie and Nettie are at a crossroads, but neither of them knows quite how to deal with it.'

They were probably working together for no more than a couple of hours and it's a huge surprise to hear that my dad felt comfortable enough to open up to Ross like that.

'When Dad is wrong about something he takes it hard. He's feeling guilty, Ross, for not giving you the benefit of the doubt. My mum, on the other hand, always said I left a little piece of me in Penvennan Cove when I left. She knew it was the right thing for me to come back, simply because you were still here.'

Ross turns, lifting me up in the air and spinning me around. 'Then she'd be happy that we're venturing forward into a life that promises to bring us even closer together.'

With the apt sound of cows mooing in the background, I gaze down at him. He's so happy and his eyes are sparkling.

'She would,' I reply, unwilling to diffuse his sense of excitement as he lowers me back down to earth. After all, if something is meant to be, we'll work it out somehow. Won't we?

# 26

## Packing Up

As I do a final clean through with a mop, I can't believe it's the middle of August already. Life has been a blur recently. Ross hurries past me with a screwdriver in his hand, avoiding the wet areas.

'No, that's staying,' I inform him, as he's about to ease the painted pine cabinet off the wall.

'But you love this, Kerra. It has some of your granddad's old Cornish mining lamps in it.'

'I know, but it belongs here.'

Ross can see it's an emotional day for me, but I'm ready and excited to start the next stage of our journey together.

'Then we're done.' He beams at me.

He clasps my hand in his and we find ourselves walking towards the wall of glass, staring out at the garden.

'I remember that Sunday you invited Sy, Tegan, Drew and me for lunch down at the bottom of the garden. Drew and I hammered together some decking as the garden was literally a building site. I ended up helping you to assemble the patio furniture. You were nervous around me,' Ross points out. 'But that didn't stop you from turning it into a challenge. Your fingers are smaller than mine and you won. All those fiddly little nuts and spacers, I didn't stand a chance.'

'I remember. Dad called in, but he didn't stay long as he was off to the pub. It was a great day, though.'

'You were so delighted to see the work progressing on the cottages. And now because of me you're letting it go.' The soulful look on Ross's face tells me he understands that I'd give up anything for him.

'It's time to move on,' I concede. 'I was high that day because you were here. And you were flirting with me – it was fun, exciting.'

'Well, this is the last run to the storage facility. Are you ready?'

'I am,' I say, determinedly, as Ross leans in to place his lips on mine. I close my eyes and so many memories come flooding back. But they're all of Ross. As I pull back I indicate for him to go on ahead and tell the removal men we're done.

Hanging back, I gaze around. We're taking very little with us and I have no regrets because it would hurt to strip this place. The things I've left are things I love. Like the massive pine table that I made Sissy sell me, even though she didn't want to. And the chairs I lovingly painted by hand.

'Goodbye, Pedrevan Cottage, Grandma, Granddad and Mum,' I whisper as I walk towards the front door. 'I won't be a stranger, but I know you're all wishing Ross and me well.'

It's a wonderful day in the height of summer. August

is my favourite month and the seventeenth happens to be Mum's birthday. Is that an omen, or what?

The van is just pulling away as I shut the door behind me. Ross is standing on the other side of the street, waiting for me.

As I look left before crossing the road, Zacky approaches.

'Hey there, Kerra. Movin' day, I see. Good luck to you and Ross.'

'Thank you, Zacky. How are things with you?'

'Champion. Me and Jared have been helping Tom and Wally setting up the exhibits. My, does it take me back. There's a boat not unlike the one your granddad used to take you out fishin' in. And we found an old pilchard net full of holes. Jared can repair it with his eyes closed and it's one of the things he's goin' to be demonstratin' on the tour of the museum.'

It's good to know that Zacky and Jared are getting stuck in. It's not just about having a few extra pounds in their pockets as it's a wonderful way to spend their time.

'That's good to hear. Right, Ross is waiting so I'd better go. Take care, Zacky!'

'Oh, I will.' He waves out to Ross before continuing his walk.

I wait for several cars to pass. They're looking for a parking space, but they need to come early to find one on the High Street. By the time I cross over, Nettie and Dad are standing talking to Ross.

'Here she is then,' Dad says, leaning in to give me a hug. He doesn't seem to want to let me go and I'm feeling tearful, which is silly. This is the right thing to do.

As if to confirm my suspicions, we both let out a poignant

sigh as I pass the keys to Pedrevan to Dad, and he passes the keys to Green Acre to me.

'The end of an era and the start of a new one, lovely!' he exclaims.

Ross and Nettie look on in silence, but they're equally as emotional.

Dad raises his hand, and the van parked a little further down in one of the lay-bys starts its engine. A lot of his old furniture has gone, and the contents are mainly personal effects from both Green Acre and Nettie's former home.

'There's a cake tin on the worktop in the kitchen with some of Mrs Moyle's saffron buns. She popped them in first thing,' I explain.

'Ah, what a kind thought,' Nettie says, as we hug each other. This is a monumental day for us all. 'Don't forget you're both coming to dinner on Saturday evening.'

Ross laughs. 'Forget? A home-cooked meal is going to be the highlight of our week.'

As we head off in opposite directions, I wonder how I'm going to feel when Ross swings open the gate to Green Acre, knowing that it's our future home. It's a shell now. Dad moved in with Nettie a little over a month ago, while we had some internal walls taken down and the whole house re-plastered, re-wired and the central heating replaced. For the next four weeks Ross and I are living in a caravan in the garden. The kennels have gone and in a way it's good that nothing looks the same any more. Tomorrow the smart new gates Tom forged for us are being installed.

I wonder how Nettie felt, handing over the keys of her house to the new occupiers. She must feel as jittery as I do. Knowing it's for the best and exciting in one way, but also hoping life will soon settle down into a routine again. I realise Ross is talking to me.

'We need to check those rabbits haven't found another way in.' His head isn't worrying about what we've left behind, or our new sleeping arrangements. 'I was thinking we should perhaps put up some sort of inner perimeter fencing. I mean they can't jump very high, can they? And two barriers are better than one.'

He used to worry about floor levels and footings, now it's the rabbit population of Green Acre. As a former market garden, they've always been here and it's their home too.

'Maybe we should plant some carrots in the ground, to keep them occupied.'

He turns to smile at me as we draw level with the caravan. Lifting me up in his arms as if I'm as light as a feather, he nods with his head indicating for me to open the door. It's not wide enough for his shoulders and with two steps to negotiate, he does a half-turn, lowering me down gently in the section between the dining room and the bedroom.

'Welcome home,' he says, sporting a huge grin.

At least it's not a farm and there are no cows. Okay, we do have three massive polytunnels, only one of which is up and running properly, but he's happy. And so am I. Well, I'll be happier once I have an office and a proper bedroom, but a caravan isn't exactly roughing it. We have a camping cooker, a small fridge, and a working bathroom. Besides, it's not forever. And next Monday Dad is back working alongside Uncle Alistair, at Shaw & Sons Joinery. His first job is to make our new kitchen. Ross is done with the shiny, contemporary finishes and now he's into simple country elegance. Goodbye to my shabby chic, hello timeless beauty.

*

As we lie on our backs staring up at the grey-tinted roof light, we're both too wired to sleep. Ripley is still confused, even though she's been with us every day while we've been setting up the grow area. She has a nest in one of the polytunnels as well as one in here now, but her favourite place is the old tree house down at the bottom of the orchard. I can't blame her, because even with all the windows open and a small fan going it's warm.

I did wonder whether she'd gravitate back to Pedrevan tonight, but Dad said he'd give me a call if she does.

'Stop worrying about her. She knows we're here now. If she misses the cottage, she'll use the cat flap and when she doesn't find us there, she'll come straight back.'

'But that means crossing the road.'

'Can you hear any traffic out there at this time of night?'

'No, but...'

'They adjust more quickly than you think. Remember when she used to make her way up to Treylya? Now that's quite a distance and who knows what animals are lurking in the woods. Foxes, big dogs off their leads nosing around. She was fine then, and she will be now.'

He's right. I'm panicking over nothing. But I'm not at all sleepy. 'Do you fancy a cup a coffee?'

'Yes, but not in here. Let's wander down to the orchard.'

Dressed in shorts and t-shirts, we stroll down to the wooden bench beneath the oldest of the apple trees. Ripley is still nowhere to be seen. The caravan was only dropped off yesterday, so there's been no time for her to get used to it.

The semi-darkness is comforting, and it takes me back to my early teen years. Mum, Dad and I would often sit out for an hour or two, chatting. Well, I didn't say much back then. Mum was always trying to figure out what was going on in my head. She knew I wasn't happy, but it took me a while to grow into being me.

'You're very quiet. Is the reality of living in the caravan for the next month sinking in?' Ross slumps down on the seat next to me, his coffee splattering his top. 'Darn it!'

I smile indulgently at him.

'It's fine, really. I'm excited to see work commence on the new façade for the house. Mum never liked that 1960's style either, but with just over an acre of land it was perfect for the kennels.'

'Then what's wrong? Something is bothering you. You haven't changed your mind about setting up Green Acre Botanicals, have you?'

'It's a challenge that I'm looking forward to as long as we start small to test the market. My head is reeling with what I've learnt these past few weeks doing research for it. Sissy says that candles fly off the shelves at The Design Cave, so it will be interesting to see how our first range will sell.'

*Miaow.*

'Did you hear that?' Ross turns his head, but I look upwards. Ripley is peering over the edge of the tree house platform.

'There you are. I knew you'd be around here somewhere.' Ross sounds as relieved as I am to see her.

Every day we've brought her over here with us to begin getting used to her new home. It's a place she always avoided in the past as she could hear dogs barking and she was nervous. But we'd bring her nest with us and once the first polytunnel was erected, she had a little corner of her own.

'Ripley, good girl. I'll go and fetch some treats.'

When I return with a bowl of water and a tube of dried salmon chunks, she's on Ross's lap looking very at home. The rattle of a tube makes her jump straight off. She's thirsty more so than hungry and when she turns her attention to her treats, she simply sniffs at them before sauntering off to see what she can find. Same old same old, as they say. Our little diva will never change.

'I'm sure there are enough mice here to keep her going for a while,' Ross points out, 'and as we're sleeping with the windows open she'll know where we are.'

The true test is when we wake up in the middle of the night to find her lying on the bed. Only then will I be able to relax.

'Shall we take a wander around?' It's obvious Ross is much too excited to sleep and I am too.

Draining my coffee mug, I stand and he takes it from me, placing it on the bench. 'Come on. Let's walk the estate.'

That puts a grin on my face. 'You know my mum would have been so on board with this idea.'

'What? Hydroponics?'

'No. You and me making this our own. Whose idea was it *really*?' I press him.

He looks at me a little shiftily. 'It was your dad's, but we need to keep that between you and me. It's a pride thing.'

'Dad came up with it?'

'It was something you said, apparently. It made him stop and think about what really makes him happy.'

'During my rant?'

'No. I think it was the day you came to tell him about Ian's brother. Anyway, whatever you said helped and that's all that counts, isn't it?'

Ross leads us straight over to our first grow tunnel, the only one that is fully up and running. He unzips the entrance flap, and we step inside. Instinctively our eyes go straight to the plants, eager to spot the new growth.

'Look!' Ross points to one of the trays and he's like a kid with a new toy. 'All these shoots are new – since this afternoon.'

I'm still learning the basics and I'm amazed to see the results the grow lights produce. Looking down the long line of tiered racking, already there is a visible hue of new green shoots everywhere. I have more questions than answers still, but I'll learn. 'Is it necessary to keep the lights on 24/7 all year round?'

'Yes. Even in summer as it does cool a little overnight, but during really hot spells we can turn them off during the day. The air-cooled reflectors on the grow lamps actually remove the heat, if they didn't it would damage the plants.' I love hearing the passion in Ross's voice. Whatever he does in life he commits to fully, well… when it comes to work. But still no mention of marriage, I ponder wistfully.

'It's a case of trial and error to begin with,' he explains. 'But I've joined this online group who share their experiences and it's been enlightening. And it threw up a contact name of a guy who will come to the site to evaluate the set-up and make recommendations for improvements. It'll be interesting to see what he thinks.' There's pride in Ross's voice as he talks and he's happy with the results so far.

It's like being in a greenhouse, not unpleasant but we make our way back out into the night air to gaze up at the sky. There's a little breeze springing up now and it's wonderful. The leaves rustle gently and the sound of snapping twigs from the swathe of dense shrubbery we've yet to clear indicates that Ripley is probably hunting. Poor mice… poor rabbits!

Down where the sad looking garages used to stand the whole area has been flattened and the rubble taken away.

'It looks ugly,' I admit, sadly.

Ross comes closer, throwing his arm around my waist. 'I know but I promise you when it's all done you'll be as thrilled with it as you were with the garden office.'

My one stipulation was that Green Acre is our home first, a business second. Whatever is visible from the house and those huge windows, must be aesthetically pleasing.

'It's going to be big, isn't it?'

Ross relinquishes his hold and paces it out for me. 'From here… to… here,' he confirms. 'Three times the size of your old office. But it will be clad in the same border oak as the house. Hand on heart, Kerra, when the house is done and you're inside staring out, I promise you this will look like a little country-style cottage. You trust me, don't you?'

He comes close, his lips hovering over mine.

'Of course.'

And when I'm busy growing our little cottage industry, I'll have the satisfaction of knowing that Ross is close by.

# 27

## The Housewarming

Who has a housewarming party on the thirty-first of October? Yes, Ross and I, but there isn't a pumpkin in sight. Tonight, we are unveiling the house and our new project to friends and family.

'Are you pleased with how everything has turned out, Kerra? It all looks amazing. Contemporary country with a homely feel to it,' Tegan remarks as we make our way down to my new home office, champagne flutes in hand.

'Ross has delivered on all his promises, and I couldn't be happier. And this is the home of Green Acre Botanicals.'

What was once two sad looking garages, a blot on the landscape at the far end of the garden, has been transformed. It backs onto the rear gates and a parking area, which was a little overgrown but is now immaculate.

'This isn't normal gravel, is it?' Tegan questions, as we step off the path and onto a wide curved area bounded by grey pavers.

'It a bonded resin, which holds the small gravel stones

together.' The door is unlocked, and I indicate for Tegan to step inside.

'It reminds me of a fairy-tale cottage, not the gingerbread variety. It has all the elements of that country feel without being twee.'

The single-storey unit is faced with horizontal planks of border oak, which will eventually turn a wonderful silvery-grey colour. The front door is a traditional stable door, although it's PVC. It's been sprayed a pale bluey-grey and, with six panes of glass in the top half, which swings open independently, and a vertical plank effect on the bottom, it's homely.

'And this is going to be where you'll be developing the new products?'

'Yes. The workroom and kitchen are through that door. This is obviously the office area. Ross has a study come office in the main house.'

As soon as Tegan arrived, she asked if she could see my new workspace. She gave Sy a quick kiss on the cheek as Nettie offered to give him, Gawen and Yvonne a tour of the house. That was supposed to be my job, but even Nettie could see that Tegan had something on her mind. We managed to slip out unnoticed, as Ross and Dad are tied up welcoming people, hanging up coats and sorting out drinks.

She smiles, warmly. 'Somewhere for Ross's books, no doubt. I did miss the library when he moved them from The Forge to Pedrevan. Sy and I have managed to fill one shelf between us, but we've taken the others down and re-painted the wall.'

'The Forge is really beginning to feel like it's yours now?'

'Yes. It felt right from day one, to be honest with you.'

It's comforting to know that Tegan isn't having any regrets about selling her old house.

'Are you going to give me a sneak peek at the candles?'

'Head this way,' I say, and she follows me through the door.

'Oh, Kerra. It's like an old farmhouse kitchen with that wall of cupboards and shelves above them. Very like...'

'Your Welsh dresser at The Forge?'

'It is!' she replies, sounding delighted. 'And I love this colour. What's it called?'

'We had it mixed specially. It's a French grey base with a soft, duck egg blue added to lighten it. The windows and front door are the same colour, just in a satin woodwork finish.'

'Has Sissy seen this table?'

'She helped design it.' Sissy is always on the lookout for furniture to upcycle, as not everyone visiting The Design Cave is looking for something brand new. 'She went to an auction at a pub that was shutting down, the other side of Launceston, and managed to pick up four large, traditional farmhouse tables. We stripped them down and Dad came in and worked his magic to turn them into one big worktable. It would have cost twice as much to have had a bespoke table commissioned. Dad was a bit miffed when I said I was painting it rather than applying wax, but I like the chalk finish and the way it wears over time.'

'It's charming and you're going to love working from here. The candles are awesome,' she enthuses as she inspects the latest batch that I made this morning.

'Let me light one. This was inspired after that little session with you at The Forge, applying those leaves to the pillar candles. When Ross was throwing ideas around of how we could use the herbs and he mentioned candles, I jumped on the idea.'

'Ooh, lavender! But the real thing, not that fake chemical fragrance that loses its smell and makes the wick burn black. I'm assuming the lavender was grown in Ross's new greenhouses?'

'It was. They're called polytunnels. I'm also experimenting with sage, fennel, rosemary, thyme and mint. I use soy wax and they look good in the mason jars. We're targeting special occasion gifts and the Christmas market. As a test run, Sissy is selling them singly to help me determine which are likely to be the most popular fragrances. The idea is that we'll sell them in sets of six in the smaller jars, in a lovely wooden trug that can be re-used for utensils, cutlery or condiments.'

Tegan's eyes light up. 'I know where I'll be doing my Christmas shopping this year!'

I raise my glass to toast, but as I take a sip she just stands there, staring at me. 'I'm pregnant,' she blurts out.

'Oh, Tegan! Congratulations – I'm so thrilled for you and Sy.' I put down my glass and throw my arms around her. 'His dream was always to meet the love of his life, settle down and have a family. Goodness,' I close my eyes for a brief second, 'this is his dream come true. You'd better tip that down the sink and fill it with water.'

As I let her go, she grins at me. 'I wasn't sure whether to tell you tonight, or not. But I couldn't keep it in any longer. This is your night; yours and Ross's, but Sy is bursting to share the news. We waited until I was eight weeks and it's been agony keeping it from you!'

'Ah – Felicity and Drew are going to be ecstatic…

Ethan will have a playmate. Sadly, he's teething and has a temperature tonight. They phoned earlier to say they won't be able to make it. You must totally share this with everyone when we head back inside.'

'Are you sure?'

I roll my eyes. 'After a tense couple of years with so many highs and lows I can't even list them, any good news is worth shouting from the rooftops.'

'Well... it's just a thought, but if you need any help with the new business, another couple of months and I'll have some time on my hands. Sy wants to take someone on now to step into my role. He's not happy to think of me constantly behind the wheel, heading off at a moment's notice to take on new cleaning contracts. Especially now that we're venturing further afield. He has the office situation under control, and he says he wants me to start taking it easy.'

'Gosh, that isn't you, is it?'

'No. So if you want someone to bounce ideas off, or to keep you company when you're experimenting, or even to get hands on...' She looks at me and laughs. 'Sy wants to run the business himself, but I can't sit around doing nothing, can I? Besides, we have a lot to thank you for, Kerra. And you put a lot of business our way recommending us to Oliver Sinclair.'

Tegan has a creative streak in her and as long as Sy is happy, to me they're family. I think we'd make a great team.

'Remember when you first returned to Penvennan, and you donned your rubber gloves to clean bathrooms for me? And the day you locked yourself out of that bungalow and got stuck in the window? Oh my... and that Saturday we had our work cut out and arrived at Treylya when Ross was using it as a holiday let? The people were still in bed, and they'd trashed every room. All those bathrooms… and those shiny floor tiles. I figure I owe you, my lovely friend, and Sy does, too. You'll always be his bestie… well, our best friend because I knew you first.'

'Where have you been?' Ross whispers into my ear. 'Almost everyone we invited has turned up. It's been crazy. Nettie is on her fifth tour of the house. And look out for Paul, he brought his wife, Hayley, along. Their dogs used to board here whenever they went on holiday.'

Paul is an old business acquaintance of Ross's. Ross reached out to him as Paul has some monster trucks, including a lorry with a Hiab on the back. We needed the crane to lift the individual dog runs over the wall. He owed Ross a few favours and I didn't even realise he'd been sent an invitation.

'I'll make a point of introducing myself to Hayley. And sorry, but I received a proposition I couldn't refuse. It put a huge smile on my face.' I smirk at him.

'Oh, Oliver's here, is he?' Ross makes a face. He's play-acting, but there's just that little hint of annoyance in his tone.

Yanking on his hand, I pull him into the downstairs cloakroom, locking the door behind us.

'I think we might be missed as it is our party,' he states, raising an eyebrow.

'Don't flatter yourself. I can drag you in here anytime I like and now is not the time. Oliver and Polly are seeing each other.'

'What?' He exclaims, sounding totally shocked.

'Shh… I'm not supposed to know. And you don't either. Right?'

As a little smirk starts to appear on his face, I can see that he's relieved. 'My lips are sealed,' he replies. 'I had no idea!'

'It's early days. His divorce is going through, and Polly told me in confidence. Sam doesn't know, either. Do you hear that? So, no leaks, because they're taking it slowly.'

'Right. Understood. And Tegan is okay?'

'She's fine. Really good, actually.'

'Everyone is impressed by the kitchen units. Your dad and your uncle might get some more work after tonight.' Ross grins at me.

'I knew the timing was right for Dad to let the kennels go and he's loving being back at his old workbench. Now, my glass is in desperate need of topping up before I start circulating again.'

'Anything to keep my woman happy.' Ross grins back at me, then grabs a long, lingering kiss that takes my breath away. Tonight, he's on a high and he deserves it.

'Is everyone ready for a candlelit tour of the garden?' Ross calls out.

Sissy sourced some wonderful, hand-held candle holders and I made up a special batch of mini candles in various fragrances. Ross said it wasn't necessary, but I wanted to be able to show off some of the results of his hard work. None of this would be possible without his vision.

'Hey, my lovely. How are you doing?' Dad sidles up next

to me and I glance around, stepping off the path to wait for Nettie to catch up with us.

'I'm good. How are you two?'

Nettie beams at me. 'I got the new contract. It's a three-book deal with an advance! I'm over the moon. The garden office has changed everything for me.'

'And I know not to disturb her when she's down there writing,' Dad adds. 'I was going to ask you if I could take a photo of that worktable of yours. Yer uncle was talking to one of our clients and he's looking for something similar for his big new house up near Renweneth.'

My stomach turns over. 'The plot next to Treylya?'

Dad nods his head. The project Ross started and didn't get to finish. 'Yes, by all means pop in and take some photos. It's not locked, but I'd be grateful if you didn't mention it to Ross.'

'Oh, yes, of course. But do you know what, Kerra? Ross wouldn't change a thing. He's a happy man and you only have to look at his face to see that.'

'I know. It's ironic that in the end Jago did us a favour. But tonight, I want this to be about Ross. He's turned Green Acre into our dream home, and I thought that wasn't possible.'

Nettie places her hand on my arm, giving it a squeeze. 'You were meant to be here, Kerra, I can just feel it. This place is unrecognisable with the vision you two have brought to it.'

Dad throws his arms around us both.

'Change is scary, but sometimes it's the only way to move forward. There's nothing wrong with being different, Kerra, only in letting other folk make you feel uncomfortable about that. Some people simply weren't made to fit in, but to push the boundaries instead and they make the rest of us stop and think. As you did when you had your little rant at me. And you were right. Your mum would be happy to know I'm back working with me brother doing a job I love.'

All three of us know that's true.

'Your uncle and auntie are looking for you, Kerra,' Nettie informs me. 'Ian and Alice couldn't make it as they're working late on a job for Polly, but they sent their regards and said they'd catch up with you very soon.'

'I'm glad things are going well for them. Anyway, you go on and take the tour of the garden and I'll catch up with Uncle Alistair and Auntie Marge. Love you both.'

Mum would understand that life goes on. But even in my wildest dreams I never saw Ross and me here, at Green Acre. Was it really Dad's idea, or was it one of those lightbulb moments? The sort that come out of nowhere and you wonder where it came from. Or even whether it was given to you by… well, who knows? But as I make my way back up the path, something tells me Mum had a hand in this.

'Kerra!' Uncle Alistair calls out and I hurry to join them as they linger behind the stream of people making their way down to join Ross.

'Ah, thank you for coming! I've been showing people around my new office. Ross says everyone is talking about the kitchen. You and Dad did a great job, Uncle Alistair.'

'We weren't going to let you down, Kerra. You're a tough client to please, but we love a challenge. And it's great working with my brother again.'

'Mum never intended for him to make the kennels his life's work, Uncle Alistair.'

'You have no idea how comforting it is to hear you say it, Kerra,' Auntie Marge admits, with real sincerity. 'I told you, Alistair. Meryn would love the thought of you and Eddie working together again.'

'I've been feeling the same way, Marge. I've a lot to thank Eddie for, that's the long and the short of it.'

We all know that he's referring to Alice and Ian. Dad gave them the space they needed to grow as a couple. And now Alice is working alongside Ian, for Polly.

'Our Alice is finally happy,' Auntie Marge agrees. 'And Ian has proven himself. He did enjoy his time here helping Eddie, though.'

My mind travels back to the day I returned home for good. The dogs were sleeping in the house, not the kennels, and it was a long haul to get Dad to turn it around. Even then I knew his heart wasn't really in it, but he gave it his best shot.

'That's true,' Uncle Alistair reflects, soberly. 'Eddie gave him a chance and that was all Ian needed. I see that now.'

'How are they settling into their new flat? It's in Polreweek, I hear?'

'Very well indeed and, yes, it's over one of the shops in the arcade,' Uncle Alistair confirms. 'It wasn't furnished, so we've given them a bit of help financially. Polly is keeping them both busy, so they're not complaining. Alice is a lot happier these days. They gave her a hard time at that salon, even though she was popular with the clients.'

It's funny, but from a distance it seemed to me that Alice's life before was devoid of any problems, but it's easy to make assumptions. She might have thought the same about me.

'We'll catch up properly soon, I promise. Wait until you see Ross's new venture, he's achieved a lot in a short space of time.'

'If it's anything like the house, then he's done a sterling job, Kerra. We're glad it's all worked out so well for you and Ross. And thanks for giving your dad the nudge he needed. Shaw & Sons Joinery wasn't the same without him, was it Marge?'

'You two always sparked off each other. They like a bit of competition, Kerra.' Auntie Marge giggles. 'They rib each other all the time, but it's only banter. That kitchen of yours was a labour of love. Every single joint, every single cut brought them closer together.'

Uncle Alistair is unable to speak because Auntie Marge is right.

'And Ross and I appreciate that. It's the heart of the home, a kitchen, and we can't thank you enough. Now you'd best hurry to catch up. Ross has put so much work into it and he's eager to show off what he's achieved.'

They can see how proud I am of him, as I give them both an affectionate hug.

*Miaow, miaow, miaoooooow.*

I look down to see Ripley, who begins to wind herself around my ankle. 'Come on girl, let's go inside so you don't get under everyone's feet.'

She dutifully follows me up the path and into the kitchen. Standing in front of the bi-fold doors, which look across to the orchard and down to the wonderful new cottage, I acknowledge that Ross has surpassed my expectations.

With the new, grey slate roof and the beautiful border oak exterior panelling, those huge 1960s style windows now look contemporary. It's a sleek building with a real sense of blending into the environment. Before it was an off-white pebble dash with steel framed windows that looked like naked gaping holes. The sort you want to disguise with blinds.

This move has taught me that it's the memories you carry in your head that are important, not the keepsakes you put on a shelf. This is my childhood home and yet now it's a totally different environment. That doesn't wipe out the old memories, it's just a reminder that an ending simply marks the start of a new beginning. That's what living is all about – looking forward with anticipation and looking back with gratitude for the good times.

# Six Months Later…

# 28

## It's Time to Hoist the Main Sail!

Getting a surprise invite for an afternoon trip on a traditionally rigged tall ship isn't something you turn down. It was from Ross's old friend and former client, Paul, and his wife Hayley. I've met Paul twice and Hayley just the once, which was at our housewarming party.

They're a fun couple and Paul is one of those entrepreneurial guys who has made a lot of money from a very diverse business portfolio. Apparently, in the past, Ross got him out of a bit of a nightmare situation when Paul bought a huge warehouse at auction, only to find there were some serious structural issues. Time was of the essence and Ross managed to re-work the schedules to send in a team of men and get the problem fixed quickly.

'Have you been on a tall ship before?' Ross asks, keeping his eye on the road ahead.

'No, why?'

'It's likely to be a bit windy and while that hat looks lovely, it probably won't stay on long.' He grins.

'Are you poking fun at me? I thought it was very appropriate for a warm day in May. It adds a touch of elegance to a summery dress.'

'Well, you look totally gorgeous, and I'll be proud to have you on my arm, with or without a hat.'

'I know why you're flattering me and no, you can't see the results of the first batch of handmade soaps until the packaging arrives. I want you to see the end-product all nicely displayed as it'll have more impact.'

He pulls a face and I reach out to touch his cheek. 'They'll be ready by close of play on Tuesday if the delivery arrives on Monday as planned.'

'That'll be four different lines in circulation. We're getting there, Kerra. Slowly, but surely.'

He's impatient and so am I but developing a new line takes a lot longer than it does for Ross to produce an entire crop. The next stage will be to increase production and Green Acre Botanicals will move to a commercial unit around the corner from The Design Cave. It's a big step but I'll still be spending most of my time at Green Acre once we are staffed up.

Life has really settled down for us over this last six months. In that time Ross signed a lucrative contract with a chain of upmarket restaurants and installed a fourth grow tunnel. We successfully launched a range of candles, lip balms and hand creams. But – more importantly – we became godparents to little Ethan.

'Is this Paul's first trip out this year?'

'Yes. He mainly rents it out to film companies. It's big money, but the contracts are few and far between. It's the first run of the season for the crew as it's being hired out next week for a natural history programme.'

'It's in good working order then?' I ask, nervously. Aside from Granddad's little two-man fishing boat, I've been on the deck of a trawler in dock a few times, but never taken a trip out to sea. 'Will it be choppy?'

Ross laughs, as he looks up at the sky. 'No, and it would take some huge waves to make it a rough ride. It's a solid sailing vessel. It'll be fun. I'm really excited about it.'

'Me too,' I lie, hopefully convincingly.

The invitation called it *a champagne cruise from Drakestown to Penvennan Cove*, which is a bit risky if you ask me. Wouldn't it be better to stay hooked up to the quayside? Even in flat pumps I imagine myself hanging on with one hand, glass in the other as I try not to list to one side. And Ross is right, the hat has to go. Still, at least I managed to buy a lightweight, long sleeved linen jacket to match my dress, so I won't get goosebumps on my arms if it's chilly as we sail along.

Parking in Drakestown isn't easy and Paul told Ross he's arranged for his guests to use the car park to the rear of the old chapel. It's situated at the top of the hill that leads down to the quay. There are only two other cars here when we arrive, so either we're early or this is going to be a very small party indeed. Before I get out, I slip off my hat and leave it on the back seat.

'If it's your favourite, then I think that's wise,' Ross remarks. 'Right, are we ready for this?'

'As ready as I'll ever be.'

'Aww… don't be like that, you're going to love it. There's

nothing like standing on deck and feeling the breeze through your hair. And watching the crew as they nimbly get *The Old Mariner* under way.'

We take our time strolling down hand in hand, taking in the view. There are a few clouds in the sky, but nothing that concerns me. The water is sparkling as the sun bounces off the rippling surface.

'This is perfect weather, as if there wasn't any breeze at all it could take all day to get to Penvennan Cove, even though it's not that far as the crow flies.'

'Oh, of course!' A sailboat can't move without the wind behind it.

'I'm teasing you, Kerra,' he admits, sheepishly. 'It's a replica, as most of them are these days. It has an engine to manoeuvre it in and out of the dock. Years ago, there would have been smaller boats with ropes to do that job. Once the boat was close enough, they'd throw out a stout line onto the pier. It would be wound around the capstan. You see that one over there?' He points to the harbourside. 'It's a cylindrical pulley, with bars that stick out of it horizontally. Lots of men would push the capstan bars around in a circle, winding the rope tighter to pull the ship in.'

'Thank goodness for engines,' I remark. He's pleased that I'm getting into the spirit of it.

As we draw closer, *The Old Mariner* is one of the sailboats I instantly recognise. I've strolled past her many times, as have most of the tourists who come here. Today she's berthed opposite The Jaunty Sailor Inn. It has commanding views out over the sea and has been there since the early 1800s.

I do appreciate that we're privileged to be invited aboard

to take this short trip. 'I can't help thinking that Dad would really love this.' I mumble, almost to myself. He'd get a real kick out of it.

'You're right, he would.'

'Hi there, Ross and Kerra,' Paul calls out. 'The weather is treating us well for our first trip out.'

'You couldn't have picked a better day,' Ross agrees, a broad smile on his face.

The ship does look magnificent as we board her, I can't even imagine what it must cost to keep it in such good condition. Hayley appears to greet us.

'Welcome, welcome!' She leans in to give me a hug as the men do a high five. 'Kerra, let's go below and grab a drink before the others arrive.'

I wonder whether we got the time wrong, but they don't seem put out to see us. 'It's like going back in time, isn't it?' My fingers trail lightly over a coil of rope looped around a stout pillar.

'Yes,' Hayley calls over her shoulder as we approach a set of narrow wooden stairs leading down into the belly of the boat. It's rather gloomy as we descend.

I wasn't sure whether a silky calf-length floral dress was going to be appropriate, but Hayley is wearing a pale pink short-sleeved dress and looks very summery.

'Is this your first time on a tall ship?'

'Yes, and it's my first time going out into deep water, so I'm a little nervous. I've only ever been hand-line fishing in the cove and that was many years ago.'

'Oh, you'll be fine once we're out to sea. Maybe we'll stay down here until we're under way properly.'

It's bigger than I thought it would be and full of trip

hazards. How on earth sailors coped during rough weather when the ship would have been rolling as the waves hit, I don't know. But it's atmospheric and a real eye-opener.

'How old is this ship, Hayley?'

'She was built in 1929 in Denmark, actually. If you're interested in the history, let's grab a glass of champagne in the captain's quarters and then I'll take you through to what we call the archives.'

Any nerves seem to dissipate as Hayley gives me a guided tour below deck and we end up in a small room that looks a bit like a study. It smells of aged wood and old paper. There's a proper desk and a display cabinet. And shelves with books and various seafaring items, kept in place by decorative wooden rails.

'This journal diarises the changes over the years.' Hayley carefully opens the book lying in the centre of the desk. '*The Old Mariner* began life as a schooner, which simply means it had two masts, the foremast being slightly smaller. Then, in the 1970s, she was converted into a brigantine. In the 1990s there was an increasing demand by film makers for period square-riggers and she underwent yet another change.'

'You're very knowledgeable.'

'I'm the main contact for bookings and the details matter when it comes to production companies,' Hayley says, drolly. 'When you see them hoist the sails for the first time it's quite something. I was hooked from the start. I'd happily live most of the summer on a boat if I could get Paul to agree to buy something sleek and modern.'

The moment my stomach begins to sense some real movement, I look a little startled. Hayley suggests we go over to the porthole window to look out. The ship moves slowly at first as the pier walls taper to a narrow entrance, but we pass through with ease.

'Come on. It's time to find your sea legs up top! I'll lead the way.'

The movement is enough to make me hold on tightly to the handrail as we mount the steps. It's barely wide enough for two people to pass and the depth of the steep treads won't even take a size four shoe. I've hardly touched my drink and it takes all of my concentration to climb to the top. But as I gaze upwards, all I can see above me is blue sky and tiny little fluffy clouds.

'Surprise!' A loud chorus of voices fill the air as Ross extends his hand to help me up the final couple of steps.

'What on earth is going on?' I glance around, unable to take it in. I spot Dad and Nettie first and then I realise that most of our closest family and friends are here. I turn to look at Ross, biting my lip.

He leans in close to kiss my cheek and whisper in my ear, 'What's more romantic than a tall ship?'

Paul indicates for Ross to head over to the main deck and what feels like a sea of smiling faces part as Ross grabs my hand and leads me forward. Hayley offers to take the glass from me as I look at her and shake my head. She laughs. I bet she couldn't believe her luck when I said I was interested in history.

'Ladies, gentleman and…' Ross glances in Paul's direction, 'our esteemed captain,' he begins. 'First of all, I'd like to thank you all for being complicit in keeping this surprise a secret from Kerra, and I'm grateful to Paul, Hayley and the awesome crew for making this trip possible.' He clears his throat, nervously.

In the background I hear the cries of the seagulls as they wheel in the air and the buffeting sound of the breeze as it fills the sails.

'Kerra my darling, my forever love.' Ross takes both of my hands and the way he gazes at me adoringly tells me more than words can convey. 'Think back to when you were eleven years old. On Valentine's Day you opened your locker to grab your exercise books and someone had posted a hand-drawn card. It wasn't very well executed. A heart with an arrow through it was par for the course back then, but the two little birds I drew in the corner weren't bad.' He pauses and there's a little ripple of laughter. 'I didn't sign it, of course. If my memory serves me right, I put something like *from your secret admirer*. I'm pretty sure I didn't spell *admirer* correctly, but I did put one huge kiss at the bottom.'

I look at him, then close my eyes for a second. Do I remember that card? Of course, I do. Did I ever consider it was from him? No, although in my heart I wanted it to be from Ross, but I had no reason to believe that was the case. I wasn't even sure whether it was someone winding me up, but that's how eleven-year-olds think, isn't it?

'I'm pretty sure I didn't get one back from you, but it was okay. The point is that while you didn't know it was from me, you knew that someone loved you.'

My eyes instantly fill with tears.

'And I still have it. It's in that box marked school stuff, up in the loft,' I blurt out.

'Why am I not surprised?' We smile at each other, suddenly oblivious to the people around us. Ross releases my right hand, pulling a box from his pocket and lowering himself down onto one knee.

With the breeze whipping my hair across my face, the gentle sway of the boat and the salty tang in the air, this is a perfect moment.

'Kerra Shaw, will you do me the great honour of saying that you'll marry me?'

I use my free hand to swipe away my tears, sniffing loudly. 'I thought you'd never ask!' I exclaim and everyone starts laughing as he slips the ring on my finger. I can't even see it for my tears and the wisps of hair flickering across in front of my eyes, but all that matters is that the day I've longed for is finally here.

Standing at the prow of the ship with Ross's arms around me, it's smooth sailing as we edge ever closer to Penvennan Cove.

'I know I kept you waiting but I wanted everything to be… settled. It's taken longer than I'd hoped and, to be honest, it's nothing short of a miracle what we've achieved in such a short space of time. Things didn't exactly go to plan, did they?' Ross reflects, and I can't disagree.

'Who would have thought that losing your job would end up giving us this incredible new start? I don't have any regrets at all, do you?' I half-turn to look at Ross, but I already know the answer.

'None at all. I've spent virtually half my life on building sites. It was all I knew. Now, I'm living my dream and you'll soon have another ring on that finger, don't you worry. I know a good partnership when I see one!' He smirks. Suddenly his voice falters. 'There's Lanryon.'

My eyes follow his gaze. For so long just the mere sight

of that church sent chills down my spine. For me, the sea became something to fear and until today I hadn't stepped on a boat since the last time Granddad took me line-fishing for mackerel.

'See the way the sun glints on the windows?' I point out and Ross pulls me even closer.

'I wasn't sure if it was the right thing to do, but I just felt you'd want them to be a part of today.'

'Thank you, Ross. I appreciate the thought you've put in to making today so special and I wouldn't change a single thing.'

'I figure your mum is happy that you're back at Green Acre, and Eddie and Nettie are comfortable in Pedrevan Cottage. That's all thanks to your dad, Kerra.'

Even a year ago, none of us could have imagined the changes that were to come. It's a good job we can't see into the future, because if we didn't have the courage to look far enough ahead, would it have felt too daunting to bear? Would we have ended up settling for less? Like Ross setting up his own building company and going through the motions? Our time apart was agonising, but I see now that it was necessary. Ross was more important to me than Pedrevan Cottage, and I was more important to him than buying a farm.

'The truth is that Mum wanted me to return home for two reasons. One was to get Dad back on track and the second was to either go with my heart or put my first love behind me. She'll be happy to see how it all turned out. You're a catch, Ross Treloar, and I know it.'

Ross is too busy kissing me to notice that we are sailing

past Treylya and the building project just the other side of it that he started, but never got to finish.

At Green Acre, Ross and I are going to grow our little business into something we can be proud of. It's beautiful now, a dream home where we live and work. Behind the stone walls, and the tall metal gates that Tom spent hours in the forge crafting for us, is our future life's work. Healthy produce and a growing range of organic products that don't put profit first, but quality and the environment.

Happiness is when you realise life's journey isn't about the pursuit of *more*, it's about realising, and being grateful, when you have *enough*. And when your cup overflows, you bring your circle of like-minded family and friends close to share it with them. Like a nest of concentric circles, it can grow exponentially. The only limit is one's imagination…

# Epilogue

One year later…

Life is one long, evolving story. It's never ending and popping back to visit Penvennan Cove some twelve months later reveals that it's been a busy time for everyone.

*The Lark and Lantern*

Sam now has a full complement of staff to run the business, which is going from strength to strength after a total renovation.

He, Sissy and Willow have settled into their lovely new home in one of the former holiday cottages. With Polly living next door to them, Sam's decision to stay was the right one.

After Kerra's injection of capital, she's now able to stand back and watch Sam once again feel a real sense of pride in what he does having shed his financial worries. And the fact that he's now able to enjoy some real quality time with Sissy is the icing on the cake.

*The Salvager's Retreat*

What had been a dying business is now a big attraction for visitors to Penvennan Cove. Tom and Wally worked steadfastly to turn it around. It has become a hub of historical interest. The tours have been a great success, even off season, and they have seven retired fishermen who come along to talk about their life at sea and demonstrate some of the old skills.

The walking tours too, are very popular with locals, as well as tourists. And Tom spends a lot of time showing people how a working forge operates. The estate agent's office has also become a central point for visitors interested in booking holiday lets, which wasn't the original intention, but guarantees its presence for a long time to come.

*Drew Matthews Architecture*

When the house known as Grey Stones, set on a large plot next to the vet's surgery, came on the market, Drew and Felicity knew it would be perfect for them. While it was a tough decision to leave Tigry Cottage, with another baby on the way there just wasn't enough room.

As they both work from home, and Felicity intends to take on a 9–5 nanny, they're very happy to have found their forever home. And Ethan, who is now an adventurous toddler, will soon have a new baby brother to keep him company.

*The Penvennan Convenience Store*

One of the biggest changes is that Mrs Moyle and Arthur decided to take early retirement. They sold the shop to Barbara and her husband, who are over the moon to be the new owners.

The Moyles, however, didn't move very far – just across the road into Tigry Cottage. Mrs Moyle works in the shop's kitchen for three hours every morning and Arthur still runs the Penvennan Cove Link-Up. Arthur underwent spinal fusion surgery two months ago and now that the back brace is off, he's able to walk without his sticks. It's hoped that over the coming months, with the help of an intense programme of physiotherapy, he'll soon be strolling down to the cove.

After a thorough investigation into the circumstances surrounding the original disappearance of Arthur's first wife, Helen Moyle made a statement confirming that she had abandoned the marriage and, in moving away, severed all contact. Because more than two years had passed by the time Arthur met and then eventually married Daphne, if he'd seen a solicitor at the time it would have been a relatively straightforward procedure. If one partner severs all ties it's desertion. Instead, his marriage to Daphne was annulled because that's the law. However, when his case was reviewed it was decided there was no criminal intent to commit bigamy and the file was closed.

Arthur and Daphne are hoping that Arthur's daughter, together with his granddaughter, will be at the small wedding they're planning next summer.

*Designed to Sell*

Polly's business continues to grow now that she no longer works for her dad at The Lark and Lantern. Ian and Alice have a third person to bolster their team and the future looks rosy.

Following Oliver's divorce, he and Polly have grown even closer. No one would be surprised if they suddenly announced their engagement. Whether he'll move in with Polly, or they'll find a new home together it's too early to tell. But Sam and Sissy accept that sometimes plans change and if it ends up being for the best and Polly is happy, that's fine with them.

*Clean and Shine*

Sy now runs the cleaning business supported by his new assistant manager.

Tegan is enjoying life working mornings helping Kerra at Green Acre Botanicals, where baby Daisy has her own little crèche for one. Tegan is happy indulging the artistic side of her nature and there isn't a pink rubber glove in sight.

*Green Acre*

Ross now provides independent advice for new hydroponic start-up businesses in addition to managing two gardening technicians back at Green Acre.

But he also has other plans for expansion. He and Kerra are hoping to start a family very soon. Fingers crossed, the Green Acre crèche will grow, as both businesses continue to bloom.

Penvennan Cove will flourish because whatever happens this little community sticks together!

# Acknowledgements

Cornwall has always been an enchanting destination for me. Whenever I visit I return home feeling renewed and uplifted. It was the perfect setting for this three-book series in which Kerra Shaw rediscovers her first love, Ross Treloar, and sincere thanks go to my Cornish friends who always welcome me with open arms.

I'd like to give a virtual hug to my new editor, the inspirational Martina Arzu – it's a delight working with you and your input has been invaluable!

Grateful thanks also go to my agent, Sara Keane, for her sterling advice, professionalism and friendship. It means so much to me.

And to the wider Aria team and Head of Zeus – a truly awesome group of people I can't thank enough for their amazing support and encouragement.

To my wonderful husband, Lawrence – you truly are my rock!

Ripley, too, gets a special mention as she is a cat with attitude and a well-loved family member.

Family and long-term friends understand that my passion to write is all-consuming. They forgive me for the long silences and when we next catch up, it's as if I haven't been absent at all.

Publishing a new book means that there is an even longer list of people to thank for publicising it. The amazing kindness of my lovely author friends, readers and reviewers is truly humbling. You continue to delight, amaze and astound me with your generosity and support.

Wishing everyone peace, love and happiness.

Linn x

# About the Author

LINN B. HALTON is a #1 bestselling author of contemporary romantic fiction. In 2013 she won the UK Festival of Romance: Innovation in Romantic Fiction Award.

For Linn, life is all about family, friends, and writing. She is a self-confessed hopeless romantic and an eternal optimist. When Linn is not writing, she spends time in the garden weeding or practising Tai Chi. And she is often found with a paintbrush in her hand indulging her passion for upcycling furniture.

Her novels have been translated into Italian, Czech and Croatian. She also writes as Lucy Coleman.